I0836838

FOURTH THOUSAND.

DICK WILSON,

THE RUMSELLER'S VICTIM:

OR,

HUMANITY PLEADING FOR THE

"MAINE LAW."

A Temperance Story—Founded on Fact.

BY JOHN K. CORNYN.

WITH AN INTRODUCTION, BY THURLOW W. BROWN.

AUBURN:
DERBY & MILLER.
BUFFALO: DERBY, ORTON & MULLIGAN.
CINCINNATI: HENRY W. DERBY.

1853.

STEREOTYPED BY
THOMAS B. SMITH
216 William St. N. Y.

Preface.

THERE was a time in the history of the Temperance reformation, when it would have been necessary, in presenting a work upon this subject to the public, to have fortified it well with apologies. That time, however, under the influence of the light "which shineth more and more unto the perfect day," has passed, and it is no longer a work of doubtful propriety. This question has passed successfully through all the stages of progressive revolution, and wherever a new era dawned upon it, there it erected its altar, offered its sacrifice of thanks to God, and marched on. Where is it now? in the keeping of comparatively the few? No! it has become the question with the masses—the question of the age. It is backed up, wished and prayed for, in every circle, save that in which the rumseller rules.

It has gathered to its aid every variety of talent, and this has been made doubly effective, by the knowledge of the fact, that it was set for the defence of virtue and innocence.

Still the work is not yet accomplished. Its vaunting enemy, who would, if it were possible, establish a Divine right to roll on his death-freighted car, is not idle. He is wary—cunning—subtle as his ancient prototype, who said, "ye shall be as gods." Money is dispersed freely—men are bought and sold, wherever there is an opportunity to do so—elections are controlled, and legislatures are overawed by them, and it is only in the broad clear face of the people's sovereignty, which has always been the terror of tyrants, that they see their merited doom.

For an encounter of this kind, earnest, determined, unyielding humanity is gathering up its armor. It is not without a witness as to what it can accomplish, when fairly marshalled for legislative strife. The "Maine Law" is the battle cry, and anything and everything which will tend to throw light upon the deformities of this shapeless monster, and waken the public mind to greater effort in this cause, will be of service. It is with this view that the story of Dick Wilson is offered to the public by the

THE AUTHOR.

CONTENTS.

CHAPTER VII.

CHAPTER VIII.

CHAPTER IX.

CHAPTER X.

CHAPTER XI.

CHAPTER XII.

CHAPTER XIII.

CHAPTER XIV.

CHAPTER XV.

CHAPTER XVI.

CHAPTER XVII.

CHAPTER XVIII.

CHAPTER XIX.

CHAPTER XX.

CHAPTER XXI.

CHAPTER XXII.

CHAPTER XXIII.

CHAPTER XXIV.

CHAPTER XXV.

CHAPTER XXVI.

Introduction.

For forty days and forty nights the rain poured down from the open windows of the heavens, until the flood covered the earth, and the sun, after the storm, smiled down upon the watery waste, where a world lay entombed. Solitary and alone, without helm, mast, or sail, like a speck on the world-wide ocean, floated the ark with its freight. The olive branch, borne upon a weary but glad wing, proclaimed the subsiding of the deluge. The sunbeams kissed the vapors as they rolled up from the retiring waters, and the bow of promise lifted its arch into the clouds.

Noah went out and planted a vineyard. He partook of its fruits, and lay in his tent in the slumbers of drunkenness. The frailties of a good man, are used to justify the drinking usages of to-day. The scourge of a world passed away, had commenced its progress again in the new. From that vineyard the tide has swept on, gathering in depth and power, until the *debris* of human ruin has been left on every shore where human foot has trodden. Stream has mingled with stream, and wave followed wave, until every land and people have been scourged. In the hamlet, the city, the country, or wilderness, the influence has been the same. Nations have been drunken to madness. New woes and keener sorrows have been sent out to stalk through the world, followed by red-handed crime and ghastly death. Beneath those oblivious waves, the brightest hopes of earth and heaven have gone down; and up and down the world the stricken millions have wasted away, and prematurely mingled with a mother dust. North, east, south and west, the plague has spread. The white sails of commerce have borne it across oceans. The pioneer has carried it across the wilderness. The trader has scaled the mountain range, and thus, in civilized and savage clime, the noon-day scourge has sped on in its mission of ruin. In the hut of the savage, or where science, letters and art have elevated and refined, the effects have been the same. The very heart of human society has been poisoned, until along every artery of health and strength, the hot currents have swept in their blighting power. The shadow has fallen across every hearth-side, and at the altar's base; and lingered there like the foot-prints of unutterable woe. Every house has had one dead in it—every circle has been broken. Homes are ruined and deserted, and fields turned to waste. The wife and the children are driven out from the home-roof, and to-day the mothers of America, like Niobe of old, as they weep at their broken altars, are attempting to shield their offspring from the shafts which fall thickly around, and quiver in the tender hearts they love. It is Intemperance that we speak of; the history of whose desolations has outstripped the wildest imagery of tragic fiction, and laughed to scorn the efforts of the tongue, pen, or pencil. If hell has one more potent enginery of human degradation and crime upon earth than another, it is Intemperance. It's very sound sends a thrill back to the heart, and a Gorgon monster slowly rises up from its heart of blood among the graves.

The gloomy night of Intemperance long rested upon the world, and no day-star in the horizon. The death slumber was deep and profound. Like the fabled city which was petrified into stone, no trumpet blast rang out to awaken to life. Woe and Want went hand in hand, Vice and Violence stalked unobstructed, and Crime laughed and reeled in its drunkenness of blood. Alone in the sky, the malign light of the death-beacon followed man from the cradle to the grave. The monster sat at every gathering. At the birth, marriage, or death; in the home, shop, or field; at the social re-union, or the festive day—in hut, palace, or council-hall, it plied its work. The mother fed rum to her babe with her own hand, or through the resources of life. The fair young bride stood at the altar in the light of her bright life-dream, and handed the goblet to him she had chosen to accompany in the pilgrimage of life. At the social board, the father followed the marriage prayer with a glass. In the silence of the night, where the living had just passed to the rest of death, the decanter kept its watch with the watchers. The friends of the deceased came to look once more upon the dead, and stopped at the sideboard as they passed out. The pall-bearers tipped the bottle and bore away their burden to the home in the churchyard. The father of the writer once lost a loved young brother. With a heart heavy with grief, he took the jug, and at the rumshop, which was beggaring the family, purchased rum to treat the friends at the funeral. What wonder, then, that Intemperance, like the red plough-share of ruin, went under every hearth.

A missionary once found a heathen mother in tears. She wrung her hands as she left her hot kisses upon the bloodless lips of a beautiful child, calm in the slumbers of death. The little treasure had been bitten by a serpent. The woman was one of the serpent-worshippers, and the reptile, which had robbed her of her first and only child, lay coiled at the hearthside of the home it had made desolate, safe from the avenging hand of the superstitious mother. She would not destroy it. Need we wonder at the superstition of the benighted heathen? To-day, America is a *nation of serpent-worshippers.* We look around us, and how many homes are there where the serpent is coiled, yet madly cherished by those who have mourned the loved and the good, poisoned to death by its fangs! And at the same time we see a great and free people hesitating about crushing these serpents! The darker rites and fearful religion of the poor Pagan can but *share* our sympathies.

We are proud of our country and its institutions. There is no land like our land; no people like our people; no lakes like our lakes; no streams like our streams; no prairies like our prairies, or mountains like our mountains, as they sit upon a continent and nod to each other in the clouds. American enterprize and American genius, inventive and literary, is startling a world from its slumbers. The heart of our Republic throbs upon two shores; and yet, at the heart of all our free institutions a cancer is tugging with never-resting energy. For its removal, Christians and philanthropists are marshalling.

It is but little over one-quarter of a century since a land so favored groaned in bondage unbroken. No light had broke in: no star had beamed out to guide our wise men to a Saviour. Humanity wept over the desolations. Patriotism saw its first stars pale and set in darkness. Religion saw its most gifted ones fall to rise no more. The strongest were in shackles, and the friend of his country and of man looked out sadly upon the scene, and saw no morning light in the dark night. Foreigners stigmatized us as a nation of drunkards. Thus, unobstructed, the work went on. The great deep of popular opinion had not been stirred by a single breath, but lay in its stillness until miasma had bred in its sluggish bosom, and rolled up to sicken and destroy. The thunder of popular will slumbered uninvoked in the ballot-box, or like the three-mouthed dog of hell, sleeplessly guarded the wrongs there entrenched. A scourge was abroad in the land, yet a free and Christian people slept over their wrongs, and yielded without an effort, to the annual conscription of Intemperance.

But a better era was to dawn upon our country. A brazen serpent was lifted. The trumpet blasts of a Beecher and a Kittridge startled the petrified city into life. The plume tossed in the conflict, the war-horse plunged and chafed, and in the light of the coming morning the BANNER OF TEMPERANCE rolled out like a beacon of hope and promise to gladden a world. A breath has swept the valley of Hinnom, and the sleepers arise. The ocean is swept by the storm, and hope springs up in the human heart. The light comes slowly, but it bears healing upon its wings, and heralds redemption to a rum-scourged world. There is joy in heaven and upon earth. The mother weeps tears of joy, and clasps her child to her bosom with a prayer of gratitude for the promise which speaks of a better day for her and hers. And so the great moral revolution has commenced—a war of extermination, ending only when the rum traffic shall exist no longer. A free people are girding for the conflict with a hoary curse, saying to its armies, as they wage the strife from pillar to pillar—" Thus far, and no farther."

The history of the Temperance Reformation is not yet written. The strife is yet in progress. But that history will occupy the brightest pages of our country's annals, and command the admiration of the world. We look back with a full heart and kindling eye upon that history. There is a moral sublimity and beauty in the record. It is like the beaming of the setting sunlight across the ocean. Storms may have swept the surface, and its waves dashed angrily upon the shore; but in its calm there is a wake of crimson and gold—a beautiful pathway, where angels might tread. The course of our reform has been marked by the most important results. It has carried blessings to myriads of hearts and homes. There is an angel in its waters, and peace, happiness and hope spring up where desolation has withered up the greenness of earth. It is destined to revolutionize the sentiment of a world. It enlists all that is lovely and noble in the human heart—the eloquence of poetry, and the inspiration of genius; the fervor of patriotism, and the zeal of religion. Its principles are as plain to the mind as the sun at mid-day, and as just as God. It is the gospel of redemption to a rum-cursed world—the John the Baptist of the Christian religion. Like the Christian religion, its fruits bear full evidence of its blessed character. When John heralded the coming of the Saviour, he did not startle the world by the brilliancy of his promises. He did not announce that Christ was coming with a crown of gold upon his head and a monarch's sceptre in his hand, with legions of conquering warriors bristling in armor, and in his train the kings and princes—the rich, and powerful, and elite of earth. No: the dumb should speak, the deaf should hear, the blind see, the lame walk, the dead be raised, and the gospel be preached to the poor. And thus along the pathway of Christianity, wherever its spirit has gained a foothold, there are eloquent records of its principles and influences. So with the Temperance Reform. The heralds did not announce that the fashionable and the wealthy, the titled great, the monied aristocracy of the land, would exclusively lend it their countenance. But the blind have seen, the deaf have heard, the stone has been rolled away from the grave of drunkenness, and the lost restored; devils have been cast out of those cut among the tombs, and its gospel has been preached to the poor. The reform was designed by a kind God to lift up and restore poor fallen humanity, and not to add brilliancy to fashion, or popularity to men. The prodigals, who have wasted all in riotous living and hungered for the husks, have turned back from their dark wanderings, and the temperance cause has met them half-way, and rejoiced that the lost were found. The so-called fashionable have murmured, and turned away with scorn from such manifestations. They would so have scorned the meek Saviour, because he called after the sinner, and wept with and comforted the poor and afflicted.

The hand of Providence has marked the course of our cause. Step by step it has moved onward, ever going deeper into the hearts and consciences of men. It has had its reverses, as has every great moral revolution which has agitated the world; but its first standard, "torn but flying," floats out prouder to-day than ever before. There is a hydra influence against it—one sleepless and gigantic. But ours is the majority, for God is with us. At times it has been beaten—its waves have rolled back and again mingled with their kindred waters; but they have returned to the shock with other waves and deeper flow, sweeping on with the strength and grandeur of its power. Wealth has opposed it—fashion has sneered at it—interest has fought it—demagogues have stabbed it, and Iscariots have betrayed and sold it; but, like the oak matured in the storm, it has taken root, until its towering trunk sways defiance to the fiercest wrath of the tempest. And it will live, and flourish, and gloriously triumph.

The blessings of the Temperance Reform are sufficient to reward for an age of effort. One home made joyous—one broken heart healed and made happy—one man restored to manhood, family, society and God—is a prouder and more enduring monument than ever towered in marble. What a change it has wrought in public sentiment! Look back—and many of us can remember it—to the time when tippling was interwoven with every custom of society, and infancy sucked drunkenness from the mother's breast. We know that intemperance yet sits like a nightmare upon the bosom of society; but there are millions of homes, and fields, and systems from which it has been forever banished. Where is now the physician that prescribes rum to the mother, or a mother who swallows such prescriptions, or feeds them to the child? Where is the family table where the morning bitters sit with the food which gives life and strength? Where is the mechanic who carries it to his shop? The farmer who furnishes it to his laborers in the field? The marriage where the health and happiness of the bride must be given in wine? The funeral where it must mingle with the tears of the bereaved? They are scarce. A blessed light has dawned upon community, and it is found that man can be born, married, and die without the spirit of alcohol.

In the progress of the reform, nearer and still nearer to the enemy, the ground has been broken. The first position was not the one of to-day. The old pledge was the entering wedge, but it did not banish the insidious tempter from our own ranks. It coiled still in the wine cup, and in the more common alcoholic beverages. Experience demonstrated the folly of chaining the mad dog, and the total abstinence pledge was adopted. Then came a war among temperance men, but the right triumphed; for, it was found that the old pledge was a dangerous ground for drinking men. Then came the Washingtonian movement, like a storm, and its floods swept on with startling intensity and power. There are ten thousand trophies where it moved; but the force of the torrent long since spent itself. The flames have died out upon its altars, as a general thing, and its legions disbanded, or enlisted in new organizations. Something more systematic was demanded. An organization more concentrated, and ever active, was called for, to retain old ground and win new fields—one which should throw a shield around the inebriate, and retain him by influences always appealing to his manhood and love of home. The exigency brought out the thing needed, and the triple emblem of the Red, White and Blue, was lifted to the world. Under its broad folds, an army of freemen has gathered, such as the world has never seen before. The tread of that army sounds the doom of the rum traffic.

In the commencement of our reform, and for a number of years, the mass of its friends considered "moral suasion" as the only means of success. It would have accomplished its work, were all men susceptible to moral influences. But it would not answer the ends designed. While human nature is such as to require penal laws in the restraint and punishment of its excesses, moral influences will never keep man from the commission of wrong. God's government is not based upon moral suasion alone. His laws are prohibitory, as are the laws upon our statute books. And against all this array of enactments, human and divine, wicked men continue to trample upon the rights of others. If laws will not prevent the commission of wrong, who would expect moral influences alone to protect the interests of society from the vicious and abandoned? And more especially would it fall far short of accomplishing such an object, when coming in contact with evils *sustained and guarded by legislation.* Never, while avarice has a home in the human heart, can bad men be influenced, by moral considerations, to abandon a traffic which law tolerates, and protects, and clothes with respectability. With a license law existing and shielding the seller from punishment, how long before he could be prevailed upon to abandon a lucrative business? Time might end and find the traffic in its full strength, and those engaged in it as indifferent to our entreaties and appeals, as they are to-day.

It was seen that the fountain must be dried—the Upas uprooted and destroyed forever. Hence the idea of prohibition and protection. And this sentiment finds a response in the hearts of the friends of the cause, enthusiastic and unanimous. Here is the great battle-ground, and around this banner the contending interests are rallying. Eloquence has been spent in vain heretofore, so far as having any effect upon those engaged in the traffic. God's truth has thundered against them. Facts have been piled on facts, until they tower in fearful judgment against them. Arguments, unanswerable, have been adduced, and appeals of the most earnest and touching pathos been made. All has been in vain. Entrenched behind law, and flanked by the unscrupulous demagogueism of the country, they have looked unmoved upon the ruin wrought by their own hands, and laughed all our efforts to scorn. A new system of warfare must be adopted, or the strife would be for time. As in times past, so Providence, at this juncture, directed the movements. Then appeared a light in the east, and clear and startling above the din of the strife, came a new battle cry, thrilling like an electric shock, and everywhere arousing our wearied hosts. A new banner out, and its magic words have filled all hearts with zeal, faith and hope. "THE MAINE LAW" is an emblem of triumph. It is the mystic writing upon the wall, announcing the downfall of the Babylon whose iniquites have so long cursed the earth, and political Belshazzars already look upon the record of sure coming doom, and tremble. The new plan is as simple as potent. It embodies, in a stringent form, the principles of prohibition and protection. Like all other laws for the prevention of crime, it strikes at the cause, leaving the streams to dry up when no longer fed by the fountain. It dispenses with arguments and appeals. It leaves no dripping heads to multiply others, but attacks the hydra in his den, and with the hot irons of fine and imprisonment, sears as it goes. It destroys *the traffic itself.* Like a complete battery, it has been planted under the very walls of the enemy. Broad breaches have already been made in the very citadel, and the flushed legions of four States of the Union are already pouring in for the last hand-to-hand conflict. "God defend the Right" in the battle.

Various instrumentalities have operated in bringing the Temperance Reform up to its present commanding position. Able men have written and spoken, and from the rostrum and the pulpit public opinion has been educated. But the great engine has been the PRESS. This giant friend of man in a free country, has scattered its light, its facts, arguments and appeals, into millions of hearts and homes. It has invoked a storm slowly, but none the less effectually. The mutterings of years past are deepening into startling peals, and the red language of popular indignation and wrath, glows ominously bright across the sky. The deep of public opinion is rocking to its depths.

The Temperance Press, at first struggling with almost overwhelming difficulties, has slowly increased in ability and power, and to-day exerts a controlling influence upon public sentiment. The literature of our reform is assuming a more refined and elevated character, and clothing great truths in purer and more attractive garb; and never was there a wider field for the exercise of intellectual effort. The wildest dreams of fiction seem tame in comparison with the stern and sober realities of our cause. Tragedies, more fearfully dark and startling than Avon's bard ever sketched, are thickly traced on the record of rum's history. Scenes which would mock the artist's pencil are of daily occurrence. The desolate home, with its heart-broken wife and mother, with her pale cheek channelled with tears of unutterable woe, as she bends weeping over the drunken wreck of her youth's idol; the child-group shivering in the blast, or clinging to that mother, as they moan for bread; the orphan turned out, with no friend but God, into the wide world; youth wrecked and palsied with premature age; manhood reeling amid the ruins of mind and moral beauty, the sepulchre of a thousand hopes; genius drivelling in idiocy and crumbling into ruin; the virtuous and noble-minded turning away from truth and honor, and plunging into every vice; the parent and citizen wandering away from a home-heaven, through a devious and dark pilgrimage, to a dishonored grave—the home-idol shivered and broken, the altar cast down, and an Eden transformed into a hell; childhood and innocence thrust out from the lovelight of a mother's eye, to wallow in all that is low and vile; Poverty and Want looking with pinched and piteous gaze upon the scanty tribute of charity; foul and festering Vice, with sickly and bloated features, leering and droolling in licentious beastiality; Madness, with fiery eye and haggard mien, weeping and wailing and cursing in the rayless night of intellectual chaos; Crime, with its infernal 'ha! ha!' as it stalks forth from its work of death, with its red hand dripping with the hot and smoking life-tide of its victim;—these, and ten thousand other combinations of warp and woof, are woven into tales of wondrous intensity and power. The hovel, the dram-shop, the subterranean den, and the mansion of fashion and wealth, have all furnished the material for tales of startling interest. When fiction even has called up its weird creations, they have been but copies of the facts already transpired. The moral is always there. Thus poetry and romance have combined to place the realities of two opposing principles in striking contrast. Such is the object of the following tale, from the perusal of which we will no longer detain the kind reader. That the Maine Law may triumph, and the dark shadow of Intemperance pass away, is the earnest prayer of him who has thus far claimed attention. The door is open, and the reader can go in and examine the structure of the author's fabric at leisure.

T. W. B.

DICK WILSON.

CHAPTER I.

FUTURE PLANS AND PROSPECTS.

"Thou who, securely lull'd in Youth's warm ray,
Mark'st not the desolations wrought by Wine!
Be roused, or perish! Ardent for its prey,
Speeds the fell CURSE, that ravages thy prime."

FRIENDS of Humanity! Heaven is in the great effort which is now being made against the rum traffic. God designs that this great national disgrace,—this plague-spot upon the pages of civil law,—shall be wiped out by a bloodless revolution. And the many voices of the same God, coming through unmistakable agencies, are summoning you to the spot where Humanity and Temperance erected their pure white standard; and where soon, by the blessing of God, and the assistance of those who love peace, you are expected to do just what others have done in Maine,— "*Rout the rumseller!*"

"Ah! then, this means me, does it?" says a distiller, hard by. "I won't read a word of it,—no, indeed! It is a shame that people won't mind their own business. I tell you what I will do,—I will fight against this effort until the very death!"

"This is agitating the subject of *white slavery!*" say the *genteel* apologists for this immeasurable curse; "*equal rights for the people*, is my motto," says the time-serving politician; "we must be up in arms against it; if we do not, our craft and our trade will go down together," says the trembling rumseller.

Yes, enemies of mankind, it is precisely so; and as Delilah said to Samson, so we would say to you,—the Philistines are upon you!

You know very well that Humanity, in all her forms, has appealed to you, and craved your mercy, —that your work is wicked, and that its tendency is brutalizing in the extreme. The ragged, starving, trembling child,—the father, the mother, the brother, and the sister, have invoked your compassion. But to what purpose?

The poor-house, the prison, the gallows, the suicide, —have, with one voice, besought you to desist. But to what purpose are these most fearful of exhibitions that can be made upon the earth, and of which you are the architect? Have they moved you to mercy? No! These facts have had no impression; but like a rival Juggernaut, you have moved on your ponderous, crushing car! and the warm, fresh blood of your vic-

still rises in your path, and is invoking the vengeance of God upon your cruelty.

Humanity has appealed to you in every form,—by every argument,—until her very charity has lost all confidence; and hopeless, and in tears, she has turned to the humane, the noble, and the virtuous; and when these are fairly marshalled in the order of legislative battle, you must disband,—disband, as did your fellow craft, in the gallant State of Maine.

Remember—Remember the battle of Maine! for it loosened your foundations throughout the dominion of civilization. The next music you hear will be the voices of little children chanting in ecstasy the rumseller's doom: "The rumselling Babylon is fallen—FALLEN—FALLEN—to curse humanity no more forever!"

Friend of humanity! are you a father, standing at the threshold of your own door, and holding in your own hand, with a warm, parental grasp, that of your son, for whom, and for yourself, the endearing assosociations of the past are, to a great extent, to be broken up forever? *You* expect to remain under the shelter of your own roof; but your boy—your proud, noble boy—the object to which your hopes are clinging—he is going out into the "wide, wide world," of trials and temptations.

But then, why do you weep? Why do you linger, as if you were unwilling that the word of parting should ever leave your lips?

Ah, yes, father, you know why it is. The big tear starting from your eye is sparkling with the interpretation. Oh! yes; it is the recognition of the rumseller's ability to cut off all your expectations; and, finally, to cut off your boy!—and you do well to weep. But remember that timely action may save you, in your old age, those bitterest of all tears—the untimely and unavailing.

Mother!—dearest of earthly names—most precious treasure which God reserves to the child on earth—mother, why do you weep, as your boy goes forth from your home? Why does that silent ejaculation, which can only find an overflowing fulness in the deep storehouse of a mother's love, so often go out from your heart?—"God bless and preserve my dear boy!"

Brother—sister—friend! Why do you weep as your several relations in life are broken up by the departure of dear ones? These may all come back again. Yes, and who knows this better, or hopes more fervently for it, than you do? Wherefore, then, dost thou weep?

Do you see—and, perchance, not far off, in the future—a loved one straying back again, a wasted wreck? Ah! if tears have the power to strengthen the weak, you do well to shed them freely; for the rumseller has a fearful power. He has the power to crush, by his cruel machinery, the finest form and the noblest intellect, and fashion the likeness of the invisible God into the similitude of a beast!

A sense of sadness always steals its way, and mingles freely in the associations of an hour, in which loved ones are called to part.

Such a sadness as this seldom fails to throw itself about the evening of a college commencement-day; and it is natural, as well as fitting, that it should be so. In circumstances like these, relations and associations, which are only to be surpassed by the endearing ties of home, are to be broken up. Hearts, which have been knit together and interwoven with each other by the intimate and sweet communion of several years, it may be, are now to be parted. Their paths are to be divided, and the pleasant seclusion of a college life, with all its local associations and life-like memories, are to be exchanged for the stern warfare of real existence,—one for which the wisest is but poorly girded,—a tournament in which, often, the lance of the generous young warrior is shivered in his hand by a powerful antagonist, and himself thrown prostrate and bleeding to the ground.

It was on one of those beautiful and never-to-be-forgotten evenings, which seldom fail to throw a melancholy, love-like radiance about the closing scenes of a commencement-day, in a dear old college in western Pennsylvania, in whose history many a one in this wide land is associated, and in whose affections it will never lose its place.

It was on the evening of one of those lovely days, in the latter part of September, 184—, that Frank Hamilton entered the room of Dick Wilson, to bid his more than "college chum" good-bye. These young men were as warm friends—not from necessity, but choice—as ever were united within the dominions of that venerable enclosure, from its rude "log cabin" to its stately pile of brick.

Their time had come to part—their college hours were all lived out, to the very end; and yet they lingered in the presence of that passing moment, as if they would fain protract, into years again, that which just then was passing with a whirlwind's haste.

It was natural enough that these young men should feel so. This same feeling has clung to a thousand partings which have taken place there. They were to part with a numerous band of other young men, whom they could only hope to meet again, if ever, on the stormy ocean of life; and whose huge billows, they knew, would at last roll over the graves of all. But did it occur to them that some would go down earlier, and some later,—that some would go down in brightness, and some in gloom?

But old Dr. B——, whose kindness was a proverb, with all his eccentricities,—to part with him—to hear that voice no more, perhaps, forever—the voice to which they had been so well accustomed to listen—the same which had given them a kindly welcome on their first arrival within its walls—the same from which they were accustomed to hear the truths of religion and the lessons of science; this voice—to hear it no more upon the earth, was far from being the least powerful of the influences with which that moment was filled to overflowing.

Frank Hamilton and Dick Wilson were classmates. They had been thrown together strangers; but strangeness had passed away before the mystic minglings of kindred spirits with kindred tastes and sympathies, and they were friends, to each of whom the "good-bye" was a cheerless sound.

It was a difficult matter for them to part. They looked at each other intently, as if searching for some portion of their future history. They looked about upon the walls of that old room, with every square inch of which they seemed, at that moment, to have a wonderful familiarity. Why did these young men hesitate to go? The homes, towards which they were about to return again, were waiting to welcome them; and yet they wept! Was the unseen spirit of some departed one at that moment communicating to them the facts in their future history? Did they see, a little way off in the future, some gloomy monster upon whom almighty vengeance had written *fiend*, rising to obstruct their path? Were they gifted at that moment, with the view of the rumseller's power over human character and human destiny? No! surely they were not, or the buoyant aspirations of their hearts would have been chilled to icy coldness.

"Well, Dick," said Frank Hamilton, after some evident emotion, "I have come to say farewell, but, my dear fellow, I did not realize, until this moment, how difficult it would be to part with you. But the fact is, Dick, our business here is all over—our work is done, and we must go, and make room for those who are to succeed us. It grieves me to think how soon we shall be forgotten on these grounds; for, with the coming of the next session the stranger will come, and some one or more, as the case may be, or as necessity may require, will take up their abode in this old third-story room of yours, in which we have spent so many pleasant hours together, and around every part of which, at this moment, I see pleasant associations clustering. With these new faces will come a train of new feeling, and new associations, and new interests; and these new creations will cluster about these walls, and mingle with this atmosphere, as gaily and as lovingly as ours do now. But where, Dick, shall we be, when these new associations are continuing to be formed here, through many future years?"

"The Lord only knows, Frank! I hope, however,

that the poor fellow who comes here next may manage to keep the *blues* off as well as I have done; but then, I am in your debt, after all, for a large share of my success in doing so."

"Well, Dick, you are no doubt right when you say that the Lord knows, but the fact is, I should like to know something about it myself, if it is good; and if it is not good, then I don't care particularly about being very wise, so far as that is concerned. After all, I tell you, this college life is rather a dreamy affair. There is but little of the hard-fisted, rough-and-tumble reality about it. Here we are at this moment, just going out into the world, and we know but little more about it than a brace of old monks, who have been shut up in their cloisters all the days of their lives, and what under the heavens do they know about its wants and its realities? Well, the fact is, we are not much wiser than they are. We passed from the nursery to the school-house—from the school-house to the academy—from the academy to this college; and I think we have kept one proverb about as well as it is possible to keep it—'salute no man by the way.' But then, with us it has been the action of necessity rather than volition. I am afraid, Dick, after all, we will be forced to a conclusion to which young persons generally do not wish to come; but old folks say it is true, and they cannot be reasoned out of it either, that 'the ways of this world are not always as pleasant as they might be.' The history of this world, if those who preceded us here and elsewhere are to be believed, is a strange and checkered story, made up of pleasures and pains, of success and failures, of triumphs and defeats."

"Why, Frank," said Dick Wilson, "what on the earth is the matter with you all at once? Come, come, my friend, shuffle off those unpleasant reflections; for this, I am sure, is no time for them. What business have they here at such an hour? I am sure we have enough else to think about and talk about, without disturbing the wisdom of our fathers. If misfortune is before us, it will be time enough for us to know it when it comes. All I will ask of the surly old dame is half an hour's notice of her coming. I am sure this is fair, and then, if she gets her paws on me, I will surrender; but I tell you, Frank, she must be ready to spring very soon after she sends her compliments, or else she will find me, eyes right, and prepared to meet her. And by the powers, Frank, there is another thing that I will just mention,—'we are not old monks.' If there were such beings as young monks, you would be a precious sight nearer than you are. But old monks! Frank, just think of that again, and you will call it back; and what is more to be observed just now, is this,—you had better not compare anything, about these quarters, to mockery, or you may find yourself minus a diploma, yet. A monk!

Why, Frank, this orthodox atmosphere would strangle him, just as soon as Hibernian soil would kill a snake; he couldn't live here at all. Monks, indeed! No, sir, I guess not. But come, shuffle off those unpleasant reflections,—wake up from this dream of yours; fling these grim spectres out of your mind, and select for your motto, what I have selected for mine —'*ad astra!*'—and Pluto himself can't keep us from winning the race. But, Frank, go on; say whatever your inclination may lead you to say, only don't sermonize; for you know we have had one of the usual dimensions to-day, already."

"Well, Dick," replied Frank Hamilton, "you have entrenched yourself pretty well,—better than I imagined you could, and much better than I am able to do. But then let me tell you, Dick, it is folly to kill by sport what may come as reality. You know as well as I do, that at least a few get what is called a short and a merry ride through life. How merry it may be, is what I could not vouch for; but there is no mistake about its being short enough, to answer those who are in the greatest hurry. Several times, since we met here strangers, our hearts have been made sad by the intelligence of the melancholy failure and fall of those whose acquaintance we first formed here; and it is remarkable, that, without a single exception, so far as I know, they were those who were amongst the first in every sense; and very unexpectedly to themselves, and to us, first in the grave! These dear fellows, graduated as we have done, and went away from here, as we are about to do. Their hopes were as bright as ours are now, and yet they perished in the very bud, and I think it is rather natural than forced, that these premature wrecks should make us thoughtful. We will leave here in the morning—our faces will once more be turned towards home; and kind friends, no doubt, will greet us, as we cross the sacred threshold. But then, Dick, home will be home no longer, in the sense of our boyish days. Things, you may depend upon it, will have changed. The love of the household will, no doubt, be as sincere as it ever was; but yet, each of us will find a change, which is both natural and necessary, although now we may not be able to conceive any such thing. I think that we had better make up our minds for hard times, and make a wise selection of our armor; and then, if they do come, they will find us prepared to meet them; and if, after all, they should not come, why, we will still be the gainers rather than the losers. I tell you, Dick, I am afraid you would find your half-hour too short at both ends, to gird yourself for an encounter with even a moderate share of adversity."

"Frank," replied Dick, "it is more difficult for me to break away from these associations than you imagine it is. In fact, it is more difficult than I thought it was. But then, I know it must be done, for we can't stay any longer here. The stranger wants to come; and now he is waiting to succeed us, as we succeeded others. Ah, yes! my dear fellow, he is waiting for an opportunity to form such sacred associations as ours have been. Yes, yes; he will spoil all their beauty for us, but then, it will be to make them beautiful for himself; and surely we should not envy him whatever pleasures he can get here. We have been permitted to paint, with the pencil of fancy, our living households upon these walls; but the poor fellow who comes here next may have nothing to paint, save what the grave has left him—the recollections of the past! Let him paint them, then!—let him enjoy them, too, and often, in his hours of sadness—let them cheer him, and have the power over him to nerve him forward. You and myself, Frank, will be architects somewhere else. I never knew until to-day, how much I thought of old Dr. B——. Those parting words of his to us, this evening, were the evidence of his solicitude for our future welfare.—No trifling circumstance will destroy his interest in us, and his affection for us; and I think if it were at all to be desired, we might be sure of his prayers. I must say, however, that while I admired the touching pathos of his parting benediction, that I did think he was rather too solicitous about our future, and especially mine. I suppose, however, that he would like to see us ministers, as a very large proportion of the crop which grows in this soil is of that kind. But this won't do for me. I think they are good enough, and useful enough, in their places, but I am satisfied that is not my place. Why do you think he made that singular allusion to the rumsellers, Frank?"

"I think, Dick, he has in all probability heard of some of your fun, as you call it—perhaps last night's *spree*."

"No, I should think not, Frank. I would rather attribute it to his hatred of the rumseller's *profession;* and, by the by, if he had the entire control, rumsellers, big and little, would soon be a rare commodity in this place. The fact is, I think he is too severe with those persons. But then, I don't want you to think that I have any sympathy with them. I think, when it is viewed narrowly, that in fact its virtue becomes so small as to be hardly visible. I mean the profession. These rumsellers cry 'accommodation, accommodation!' and old Dungy* cries precisely the same thing. When he comes in with his basket of *taffa*, he cries 'accommodation, accommodation!' and says, it is good for colds, coughs, and consumptions, and empty heads, too; and when he has succeeded in emptying his basket profitably, and has his change in his pocket, I guess he could, if he would, tell who, according to his judgment, was most profitably ac-

* A well-known hawker in —— College.

commodated. Just so with the rumsellers here and elsewhere—they are mighty free to accommodate! Oh, yes; nothing but accommodation! It is their profession, and they are ready to spring, like lamplighters, whenever there is a prospect of a sixpence or a shilling; but the misfortune is, when they accommodate in rum, the accommodation is all on their side, and no one knows it better than they do. No, sir, I have no sympathy with them, and I want no place in this rum army. I intend to let them alone. I will attend to my business, and they may attend to theirs. Here is where I object, principally, to the old doctor's advice. He wants us, as he says, 'first of all, for our safety, to array ourselves against it.' Well; first of all, I can't believe it can harm us; and then, I have no disposition to do it. It is a fine idea, indeed, that two young men, who are just going out into the world, and who have the profession of law in view, should be called to take the unpopular side of any question, and then make it a hobby upon which to ride themselves out of reach of every reasonable prospect. I won't do it. I expect to be in Congress, or somewhere else, some day, and marching after that music would lead anywhere else. No, no; not I! If he wants that done, he must turn out the *black coats*, and if they fail, no one will mind it. Don't you think I am about right, Frank?"

"Dick, I must be candid with you. Words live

forever, and it is better to speak them wisely. I must say that I think you are wrong, all wrong in this matter. You intimated that if it were a matter of importance, you thought we might safely reckon on the old doctor's prayers. Do you think, that the prayers of that good old man, following us out into the world, would be likely to do us any harm? For my own part, although I am not religious by profession, there is nothing which I would more desire; and I must tell you, that the knowledge of the fact, that I have a home, where prayers are offered for me daily, has made me feel safer; and I should feel all the better if I knew that many more were praying for me. Such things will not be likely to do us any harm, and I am sure that good advice will be just as unlikely to injure us. I have as good an opinion of myself as I ought to have. My hopes are as sanguine as I would desire them to be. I have painted my future as bright as I dare paint it. There is danger! True, it may never come to us. I hope, Dick, it never will. And here is where I think the prayers of that old man, following us out into the world, would be likely to do us good. But then, there is danger; and if it does not come to us, it will come to others. There will always be danger, while rumselling is permitted —and circumstances favoring it, it will be just as powerful to accomplish our ruin as that of any one else. This is one of the subjects for which a fitting illustra tion is always furnished to hand by the monster. Take those two boys to whom this evening we have given our old clothes. They are sweet, lovely children. How have we pitied them, whose wants we have often tried to supply? How many times have we seen them, when it was our conclusion that hunger had driven them from home? Think of that, Dick—driven from home by hunger! Then, who occasioned it? You know it was the rumseller. You know that it was their father's familiarity with the *bar-room*, that made poverty reign in his house,—that sent the inmates out to beg. How often have we looked at the apparently happy group of boys, engaged in play? But these little fellows, if they were there, were generally at the outer edge of the circle. Often have I looked on, when every countenance in that group was lit up with smiles but theirs—every heart appeared to be leaping with joy but theirs. Every one in that crowd but those two, little more than children, knew that they had comfortable homes, to which, at the end of their sports, they might retire. These children had a shelter—but who would call it a home?—only that a mother's love was there. When I have looked at this, again and again, I have asked myself the question, 'Who has robbed these children?' and my better judgment has answered, 'The rumseller!' These boys were the back-ground to every youthful sport in which they mingled, and as sometimes a rude, unfeeling lad would taunt them for their poverty, they would make no reply; but their countenances would seem to say—'Mock us not! It is not *our* fault; we are not to blame. This misfortune is the rumseller's work, and not ours. We do not love these ragged clothes; but necessity, of the rumseller's creation, compels us to wear them. If we are hungry, and cold, and naked, and unloved by all, save our dear mother, oh, do not reproach us for it—for we are innocent! Some of your fathers are warming and feeding the serpent which is stinging us to death!' To me, Dick, those little fellows, with their bright eyes and pale cheeks, seemed to realize their loneliness. I have sometimes thought that they seemed to feel as if they were uncared for; and if such were the feelings of those little boys, I know of nothing which would so much tend to harden, to vitiate, and deprave their young minds. And is this all? Oh, no! they are but two out of the thousands with which the land is teeming. These boys need a defence—the most powerful defence; and where are they to find it? They will not be likely to find it in the same channel where they find their father's ruin. Ah! no, indeed, these are not the agencies to whom they can confidently look for lessons of virtue. No, no! They must look somewhere else than to the rumseller. Now, Dick, they have a right to your aid and mine. Whenever there is necessity, they shall have mine! This appears to me to be a work of the most exalted character in which a human being could engage,—a work in which talents of the most brilliant order might do honor to the possessor, and immense, immeasurable good to the little *unfortunates*, with whose wail of sadness the land is becoming vocal. In my own State there are about twenty-five thousand drunkards! Most of these have families, making the aggregate number of sufferers at least one hundred thousand in that single State. One hundred thousand sufferers bleeding at the hands of rumsellers! What an army this, which is being swept on to ruin! Collect it in your own mind, and then look at it, and then tell me what work of earthly character can be so truly noble as that which would seek to restore them to happiness? You are mistaken about this matter, or else I am; for I believe the finest abilities and the rarest accomplishments will do their mightiest work and get their most signal renown on this very field; for God will help them. The conquerors on this field will bring away with them such laurels as will never fade. Their fame will be a living, cheering, soul-inspiring fame! It will ascend up with morning and evening orisons,—from altars whose base the rumseller has caused to be saturated with tears!—the widow's and the orphan's tears! From homes where children have starved, and from solitudes where beauty has pined. This is the heaven-born and the heaven-given meed, which is awaiting the victors in this war. Can it be possible, Dick, that you intend to plead no cause for which you are not paid in money, as you once intimated to me? Is it possible that you intend to leave the fate, the character, the everything belonging to this class, to other hands than yours; and that you will have nothing to do in aiding to heal their wounds,—in wiping the tears from their eyes? If so, I tremble for your future. I am convinced that it is your duty—that it is my duty—that it is the duty of every man, woman and child—to war with everything which tends to disorganize human society, or taint it with the breath of putrefaction—whatever may tend to depreciate morals—to squander property—to destroy health—to wither reputation, or to insult God!"

"Well, well, Frank, you will find, I imagine, and I am sorry for it, that this philosophy won't be very profitable to you. It would do very well in the pulpit, but it will never do anything for you at the bar."

"Well, then, Dick, this is my principal philosophy, and if it should not be current at the bar, I will try its currency in some other avocation. But I apprehend no such difficulty; and I do believe, farther, that the best way to secure our safety, is to do all in our power for the safety of others. This, I am sure, will be our safest plan, and it will secure our dearest interests, and I advise you to adopt this principle. But, I must go. Will we ever meet again?"

"I hope we shall, Frank; and then we will talk more about these things, and be better able to tell whose philosophy was best, wisest, and safest. Keep the portrait my mother gave you. I know of no other person to whom she would have given it. It may at some future time serve to revive by-gone recollections. I shall always remember you,—I cannot forget you."

"Nor will I ever forget you, Dick. Wherever you find me, you will find Frank Hamilton still. Remember me kindly to your family. Tell them I never shall forget them."

The good-bye was uttered, and the young men parted, to meet again—they could not tell when, where, or how.

CHAPTER II.

NEWS FROM HOME.—A SAD CHANGE.

"Fair was the blossom, soft the vernal sky,
Elate with hope, we deemed no tempest nigh;
When lo! a whirlwind's instantaneous gust,
Left all its beauties withering in the dust."

How often—yes, how continually—in the midst of life's pleasantest ways and most winning prospects, are we, seemingly by a Providential declaration, taught that it is not in man that walketh to direct his steps. How often is it made plain, on a wide scale, that the circumstances by which we are surrounded, and which we often create, or tacitly endorse—be they propitious, or unpropitious—are the mighty levers, under the agency of which we are impelled onward, and often with a tyranny more absolute than that which presses the fainting slave through his years of toil; and this, often, when the voice of a living consciousness tells us we are wrong, and that destruction and misery are in the way, and its end death!

There are none who are more frequently or more fearfully startled, in the ways of life, than the young —especially the young man. He is just lifting the curtain, and feeling his way, cautiously, or recklessly, it may be, to the stage—the stage on which innumerable actors have played their part, and for whom another curtain has been lifted, and through whose opening they have passed to other scenes! How fearfully variegated is the *comic* and the *tragic* of this drama! Such persons have no experience—their knowledge of the world is second-hand—and hence they enter upon this stage, crowded with as much uncertainty as that which crowded the entrance of the gladiator, when, for the first time, he braved the dangers of the Roman or Ephesian Amphitheatre. He knew not how it would result. The Tuscan boar, the Numidian lion, or the Hispanolian bull, after a feeble defence, might overcome him; or it might be that a well aimed blow from the battle-axe, or thrust from the spear, might lay his savage antagonist in the dust, and win for him a conqueror's meed. But everything trembled upon the wheel of a hazardous uncertainty.

How little do those who are experienced in the warfare of life—who are rich in the history of its joys and it sorrows—seem to understand how much they may do in equipping a young warrior, that he may reach at last a more brilliant fame than that which graced a Roman holiday!

How seldom do we dream of the infinite, the indestructible duration, of those far-reaching pulsations, which come in quivering, lisping echoes, from the slight vibration which a touch may waken into life! —a touch, a breath, a faint articulation—hallowed, or unhallowed, for good or for evil, for fame or for infamy! Who shall measure the power which that single touch may give to one of those fragile human barks on life's stormy ocean—or how it may allay its storms, and assuage the fury of its madness, by carrying with it an ennobling sympathy, containing the elements of "peace, be still?" The earthquake sends the tremor of its wild pulsations farther when it is deepest buried in the bosom of the earth. So does the element of virtue. So, too, does the element of vice.

It is human nature's great misfortune, that its sympathies are not more generally on the side of virtue. By the unhallowed touch of an ingeniously wrought mystic influence, the seeds of corruption easily affiliate with the soil of the human heart, and when left to act of its own accord, what fearful desolations mark its path!—desolations which are not measured by days, but by the unravelling thread of a whole existence.

One year had scarcely passed away since Dick Wilson had parted with his friend, Frank Hamilton. Then his countenance was expressive of the most ardent hope—now it was expressive of sorrow and disappointment. Dark storms had suddenly swept over the roof, and howled in the halls of his princely home, and before their driving fury it had become desolate indeed. Already the stranger named it by another name, and Dick Wilson had no home! His father—a kind, indulgent, but unfortunate man—had fallen into the rumseller's hands, and then, ah! how suddenly, changed his earthly for an eternal home. He needed no longer the well-attired parlors, or the company of his brilliant guests; for his cup was drained—his banquets over. Close by the side of that father—in the spring-time of her existence, in the blooming freshness of her young life—reposed a lovely daughter; and while other hearts were beating high with hope, her's had ceased to throb. One morning's sun saw her, still in beauty, but with a deep shade of sorrow on her brow: that evening's setting sun looked forth again, as it was departing, through the crimson drapery of a quiet room, and again its golden tints fell upon the same brow. But now, gloom had disappeared—the traces of sorrow were gone; her features were clear, her heart moved not—for her form, girt about with the pale livery of death, was ready to be laid by the side of her father, on whose premature fall, through the rumseller's agency, the young heart had broken. Fortune had failed, with her train of fickle attendants.

All this, to Dick Wilson, had come suddenly. He had not received even his half-hour's notice of its coming; and it came just at the time in which, with greater buoyancy than ever, he was aspiring towards future fame; and, more than ever, he was unconscious that the wings, to whose capacity he was too confidently trusting, were about to be broken off.

It was a night of merriment with Dick and some of his young law companions, at C——; but it was a night of wasting sadness in his home. *Wine* had entered the room where these young men were holding their conviviality—but *intense sorrow* had borne itself to the doors of the home he loved, to banish its joys and wipe out its happiness.

These young men were nearly frenzied with ecstasy as the wine cup, the great mocker, with all its deceptiveness, pictured to them a glowing future—a future, in which the dullest and most stupid, as well as the most brilliant mind in the throng, saw the doors of fortune and fame hard by each other, and both wide open to admit them, inviting them to come at once—to come hastily—to come by the nearest way, and to discard from their minds the tedious idea of building up a temple for themselves, and placing and fitting each stone with their own hands. Ah! yes; to come by the bleak and blighted path, along which *wine* has led her fame-aspiring votaries.

While these things were passing before the minds, and whirling in the brains of those young men, Dick Wilson, to all appearance, felt it to be a night of cheer—of rich, innocent enjoyment. But then he knew not by what a fearful voice he was soon to be awakened from the embrace of the charmer; little did he dream at that moment a mother and two sisters were watching the fast glazing eyes of a dying father, whose pleasant words and gentle smiles had greeted him for the last time. While *he* was looking at the beauties of a picture which *wine* promised to draw for him, his dear ones *at home* were looking upon a cheerless reality, which wine had painted for them, and to which the privileged rumseller had added the last touch of his scathing pencil.

When Dick Wilson returned to his own room that night, he threw himself down, with apparent unconcern, upon a lounge, and while musing there, he sud denly caught a glimpse of something suspended to his mirror. He looked at this a moment without moving, and then rising hastily, he advanced to examine it, and found it to be a letter from his mother, which some thoughtful person had brought from the office, and placed in that position, that he might the more easily find it. On opening it, he exclaimed, "Why, this is from mother!—something must be wrong." The letter contained a simple request for him to come home immediately, and bring everything with him. "This," said he, "is strange indeed. Mother has written to me to come home at once, and to bring everything with me, and there is not a word of explanation about it. They can't have any prejudices against this school, and intend sending me some where else. No, this is not the reason; for in that case father would have written. They can't be sick; for it was only the day before yesterday that I received a letter from them, and they were all well. I must look again at the other letter." He ran his eye over it carefully, and at length he said, "Yes; here it is—little Harry is slightly indisposed. Yes, here is the secret," he continued; "my poor little brother, very unexpectedly to them, at the time of writing this letter, may since have become very sick, and perhaps he is dead; and if this is so, my arrival at home will not be greeted, as formerly, by smiles and joys, but by a heart-broken household."

Just at this moment, and while Dick was still trembling in uncertainty, a young man who had made one of the company during the evening, entered his room. It was evident enough that this young man's brain was still restless, and he determined to say nothing to him about his letter. After some time his friend observed Dick's uneasy manner, and inquired what was the matter. Dick at once informed him.

"Well, if I were in your place, Dick Wilson," replied the young man, "I wouldn't go—at all events, I wouldn't go for my mother's saying so. Yes, yes, indeed, a mother—she is the last person I would think of obeying, or whose right to command I would acknowledge. 'Come home, immediately, and bring everything with you.' I'll tell you, Wilson, that's a sweeping command to come from a mother. But I suppose you won't be fool enough to go."

"Yes, I will," replied Dick, sharply; "I will leave by the stage in the morning."

"Well, now, Dick," continued the profligate young man, "I would not go—at any rate until I should receive another letter; and if they want you badly it will soon come, and your father will write it, and he will give you the whys and wherefores. What do you think is wrong at home, Mr. Wilson?"

"I don't know," replied Dick; "but I fear a little brother may be very ill, or perhaps dead."

"And you will go home for *that?*"

"Certainly!" replied Dick.

"Well, I guess I wouldn't do any such thing—not for a mother's command, nor to see a little dead brother, either. Why, my folks, I don't believe, would send for me, if all the family should die; for they have come to the conclusion that I will have my own way, and necessity has compelled them to give me free passes, and I'm my own man, and independent of mothers and dead brothers. I'm bent on enjoying myself."

Here the conversation ended. Dick slept none that night, but busied himself in making preparations for an early start in the morning. He was thinking of home, and trying to satisfy himself as to what the cause of this unexplained request could possibly be.

And often, as he looked upon that sleeping figure, with hat and boots and all on, upon his bed, the perfect picture of hardened recklessness, did he think of Frank Hamilton, and of the contrast. And sometimes he almost concluded that the philosophy of Frank should be his philosophy. He hesitated, however, and excused himself by saying, "This fellow would have been a brute if wine had never been made!"

Dick Wilson arrived at home, and was greeted by the wail of a weeping family. Just as he entered the door, his sister Eliza threw her arms about his neck, saying,

"Dear, dear Dick, poor father is dead!"

The shock was sudden and appalling. He felt in a moment how insecure were the hopes of life. But he did not know until the next day that they were to be driven into the street by *the law* which protects this species of murder, and which in so many cases gives the administrator of rum complete control over the estate of his victim.

Who calls this innocent? Oh, if it be, whisper it not in the hearing of the lisping child! Whisper it nowhere, but among the hopelessly depraved! Go where humanity has erected a shelter for the rumseller's worn-out victim, and if you tell that poor creature that it is innocent, he will tell you that it is false! Here stood Dick Wilson, with this appalling evidence staring him in the face. Could he say, as he looked upon this dark picture, and saw it in all its horror, that no blame could be attached to the rumseller? No! But as he saw the change, for which he was unprepared, is it not probable that in the depths of his own heart, bitter, burning curses were muttered against the cause and the agencies which had so early blighted his fair prospects, and withered the hopes of his home? It would be strange, indeed, if he did not. God himself looks with abhorrence upon such agencies, whose fearful ravages cover the land. And must they still go on? Is there no way to check the fearful flood of ruin? There is. A light looms up in the east, full of hope and cheer to the friends of humanity! By it you may read the *mene, mene, tekel, upharsin*—the rumseller's doom! THE MAINE LAW IS ENACTED!! Already have its benignant influences pervaded the border State, and have swept, with electric rapidity, over every State of the Union. On this, Humanity fixes her hope—a foundation firm as the rocks of its parent State.

* * * * * * * * *

Dick Wilson had just carried into a very small house, situated in a part of the city frequented by the inheritors of poverty, the last articles of their scanty furniture—all that the *law* and the *rumseller* had left them. Deep agitation was visible in Mrs. Wilson's countenance, as her eyes fell upon the few precious relics which remained of her once ample establishment. With them were connected the fondest and most endearing, as well as the bitterest recollections of her life. *Here* was a memento of the sunny period of her existence, the sight of which brought vividly and at once to view, the love, the devotion of him who was then the fond father, the more than devoted husband,—*there* a relic, reminding her of the many years of domestic happiness which she had passed in *that house*, from which she had been so suddenly and ruthlessly driven.

There may be some who cannot realize the feelings of this family at that moment, and others still who may say, "It is well enough, for aristocracy ought to fall." Well, you are supremely cruel. If you had been a beggar at Mrs. Wilson's door, in the time of her prosperity, she would not have turned you away empty; but she would have supplied your wants, and given you a kindly word. Nor would she have forgotten to ask you if there were others in your home who needed her assistance. Even the old drayman, with his rough exterior and sun-browned face, could feel for them. He had known them in the day of their prosperity, and now, in the day of their adversity, he was doing what he could to assist them, and one could see, in his cheerful movements, the character of his heart.

There is something noble in a strong man's tear. It bespeaks a cause, under the influence of which it has been forced from its hiding place. A tear, denoting the true nobility of his nature, stood in the eye of old Donald, as he spoke his word of cheer to Mrs. Wilson, before leaving the door:

"Many, aye, many a time, Mrs. Wilson, has ould Donald seen the like of this. Yes, sure, madam, they're sorry days, but they must be borne; but it's weel to trust in God—it's always weel to do so, in riches and in poverty. Yes, madam, God will pay these workers of iniquity for the sorrow they have brought to you;" and brushing the tear from his eye with his sleeve, he spoke gently to his horse, and departed.

"Mother," said Dick, as he seated himself in a house which gave unmistakable evidence that for a long time it had been consecrated to poverty—"mother, dear, dear mother, can it be possible that we are really in this situation, and that this is all that is left to us? Is it merely in a dream that I see this misery? Is this my mother, my sweet sister, my dear little brother? Then where are the rest? Ah! yes; but it's not a dream. I understand it—it's only too real. The rumseller—the rumseller! What a name! —what a power!—what a destroyer!"

"My son, be calm," replied Mrs. Wilson; "let us give this dark cloud an opportunity to pass over. We are here, my son, alone; and this is all that is left to us. But, my dear children, you are spared to me, and we to each other, yet. Richard, I saw this storm coming. I saw it when it first appeared in the horizon, and I labored to arrest it; but I failed. It came to me, my boy, after all, nearly as suddenly as it did to yourself. For some time I vainly hoped that if I could not prevent it entirely, I might at least be able to make it linger in its coming; and what you see, with the exception of seven hundred dollars, which was in my possession at the time of your father's death, is all that we have left. But, with this you can finish your profession, and when once you are admitted to the bar, I think I may hope, my dear son, that you will be able to make some provision for us all. Richard, my first born, our staff and stay is broken off, and we must lean upon *you*. You must be our protector: you must be our defence. It seems to be too hard for you: the load is too heavy. A mother, and sister, and brother, all helpless as children. Oh! it was cruel in the rumseller thus to torture us."

"Yes, yes, dear Dick," exclaimed his sister, throwing her arms about the neck and kissing the fine forehead of her brother, whose spirit seemed indeed broken; "yes, my brother, you are our only dependence, and to you we must cling. You are our only earthly protector, my dear brother. This change has been severe, Dick; but still, it might have fallen with greater severity. God is good, for he has spared you to us yet, and we will pray for you continually, that you may not be taken from us. Poor dear Ellen, it is well that *you* are gone. I am sure your gentle spirit is in heaven. I see still the sweet, serene smile which death left upon your lips, and memory, dear Ellen, will ever fondly cherish it. Yes, Dick, she is gone. She is done with the sorrow of this toilsome way. And I have just been wondering with myself, whether it may not be entirely consistent with the Divine government, that the spirits of the just made perfect by the blood of the everlasting Covenant, may not have some knowledge of this world still; and also whether they are not sometimes sent on errands of mercy, to brighten the hopes and lighten the toils of the earthly pilgrimage of their friends. If such permission is given in the courts of the redeemed, then we will have the gentle spirit of a glorified sister to sympathize with us in our gloomy path, and He who has been her friend may be ours. But oh! Ellen, I miss you much. Your departure has loosened my hold on life; but I am glad that you are safe—safe where the cruelties of earth can never reach you—safe in the possession of an enduring home, where wickedness will never disturb the harmony of your society. Precious sister! the cold, cheerless storms of life will never beat upon thy pearly path, or damp thy fervent joys."

Here poor little Harry suddenly joined the group.

It was not to be expected that this child would realize the effect of the change. Indeed, it was all the better that he did not. But still, he read in the expression of the rest of the family, the meaning of the double inheritance of orphanage and poverty.

"Come here, my poor child," said Mrs. Wilson, noticing the evidence of melancholy which shaded his dimpled cheeks. The little fellow sprang at once into her arms, exclaiming, as if he knew his mother's need of consolation,—

"Dear mamma!—little Harry loves mamma!"

"Ah, my poor child," said Mrs. Wilson, "I am glad that you do not know the sad realities of this hour; but if you live you will know them. I hope, my child, that if God spares your life, that it will be your privilege to live and act with men who will be much wiser than their fathers. I hope that in your day, the luring temptation which has scathed us will be better understood; that defenders of the right will band together for its extirpation. My prayer is, that my dear boys may be workers in the noble cause. It would make up, in some measure, for the troubles of this hour, if I could see my children safe themselves, and then, with a noble magnanimity, throwing out their influence to save others. Poor child! If your mother can only be permitted to keep you under her own protection until your character is formed, she will try to bear up under the burdens of life with resignation. But—O God!—Father in Heaven! spare, oh, spare, if in the wisdom of thy counsels it may be done—spare my life, until these dear ones, whom thy kindness hath given me, are safe from the tempter's snare! Teach, I pray thee, O Father in Heaven! a broken-hearted mother to say 'Thy will be done!'"

At this moment, while the eyes of that broken-hearted mother were intently fixed toward heaven, as if waiting some answer, or the assurance that her prayer was heard, and while mute and melancholy despair was depicted upon the countenances of her orphan group, a tall, well-dressed, but uncouth looking man entered the room To this family, at this moment, he was a revolting object, and they shuddered as he seated himself. His swaggering air, and his cold, unsympathizing countenance, pointed him out as belonging to that class of men to which their bitter sorrows were directly traceable. The manner of his entrance pointed him out at once as one who was lost to all the finer sensibilities of humanity. An unannounced entrance is a privilege which none but the meanest will avail themselves of, any more at the threshold of poverty than at the door of munificence.

"Is this where Mrs. Wilson lives?" inquired the intruder.

"It is, sir," replied Mrs. Wilson.

"Well, ma'm," continued the man, "I've had a

devil of a time in finding you out. I guess you don't know me, ma'm."

"No," replied Mrs. Wilson, "I do not."

"Yes, I see—just as I supposed. People never know me when I want to get my own. This ain't the first time widows haven't known me; and this ain't the first time, neither, that I've seen children holding on to their mother, as if I was the devil. Your husband knew me, ma'm; yes, he did, devilish well. I wish to the Lord he had made it convenient to have paid me his rum bill before he went off. But I guess he didn't think of going off quite so soon. Your husband, ma'm, was a very clever man—indeed, he was an excellent man; and if it hadn't been for them infernal gambling scoundrels at the ———, he would have stood it a good while longer. I have a matter of fifty dollars against your husband's estate, Mrs. Wilson, and I called at this time, supposing, perhaps, that there were some valuable articles which you had kept back, and some of which, perhaps, I could get. I would take anything you can give me, to make up the amount. I'll not be hard, Mrs. Wilson, for God knows you've suffered enough already. Some people think it ain't wrong to hide property; but I'll tell you, ma'm, its all wrong to do so—and people who do it can't expect to prosper. I should think, from your appearance, Mrs. Wilson, that you wouldn't do anything that's wrong, if you only knew it. Now, I declare it's a

God's truth, if you have anything laid away, in money or goods, it's very wicked in you to do so. When I saw Mr. Wilson last he had an elegant gold watch, and I tried hard to get it of him, but he said it was for his son. Now, Mrs. Wilson, I suppose you are a Christian; then just think of this."

"Then, sir," replied Mrs. Wilson, "I understand my husband was in your debt. Is this the entire claim that you had against him?"

"No, indeed, ma'm, it is not. I have recovered fourteen hundred and fifty dollars. I took your piano, at the hands of the auctioneer, at three hundred dollars. It's an excellent instrument, Mrs. Wilson. I think I made something there! I bid off a good many articles that I ain't a judge of, and can't tell how I've done."

"Will you have the goodness to tell me, sir, what my husband had in value to the amount of fifteen hundred dollars?"

"Well, madam, I'm an honorable man, and I wouldn't cheat; but your husband had full value for the amount."

"Will you then tell me in what business you are engaged?"

"I am engaged in the coffee-house business, if you must know, and it's a respectable business too, as well as a living business."

"Ah, yes, sir," said Mrs. Wilson, "you are a liquor-dealer."

"I have my father's watch," said Dick; "we have a little money; you see our furniture,—we have hid nothing. Here you see all that your traffic has left us of earthly goods. Here we are, clinging to the wreck that you, in part, have made, and your heartless avarice would lead you now to sink us if you could. Ah, sir, we detest your vocation. You can leave as soon as possible. We are not in your debt, except for the bitter cup of misery which you have placed to our lips. The *law* has paid you too much already."

"Richard, my dear son," said Mrs. Wilson, "suffer not this man to excite you to anger."

"My dear mother," said Dick, wiping his eyes and brushing back his hair with his hand, "I am not angry—there is no room now in my heart for anger. I am only telling this man what he ought to know. There are thousands in this city who think as we do about this business, and who know the mischief he, and others like himself, are doing; but for some reason others regard them as public benefactors! I wonder, mother, that the love they bear their own children does not compel them to wake up, and make war upon this great scourge of the race, which has filled every path of vice to overflowing."

"Madam," said the liquor-dealer, drawing himself up with a peculiar dignity, "I don't want to quarrel—I love peace: I only want my pay."

"I am unable to pay you, sir," said Mrs. Wilson,

"without distressing my family, and that I am unwilling to do. They are now distressed, I fear, beyond their capacity to endure. Besides, sir, it would be paying you for the commission of a crime—one which God has now charged against your soul! Have you a family, sir? And if so, try at this moment to put yourself and them into our position, and then ask yourself whether you would feel as you now do!"

"Yes, ma'm, I guess I have a family, and a big one, too! But they don't give me much trouble, I assure you. I have set it down as a fact, that children raised about a house like mine, never amount to much, unless by accident. While I live, I suppose they can live, and when I'm dead they must scratch for themselves. I never look forward."

"I should think not," replied Dick, sharply.

"Well, sir," continued Mrs. Wilson, "as for my little family, they are very precious to me. I love them as I think a mother ought to love her children, and if it is possible to do so, I want to keep them together, that their affection for each other may not be sullied, and that they may grow up to usefulness and respectability. Thus far, they know nothing about a bar-room, and I trust in God they never will! I hope they will learn to look upon that room, wherever it may be—no matter how well its hideousness may be masked; no matter how its deformities may be covered over, by the witchery of fashion—I hope they will regard it as a room containing the element of every vice."

"Now, let me tell you, madam, as a *friend*, you can't keep your family together—that's impossible! After all, it ain't worth doing, any how; and if you could do it, it wouldn't pay! Children never pay for the raising of them; and *natural affection*—it ain't nothing at all. There is nothing in it; it's all moonshine! I suppose it's about the same kind of affection which two horses, or two oxen, which are fed together, and drove together, have for each other. This natural affection is off the same web with preaching, and praying, and psalm-singing, and the like. It's all folly; and you find mighty few in my business who are fools enough to follow in this road. Hadn't you better pay me, Mrs. Wilson, and let me be going?" Without waiting for a reply, he turned to Dick, and said: "That young boy sitting there would be squire, I suppose. Now, Mrs. Wilson, if you would just do your duty, and get these notions of high life out of his head, and let him know that he has to dig for a living now, and start him out, just at once, to begin it; and that little one," pointing to little Harry; "if you would give him to some one for his keeping, it would be the best thing that you could do."

Here little Harry, as if terrified by hearing his name articulated by such lips, bounded at once into his mother's arms, exclaiming—

"Mamma won't let man take me—little Harry love mamma."

"No, my poor little son," said Mrs. Wilson, "not while life lasts! I thank God fervently, my orphan boy, that you are not a little slave. If you were, you might be wrung from my bosom—torn from my embrace, or flogged at my feet. But thank God, you are a little *freeman*, and if you are the heir of orphanage and poverty, the rumseller can neither buy you nor sell you. 'Heaven be praised for kindness in giving to you a *white* skin.'"

"Oh, yes," continued this wolfish intruder, "I've heard all this a great many times. It's lost all its effect on me, I assure you it has. It's no use to argue in that way with me. I say, ma'm; if you will give him away, it will be better for you. He will soon forget you; and then it will be just as well for both of you. And your daughter! She is big enough, and I dare say old enough, to earn her living; and it is your duty, as a *good* mother, to put her out to work, and if you do not do it, I think the poor-master ought to do it for you. That girl is pretty, and after some telling, she could wait at a table nicely. If it wasn't just for one thing, I should like to have her in my house. If I did take her, to work out this bill of her father's, I suppose she would want to stand on a level with my girls and my wife. They are real high-fliers, and wouldn't stand it nohow; and what's more, I wouldn't be able to get no good out of any of them. Just open the door and tell them to go. I'll go bail, they will do something before they starve! What do you say, Mrs. Wilson?"

"I say, sir," said Mrs. Wilson, while her features glowed with a consciousness of princely superiority, over the ruffian in her presence; "I say, sir, you are as mean as you are murderous. You are as insolent as you are vile; and you are as sure, as you are deserving, of your place at last! Know, then, that Mary Wilson, once the wife, and now the widow, of him whom she tenderly loved; whose memory she still cherishes; whose children she loves better than she does her own life, and whose natural affection for each other rises far above your brutal apprehension—know, then, that these dear ones, to whom your wanton agency has brought a filled chalice of misery;—yes, sir, or *villain*, as you may choose, know that only God can part me from children! Give this boy away! Turn him out into the street to beg, and force him to become a thief! Sooner would I give the last drop of blood which circles in my veins! Give *my* daughter to *you*, to wait at your table—to be on a level with your daughter! No, sir; rather would I follow her to the grave! I want you to leave this house if you will do it. Do not, I beseech you, kill us by your cruelty."

"Yes, ma'm," he replied, "I wouldn't stay long

with such dishonest folks. 'Nice Christianity, this!' —but it won't pay honest debts."

He rose to depart, but turned when he reached the door, and fixing his eye upon Dick, he muttered—

"You young devil, you! If you had been away, I should have got my pay; but I shan't lose it, I'll go bail for that. I'll get it out of some other fool—yes, that's what I will. Good-day, madam. Keep your natural affection—maybe it will make you rich, and then you will think of honest debts; and maybe you won't call decent people *rum-mongers!*"

Here Mrs. Wilson had a new insight into ways of misery, of which before she had not dreamed. She knew how, and by whom, these miseries had been produced. She knew very well who were the cause of her sorrow, but until this moment, she did not dream that even amongst this class of men, there were any who were wanton enough, willingly, much less maliciously, to add a single pang to her overflowing grief.

But Mrs. Wilson was mistaken. The path along which, hitherto, she had travelled, was one peculiarly exempted from the insults of the rude and unfeeling, but now the barriers of fortune were swept away, and already the beasts of the field had well-nigh destroyed everything.

"I suppose, my children," said Mrs. Wilson, "we must now make up our minds to be governed by the straitened laws of poverty, and we will no doubt find them severe enough, until we get familiar with them.

I suppose, too, that our *caste* has gone with our wealth, and that we will be excluded from the society in which we formerly moved. This I think is cruel. I have, when a child, stood by the hive, when as many bees as could find a share in the work, were carrying out a dead one, but I never saw them carrying out a living one, unless it were a drone, or a thief. In their misfortunes they protect each other; and what a rebuke do they, by their simple instinct, give to the cold formalism of reason! We are not *dead*, my children—neither are we drones; and most of all, we are far from being *thieves;* but yet, I apprehend we must make up our minds that there is but little sympathy for us. Those whose protectors perish, as your father did, my children, I suppose are very much like ourselves—*widows* and *orphans*, for whose protection there is but little civil or social law. But it is not so with those who have brought this affliction upon us; they are protected; their business is legalized; they are privileged to work wickedness with greediness, and to wring, even from penury, the last cherished article, around which the affections and associations of the household have fondly clustered. Ah, but the widow! Where is she? And where her orphan children? The fox and the wild deer can find a covert in the forest's shade—but where is her's? Where the repose for her dear, dependent orphans? Only in Heaven! O God, preserve them! Relieve their bitter agonies, and minister to their many wants!"

CHAPTER III.

LEAVING A DESOLATED HOME.

"And I—but ah! can words my loss declare,
Or paint th' extremes of transport and despair!
O thou, beyond what verse or speech can tell,
My guide, my friend, my best beloved—farewell!"

It was now out of the question for Dick Wilson to return to the law-school at C——, where he had commenced his legal studies, and at which he had spent one year to good advantage. With this impossibility before him, he had entered into correspondence with a lawyer about one hundred miles distant, in a small country seat, and had succeeded in making satisfactory arrangements with him; and all that was necessary now for him was, as soon as possible, to be on his way.

He had been from home many a time, and long. Nearly all this time, with occasional vacation intervals, had been spent among strangers for several years; so that Dick's empty chair and unused plate at the family meal, were no strange things to the family.

To see him preparing to go, and going, was nothing

new. This time, however, it was peculiar. When he left formerly, it was from a princely dwelling, and an unbroken, happy household. These now were changed. Friends, too, came forth to cheer him on his way, and bid him God-speed. Now, he was about to leave, lonely and alone, to seek a temporary home among strangers, and with scarce enough of money to bear him to his journey's end. He was too noble to take his mother's money, further than was absolutely necessary to enable him to reach the end of his journey.

"Mother," said he, "I do feel *sad* this morning."

"What is the matter, my son?" said Mrs. Wilson, tenderly.

"Ah! mother," he replied, "you cannot hide your heart from me. I have noticed your struggle in preparing for this hour. It has been a mutual struggle between us all. I have tried to smother my feelings, but I cannot. We have all failed to hide from each other the sadness with which this parting hour is necessarily filled. My parting with you now is so new and so strange, that I cannot but feel it, and painfully I find myself unable to banish sadness. I am going now, and I look about me for my father, and am reminded that he is dead! I look for Ellen, and she too is gone! When I left you last, they were here, and came out with you to cheer me on my way. I look—yes, and for days I have looked for friends, who never failed until now to come, and but three as yet have *dared to venture* within this enclosure of poverty. These absent ones, mother, are *not* dead, but they have lost their friendship for us. Why is it that no one comes to see me before I go?"

Mrs. Wilson and Eliza were mute from emotion, and Dick continued:

"Mother—Eliza—can you tell why it is? Have I done anything to merit this? No, no; you all know that I have not, and they know it too. They ought not to hold me responsible, and make me and you sufferers for the *rumseller's crimes;* for already we are suffering at his hands all that we can endure. It is indeed cruel that the widow and her orphans, already sorely smitten, should be still deeper wounded by the indifference of those who were formerly friends. I am now about to leave the few who are dear to me—all that I have left to love in the midst of averted faces—with those with whom you are as well acquainted as you are with me, and who, to all appearance, but a few weeks since, were your best and warmest friends. Ah! mother, where are *they* now? I have seen enough in a few weeks—much that I have not told you—to convince, not only my judgment, but my very heart, until it has sickened at the sight, that whatever we may have been, it is now all over! Yes, the dark side of a dark picture is shading us now, and with a few exceptions we are friendless, uncared for, and alone, only because the rumseller has robbed us. If this were all, it could be endured. Oh! yes; we might afford to part with such heartlessness without a tear or a regret. But this is not all. When necessity compels you to go into some fashionable street, you will meet many of these persons who will take no notice of you—at least they will affect not to notice you, lest they should compromise their dignity! As soon as they have passed by you, they will whisper to their companion, 'There goes the drunkard's widow!' And you, my dear sister, as you meet them in the street, without any tokens of recognition on their part, they will say, 'There goes the drunkard's daughter!' And of poor little Harry, they will say, 'There goes the drunkard's son!' This, mother, to us is an insupportable load; for at this time a generous sympathy of that kind, which I think human beings are under obligations to share with each other, is absent entirely; and the voice of the multitude articulates the withering sentence, '*This is the drunkard's family!*' To me, mother, while I hope it may not be my sad misfortune to fall a victim to the rumseller, and be an inheritor of the fortunes which always follow *his victims* to the grave; it is no strange thing that the drunkard's son, with his cheerless heritage, so often follows in the path of his father, and becomes a drunkard too. It is vain to attempt to attribute this entirely to hereditary causes, for surrounding influences are the most active agencies, and effect more than the mere force of instinct. No, it is not strange. It is rather to be expected. It is just that, for the coming of which those deepest read in human nature would fearfully look. They would not regard its coming as a mystery. There is no mystery about it. Self-respect—the guardian ægis of society—is withdrawn, and tempters are often but too successful. Who cares for the drunkard's orphan? Only the few. Who cares for the widow? Who speaks kindly? Only the few. The language of the many is the language of harshness. Is it strange, then, that a pupil in such a school as this—with the tempter on the one hand, enticing to ruin, and society on the other, repelling the victims—is it strange that he should fall, and fall irrecoverably? Kindness and sympathy have a marked and powerful influence for good over the minds and hearts of the young; and if we ever hope to reclaim the erring, we shall find these the most effectual agencies which we can employ for that purpose. On the other hand, unkindness and indifference have directly the opposite effect: they impel its victims rapidly onward in the paths of vice and and crime. Yes, mother, until the drunkard's family become the objects of tender sympathy, a *succession* of drunkards may be expected. How much more cheerful would our hearts have been this morning, if some kind friend, as heretofore, had come to speak words of kindness to us! What a power it would have had to help this poor boy on his unforeseen way! What a power perhaps in shaping his destiny! Ah, mother, it is not Mr. Wilson's son who is leaving for college this morning. No, no; it 's the '*poor drunkard's son*' who is leaving—for *where* and for *what*, God only knows, and if Heaven cares no more than men, he must inevitably be lost!"

As Dick Wilson, from the fulness of his heart, was giving out these truths, under the influence of which his heart was smarting, he was suddenly interrupted by the entrance of one whose visits had always been welcome, but now they were especially so. It was an old minister who had known the family for years, and who had always been on terms of intimacy with them, and who had spent several days in searching out their place of retreat. The old gentleman entered with his kind "good-morning," and seating himself hastily, he burst into tears. The transition was too sudden for him. He was not prepared to witness such an entire desolation as that which stared him in the face and chilled his heart as he entered. After some time, letting fall his trembling hands, which covered his face, and then wiping his eyes with his bandana, he slowly raised his head and surveyed the room; and after a moment, he said,

"This is surely the winter of your life. This, Mrs. Wilson, is severe;" and then casting a glance mingled with love and sorrow, at each of the family, he continued—

"Mrs. Wilson, this is a severe affliction through which you and your dear children are now passing. You have been made to feel the fury of a storm for which you were not prepared, and you have been smitten by it to the earth. But such storms as these are more frequent than you may suppose. This one has carried you and your children far out upon the cheerless ocean, whose billows are first created and then maddened by rum. Your position in society has not given you as good an opportunity to observe and know what is passing, as mine has given me. For fifty years I have been a watchman upon the wall. I have been unfaithful; my heart has been harder than it ought to have been; and yet, (to the praise of His grace be it spoken,) I think He has sometimes enabled this stammering tongue to lift up the voice upon the wall, and win a few from the paths of vice to the pleasant ways of virtue. I have seen much—much, at at the recollection of which I shudder. But surely, Mrs. Wilson, it is a great consolation, and one with which none should fail to familiarize themselves in the day of prosperity, that there is a God. It may do when fortune is smiling, and when friends in name are flattering, to trust in this world; but when the long day of bleak adversity gathers about our path, God then is our refuge—God, in whose presence the selfish inequalities of earth dwindle into insignificance. You are not alone, Mrs. Wilson, in this suffering. Would to God that you were. But you are not. Thousands upon thousands of such wrecks as yours strew the beach of this ocean! Yes, the land is flooded with widows and orphans whose husbands and fathers perished in its bottom. But these mingling prayers and groans—these tears and screams—these terrible *anathemas* against the rumseller, are daily ascending to heaven; and God will answer them, and his avenging fury will be poured out upon its authors and abettors. It has often brought sadness to my heart, as I have looked at this systematic destroyer of the human family, to see the influences by which it is upheld, and without which, *of its own rottenness*, it would fall to pieces. But, Mrs. Wilson, you have yet much to live for. You are not only a widow, but you are the mother of orphans, and you have before you at this moment a treasure for which you would not take the world in exchange. Here you see where the goodness and severity of God mingle, and where, notwithstanding these calamities, he still is love. Your relations to these dear ones has a fearful importance; for they will wear some impression of yourself forever. It is not improbable that these children, now sitting by your side, will keep some memento of you throughout eternity. Poor things! They are pale and dejected now; but they may become strong again when this storm has entirely passed over. But still, sooner or later, like a rose on its fragile stem, or the full-grained corn in the ear, they will bow their heads, and lisp their mother's name for the last time upon earth. Yes, mother of this riven group, your tears, your breaking heart manifest the keen agony of your grief. But it is not improbable that when sun, and moon, and stars shall fail, and when eternal *noon* shall abide in its own sublimity—its grand manifested reality upon the engulphed wreck of all physical existences,—that still, far on through the mysteries of that eternal being, and still on through that to which eternal being shall aspire—aye, in the whispers of that still beyond—is it not improbable that in light and joy, or in gloom and sadness, the name of mother, *mother*, MOTHER! will still be lisped. As a mother, what a charge and treasure has God committed to your keeping! What a fearful combination of mortal and immortal has he entrusted to you for education! Then strive, as you love those immortal beings, and are solicitous for their present and future welfare, so to touch the gentle chords of their young being, that each vibration may have an upward tendency—that each echo may have the still small voice of love for all, and they will be *safe*—safe from the rumseller, and safe from the master of *his feasts.* We do not live in this world for ourselves alone. No such prescribed existence belongs to our being. There is no doubt that we live, in part, for the whole human family—certainly for those who are walking in the same path with us—fearfully for those of our own households. I pity that poor creature whose hopes and whose fears, whose thoughts and anxieties all centre in himself, as if he alone were the whole creation. Mrs. Wilson, so teach these children, that every aspiration of their hearts may be for 'whatsoever things are lovely, whatsoever things are pure,' and they will never dishonor the sacred name of MOTHER."

—Turning to Dick, he said:

"And Richard, my boy, I understand that you are about leaving home again; you are now leaving it as you never left it before, and you will every day get new insights into the mysteries and mischiefs of the world. You will meet temptation in new forms, and coming with new power, and the only way in which you can hope to save yourself from being contaminated, is to begin at the beginning, and resist the *first*, and this will give you new strength to meet and vanquish every subsequent temptation. You cannot tell what form the temptation may assume, or how beautifully it may array itself, or how eloquently it may plead, or how sternly it may menace you. But remember, and be apprized of one thing, 'temptation will come;' and if you yield once, you will probably yield again, and I may ask, but you cannot tell me, where it will end. You are one of those young men whose character I have often tried to analyze; you are fortunate, and yet you are unfortunate. Your nobleness will win for you distinction, if you live and adhere to the ways of virtue—in which only is safety. But nobleness has a back-ground; and this very thing, which is so desirable in human character, unless you guard it well, will give the polished viciousness of the world a great advantage over you. You expect to meet temptation at the hands of the *rumseller,* and of the *winebibber,* but you cannot tell how they will approach you, or how eloquently they may plead for your successful distinction. If vice had *vice* written on its *forehead,* if the bar-room had 'THE BROAD WAY TO RUIN,' written over its threshold, if the accomplished knave had *knavery* branded on his brow, if the merely pretended friend of humanity had hypocrisy stereotyped on his countenance, then there would be less danger, my boy, for your future. There is but little danger that the poor degraded drunkard will be able to tempt you; his influence, so far as it would go, would tend to repel. He, poor fellow, an object of compassion rather than reproach, is the object upon whom the rumseller has painted, in vivid colors, the fruit of his vocation. Many of them have left the touch of their merciless pencils upon his trembling frame; they have parched and withered and burned up his character, and have imprinted their own in its stead; and no matter what he was, or what he might have been, he is a blank now, and he cannot tempt you. But if you are in no danger here, do not apprehend that there is no danger. You will meet the gentleman in *appearance*—you will meet the friend by *profession*—you will be met by beauty in disguise, full of professions, but false at heart—you will be met by those whose words are flattering, but whose influence is as the poison of asps. These are terrific temptations, when the agent is bold enough to filch an angel's being, the better to subserve his master's purposes. Richard, I tremble as I see you going out with your noble nature to confront such agencies as these, and all the advice I can give you, is to remember to engrave it upon your soul, that by whomsoever the sparkling glass is urged upon you, to account *that individual* your enemy. Ah! but do you say, 'Who is this enemy?' It may be beauty in the freshness of its bloom, or it may be manhood in the vigor of its prime, or it may be genteel-looking, but depraved old age, in its tottering imbecility. If any or all of these should conspire to tempt you, think of the *past*—think of the future—think of those whom your going out at this time will leave lonely indeed. Think, young man, of God; for, after all, no other power can save you. Remember this, and you will do well." And here the old man, true to a good old custom, knelt down and offered up a fervent prayer for the afflicted family, and for the safety of this young man, who was going out from their presence to try his fortune, under circumstances which the rumseller had imposed upon him.

"Mother," said Dick, "I feel better now, and you look more cheerful too; I shall leave you with a lighter heart than I expected, and oh! mother, I shall be often with you, and if I only succeed, you will soon be better provided for than you are now. And you, my sweet sister; and you, my dear little Harry —Dick will help you. Mother, when Mrs. Livingston and Mrs. Eagleson call, remember me kindly to them."

The hour at length arrived which was again to separate him from his dear ones. His old trunk, the same that he had often carried with him across the Alleghanies, was laid down at the door, and little Harry was seated upon it, looking intently at his brother. Eliza was standing by his side, with her hand resting on his shoulder, and Mrs. Wilson stood before him, with one hundred dollars, urging him to take it, but with a filial tenderness he refused it, saying, "I have to begin some time—I may as well do it now." His trunk was placed upon the dray of Donald, the good-hearted old Scotchman, who was always to be found when they needed him, and already his faithful horse was moving off.

Dick lingered for a moment, as if loath to leave the spot, and then beginning with little Harry, he kissed them all, and without a word, for their hearts were too full for utterance, this poor boy turned upon his unforeseen way.

They watched him until he disappeared, and then Mrs. Wilson fervently ejaculated, "O God! preserve my boy from the *rumseller's snare!*"

CHAPTER IV.

THE CONTRAST AND ITS CAUSE.

> "And is this all? Can reason do no more
> Than bid me shun the deep and dread the shore?
> Sweet moralist! afloat on life's rough sea,
> The Christian has an art unknown to thee:
> He holds no parley with unmanly fears;
> Where duty bids, he confidently steers,
> Faces a thousand dangers at her call,
> And, trusting in his God, surmounts them all."

FRANK HAMILTON, the former friend and classmate of Dick Wilson, had just returned from the law school at A——, at which place, without any interruption, he had spent the required time, and was ready to be admitted to the bar at the next regular term of court. On his return, he had received the cordial and endearing reception which loved ones are sure to receive when they return home, after an absence from its cherished endearments. Who does not know the inexpressible joys attendant upon the return of an absent one, when death, so often the relentless spoiler of domestic peace, has not been permitted to invade the sanctity of the home circle? The home of Frank Hamilton was just what it had always been, and than his own family there was none pleasanter on the earth, and than his own sweet sister there was none whom he accounted dearer or lovelier. They had all the elements of a happy and prosperous family. They had wealth in abundance; but even this, without wisdom, is oftener an element of ruin than of success. They were somewhat singular; for with all their getting, they had managed to get *understanding*. Possessing in an eminent degree that rare commodity, the goddess of Fashion never found in them obsequious worshippers.

Mr. Hamilton was—and Frank bid fair to be just like him—a remarkable man. He usually heard all the sermons which were delivered in his own church on the Sabbath day, and so did his family. No excuses were heard about that house on Sabbath morning. Kate never said, "Mother, it's really too warm," or, "It's really too cold," or, "I have a slight indisposition," or, "My bonnet is not in order, and I believe I sha'n't go." No, no; when the carriage was brought to the door, Mr. Hamilton was always careful to see that all the passengers were aboard. He was a firm believer, according to the Scottish style, in the "covenants of promise." If he dissected a sermon—and this he usually did, if it were worth dissecting—he portioned it out to himself and his own family, and not to his neighbors. When the gentle shadows of the evening twilight were closing the Sabbath day, Mr. Hamilton would take his accustomed seat, and then the whole family knew what was coming. Seated there in the usual order, Mr. Hamilton would first help himself, and then from the same sermon or sermons, as the case might be, he would mete out a portion to each of his family, and endeavor, by explanation, to make them understand and apply it. This done, Mr. Hamilton would kneel down with his family and invoke the blessing of God upon them; and here he seemed to realize that he did not live for himself and his family alone. He prayed for everything for which it would not be wrong to pray. He prayed for the poor drunkard and his little helpless children, and for his heart-broken wife, and that the rumseller —*the occasion of all this*—might be brought to repentance, or else be cut off.

When Mr. Hamilton met the poor drunkard in the street, whose appearance indicated the excruciating agony of the dread spoiler, then he had time and he had a heart to stop and remonstrate tenderly with him; and often from the lips of the victim, tottering upon the verge of the grave, and supported by the hand of his *unfed* and *unclothed* child, did Mr. Hamilton hear the interrogation, "Why do you keep these adders in the street? Why do you permit these wholesale curses to exist? I cannot help it. I am the rumseller's slave. This child is the rumseller's slave. My wife is the rumseller's slave. Why don't you help us to break our chains?"

When Mr. Hamilton met the boy, about whom the fruits of this curse was hanging in gloomy profusion, with a "Please, sir, give me a penny to buy some bread," then he had an open heart and a kind word. He never stopped to say to himself—"Well, I don't know. This boy may be a little thief, or a little imposter," and then bid him be gone. He was always careful that his influence should never mingle with the rumseller's, in driving an almost *infant* beggar to the commission of crime. The great pity and the great misfortune for the poor drunkard is that so few have a heart to do what they have plenty of time to do.

In the midst of these associations we meet Frank Hamilton at home, enjoying them to the very full, delighting himself with the pleasant and familiar appearance of everything about him, the most of which had been there from his earliest recollection. While he was musing in the midst of these associations, and contemplating the beneficent influence which they had exerted over his life, he was suddenly interrupted by the entrance of Kate, who, with her loud, hearty laugh, was making everything ring. She approached to where Frank was sitting, and laid her hand upon his head. It was plain enough from her mischievous appearance that there was fun in the neighborhood, and it was just as plain that she knew all about it, and couldn't keep it half a moment longer. Suddenly taking from her pocket a beautifully embossed note, she held it before his eyes, saying—

"Here, Mr. Frank Hamilton, Esquire, Junior—for this is the direction—here, I apprehend, is something especially sweet for you; for it is a mark of very great consideration for your precious self from Mrs. B——."

Frank at once opened the evidence of Mrs. B——'s consideration, and then tried hard to read it; and at length he said to Kate, smiling:

"This may be my death warrant, for all I can make out of it. Suppose you take it, and see what you can do with it."

Kate took the note; but all her ingenuity could do, it wouldn't read. She turned it right side up and right side down, and every other side; but to no avail.

"Well," said Kate, "what's the use of trying? I guess it wasn't intended to be read. Still, they were thoughtful enough to send the interpretation thereof by the black Daniel who brought it. He said it was an invitation to attend a mighty *select* party at Mrs. B——'s, on next Thursday evening, at half-past eight o'clock."

"Kate, who is this Mrs. B——? I have no recollection of any such person."

"Oh, she has sprung up since you left; or at least, she has but recently come into notice. They have been in the city for many years, but their business was not very reputable, and hence they were not known. But they became wealthy, and retired to private life. This accounts for that *stubborn* note."

"What was their business formerly, Kate?"

"Rumselling."

"Ah!—rumselling? And now, because they have retired wealthy, at the expense, it may be, of a thousand wretched homes, they are *very* respectable! Kate, I don't want to go there."

"You must go. There is no way in the world that you can get out of it."

"Well, Kate, you havn't seen all the world yet, nor all the ways of it, either. I guess I could get out of it if I set myself about it. I suppose, however, it will be best to go."

"That's right, Frank; be cheerful now about it. These people have abandoned that business, and if they want to do right during the remainder of their lives, they ought to be encouraged."

"That depends on the motives by which they were prompted to give it up. If it was from policy, in order to find their way into fashionable life, I wouldn't give much for it. If it was from a conviction of the pernicious tendencies of their business, then certainly they ought to be encouraged."

"You will find *wine* there, Frank, plenty of it, and if you should be taken with sudden *pains*, I have no doubt that you could be accommodated with something stronger."

"That's the devil's own kind of repentance, Kate. I see through the whole thing now."

"They have a beautiful daughter."

"She has been brought up in a bad school, Kate."

"She is rich, too."

"Her riches came through a bad channel, my sister."

"Caroline will be there. What do you say now?"

"Nonsense, my sister. I understand you very well. You have the same opinion about this matter that I have. But Caroline!—Why, if you had seen what I have seen amongst the hills of western Pennsylvania, you wouldn't speak of her in several moons! I have no peculiar attachment in that way, and I don't think I ever shall have."

"Heigh-ho! Frank—you don't know what you may have before you."

"That's true; but I know what I will try to keep from before me—anything that savors of the rumseller's temptation."

"Frank, what objection can you have to Caroline? She is rich, handsome, and well educated."

"For several years I have been out beyond the restraints of fashion, amongst those whose young spirits, when once they have tasted of freedom from its chains, are too noble to be bound by it again. This is a good place to see and study human nature, and I have tried to improve it. I have formed, or have tried to form, some idea of what a real life is. I do not mean a sleepy, dreamy life, in which *formality* is an abiding law; but I mean an active, sober, industrious life—a life which in some sense may be beneficial to others as well as to one's self. Now, my objection to Caroline is precisely my objection to going to this party. As you say, she is rich and well educated; but you must excuse me when I say that I do not think her beautiful. Caroline has been educated in the school of that great mocker, the wine-cup. She has had the example of her parents, in this way instructing her that it was harmless, and not only harmless, but reputable. I have laid it down as a rule, or rather as a principle for the government of my life, that on all occasions wherever it is possible, I will fly from *this* temptation. This, I apprehend, is the safe way; for when persons recklessly, and in opposition to the dictates of their own better judgment, put themselves into the way of temptation and danger, they cannot tell how it will result, or how far the consequences may reach. I apprehend, Kate, that in this path you will find more captives than conquerors. My sister, you love your brother, and you think that he is perfect. This, let me assure you, is a great mistake. Your brother has still with him the impulses of youth, with many of its indiscretions; and he could be led astray, tempted, ruined, and drawn by an irresistible power to the door of the lowest rumselling den in this city, if he would suffer himself to take the bait which the rumseller manages to throw out, often, in the social circle of high life. I believe, if it had not been for this sacred book, and what I have learned from it, and the fervent prayers of my father and mother, that I should have been ruined. Kate, I have thought that you prayed for me too—I know you did."

"Yes, Frank, I have. Could I forget you? Could a sister forget her brother?"

"Many are thus forgotten, Kate, not only by sisters, but by entire households. I know many a poor young man who never heard a prayer in his father's house, and for whom, in his absence, no prayers were offered. I knew that I was remembered by my household. These, my sister, were the influences which heretofore have enabled me to withstand temptation, and now I would not have Caroline, and risk the consequences, for her weight in gold. Suppose I had returned to you a drunkard—for such a thing would have been possible. Many a young man returns home in this way. Many an one in this way goes home again with blighted prospects and a heavy heart. If this had been my lot, what would have paid you, my sister, and my dear father and mother, for the sacrifice? You could not name the price."

Frank, you are certainly right. But do you think,

my brother, that in the simple form of wine, the *pure* juice of the grape, there can be the danger of which you speak?"

"*The pure juice of the grape!* Kate, there is not a more systematic counterfeiting organization in the world than belongs to the rumselling business. *Pure wine*! Why, in the whole system of adulteration, this is the most poisonous and nauseating article they make, and yet on this miserable stuff, filthy as it is, many commence their career of dissipation. Ah! Kate, if the gloomy horrors, the unapproachable miseries of that dark monster-mocker could be painted out before you on the canvas, you would tremble. If you could hear, as they have been heard, the touching pleas which misery, in all its grades, has made to the agents of the monster wickedness, to cease, and spare their friends,—to save them from premature death and a drunkard's grave,—you would more than tremble. Many an one who has tasted wine for the first time in a gay group, has finished in the lowest den. I suppose we had better go to that party, as it may give offence if we do not. But I do most fervently hope that the time may soon come when an intelligent and sympathetic humanity will no longer permit this mischievous business to be carried on under the sanction of law. The Italian mode of licensing the assassin is not productive of so much misery as this is; for at his hand the victim dies quickly. A groan—a struggle—a gasp, and it is over; but his character survives. But the *rum-monger's* dagger is like the lightning's fiery bolt: it selects often the loftiest and finest tree in the forest, and then comes down in its fury to rend it; and its beauty is gone long ere its decay. Here is the drunkard's great misfortune, and the rumseller's great crime: *the character dies first*, and often the immortal being waits the *slower process* of constitutional decay."

CHAPTER V.

THE CONTRAST AND ITS CAUSE—CONTINUED.

> "If hindrances obstruct thy way,
> Thy magnanimity display,
> And let thy strength be seen;
> But oh! if fortune fill thy sail,
> With more than a propitious gale,
> Take half thy canvas in."

THE evening on which Frank Hamilton was to be introduced to Mrs. B——, her pretty daughter, and a very select party, at length came.

"Well, Kate," said Frank, "are you ready to go? If we *must* go—and I suppose Mrs. B——, as a special favor to us, has decreed that,—I think we had better be moving soon; for if possible, I should like to get there at an early hour. Some persons manage to be the last to arrive on all occasions. This, I suppose, is to give as good an opportunity for observation as possible."

Frank had been poring over the pages of a late monthly, and during all the time in which he was speaking to his sister, he did not once raise his eyes from the page, and he started in surprise when Kate informed him, that already she had been waiting his movements more than half an hour.

"Well, then, if we must, let's be off quick. I'm sure I don't want to be late; though the fact is, I should rather not go."

"You would look much better, my brother," said Kate, "if you would turn your attention, with as much expedition as possible, to making some arrangements in the way of improving your personal appearance, before you go."

"What's wrong now?" inquired Frank.

"Nothing; only I would like to see you brush off a little of your 'back-woods' carelessness."

"That's the way it goes, Kate; but I do wish that you had a great many things in this endless city which belong to 'back-woods' life. If you had, you would not be quite so particular about shining collars, boots, &c. But, what do you want me to do, it's getting late; we must be in a hurry."

"Frank," replied Kate, "your own taste must direct you;" and off he went, to make his preparations. In a few moments he returned again; and to the eye of an exquisite, it would seem, not much improved; and just as he entered, he exclaimed:

"Kate, how will this do?"

"Very well, my brother."

"Now, let us go. I will try to equip myself in the robes of fashion, and arm myself to the teeth with formality. But I declare, it is so long since I have made any attempt to change myself into anything else than a human being, that I am afraid now I shall make a failure. I am sure that this *harness* will be a mighty bad fit, and I don't believe that I shall be able to keep it on; but perhaps I may do so.

"Just look here a moment, Kate, and be sober about it, if you don't I'll call mother. Has this collar a fashionable sit?"

"Yes, Frank."

"How do I look?"

"Very well, I think."

With this they started for Mrs. B——'s, whose wealth rather than worth had brought her into notice. Frank felt uneasy, for it was the first time in several years that he had made one of a fashionable party, but still, he had his "wits," about him, and a good, well-founded principle, to assist in giving point and effect to them.

"Kate," said he, as they tripped along the smooth pavements, which reflected in their faces the glare of the street lamps—"if my preferences were consulted, I should much have preferred to remain at our own quiet home, where we would have enjoyed the free communion of kindred and congenial spirits; while here we must be tortured by a cold and heartless formality—by grossness flimsily hidden by external glitter, and be compelled, by the merciless forms of social despotism, to meet and mingle with those with whom we have no sympathy, and for whom we have no respect."

"Stop, stop this nonsense, Frank, we are just at the door," said Kate.

"I declare," said Frank, "Mrs. B—— has got up pretty well. By my word, this is a *lift* for a superannuated rumseller. How in creation did this come about? It's a perfect *phenomenon* to me."

"Stop, Frank, they'll hear every word," said Kate.

At this moment the brilliant hall, filled with fashion at the bidding of notes which none could decipher, broke fully upon him, and at the next moment he stood in the midst of the crowd, going through the ceremony of greeting old acquaintances, and being introduced to new faces.

At length Mr. and Mrs. B—— came to pay their respects to Frank, and as they were on their way, he almost smiled to see them coming. They were elegantly dressed; but their dress, their gait, and their manners were perfect *antipodes;* between them there was no agreement. Frank's eye was quick—and silk, and satin, and all the rest couldn't hide from him, the "old times" of their history. They paid their respects and retired across the parlor. He had just concluded to seat himself, when suddenly a group of young ladies, numbering about half a dozen, were seen bending their way towards him. He knew them every one, and Caroline A—— was of the number. The ladies at length reaching him, by a kind of *dead* march pace, said,—

"It gives us much pleasure to see you, Mr. Hamilton; we hope you are well."

"Thank you, ladies," replied Frank, "I am glad to see you, and hope you are also well. But come, girls, don't call me mister, if you please—call me Frank; I do believe it is the first time in my life that I have been called Mr. Hamilton."

"Your wish shall be our pleasure," they replied, as they turned to leave, in a style which was as much as to say, "you are not done with us yet, young gentleman." Perhaps, Frank thought, they were glad to see him; yes indeed, but they were a great deal better pleased to have an opportunity at his expense of exhibiting themselves!

"Good evening, Misther Frank," said an old man, by whom he had seated himself. "I hear you're but jist now got home from the larnin'; and they tell me you're done man, and that ye ain't a collegian any longer. It's a bad place for boys, isn't it, Misther Frank? Faith, thin, I expect you had good times there, hadn't ye?"

"Oh yes, Uncle Peter," answered Frank, "I guess I had fine times—finer than I shall most probably ever have again."

"I thought so, Misther Frank. Ye see, ye had nothing to do in the first place but to act the gintleman;

and thin, by me soul, what's a great deal bether—ye had plenty of money to do it with. You see, Misther Frank, yer father, like meself, he's rich. Is it the law that ye thinks of larnin' next, Misther Frank, or does ye think to be a ministher? It seems to be a great pity, Misther Frank, if ye thought to be a ministher in these times. In my poor ould counthry, it was a brave business, and if poor men got into it there, they were sure to get rich; but in this country, if rich men get into it, they're sure to get poor. Now, Misther Frank, don't be a ministher! If ye have a fancy for the 'law,' it will do very well, and ye'll make money too—and ye'll get rich, and ye'll be a great man—and ye'll be able to keep in yer house the best *wines* in the country—and ye'll be able to do jist whatever ye may like to do; indeed, Misther Frank, ye will, if ye only takes up the 'law!' But Misther Frank, if ye takes up the ministhry, as it's called, thin ye'll be poor all the days of yer life. Ye may git to Heaven yer-self, after a while, perhaps, when you've tugged and strived till yer tired of life, but ye'll not git many with ye, indeed ye won't, so ye had better make up yer mind to do jist what the most's doing—look after yerself first, and don't trouble the 'ould book' too much."

"Well, Uncle Peter," answered Frank, "I cannot tell what I may make, but I have studied law already, and I have studied human nature some, and the 'old book' some too, and I think it's better than any or all of them put together."

"Thin, Misther Frank, yer going to be yer father upset, and every one to their likin'," muttered Uncle Peter, apparently not satisfied that he had failed to produce conviction on Frank's mind by his eloquence. Poor Uncle Peter knew all about a dray and a dray horse, and how to manage a hogshead or a large box to the best advantage. Here he would have been at home, perfectly so; but for his present position, he needed a whole new creation, which money could never give him, and like Mr. and Mrs. B——, he was most profoundly awkward, and equally ignorant.

During Uncle Peter's harangue, Frank was by no means an attentive auditor, for in another room he thought he saw a disposition manifested to bring mishap to some one. They were the same persons who, on his entrance, had greeted him last, and who, on leaving, had given him more than half a promise that they would call again, and hence it was that he divided his attention between them and Uncle Peter.

It very often happens that temptations suddenly beset us, and come with such force, while thus unprepared, as to make us their captives. Such was the object of the young ladies, whose sudden presence and absence have been noticed. They had determined to try their powers over Frank, to see if his reputed firmness, from *all that can intoxicate*, could withstand the persuasive voice of the fashionable young lady, and the fashionable wine-glass.

The next moment they stood before him, and there was no difficulty in reading, in their manners and features, that some plot had been concerted, and was about to be put into execution. They stood in such a position as to receive the fullest attention of the company; and one of the number, turning herself in such a way as to command the best possible view of the guests, and of Frank too, displayed a goblet, in which *the fiery eye of wine* was sparkling and delighting itself, in the prospect of adding another victim to the gloomy *caravan* of its maddened votaries! She said,—

"Will Mr. Frank Hamilton please to give the company a sentiment?"

Frank replied—"It will afford me a great deal of pleasure to give you a sentiment, ladies; but the company have made no such request."

"Well, then, give us a sentiment, and that will do for the whole company; it will be like saying grace at the table—*all can partake!*"

"With pleasure," said Frank, fixing his eye upon the *charmer*, and holding it there until he was sure that every one in the house, including Uncle Peter, gave attention, and then he said, in a clear and distinct voice, while the wine sparkled in the presence of the company—"'FOR AT LAST IT BITETH LIKE A SERPENT AND STINGETH LIKE AN ADDER!'"

The effect was electric, and the column of attack quailed for a moment, and many, whose lips were longing for it, were amazed. They were not routed, however. They were in the house of a veteran commander, who had been in the habit of doing small things for a *sixpence;* and they had great courage, and came again, saying:

"Perhaps, Frank, you can't relish wine."

"You are mistaken, ladies," said he, "I do relish it; but I have seen so many bad consequences resulting from its use, I have put myself into a school of abstinence for safety; and on every occasion I will try to say what I now say—'Get thee behind me, Satan!'"

"Taste this, Frank; it will do you no harm—I am very sure it won't. What! a taste of wine injure any one? No, I'm sure it won't."

"So thought many," replied Frank, "who are at this moment writhing under its cruelties—who are weeping while you are laughing over it—who are cursing while you are praising it."

"It won't kill you, Frank. Just taste it."

"So said its master," replied Frank, "on another occasion: 'Thou shalt not surely die.' Did he speak the truth then?"

Here the entire column was broken, and they retreated amidst the illy-suppressed titters of the better part of the company.

Uncle Peter, who was seated nearest Frank, looked

dumb-founded. It was plain enough that he wanted at least to wet his lips, and he rose to leave, muttering—

"Misther Frank, that's the effect of yer *rasin'*, and it's bad."

Uncle Peter's place was supplied in a moment by a gentleman, who, as soon as he was seated, said to Frank:

"You are a noble fellow. You have done yourself great credit this evening, for the noble stand you have taken against *fashionable* wine-bibbing."

"I am gratified with your good opinion, sir," replied Frank; "and of *all others*, it is the compliment which I would soonest merit. I am very sure that if I remain unscathed by this pestilence, I must not listen to the philosophy of fashionable wine-bibbers, or put my life in the keeping of the rumseller, for the one is synonymous with the other, and the end of both is destruction."

Frank had spoken firmly, but not harshly. His speech was characterized by a courteous dignity of the true gentleman, and even those who were intensely mortified by it could find no fault.

"Mr. Hamilton," said the gentleman by his side, "in this case you have done your duty well, and I think that every one present is under obligations to you for the good example you have given, of principle triumphing over pride, and its tendencies to vice. Will you tell me, Mr. Hamilton, how it is possible for persons occupying places in such society as this, or indeed in any society, to encourage the use of that which they know to be the most prolific source of crime and misery? These people can hardly put their heads out of their own doors without seeing the fearful consequences."

"Well," replied Frank, "I do not know that I can give you a satisfactory answer; but to my own mind it is clear enough, that this apparent recklessness is the result of one or more of these causes, namely: *indifference*, *ignorance*, *cupidity*, or *viciousness*. Who can pass along these streets and be ignorant? Who can live in the midst of these consequences, which startle the stranger as soon as he enters, until his very heart sickens, and not abhor it? I tell you, sir, there is something horrible about this business. Charity will hardly believe that it is ignorance. I believe it is indifference; and what kind of indifference? The same that may be laying the foundation of their children's ruin."

Many things, of course, had occurred during the evening; and when all was over, the sister and brother were making their way toward home. Frank was anxious to know what his sister thought of his management of matters, but did not venture to ask her until they were quietly seated at home, and even then he dreaded to do so. At last he mustered courage and said:

"Kate, how did I manage matters this evening?"

"Admirably, my brother."

"Upon my word, Kate," he replied, "those are comfortable words to me. I am glad to hear you say that."

"Frank, you mortified those girls almost to death, and I think they will not try a prank of that kind very soon again. They had the matter pretty well arranged. There was an abundance of wine on hand, and Mrs. B—— and the girls were very anxious to have it going around; and they thought if they asked you for a sentiment, you could not help giving it, and you could not avoid drinking with them, and then it would have gone round merrily. I heard most of the plan when they were arranging it."

"Well, Kate, I gave them a sentiment—the most appropriate sentiment in the world for the occasion, and I hope it will do them good."

"But, Frank, your sentiment tumbled Mrs. B—— into perfect confusion and mortification. She was very angry at the girls, and said some pretty hard things, I tell you, about their destroying her select party, &c. I can't tell you how she did go on. She told them that wine wouldn't be a guest at her parties any more."

"Good!" exclaimed Frank; "if she only keeps her word; but that's among the doubtful things, I imagine. I am really glad, Kate, that they commenced with me. It is a fine thing, my sister, to have a principle, and then to make it a foundation of one's action. Here, I apprehend, is the great misfortune: too many make their principle a matter of convenience, and they can put it into their heads, their hearts, or their pockets, as the case may be; and then their principle is never found interfering with their desires or their interests. But something rich occurred there this evening. As soon as I went in, I found myself seated by old Uncle Peter, the identical old Irishman who used to drive a dray for father, about fifteen years ago. I recollect him very well. He is mighty consequential in these days. He says he is rich, and I thought some accident of that kind must have overtaken him, or he would not have been there; and I shouldn't be much surprised if we were invited to his house to drink wine before long. The old man took it upon himself to charge me straitly not to be a minister—not even to think of it, and that I should not be too familiar with the 'old book,' as he called it. I have no doubt, Kate, that he would have taken wine quick enough. I did not like to hear that old man talk so lightly of that book. But it is hard on this rum business, and those who are in favor with the one are but little in favor with the other. Those whose lives are governed by the precepts of the Bible are armed against temptation. The rumseller's *angel* may offer them the world, and they will withstand it.

To such persons, virtue may ever cling for protection. They are in no danger of becoming drunkards. They will not leave widows to weep over the graves of drunkard husbands; nor children who will be ashamed of their memory. Kate, I should like to see Dick Wilson. That portrait is himself, exactly. I think it very strange that he has ceased to correspond with me entirely. We were intimate friends at college, and he was a noble fellow, too. I do not think I ever knew such a generous-hearted young man, and I should like to know how he succeeds with the temptations to intemperance, which must necessarily have surrounded his path. He has had to contend with misfortune, and it is more the fault of his parents than his own. His home education was not what it ought to have been. His mother is an excellent woman, but she was so pressed by the continued calls of fashion, that she was robbed of those precious hours to which her children, before all others, had a claim—those hours for which you, my sweet sister, and myself, can never be sufficiently thankful. My mind has often been puzzled to know if, after all, there are not many parents who care but little about their children. If they loved them as they ought to love them, they would certainly be unwilling to send them out into the world without that *priceless treasure*—home preparation.

CHAPTER VI.

RUMSELLERS.—CAUSES AND CONSEQUENCES.

"Whose mind can tell what the heart must feel,
That is doomed to die by the rumseller's steel."

IF Dick Wilson now felt, in all its bitterness, the dire results which flow from intemperance, he had at least been spared the painful ordeal through which those results are commonly attained. If his father had fallen a victim, and his family been beggared, the result had come to him quickly, without many of those harrowing concomitants which are usual in such cases. He had, in the history of his own misfortunes, been spared the cheerless view of the *progress* of intemperance. He had not seen, week by week and month by month, the inroads which it was slowly but surely making into his beloved home, or marked the progress ive yet fearful ravages it was making upon *him* whose name he bore. His experience of the evils of rum-bibbing and rumselling had been indeed severe—as much so as he felt himself able to endure. Yet they had been too circumscribed in their range to give him a just view of the aggregate enormity of the evil, or to impress him with just views of its causes, or of the proper remedies.

He thought, as many now think, that these results were in certain cases unavoidable; that it was the destiny of some to be victims, and that, though the consequences were deplorable in the extreme, still nothing could be done to prevent them. Yet the change in his own circumstances, which had driven him from those plans which he had intended to pursue, and forced him to take up his residence in the village of B——, was rapidly changing his views, and showing him clearly the dangerous tendency of his former opinions. In that village, he had a fine opportunity to witness the various manœuvres of those who were attached to the rum interest, either by sympathy or by being dependent upon it for support. In a village, all that is going on is generally known to its inhabitants, and there are here no dark, secluded dens, into which the rumseller can thrust its victims, and hide from the public gaze the evidence of the ills of the pernicious traffic. Unfortunately for the village to which Dick had resorted, while it contained many excellent citizens, it also contained a large number of rumsellers, and many who sympathized with them in their pernicious employment. To the countenance and influence of the latter, was the rum interest indebted for its profitableness—indeed for its very existence here. There were many of them men of wealth, and of good reputation among their neighbors. Their opinions were respected, and they were among the first in seeking political preferments and honors; and "help me and I will help you," was the maxim which governed them in their intercourse with the rum interest. With Judge L—— for a leader, and the crime-polluted Stevens for a companion, they were prepared to look with complacency upon all the ills and evils which are inseparable from the rum traffic, and quiet their own reflections with the pottage which their votes and favor might give. In whatever might be attempted by the friends of temperance, to diminish the sale and use of intoxicating drinks in the village, these men were found strongly opposed, and were ever ready and prompt in argument to maintain the *constitutional*, *inalienable*, and *natural* rights of those who chose to do so, to sell rum; and whatever the consequences might be, it was not the fault of the wily *tempter*, who held out the gilded lure, but of the luckless wight who suffered himself to be enticed to his ruin.

Dick Wilson, surrounded, as he was, by what to him appeared a new existence, frequently suffered his thoughts to wander to his desolated home, and to picture to himself its sadness. Unbidden it would rise before him. A mother in rags and in wretchedness, lifting her streaming eyes to heaven, invoking God to send deliverance! He seemed to hear the faint scream —almost the death-shriek of the starving child, whose soul and body seemed to be engaged in rending the ties by which they were held in their mysterious union, and thus escape the cruelties of the destroyer. But Dick's image of a drunkard's home did not depart.

He was just rising to close the office, when a person whom he had frequently met in the street, entered. For a moment he looked at Dick, and then seated himself. There was, to Dick, in the person of this individual, at that moment, something surpassingly amiable. His plain drab coat, round-breasted, according to the fashion that has passed away, his broad-brimmed hat, his white cravat, with his collarless shirt, and care-worn yet calm expression of countenance, pointed him out to be, what Dick knew he was—a Methodist minister, of the old pioneer stamp. After a few common-place remarks, the old gentleman said to him,—

"Mr. Wilson, your countenance had a very sad expression when I entered, and it is not yet entirely gone."

"Yes, sir, I feel so at times."

"There must have been a fearful picture in your mind, Mr. Wilson, to have left such an expression on your countenance."

"Well," said Dick, "it may surprise you a little, but I have been trying all the evening to put together, in my own mind, the picture of a drunkard's home.

It is a gloomy subject, sir,—one upon which peculiar circumstances only could compel me to linger for a moment. I think it appeared to my imagination even more vivid than the sad reality itself."

"Do you think you have succeeded, Mr. Wilson, in painting that most horrid and revolting picture?"

"I do, sir."

"Then you have done what our artists have not been able to accomplish. You have painted a drunkard's home? Oh! no, sir, you have not done *that*. It cannot be painted upon the earth. Where did you put the *soul?*"

"I was only trying to paint an earthly picture," said Dick.

"Where did you paint the rumseller?" continued the old man.

"Nowhere," said Dick, trying to smile. "I would not have his countenance on one of my pictures: it would *mar* it."

"Yes, truly it would, Mr. Wilson. It *mars* and *degrades* everything it touches. The universe of God is less beautiful and harmonious than it would be, were there no rumsellers. They are doing harm everywhere; and if the evening were not so far spent, I would paint the double picture of a rumseller and a drunkard's home, as I have seen them together. I understand, Mr. Wilson, you are from P——," said the old gentleman.

"That is my native place," said Dick.

"I was once acquainted there," said the old minister, and then added—"Do you know anything of a gentleman of your name, who was a merchant there?"

"I did know such a person," said Dick, with an involuntary sigh.

"Ah!" said the old man, "I knew him well when he was a boy, and often have I seen him sporting on the banks of the Delaware. Many a time have I enjoyed the hospitality of his father; and although our religious views were different, yet they were excellent people, and I spent many pleasant hours with them. They passed away many years, and from a brother, who tarried with me last night, I learned that Mr. Wilson, their son, who had established himself in P—— as a merchant, had died at the hands of the rumseller, and I was sorry, very sorry, to hear it."

"Yes, sir," said Dick, "that was my *father*."

The old man started in surprise, and said:

"And you are the son of Richard Wilson, and one of the *heirs* of his deep misfortune and disgrace."

"Yes, sir," said Dick, "I am, and I feel it every day."

"Well, young man," he replied, "I am glad that I have found you out. But you have come to a very bad place. Many a young man has been ruined, and lost everything by coming here; and still rumselling is continued, and the annual sacrifice of health, life, property, and the peace and comfort of families, goes on undiminished. I have talked with most of the rumsellers here; but whatever they may have been when they commenced this business, it soon blinded their eyes, and hardened their hearts, so that they could neither see nor feel the mischief they were doing. I have gone into a bar-room, when it was filled to overflowing with men who were merry over the maddening bowl, and when women and children were trying to tear away husbands and fathers from this vortex of ruin, and then I have remonstrated with the rumseller, and his only reply was—'I violate no law, and if I should stop, others would continue the same business.' I have asked them if God would be satisfied with this answer, and I was once answered, by a poor fellow who has since gone to his account—and miserably too—'It will be some time before I am called upon to settle that account.' You will have to move here with great caution, Mr. Wilson, or you will regret your coming to this place."

The old gentleman said that it was past nine o'clock, and was making a motion to depart, when Dick said to him:

"If it is not too late for you to do so, I should be very glad to hear from you your history of a rumseller and of a drunkard's home. I am here in the midst of them, and anything that will tend to increase my fear of these men, will be of service to me."

The old gentleman was on his feet, ready to leave, but as Dick concluded, he seated himself; and without promising to do so, he seemed for a moment to give himself up to reflection. Dick was watching and admiring the calm, dispassionate movement of every muscle in his face, when the old gentleman broke the silence, and commenced by saying—

"Mr. Wilson, fifteen years ago I was located in this place. It was then just about what it is now. So far as the improvement of the village is concerned, there are more religious people here now than there was at that time. I became acquainted with a young man, in the prime and vigor of life. He was not what may be called rich, yet his circumstances were very comfortable, and his prospects were exceedingly fair. I became very much attached to him, and I had every reason to think that it was fully reciprocated. During the early part of my first year in this place, I was called on to perform the marriage ceremony for him, which I did. His father died soon after, and left him a very handsome property, two miles from this place, and every one who knew him said that he would do well. I spent two years here, in an almost continual state of warfare with the rumsellers, who were so intent on breaking up everything which might exert a restraining influence upon their trade, that they would employ boys to *run horses* by the door of the church on Sabbath days. This has often been done by them. At the end of two years I was removed to another field, but subsequently returned here. When I came back I saw nothing of George Handy, and thought it strange that he did not come to see me. A few days after my return, in conversation with a gentleman, I expressed my surprise that I had seen nothing of George, as he was familiarly called.

"'Ah,' said the gentleman, 'poor George is *ruined!* Our rumsellers have overcome him; and Smith, at the Corner, has a mortgage of his whole property.'

"'How is this?' I quickly inquired. 'George Handy *ruined* already! How does it come?'

"'God only knows,' he replied; 'the people here can't understand it. But then, it is true. It does not astonish me much; for our rumsellers, with Judge L—— to aid them, have done many similar deeds.'

"One day, soon after this conversation, I was walking along the street, and happened to see George, just entering Smith's bar-room. I immediately followed him, and heard Smith say, 'If you have no money, you can't have a drop of *whiskey!* If you have anything about your house that I can use, I will exchange you whiskey for it.'

"'You have all my property already!' said Handy.

"'You have had pay for it,' said Smith.

"'In what?' inquired George.

"'That is no matter, Handy,' replied Smith, in an

angry manner; 'I have the mortgage, and that is the evidence that you have received value for it.'

"'Do give me something to drink, Mr. Smith,' said George.

"'Not a drop without the money, and for that you can have just as much as you want.'

"George,' said I, 'come with me,' and he started in a moment. I suppose he knew my voice, and as soon as he saw me, he walked up to me, saying,—

"'Mr. Shepard, this is not George Handy!—George Handy has been in the grave nearly a year. Oh no, sir, this ain't the image that God made! This ain't the young man over whom, and his smiling bride, you exercised such tender care! This,' said he, trying to straighten himself, 'is a poor, miserable thing, which the rumsellers here have made, and this is the place of my ruin.'

"'None of your lying here, George,' said Smith.

"'I am not lying,' said George; 'you know what you have done, and God and my poor wife *know* what you have done."

"I asked him how his wife was, and where she was.

"'Her health is very poor,' said he, 'and it will never be better. She is yet in our old house, but God only knows how soon this man will drive us out of it, and then if death, which would be a mercy to both of us, and to our little girl, does not come, I don't know what will become of us. The thought of the poor-house makes me shudder.'

"I asked him to go home with me, and he refused to do so, saying, 'I cannot see Mrs. Shepard, and I tried to keep out of *your* way.'

"I saw that Smith was very angry, but he did not wish to commence an encounter, in which he feared he might be worsted. I was well satisfied that he hated me as perfectly as I despised his wickedness, and I was quite sure that he had robbed George, in a way which was more dishonorable than the direct theft of his estate would have been. I told George that he had better leave with me. He came to the door, and then stopped, saying,—

"'You won't ask me to go home with you, Mr. Shepard?'

"I told him that I should be glad to have him go, but that I would not insist, if he did not wish to go. I parted with him then; and, without telling him, I had made up my mind to ride up to his house in the morning, and see if the ruin could in any way be repaired. From what I saw of George, I feared that it was hopeless. He said he was in the grave, and I thought it was true; and only the *Power* that raised Lazarus could raise him again.

"As soon as I entered his house the next morning, my heart was chilled. There sat his wife, wrapt in the pale, quiet melancholy of a broken heart. My entrance was to all appearance unnoticed, and yet she was looking me full in the face. At length she said,—

"'Mr. Shepard, I am glad to see you. Do not be frightened; all that you see is a reality—there is no mockery about it. Poor George has been crushed to pieces under the *iron hoof* of the rumseller, and everything is gone. Oh! if I only knew that sweet child was provided for,' said she, pointing to a little girl, a little more than two years of age, 'I should die in peace.'

"I asked where George was, and told her that I would be glad to see him.

"'I can't tell,' said she; 'perhaps the poor fellow saw you coming, and if he did, he will not come in until you are gone.'

"I asked her if I should read a portion of Scripture, and pray with her, to which she assented; and after which I took my leave, with feelings such as I never experienced before. For several days after this I was confined to the house by indisposition; and during this time I found it almost impossible to think of anything but poor George and his wife. About the middle of the third day, the sheriff called on me, and informed me that George Handy wished to see me. I was startled at this announcement, coming from the sheriff, and immediately inquired where I could find him.

"'In prison, sir,' was the reply, 'and his heart is almost broken.'

"'For what?' I inquired.

"'Well, sir, I believe it is a matter of debt. Smith, the rumseller, has worked himself into George's fine property, and no one believes that he did it honestly; and *this* does not appear to satisfy him.'

"'Do you know how much his claim against George is?—I mean the claim for which he has been imprisoned.'

"'I believe it is about two dollars. Smith says he can afford to pay his board, and that he intends to keep him there until he gets to be an *honest* man!'

"'Has George no friends here,' I inquired, 'who would do this much for him?'

"'I think, sir,' said the sheriff, 'that but very few know it; and I do not think Smith wishes it to be known.'

"I rose, and taking from my drawer the money, which I could but poorly afford to spare, and most of all to a rumseller—hastened to the prison, and was at once conducted into the part where George was confined. He rose to meet me, saying,

"'Mr. Shepard, you never expected to meet me in a prison, where none but *felons* should ever be confined.'

"I told him at once that he must come out, and that I had come to take him out.

"'Oh, no, Mr. Shepard!' said he, 'you cannot afford to pay the claims of rumsellers against me. I would rather remain here, for my poor wife is dying at home with a broken heart, and I cannot endure the sight.'

"I took him by the hand, and told him that he must come with me; that the scoundrel who had robbed him of his property, his health, and the peace and happiness of his family, should not now, for the *mere sum of two dollars*, be permitted to degrade him farther. I walked home with him, and as soon as we entered, he said:

"'Well, Mary, the cup is nearly full. I have been two nights in the county prison, on a rumseller's claim.'

"She leaped from her seat when the arrow, for which she seemed to be waiting, pierced her heart, and throwing her arms about his neck, exclaimed:

"'Poor George! poor George!—it is all over.'

"Reason had, in the keen agony of that moment, sought a shelter in the gloomy night of insanity, from which she never recovered. She is sleeping in the church-yard. George—and you have seen him often in the street—is also the victim of insanity, and an inmate of the poor-house; and their little daughter I brought home myself, and she is with us yet—a beautiful and lovely girl. Mr. Smith, the rumseller, has had his triumph. God's justice will yet have its triumph!"

CHAPTER VII.

PRACTICAL SYMPATHY.—DIFFERENCE IN CHARACTER.

"True dignity is hers, whose tranquil mind
Virtue has raised above the things below;
Who, every hope and fear to Heaven resigned,
Shrinks not, though fortune aim her deadliest blow."

THERE is no other desolation which, for the gloom and cheerlessness by which it is pervaded, can compare with that which the rumseller can make. He, more than any other agency, distributes, with a wanton liberality, the bitterest *curses* which can be mingled with the cup of human life, and before which its richest hopes and tenderest associations are crushed.

Some time had elapsed since Dick Wilson, to his little but beloved household, had said good-bye; and to persons feeling, as they did, the effect of the dire consequences which the rum traffic had gathered around them, there was nothing to give wings to time. So far as the consolations of this world were concerned, it was sadness and loneliness when he left, and excepting the kindness of a very few, it was sadness and loneliness still.

During the afternoon, little Harry had been scampering about with more apparent pleasure than he had felt since they entered that house; and like children of his age, his conversation, which was rambling, embraced many things which touched Mrs. Wilson and her daughter to the heart. Often they would respond to his childish simplicity with the "deep-fetched" sigh and an apparent smile, when it would have been more in consonance with their hearts to have answered with a tear.

Now, this child of misfortune was sleeping, and his little sorrows, if his tender heart knew any, were sleeping with him. Mrs. Wilson was reverently engaged in reading, as for several months she had been accustomed to do, at stated intervals, from the word of God; and Eliza was sitting by her side, with her cheek pressed close to her mother's. When Mrs. Wilson had finished, she said to Eliza:

"My child, God is closing the history of another day, and oh, what heart-burnings have this day ascended up, to claim a record, which shall await the judgment of the great day."

"Yes, my dear mother," said Eliza, as she approached the little window where, perhaps, from other hearts, many a bitter sigh had been breathed into the ear of God—"yes, my dear mother, the draymen who live on this street are beginning to return from the toils of the day, to spend their hours of rest in the society of their poor families. Mother, we know something about the joys of home—its pleasures, its holiness, its love. Oh, mother! if God shall judge the rumseller and his friends according to their criminality—according to the wrongs and the outrages which they are daily committing—how withering will that judgment be! How sweetly little Harry sleeps. He does not appear to have any realization of trouble. See how sweetly he smiles; nothing disturbs his calm, dreamy life. His little lips move and quiver, as if angels—the spirits of little children, young and lovely as himself—had come down to bear him company. I wonder if he has any idea of his present situation, or of what he has lost! I hope he has not. Don't you think, mother, he looks like father and Dick very much?"

"Yes, my child, I do. I never look at him without seeing the image of your father. Have you any idea, my child, who it was that purchased your father's and my portrait, at the sale of our property?"

"No, mother," replied Eliza, "I have not. When those precious things were brought out, and handed to the auctioneer, Dick and myself left the window: we could not look on, while the images of those dear to us were being disposed of in that manner."

"Well, my child I do think that was cruel. I care nothing for my own, only for the sake of you and your brother; but your father's portrait I would like to have kept, and one would think that respect for the dead would have deterred any one from attempting to remove it. I have no doubt, that at this moment they may be gracing the parlor of some one of those rumsellers who have ruined us. If any respectable person had purchased them, Mrs. Livingston would have known it."

"My dear mother don't let this grieve you. I hope poor Dick will soon be able to find them, and purchase them back for us. We are wounded deep enough already, without permitting these precious mementos of the living and the dead, to grace such a place as that."

"Eliza," said Mrs. Wilson, "you must write to Dick to-morrow. Cheer him up as much as possible. Tell him, when you write, that the old minister comes often, and that his conversation is just what we need. Tell him that Mrs. Livingston and Mrs. Eagleson are remarkably kind and attentive to us. And don't forget to tell him that little Harry talks much about him. These things, my child, will encourage him very much. They will tend to strengthen him against temptation, and this is necessary; for his path is filled with peril, and the cheerless inheritance of a drunkard's son will cling with great power to his heart, but not to strengthen it. Now my child, let us note down every pleasure we may feel, and then, at the begining of every week, transmit it all to him, and it will do him good, and make him feel happier."

"Yes, mother," replied Eliza, "if Dick thinks we

are happy, he will be happy too. I always write to him in a cheerful manner, and somehow or other, Providence has given me some pleasant thing to tell him every time I have written yet, so that I have almost become selfish in this respect, and am looking for a continuance of the same kindness."

"Well, my child," replied Mrs. Wilson, "if you look in a right spirit, there is no selfishness about it; but it is the evidence of faith in those precious promises to which, for consolation at this moment, we are deeply indebted. 'Ask and ye shall receive.' How comprehensive that invitation. It is just what we need, and what poor Dick needs as much as we do."

"Mother," said Eliza, "has it occurred to you, since our misfortunes, how very easy it is to be deceived in persons?"

"Yes," said Mrs. Wilson; "I could hardly, in our situation, be insensible to such reflections. But why have you asked that question?"

"Well, mother, my mind has been running back. I am afraid, after all, it is more prone to go backward than forward; but I will try to subdue this disposition, except when I want to hold communion with dear Ellen. I have been thinking of times past, and the changes which have taken place. There was a time in our history, when the slightest indisposition in our family would have called to our door those who, under no imaginable circumstances, would come now. This, I think, is what we have learned,—that it is not what people wear, nor the society in which they move, that gives the true index to their characters. There is Mrs. Livingston and Mrs. Walston—they are both very wealthy. Now, mother, look at Mrs. Walston; I do not think you can remember two days together, for several years, when she has not been at our house. Many an hour, mother, have I listened to her, while she was trying to flatter you in every possible way. At one time she would speak in raptures of father—his wealth—his fine disposition—his brilliant prospects, and so on. Then, she would tell you what a fine boy master Dick was; and then she would turn to poor Ellen and myself; and that dear little fellow lying there in the cradle, has not escaped her *flattery;* for she has said of him that he was the sweetest of all your children. Don't you think, mother, that he is just as lovely this evening as he ever was?"

"Oh yes! my dear, surely I do."

"And so do I, mother; but Mrs. Walston don't think so. He is now the heir of poverty, and with her my dear little brother's loveliness is gone! Mrs. Walston, mother, you know, was always dressed in the height of the fashion. No one could recollect to have seen her when she was not. Her great business was to see what was to be seen, and hear what was to be heard. She had always use in this way for her eyes and her ears. She was never known to be in the nursery with her children when she was able to be out of it: all this business was intrusted to her ignorant domestics. Yourself and Mrs. Walston, mother, used to call me a little girl, but that little girl had her little thoughts, and those little *noiseless things* said that it was cruel—that she ought not to do so; and that mothers who were faithless to their children could not be expected to be very faithful to out-door friends, only as circumstances dictated. We have not seen her since our affliction; and I apprehend we will never see her in this house. We may chance to meet her in the street, but I hope we shall not, for I am sure that she does not want to see us. If she did, she could easily find us. Now, mother, there is Mrs. Livingston, who is very wealthy. She never knew what it was to want a single thing that money could purchase, and she can be fashionable too. Indeed, in every respect, she can throw Mrs. Walston into the shade. But then, Mrs. Livingston does not permit these things to take the place of her family in her affections. She has been often at our house; and yet she has hardly been there *once* for Mrs. Walston's *twenty times.* But when she did come, her demeanor was always dignified and pleasing, even to children. There was nothing about her to make children dislike her coming, and if she chose to caress them, as she often did, she did not appear, like Mrs. Walston, as if she was afraid that her fine things would get soiled. This could not very well have been avoided at Mrs. W.'s house; and she seemed to think the same kind of house-keeping prevailed everywhere. Misjudging, mother, is part of our experience, and a thrilling part of it too; and to me it is a matter of astonishment how, under any circumstances, we could have preferred Mrs. Walston to Mrs. Livingston. When Mrs. Livingston came to our house, she had always about her a mark of true, genuine affection, and she professed to be a Christian of more than mere fashionable style, and I presume no one ever doubted her sincerity. I think that there are places and circumstances in which religion shines with more lustre than it does in the large congregation; and one place is the nursery, when a mother, with a heart full of intelligent, burning love, consecrates herself to her children. When Frank Hamilton was spending a vacation once with Dick, he told us what his mother was in the habit of doing. He said that she spent an hour daily with them in the nursery, and that nothing would tempt her to neglect it; and surely this is a precious retirement for both mother and children; but of these hours, mother, you were robbed by the tyranny of a morbid fashion, which has mingled itself with the rumseller's doings. For this, Mrs. Livingston was remarkable; and wherever her children are seen, they carry with them their mother's likeness in their faces, and her goodness in their actions. This was Mrs. Livingston's character in the time of our affluence; and now, in our adversity, she is, if possible, still more kind. Ah, how we were deceived! The one lit up the morning of prosperity with a false light; but the other—and she the nobler one—has brought peace to the evening-time of adversity; and how kind she is to those, of whom poor Dick said, they would be called 'the drunkard's family!'"

"Eliza," said Mrs. Wilson, "is not that Mrs. Livingston crossing the street just now?"

"Yes, surely it is, mother, and she is coming here. What can have brought her out at this late hour? Why, it's almost dark!"

"Go to the door, quick, Eliza, and let her see that we love her, for indeed she is a lovely woman."

Eliza had the door open in a moment, and Mrs. Livingston drew near, with a pleasant smile, saying,—

"Good evening, my dear child."

Ah, that does not grate so roughly—it does not tear so unmercifully—it does not wound every nerve and fibre of the spirit, as does the *harsh*, *ungentlemanly*, and *unlady-like* expression, 'The drunkard's family, or the drunkard's son or daughter.'

Both were at the door to meet Mrs. Livingston, and as she entered she imprinted a speaking, eloquent kiss upon the cheek of each, and then, walking directly to the cradle, she looked for a moment into the little sleeping face of Harry, and with her kiss she left a tear upon the little fellow's cheek, the sparkle of which seemed to say, "My poor child, your lot is the hardest!"

"Mrs. Wilson," said Mrs. Livingston, "this makes my heart sick. I can hardly convince myself that your situation is a reality; and yet, it is too fearfully plain to be a dream. But tell me if there is anything I can do for you,—and I hope you will be candid. Throw off all delicacy about these matters, for your change is so severe, I think it would be wrong in you to wrong yourself by refusing to make known your wants. I assure you, Mrs. Wilson, a reverse of fortune has not lessened my respect for you; and anything I or mine can do, will be cheerfully done. Do tell me all, and I will try to sympathize with you, as I ought to do."

"My dear Mrs. Livingston," said Mrs. Wilson, "you are too kind, too generous already. We are deeply in your debt. In such circumstances as ours, the voice of human kindness is sweet indeed; and I thank you, my hitherto unprized friend, for the generous kindness and tender sympathy with which you have visited us. You have preserved your affections amidst those disastrous circumstances in which others have lost them, and of which loss they seem to be insensible. But, we are not entirely destitute; and I think, by proper management, we will be able to get along until Dick is admitted to the bar; and then, I hope, our situation will be more comfortable. That poor boy, Mrs. Livingston, is our only earthly dependence now; and I do most fervently hope that he may be spared to us. It is a great pleasure to us to receive his letters, for he tries in every imaginable way to make us feel happy. But I am sure, although he is not a child, that his heart many times is sad—that he will often weep himself to sleep in thinking of us. Little Harry is now our great comfort. He has been unusually happy and cheerful this afternoon, and went to sleep earlier than usual. I think, Mrs. Livingston, that there are for us some wise and precious lessons in these afflictions, and particularly so far as my children and their best interests are concerned; and if I am spared, I will try to lay unsparingly in their minds, the foundation of a good and useful life."

"I hope, indeed," replied Mrs. Livingston, "that you will do this unsparingly. The training of our children, Mrs. Wilson, as mothers, responsible to God, in a fearful sense, is, after all, the great consideration; and here, I apprehend, is the cause in which thousands of both sexes find their ruin, and entail a fearful responsibility upon unfaithful parents. It was the rumseller, Mrs. Wilson, who brought this heavy affliction to your family; and while God, of his mercy, may overrule it for your good, can he suffer the cruel *cause* of all this to prosper? Will the rumseller be permitted to go forward in his desolating work, slowly but surely infusing his deadly poison into the heart's blood of the community, and prostrating to the earth his myriads of husbands, fathers, sons? No, no! this cannot be. I tremble even for him, when I reflect that God is just, and that his justice cannot sleep forever. He has thrown a blight upon yourself and your precious children—can he and his escape? If there is an object of pity upon the earth, it is the child whom a callous-hearted rumseller calls his own. To be a drunkard's son, is an inheritance which is only rich in the thick gloom of its insufferable cruelty. But to be a rumseller's son, and wear the impressions of that business; to be assured that one is eating the bread and wearing the clothes which, in justice, belong to those who are starving, and who are in rags! To be conscious that the very things which are making their hearts glad, are making other hearts sorrowful! To be conscious that these things, covetously torn from others, are the price of peace, happiness and life in other homes!—homes which were once lit up by love! Yes, my dear Mrs. Wilson, the rumseller has cursed you with all his fury! But will he enjoy his ill-gotten gain? I think not. Mrs. Wilson, do many of your former friends call on you?"

"Oh no; yourself and Mrs. Eagleson, and our old minister, are the only ones who have called."

"Is it possible?"

"Yes, Mrs. Livingston, only three have outlived the storm, as yet: they are all who have come to see us."

"I feared that this was the case; but let them go. I have no doubt this has disappointed you severely. Let them go, for in their going you lose nothing. These persons have lost more than you have, and when they meet you by accident, a sense of personal inferiority will wring from them the acknowledgment in the truth-telling blush. This is one of those revolutions in which, with what they have lost already, it is almost impossible for self-respect to survive. Some of these persons may live to hear the stern rappings of adversity at their own doors. They may live to see it entering and laying its rude hands upon the domestic and social relations, upon which they are now staying themselves; and if such should be their fortune, I hope they will find that God is more merciful than they are. With some of those amongst your former acquaintances, there is at this moment a much more certain prospect of such a calamity than you had a year since. I do sincerely hope it may not come to them; but they certainly seem to be rapidly drifting to the same dark port. Have you been out any yet, Mrs. Wilson?"

"I have scarcely crossed the threshold since we came here to live."

"Now, Mrs. Wilson, remember—I will take no denial—I want yourself and Eliza and little Harry to come and spend the day with us to-morrow. Mr. Livingston will send the carriage for you to-morrow morning by ten o'clock, and you must come; and those *extra genteel folks*, who suffer the rumseller to break their friendship just when he has broken the heart and the hopes of his victims, will see that I am not ashamed of you, at all events."

"Oh, Mrs. Livingston, do excuse us."

"I can't, Mrs. Wilson."

"I would—"

"No use; no excuse taken this time. Say yes. What do you say, Eliza? If little Harry were awake, I would be willing to leave it to him."

"What would the people think, Mrs. Livingston, to see your carriage in this street?"

"No matter about the people, Mrs. Wilson—say yes, quick."

"Mrs. Livingston, suffer me to ask you if you in tend to have any other company?"

"I do, Mrs. Wilson. You would have thought it very strange, a few months since, if you had come on a visit to my house, and found no other company."

"Whom may we expect to meet, Mrs. Livingston?"

"No person better than yourself, except our old minister—and I call him better than any person else.

I have been thinking that I should ask Mrs. Walston. I think it might do her good."

"Oh, Mrs. Livingston!" exclaimed Eliza, before she could control her feelings—"for our sakes don't ask her."

Mrs. Livingston looked a little surprised, and then smiling, said:

"Why not, my sweet child?"

"I ask your pardon," said Eliza, blushing deeply; "I ought not to have made that remark."

"Would you rather not meet her, Eliza?"

"If I had my choice, I would prefer not meeting her; and it is as much on her account as on our own."

"Well, then, my child, you wont meet her at my house. What makes Donald stay so long?" ejaculated Mrs. Livingston, as she turned to look out of the window. "Yes, he is coming at last. Just let me go to the door for one moment."

There was something in the name of Donald which brought Mrs. Wilson and Eliza at once to the window, and there they saw the trusty old Scotchman backing his dray up to the door, and, as might be supposed, they were a good deal surprised.

Mrs. Livingston whispered to Donald not to leave until his load was safely put away.

"No, madam," replied Donald, "I'll na leave the house until Mistress Wilson hae all these things put to hand. Ould Donald has seen women alone with poverty before, and he won't do anything that's mean."

"Why," exclaimed Mrs. Wilson, "what have you been doing, Mrs. Livingston?"

"Not a word of blame, Mrs. Wilson; if there is anything wrong, you must blame my family this time. Don't scold me; you can settle it with them to-morrow. Just let Donald carry these things into the house: it will be a pleasure for him to do so."

And Donald, smiling and looking happy for the moment, like the rest, said,—

"Yes, Mistress Livingston, surely it will be a pleasure to me to do so. Mistress Wilson's done me many a kindness."

"Here," said Mrs. Livingston, "is a trunk, which you can open, and you will find that it contains all necessary explanation in reference to its contents. When you are through with it, close it up again, and Donald will call for it early in the morning, before the stage starts for B——, and Mr. Livingston will see that everything in relation to its destination is arranged,"—and bidding them an affectionate good-night, she left for her home.

"Mother," said Eliza, "what does this mean?"

"Don't you recollect, my child, that you said a little while since, that Providence seemed to give you some good news to tell Dick every time you wrote to him?"

"Well, mother, God is good! How kind his counsels are, after all! I will believe him now, more than ever."

"My daughter," said Mrs. Wilson, "we must see what is to be done with this trunk, as it will be called for early in the morning. Light a candle, my child, and move softly, so that you do not disturb Harry."

In a few moments the trunk was opened, and on an examination they found it to contain a number of articles for themselves and Harry, and the remainder for Dick. In a package, marked, "*from Mr. Livingston,*" they found the material for an elegant mourning dress, such as is worn by the better class; and in a slip of paper in the inside, they found fifty dollars in gold, with this inscription upon the paper—"*The rumseller can't take this.*"

Eliza found a similar passage, marked, "*from Lucy Livingston,*"—and there was one for little Harry, marked, "*from Master Tommy Livingston;*" and then a good many little affairs not marked at all.

Dick's portion was a fine one—enough to fit him out in the best style, and contained more than a sufficient amount of money to defray all expenses of making up. Mrs. Wilson understood that it was not the wish of Mr. Livingston that Dick should know the donor, and propriety, rather than a desire, induced them to keep it from him.

After the whole cargo—trunk, provisions, and so

on—had been examined and arranged, Mrs. Wilson said to Eliza,—

"My daughter, God is on the side of the afflicted; and if most of our former friends were willing to abandon us, and leave us at the mercy of the rumseller, let us thank him that he has kept a few for us, and best of all, that He is our friend."

After offering up a fervent prayer, in which Dick was feelingly remembered, these weary ones retired to rest—rest, sweeter and more refreshing than the rumseller can ever know.

CHAPTER VIII.

NEW HOME.—ITS CHARACTER.—ITS DANGERS.

> "Yet turn, ye wanderers, turn your steps aside,
> Nor trust the guidance of that faithless light,
> For watchful, lurking 'mid th' unrustling reed,
> At those murk hours the wily monster lies."

THE office of a country lawyer is generally an admirable index of the community by which it is surrounded. In a good and well-regulated community, a lawyer, as well as all others, is permitted to have a portion of his time to himself, in which he may meditate upon his *own* and his client's interests. When the community is of a different character—idle, inquisitive, and ignorant—attending to all matters but such as strictly concern themselves, and especially if there be a surplus of rumsellers or rumbibbers there—a lawyer's office becomes a mere haunt of idlers.

Here we find Dick Wilson for the first time since we left him at his mother's door, with the good-bye trembling on his lips.

The community, into the bosom of which Dick had come, was far from being what it should have been. The social influences which surrounded him here were unfavorable, though we find him in the office of one of the best lawyers of the place. In this office, on the evening of his arrival, we find him sitting alone in the shades of the gathering twilight, and dwelling with absorbing interest upon the marked contrast between his present and his former home. Twilight is the hour for contemplation. Then it is, as the eye of day closes and shuts out the images of the external world, that the thoughts rush home from their varied wanderings, and dwell with concentrated energy upon those scenes in our own history which are the most impressive. Thoughts of home, sweet, sweet home, and of loved ones at home, were consecrating that hour at the shrine of affection. Thoughts of home—a mother, a sister, and a little infant brother, from whom this poor boy was separated by the cheerless hand of poverty—had a claim, endorsed by nature, upon that hour!

He knew that at that hour they were sending forth their thoughts—the angelic messengers of their hearts—freighted with love to meet his own, and together, upon some intervening mountain cliff, to hold there the feast of love and sadness. And it might be that a mother's and a sister's prayers were also ascending up to heaven in his behalf—for the twilight hour is as sacred to prayer as it is to the cherished recollections of earth.

What a holy thing that prayer is, when it rises from

the smouldering ruins of a broken heart, to pour its wants into the attentive ear of Heaven! How pure it is, when it goes up for a beloved one, and how mighty it is too—for,

> "Prayer ardent opens heaven—lets down
> A stream of glory on the consecrated hour
> Of man, in audience with the Deity."

Dick Wilson had now been several months from home, and although he was not more than one hundred miles from it, yet from the morning he left he had not been there.

Do you think, my friend, that he had lost his love of home? Do not chide this young man with indifference, for it were cruelty to do so. Remember, he was poor, and that poverty has its laws, and they must be obeyed. He was unable to spare the little sum which it would have required to carry him to those, for whose sake more than for his own he was contending with poverty.

The day to Dick had been one of more than usual gloom, and yet he could not tell why it was so; but ever and anon, on that day, which had been one of a public character, one and another of those young men of the village, with whom he seemed to be a general favorite, would dash by the office where he was sitting alone, in a fine buggy, or mounted on an elegant horse, a cloud of sadness—not of envy, but of genuine sadness—was seen to pass over his features, and then again it would disappear, leaving in its stead a strange though beautiful serenity.

He was thinking of the time when poverty had not the power to make him a recluse, and banish him from all society, and from all the enjoyments of which a well-filled purse would have enabled him to partake.

The contrast between his present and former situation deeply affected him. This was not fully appreciated even by those who knew him most intimately. His hopes had been high. He had felt himself equal in position, wealth and talent, to those who now passed him with averted eyes, and reflections upon the change were continually lacerating his feelings. Though poor, he was nevertheless proud; and his sensitive and deeply wounded spirit still clung to his ruined hopes. Better were it otherwise. Better if the rum traffic, while it strikes to the earth the hopes of its victim, should at the same time annihilate all sense of the painful fact.

Dick's revery was broken suddenly by the entrance of several young men of his acquaintance, but not his most intimate companions.

"Dick," said Horace Stevens, "you appear gloomy this evening. What the deuce is the matter with you? We have been looking for you out all day. I'm sure a chap with your prospects never ought to be gloomy, and should never keep himself away from the *fun* and *frolic* of the day. There is a time for everything under the sun—so says the 'big book'—and there is just as much a time to *spree* as anything else. House myself up in a law office on such days as these? By George, I guess not. It would surprise everybody in this village to see me doing such a thing as that; and the case stands about in the same way with these other young gentlemen. 'Birds of a feather flock together'—and so you see we are all here; and I'll tell you we had a round time to-day. What's the matter, Dick? You look blue. Do you feel so?"

"I do feel rather gloomy this evening," replied Dick, "but I am sure I cannot tell why it is. I do not wish to feel so when I can avoid it, but sometimes a predisposition in this way will get the better of me."

"Well, Dick, you would have felt a great sight more cheerful this evening, if you had gone with us to the pic-nic to-day. If Squire B—— wanted his office kept open, he ought to have done it himself. We had a glorious time, Dick, and lots of fun. Judge L—— and my *old fellow* was there, and they got up three sheets in the wind devilish soon after they got there; and I thought in my soul, at one time, that they would have to be carried home. All we wanted, to make a polite finish of it, was a respectable row!"

"I am surprised to hear that Judge L—— was intoxicated. It is only a few weeks since he pronounced the sentence of death on Edward H——, who murdered his wife and two daughters while he was in a state of intoxication. You all remember what a *temperance speech* he made on that occasion. I am surprised that a man who holds the position he does, should set such an example."

"O Lord! Dick, you don't know that *old coon* as well as we do, or it wouldn't surprise you at all. I question if he has thought of Edward H—— since the sheriff took him out of the court-house, after the sentence of death was pronounced. Dick, do you remember how sanctimoniously he mouthed the conclusion of the *form*—"may the Lord have mercy on your soul?" Well, he wasn't *over* sober then—I'll be bound he wasn't. After all, he is just the kind of a chap that's needed here. The rum interest think he is *perfection* itself; and they ought to think so, for if it wasn't for him, they would soon be mighty scarce here. You see, we have a good many religious people here, and if it was not for Judge L——, the rum interest would scarcely maintain a living existence."

"I declare, Horace," said Dick, "if these things are really so, the Judge is hardly fit to decide upon anything, but rum; and the law, and the evidence must suffer amazingly in his hands."

"Well, Dick, let Judge L—— go for this time. Do you know that we have a 'belle' here from New York—a real eastern beauty? She was at the pic-nic, and she has been as spry as a cricket all the day—

part of everything, and almost the whole of some things! I don't know how the mischief she's heard of you so soon. You had better be scraping acquaintance pretty quick. There is no time to lose. I would give my head for her. I tell you, Dick, you would have enjoyed yourself."

"I suppose I would have enjoyed myself, Horace. At least, I should have put on the *appearance*."

"The appearance! Well, Dick Wilson, you're the last fellow I should have shot at, expecting to kill a hypocrite!"

"I think, Horace, your expression will hardly rank me amongst that class. In everything, I move under pressure. Tell me who is this young lady?"

"She is Miss Lucy S——, from New York, and is one of the liveliest beauties you ever saw. Why, man, she's an angel, all but the wings! and let me tell you, she intends giving you a chase, and I'm mistaken if it won't be a merry one, too. You must be moving early, Dick; for if you want to catch her, let me tell you, you'll have all kinds of obstacles to contend with; and you had better prepare yourself for it, and don't say that I didn't give you fair warning."

"Horace," replied Dick, "you can have her with all my heart, and if you think it will make your chances any better than they are, I will give you this moment a quit claim to all my right, title and interest in the beautiful bird. But I won't guarantee the *catching*. You must look out for that."

"That will do very well to talk about; but she's an archer."

"That's just what I've been thinking, Horace; and I advise you to approach with all possible caution, and be sure, as you go along, to keep a path open, in case of retreat, for such a thing may be necessary. And further, if what you say is true, I don't believe that she is worth catching."

"I tell you, Dick, if what you have said were to reach her ears, you would find yourself in a predicament! I'd like to know what kind of stuff you are made of."

"I fancy, Horace, it's pretty good. It has stood hardships already. And so far as knowing what I have said is concerned, I have no objection to your telling her, if you will only be thoughtful enough to tell what you said yourself."

"Yes, indeed! I ain't fool enough for that."

"Do you not know, Horace, that it would be very ungentlemanly in you to accuse me before that young lady, with having spoken disrespectfully or unkindly of her, when you have opened every inch of the way? Suppose I should go to Judge L—— and your father, and tell them what you have said about them?"

"Yes, Dick, I know. My father and Judge L——,

(if you don't know it, I will tell you,) 'rule the roost' about these 'diggins.' Come, come, boys, let's be off. Let's go right up to the Judge's;" and these worthies started, much to Dick's satisfaction.

The visits of these young *gentlemen*, who were, for the most part, what may be called well-dressed, poorly-cultivated street-loafers, who seemed to think that wealth would make up for empty heads and bad hearts, with the consequences necessarily flowing from them, rather increased than allayed Dick's sense of sadness. They had rudely broken in upon and scattered the beautiful imagery which, in spite of his depression, he had pictured to himself, and in which again he saw his mother, his sister, and his little Harry, whom he tenderly loved, in the enjoyment of happiness. He threw himself back in his chair, and said to himself:

"This is strange. These fellows are not in the habit of using such familiarity with me, and they are not by any means amongst my intimate friends either. This gives me a clue to some of Mrs. Watson's hints. I wish I knew what it means. But it is my best plan to be careful. Well, at all events, they can't drive me from my independence: that is something which, in spite of the rumseller, and misfortune too, I have been able to keep, and keep it I will, while there is a single crag to which I am able to cling. If there is treachery in this, I will defy them to move me. If this is their game, it is a pretty cool calculation, and the whole of it is not visible yet."

When Dick Wilson entered the village of B——, where he designed finishing his legal studies, preparatory to admission to the bar, it was with the consciousness that he was very poor and wholly dependent on his own exertions. This consciousness, if he had been accustomed to poverty, would have been all the safer and better for him; but he was not accustomed to it. Poverty on his shoulders was an *awkward fit*, and he had never learned those arts which *early necessity* alone can teach.

When the stage stopped at B——, to get a new set of horses, as usual, quite a number of those who were in the habit of doing so, collected at the stage office, and remained there until the last horse was hitched, and the last passenger in the stage. Dick was looking on while these things were transpiring, and just as the driver snapped his whip, a *rosy*-cheeked gentleman cried out:

"Halloo, driver! you've lost a passenger."

"I guess not," said the driver, and off he went, flying at the rate of three miles an hour.

When it was understood that a passenger had been dropped from the stage at B——, many persons flocked to the favored rumseller's quarters to see him, for peradventure it might be some distinguished man; and if all the curious who were fond of rum and strange faces didn't see him, they would have thought themselves behind the time sadly. Dick was considerably annoyed by this demonstration of inquisitiveness, but at once set about finding some employment, the proceeds of which would enable him to pay his boarding and defray contingent expenses. This he was soon able to accomplish, and a day or two found him very comfortably situated in this respect. He had engaged with a gentleman who was in a large business to keep his books for him, and in this engagement he was exceedingly fortunate. The family to whose acquaintance and to whose confidence very soon this introduced him, was just the kind under whose guardianship a young man like Dick Wilson, or indeed any young man, would, if anywhere, be safe—a much better and safer place of resort for a *young man* than the hotel with its *bar-room.* Dick was not long in making the acquaintance of this excellent family, and then he freely and fully committed to them the history of his and his family's misfortunes; and who does not know how soothing it is to have a few faithful ones to whom the joys and sorrows of the heart may be committed, and where it is certain they will be safe? Here Dick felt that he was safe, and this feeling introduced him at once into the affections of the family, so that in his hours of gloom and despondency he always turned towards their door for sympathy.

At the end of Dick's soliloquy, where we left him, he found himself in the cheerful sitting-room of Mr. Watson's family, where everything—children and all—were so well in keeping that he could not but feel that this was something approaching to home. In a moment he found himself surrounded by all the children in the house, for with them he was an especial favorite; and few people are better judges of real goodness of heart than children. Mrs. Watson tried to get them off him, but it wouldn't do: they were accustomed to regard Dick's coming as a holiday, and they would have their fun, let who would scold.

"Mrs. Watson," said Dick, "do let these children alone. I assure you it is a pleasure to me to have these demonstrations of their innocent affections. The childlike simplicity of life is a lovely thing, and it is a pity that it cannot be preserved through life. Mrs. Watson, I have been afraid that I have intruded myself too much upon your family; but I feel at home in your house, and I know that if I should make an unadvised remark, as I often do, that it will not be echoed from ear to ear under the stealthy garb of a *leaky* secrecy, until the whole community is in possession of it."

"We are always glad to see you, Richard," replied Mrs. Watson, "and we hope you will come to our house with as much freedom as you would if it were your mother's. You seem to feel unhappy this evening. What is wrong? Have you received unpleasant news from home?"

"Oh no, Mrs. Watson; I had a letter from my sister yesterday, and they are all well, which is all I can expect. Since the death of my father, I have hardly been free from melancholy; and it seems to grow upon me. I have tried time and again to tear myself away from its embrace, but I cannot. There is a mystery about it, for to me even this melancholy at times has an attraction about it, which holds me like a charm."

"Well, Richard," said Mrs. Watson, while a mother's affection brightened her countenance, "that may be true, but you know that after the natural appetite is satiated by the feast, the rarest delicacies are insipid. I think it is just so with the mind; and a feast of melancholy, while it is unsafe and unnourishing, will render substantial food unpalatable, and at last itself will turn into a nauseous insipidity. It was so with Lord Byron. He feasted upon melancholy; and the wild strains of his Alpine song, as it mingled with the roar of the cataract, and chimed with the screams of the eagle, are the evidences of the power by which it had been a prisoner. He feasted upon its poison, until every fire which burned at the source of that lofty genius went out in gloom. This, Richard, is the history of a cherished melancholy, and it is possible that we may cherish it with the very breath by which we think we are trying to expel it. But few of those who have given themselves over to its companionship, have ever been able to give a good reason for doing so. Be assured that it is begotten in the mind by an evil genius for an evil purpose, and Eugene Aram and Lord Byron are fearful evidences of its ulterior consequences. I would advise you to break away, if it is possible, from that which will overcast with gloom the brightest vision your imagination can conceive. A little poison may be good for the system at times, but too much will kill—a little melancholy may be good for the mind at times, but too much will ruin it. You have told me, in the history of your troubles, that your education from the nursery was rather fashionable than religious. This is your great misfortune, and it has been the misfortune and the ruin of many thousands. What shall that be called which robs the child of its *priceless* birthright? What name does that omission wear which fails to do what *reason* and *revelation* imperatively command? So far as your worldly prospects are concerned, I am sure you have no reason to be cast down. Your winter is nearly passed by, I hope, and the joyful spring-time is near at hand. It is true that your earthly prospects have been wickedly and wantonly blighted by the rumseller,—the all of earthly competency upon which yourself and your loved ones were dependent, is in the pockets of those who more than murdered your father, and with whom God will yet reckon! You have had domestic afflictions of the severest character. The home of your childhood has been broken up by a most *wicked* robbery. Your dead have been buried out of your sight, and the cold damp grave encloses their forms. You will see them no more. Beware of that *monster* through whose influence this tempest of desolation has been brought to your door. Fly from it and its *smooth-tongued* abettors as you would from the very gates of destruction! Why, Richard, you ought not to feel gloomy. Just see what you have to live for—and you have a prospect very soon of having your dear ones with you."

"Mrs. Watson, my sadness is more for them than for myself," replied Dick.

"I know that, Richard, but why should it be so? Your talents and education, with your amiable disposition, will bring you a reputation and a fortune at any bar. You have many warm friends here, who will do anything for you that may be necessary. But I will forewarn you—and I do this for your greater safety—that there are some who appear to be your friends in your presence, and whom it would be very unsafe for you to trust too far. These persons have been trying, and they will still try, to accomplish your ruin. They are not particular how they do it—to accomplish it is the end; and any means which promises to bring it about will be unscrupulously used."

"Ah! is this possible, Mrs. Watson?"

"Yes, I know it to be the case, and my husband and myself have talked much about it, and concluded that it would be best to put you on your guard against them."

"Do you know the cause, Mrs. Watson?"

"Well, Richard, in the first place, all the rumsellers in the place, but one, are your enemies, and only, I presume, because you do not frequent their bar-rooms!"

"Well, Mrs. Watson, that is no loss—that's a clear gain, and I am just that much safer; and if the other one, who in some respects is a pretty clever fellow, hated me too, then I should consider myself safe. Mrs. Watson, I need not explain, but it is not a strange thing that the drunkard's *son should himself become a drunkard!*"

"Well Richard, that reason, in connection with a spirit of jealousy, is all that I know."

"This," replied Dick, "is hardly a sufficient ground of action against a young man who is as poor as I am, and who has such responsibilities as mine."

"*Meanness*, *vice*, and *duplicity*, Richard, always act without a reason, and hence it is that so much of their action is in the dark. There is Horace Stevens—you must watch that young man narrowly, as well as the few who associate with him. He has, as you have no doubt learned, been raised in this place, or rather he has *grown up* here. His father is one of our wealthy men; but if you should ask him how and where he accumulated his wealth, he would be ashamed to tell you. He has become very proud now, and thinks, I have no doubt, that his *gold-headed cane* and spectacles will dazzle people's eyes so much, that they will not look to see where these things came from. I will tell you something about him. He accumulated his fortune in that 'old stone house' where black Jim's family live now, and it was one of the worst places within many miles of this place; and twenty years ago the better part of this community thought himself and his family unfit to live in civilized society. Most of his family perished by intemperance! Yes, that same *proud*, *ignorant* man, whom you will now meet flourishing his cane in the street, has been the cause of more tears, and griefs, and the loss of more lives in this community, than all the other causes combined; and he is strongly suspected of having committed murder with his own hand. About twenty-five years since, a drover mysteriously disappeared from his house, and there is but little doubt but he knows all about it. His son Horace, as might be expected, is worthless. His father and Judge L—— together, have managed to make him a lawyer, and he intends opening an office here again, as he has several times before in the course of three or four years; and he regards your plan of opening an office here as prejudicial to his interests; and the fact is, Richard, the poor fellow knows no more about law than my *little Willie* does."

"Do you think, Mrs. Watson, that Judge L—— is in this matter?"

"I think he is; it is amongst the kind of people with whom he always acts, and it would be a strange thing if he should forsake the rumsellers and their *pets* now."

"Well, Mrs. Watson, do you know a young lady who is visiting at Judge L——'s, from New York."

"Oh yes, I know her very well—have you seen her?"

"I have not, but Horace Stevens called on me this evening, and spoke of her."

"I hope you said nothing that will flatter her; for she will hear every word you said, and probably more."

"I rather think she won't call it flattery. I must go. I feel better than I did when I came in. But I must call again, and hear the history of the drover. Mrs. Watson, if I do rise, and get the better of poverty, treachery, and the rumseller, I will ever remember with gratitude your family; and if I fall—for I feel the possibility of this every day; for I once loved wine, and drank it freely—then let my memory sleep in the grave!"

CHAPTER IX.

TEMPERANCE MEETING—ITS RESULTS.

"Sirs, ye know that by this craft
We have our wealth."

THE rumsellers at B—— were thrown into great perplexity and consternation when they heard that on the previous Sabbath Mr. Smith, the minister, had the boldness to announce that on the following Wednesday there would be a meeting, to take into consideration the best means of lessening the evils of intemperance in the place. Such things had been attempted there before, but, unfortunately, the *craftsmen* had generally managed to break them up in some way or other, so that little, if any, benefit resulted from them. This time the matter had been well considered by a few before it was made public, and for that occasion they had the promise, from a very eminent lawyer at a distance, that he would be present; and when this was understood, their consternation was greatly increased. They did not like this *impudent lawyer*, as they called him, and they were afraid of his influence and his speech, which they knew would be a plain one, if he should come; and many of them hoped that something would occur to prevent his coming.

Mr. Stevens and Judge L——, the one superannuated, and the other worse, were seen, during the whole of the afternoon on Monday, parading the streets. Early on Tuesday morning they were doing the same. The rumsellers were all at their doors. Their *ostlers* and *boot-blacks* seemed to have a holiday, and their masters were watching the signs of the times. They were in a wonderful state of excitement, and in their imaginations, already they saw the *dimes*, whose jingle was more familiar to them than anything but profanity, sliding noiselessly into an honorable channel.

As Judge L—— and his particular friend, Mr. Stevens, were passing Mr. Smith's quarters, apparently as much in a hurry as usual, Mr. Smith said to them:

"Havn't you got one yet?"

"We havn't got any, and I don't think we will," was the half-growled reply of Mr. Stevens.

"Have you tried Squire B——?" asked Smith.

"Yes, we have," said Judge L——.

"What did he say?" continued Smith.

"Just what we might have expected," replied Stevens; "that we might go to the devil, for he wasn't going to disgrace himself with *such business*."

"Where else have you been?" said Smith.

"Well, the fact is," said Judge L——, looking as if he had got to the end of his judgment, which was a very short distance by a *straight line*, "we have tried everybody but Dick Wilson, and I doubt not that he will serve us just as his unmannerly preceptor did. If he will consent to appear on the stand for us, I would rather trust him than any man in the village."

"Do you think you can get him?" said another rumseller, who had just come up, almost breathless and trembling with agitation.

"It is doubtful," said Judge L——; "but we will make the effort," and off they started to test the power of flattering words in winning him to their service.

When they entered the office, they found just the person who had a better right there than any other person, and yet the very one they did not want to see—Dick's preceptor, who half an hour before had recommended them to the devil for suitable assistance. Squire B—— was sharp, as lawyers usually are, and it didn't take him twenty-four hours to guess what they had come for; and taking his cane in his hand, he marched out of the office.

"This is a pleasant morning, Mr. Wilson," said Judge L——, and then added, "How does the law go, Mr. Wilson?"

"Rather slowly," said Dick, carelessly.

"I'll be bound," said Judge L——, "you ought not

to say that, with the prospect you have before you. Such talents as yours will win a reward anywhere. Speaking is an indispensable qualification for a successful lawyer, and if I had been a *natural* speaker, I shouldn't have thanked the Governor for the Judgeship. You are a fine speaker, Mr. Wilson, and you ought to improve all the opportunities you have to let the people know it, and then, when you come to the bar, you will at once be crowded with business. You have heard, I presume, that the officious part of this community are arraying themselves against those whom they tauntingly call *rumsellers*, and that they are to have a meeting to-morrow. We design drumming up one for the next day, and have called on you to see if you will agree to take the stump for *our cause* on that occasion."

"No, Judge, I will not," said Dick, peremptorily.

"You had better do so, Mr. Wilson: it will be to your advantage in more ways than one," said the Judge, in a half-pleading and half-menacing tone.

"Why didn't you ask Squire B——, before he left the office?"

"We don't want him," said Mr. Stevens; "he would do us more harm than good."

"No, no," said Judge L——, "rather than try him, I will risk the stump myself."

Just as the Judge finished his negation and his *lie*, Squire B—— entered the office, and said,—

"Dick, this is a rare chance to *immortalize* yourself. Go to the meeting, and speak there, and every respectable dog in the village will show you his teeth, and every high-minded young lady, when you enter her house, will show you the door. I would like to see you going to Mr. Watson's or Mr. Shepard's after that. They asked me to go, and I recommended them to go where they get *all* their *assistance* in carrying on this business."

"Why, Squire B——, they have just told me they wouldn't have you," said Dick, laughing.

"That was true, sir, when they found they couldn't get me. I will defend a murderer in court whenever I am called upon to do so, however aggravated the case may be; but I will not let myself down to become an apologist for, or plead that cause which is the origin of so much misery."

These gentlemen were chap-fallen, and left much disappointed. The village was soon filled with handbills, calling together the worshippers of rum, on Thursday afternoon, in the court-house, and to which the announcement that Judge L—— would address the meeting, was appended in capitals.

"This is a pretty piece of business," said one of a company of rumsellers who had established themselves about an advertisement which graced the town-pump, "that we, for our own safety, should be compelled to resort to self-defence in this way; for if it were not for us, the grass would grow up in the streets of this village."

"Yes," said another, "and it is a high-handed, daring act, for we have the *law* and the *constitution* on our side. Judge L—— told me so, and he is right, I am sure."

"Aye, aye," said a third, "but we'll fix this matter. I'm up to games of all kinds, and I sha'n't fail this time. I'll tell you what I'll do: I'll make Jim Watkins and Pete Hany just drunk enough for them to make their way to the church, and then I'll pay them for going there; and as sure as guns, if they see each other, they will kick up a fight right in the house, and it will trouble them to part them."

"Do you think you can do this, Smith?" said one.

"Never mind, if I can't. I'm an old bird in that work, and if I can't, nobody else need try. I'll go myself, and watch the fun."

"Then, Smith," said one, "you must be hunting up your birds. It is only about three hours now until they meet."

"I'll be ready. It won't take me long to *prime* them."

Just then they saw a man coming into the village on horseback, and riding in a very easy, careless manner.

Judge L—— had, sometime before this, joined the company, and suddenly looking up, and fixing his eyes on the advancing figure on horseback, he said, "Good Heavens! boys, it's lawyer B——! I must be getting out of this crowd."

It was too late, however; for in far-sightedness he had no advantage of lawyer B——; and he was, at the very beginning of his retreat, greeted by the shrill voice of the mounted man, calling him to stop. As he brought his horse's head alongside, he said—"Judge, I came here, by particular request, to make a temperance speech to-day. This I know to be a very disorderly place, and I will hold you responsible for any annoyance or blackguardism which may be witnessed at the meeting," and touching his horse, which was like himself, of fine blood, he swept by the crowd of abashed rumsellers, like a *superior* being. After he was out of sight, a few steps brought Judge L—— into the gang again, and then he said, "Smith, you must not send those fellows there to-day; that lawyer has great influence, and can kill this place if he wishes to do so."

"How the devil can he do that?" inquired Smith, in a rage.

"Why, he can kill me!" said the Judge.

"Well, I can't think you are all the place, by a long ways."

"Well, if you do send them, Smith, remember I won't speak at *our* meeting to-morrow."

At the appointed time, the meeting was organized,

and the business commenced in the old way, on the general principles of voluntary abstinence. These people although heartily sick of the rumseller's work, yet they never dreamed that such a thing as the modern "Maine Law" could have an existence, and this was not strange. Nobody wondered that Franklin could not catch the lightning for which he was fishing with his kite; but every one was astonished when it became, from his experimenting, a common medium of communication.

If there had been a possibility of procuring any such law as the "Maine Law," they would have *dropped* at once the *voluntary* system; and they would have seized the *true* instrument of success, and stamped *felony* upon the traffic; but they had not reached, by several years, the *perfect day*, and they intended to do the very best they could, and oppose as mighty an effort as possible, to those withering curses, before which youth, manhood, age and innocence were being prostrated, and whose very hearts were being torn out of their bodies.

The lawyer, without any resolutions being before the house, rose, and commenced his speech by giving a glowing description of the squad of rumsellers who had gathered about, and were hugging the town pump, and how he had cut off Judge L——'s retreat, and secured good order for the occasion.

"Gentlemen," said he, "if you ever saw a rumseller who was a good man, you saw a man whose daily practice was immeasurably overbalancing for evil, both his profession and your opinion of his goodness."

This seemed to startle some of the audience, for it was a strong expression, and some thought it was going too far and too fast. If the lawyer had spoken restrictively of the rumsellers of B——, they would not have questioned his opinion; but as it was, they didn't know but he included the whole world, and this they were sure was a wide sweep. Said he again —"If I were selling your sons and your daughters bread with one hand, and double portions of *poison* with the other, you would have a poor opinion of my *goodness*—the rumseller, however, sells you *no bread* at all, but poison and only poison."

The thing was becoming more reasonable, and even those who were somewhat sceptical, in reference to the proposition at first, when they saw the illustration, said to themselves, "I guess he is about right."

"Never fear," said an old man, audibly, in answer to some doubtings which he had overheard, "he is no fool; he know'd every word he was going to say for this week past."

When it seemed to the speaker that what he had said had been digested—and this he understood by the expression of their countenances, in which he could read their hearts—for he had spoken too often to juries to be out of tune or out of time with anything by which he wished to accomplish an end—he said,—

"The rumseller has no more right, *natural*, *acquired*, or *vested*, to engage in measuring out ardent spirits to a human being, than he has a right to open a *shop* for the sale of *arsenic;* for although the latter acts quicker than the former, still its effects are none the more certain or fatal."

"I'll tell ye he's right, John," said an old lady who was sitting by her husband, who was a friend of the rumsellers—"jist wait till he gets to the point, and puts the saddle on."

"You are all acquainted with George Handy," said the speaker, "you see him in your streets every day—without character, the victim of insanity! The parents of George Handy were to my knowledge amongst the most respectable of your community, and George himself started in the world with as good prospects, and as fair a character, as any young man could wish. He is yet young in years, but an old man in everything else! Where is his wife? Where is the heritage that should have been the portion of his lovely daughter? Did the assassin, under the cover of a dark night, as he was on his way to his wife and child, plunge the dagger into his heart? Oh no! for compared with the *truth*, this would have been merciful, for it would have left competency and reputation to those who survived him. I say merciful, when compared with the lingering tortures which was perpetrated upon his entire manhood by the rumseller's hands. To his bar, and I will mention the name, I mean Smith's rummery, he came, and came again, and at each coming, while his property and his character were being filched from him, he in return received the lingering poison—the *warranty* of disgrace! Am I right?"

"Oh! yes," said an old man, "fifty murders could not have killed poor George as dead as he is to-day."

"Ah! John," said the old lady, "I told you to wait until he got the saddle on. What do you think now?"

"I guess he is right, Jinny—Smith is a bad man, and I guess it would be better if the *law* would *license* him to *sell poison,* and take away his whiskey from him. I don't believe he would do as much harm."

After the usual interval for digestion had been given, with a great effort he grasped the foundations and the climax, and shaking them in a manner that was terrifying to some, he said,—

"Those who are aiding and abetting the rumseller in this business, are no better than he is, and I will add, that in my estimation they are *worse!*"

And this, instead of following with a continuation of his speech, as he had done before, he followed with a pause, in which he seemed to be reading the hearts of some in the assembly who were not *duly sincere*, and whose *marks* and *scratches* it would not have been difficult for a rumseller to have appended to his application for license—setting him forth to be a man famed far and wide for *temperance* and *sobriety!*

"I ain't the rumseller's friend," said one who thought the eye of the lawyer was in his heart, looking up its character—"It's true I did sign Smith's petition the last time, but I tell you I don't do that mean trick any more."

The speaker was a good deal circumscribed by the time in which he was speaking, and concluded thus:

"Who sign those applications for license? They are the rumseller's abettors! Who are willing to apologize for the wrongs which he is entailing upon humanity? They are his friends and upholders! Who look on unconcernedly, when he is trying to trap a human being? They are his friends—in them he lives, moves, and has his being."

If that speech had been made in these days it would have been moddled and modulated to suit the times, and he would no doubt have said: Who is opposed to the 'Maine law'? Who will plead for intemperance? Who is in favor of rum legislation? These are they who give aid and comfort to the rumseller, and inflict upon society the bitterest wrong.

After he had succeeded in making every one believe that everything he had said was true, he left the stand, and was succeeded by Mr. S—— in a style which although it had not all the vigor, yet it had all the *truthfulness* of the one which had just preceded it.

After running over many of the points at which the first speaker had only glanced, and presenting them in a very clear light, he entered a little into the *private* rum traffic of the village, by persons who would have been ashamed to be called rumsellers; and yet in fact they were, and are doing a great deal of injury by it. He said it was not only at the hands of the *professional* rumsellers of the village that the community, in every sense, were suffering, but that even merchants, for the sake of adding '*ill gotten gaiu*' to their treasure, had, to some extent, enlisted in the business, and if they did not sell it by *drams* they sold it by quarts, gallons and barrels; and that it was carried home to gratify the perverted appetites of those who loved it, and to form in the young a taste for that, the use of which will but destroy. These *semi-grog shops*, he thought had a very ruinous tendency in whatever light they might be regarded, and that they ought to be included in the system, and to be held responsible for the consequences.

After the business was all over, the people departed quietly, having heard more truth, and having enjoyed themselves better, than they had ever done at a temperance meeting before.

The street was perfectly clear. The rumsellers—there was not one to be seen. Some persons did think that they were making their observations from *loop-holes* in their houses, and that probably they were trying to hunt up something which might give their meeting on the morrow a sprinkling of decency. In the evening the street was filled again with them and their friends, looking up the elements of the coming meeting.

It was pretty well noised abroad that on account of their failure to get any other person, Judge L—— had consented to make a speech, and this was quite a curiosity in itself, and would be likely to collect a curious crowd of spectators, and amongst them, many who would not like to be considered amongst the rumseller's friends; and, above all the rest, though it was to be kept a secret, the lawyer made up his mind to stay too, and hear what the Judge might have to say on the occasion.

Dick Wilson made up his mind that he would go too, and take with him, if he could persuade her to go, Miss Handy. He called at Mr. Shepard's, and as soon as a convenient opportunity offered, he asked her if she would be willing to go to that meeting.

After a moment's hesitation she said, "Mr. Wilson, how can I go there? These are the people who have robbed me of father and mother, and who have thrown me upon the charity of this good family; and now they are laying their plans to practice the same cruelty upon others!"

"You will not be regarded as taking part with them, Miss Handy," said Dick; "and if I thought so, I am sure I would not go myself. For, so far as these people have given *me* reason to have an opinion of them, my opinion would hardly be more flattering to them than your own; and while my reasons for thinking meanly of them are not resting upon a foundation so fearful as yours, yet God knows I have no reason to think well of them. They left me a little, but I am not indebted to them for it; they took all that they could, and the law measured it out to them—more I think than was meet or merciful."

"Mr. Wilson, they have wounded me deeper than a stranger's heart can ever know. My poor mother's heart was broken into atoms by these men, and her life went out amidst the wild dreams of insanity! And my father—I meet him almost daily. I try to get from him a single look of recognition, but I cannot—he does not know me. I am as a stranger to the one who, but for the rumseller, would have been the protector of my youth. I am alone in this world now, so far as the ties of kindred are concerned; and at the door of the rumseller I lay this charge of fearful robbery, knowing that he must account for it to God! No, No! I *cannot* go!"

CHAPTER X.

RUMMIES IN COUNCIL.—THEIR DOINGS.

"Should he, when he pleases, and on whom he will,
Wage war, with any or with no pretence
Of provocation given, or wrong sustained,
And force the beggarly last doit by means
That his own humor dictates, from the clutch
Of Poverty; that thus he may secure
His thousands, weary of penurious life,
A splendid opportunity to die?"

THE day which was to signalize the triumph of the rumsellers at B——, at last arrived.

This was to be a *mighty* affair! It was to give a *death thrust* to the temperance reform in that village, and its friends would then look on, and smile to see it die! On the preceding evening, when the sweeping propositions of the "*big lawyer*" were generally known to the rumsellers, they were filled with fire and fury, and determined to deluge the place with rum. They happened to meet under the awning of a miserable grocery compared with the keeper of which even Smith was a *prince*, and there *they had it* in a manner which, to relate, would be offensive to the ear of decency—and we will pass it.

On the same evening, in another place, another

company were gathered to consult on the best means to be used to give the meeting an appearance which would not frighten their friends, who might come from a distance to aid them in striking their terrible blow. This company was small and noiseless, when compared with that under the awning. It comprised Judge L—— and the superannuated Stevens, the file-leaders of the whole matter. Said the Judge, as he removed from his lips his glass of brandy,—

"It would be bad for us if the time should ever come when this delicious stuff should be taken from us."

"Yes," said Stevens, sorrowfully, "I don't want to live to see that time, for I couldn't live long after it."

"The rumselling business," said Judge L——, "is a fine business in this village. I suppose one half of the money in the township passes through their hands."

"Yes, fully that much; and it takes nearly the other half to pay *contingent* expenses."

"If you value your *rum*, Stevens, you musn't whisper such a thing as that where any of our enemies can get hold of it," replied the Judge. "But, come, it isn't our business to furnish arguments for these people. Let them take care of themselves. We must prepare for to-morrow. Do you know if that *big lawyer* has gone?"

"Yes, he has," replied Stevens; "I saw him dashing over the hill this evening. He wouldn't venture to show himself here to-morrow. If he did, he would be carried on a rail."

"Good Heavens!" said the Judge, "I am glad to hear that. You'll hear a speech from me to-morrow that will knock the brains out of everything he said. I've got the *legal* and *constitutional* side of this question, and I tell you, I'll make the fur fly. Ha! ha! indeed! That impertinent scoundrel to come here and say that decent men, because they are the friends of the rumsellers, are aiding and abetting in murder! I'll show him which side of the bread is buttered! Stevens, we musn't make any calculation that we are going to have this meeting to ourselves; for this will not be the case. I met Dick Wilson, and Watson, and Shepard, and Squire B——, this evening, and every one of them looked as if they had the devil in their eyes. They are up to something, and we had better be prepared for it. George Handy will be there. He never misses these kinds of gatherings, and if he should appear there to-morrow as I saw him in the street to-day, he would prejudice our cause very much. I tell you what I will do: I will hunt up a suit of my old clothes, if you will find a boy to carry them up to the poor-house in the morning."

"Your clothes are too big for him, Judge," said Stevens, "and everybody will know them."

"That is just what I want," said the Judge, "and

this very thing will give *point* to my speech. I will send a note to the steward to compel him to put them on."

"I'll do it," said Stevens, triumphantly.

"Now," said the Judge, "there is one thing yet which is of more consequence to us than George Handy. Mrs. Armstrong, you know, is very poor, and is to a great extent supported by the charity of our enemies. Now can't we do something for her that can be pretty well *noised abroad* before to-morrow noon?"

"Yes, we can so," said Stevens, with a very *charitable* look. "I will give the half towards buying her a calico dress, if you will give the other half."

"Come, come, Stevens," said the Judge, "on this occasion you will have to go further into your generosity than that. Now, I'll tell you what I will do. I have got a *cow* that is worth twenty-five dollars in any man's money, and if you will insure me two-thirds of that amount, I will send her down to Mrs. Armstrong in the morning, and I will send a *bag of bran* into the bargain."

"She must be a good cow," said Stevens.

"There never was a better one," continued the Judge, "and *you* can well afford to give the half yourself. You know where that woman's property went."

"Well, Judge," said Stevens, "it's a devil of a *lift;* but I suppose we must stand it. I'll agree to raise all

I can out of Smith and Fritz and the rest of them; and I'll call on some of the *store-keepers* too: they ought to aid; and then I'll pay the balance myself. But if it wasn't for the meeting, I wouldn't give one cent!"

About nine o'clock in the morning everybody in the village knew that Judge L—— had given Mrs. Armstrong a cow, and, as might be expected, it was a matter of much curiosity to many.

As the hour of the meeting drew on, troops of the rumsellers' friends were seen crowding into the village, and, taken all together, they were a very fair representation of the trade. The quarters of the different rumsellers of the place were filled to overflowing, and a majority of them were in the process of being filled with rum. Crowds of boys were in the streets, admiring the appearance and occasionally the *swaggering* dexterity of the jolly host.

A new object of attraction suddenly arrested the attention of the boys. It was George Handy, arrayed in Judge L——'s old broadcloth. The poor fellow looked unusually bright this morning, and the cheerlessness of insanity seemed to have partially passed away. He halted in front of Smith's door, where the cruelty of the boys, encouraged by the *grimaces* of the bystanders, most of whom were passing through the very same process through which poor George had passed, and which had made him what he was, soon set George in a rage. Smith came to the door, and as he was attempting to lay violent hands on the poor fellow, George, by what some would call a *luckless blow*, left him sprawling in the gutter beside him, which was a very fit place for him.

The bell of the old court-house, whose walls were accustomed to the recital of events connected with the rum traffic, at last told the community that the magnificent spectacle was about to concentrate in the court-room. The room was soon filled, so that not another one could get in. Those who were merely spectators, who had gone early and without any preconcerted plan, were seated on one side of the house, and that side contained the well-developed proportions of the "big lawyer." The other side contained the *bone* and *sinew* of the rumsellers' forces in that region, and amongst them, very conspicuously, sat George Handy, the man whom they had so cruelly cursed. The contrast between the two sides of the house was perfect, and some one, on the side of the spectators, was heard to say—"*Deliver me from this body of death!*" The *bar* on this occasion was crowded with rum-manufacturers and rumsellers, and constituted the pageant toward which all eyes were directed.

After a few moments, at the instance of Judge L——, who had not noticed that lawyer B—— was in the assembly, an old and, as the Judge said, a *very respectable* manufacturer of rum, was called to the chair; and in answer to the question as to where the presiding officer should sit, George Handy called out —"In the *prisoner's box!*" After this officer had found a place where his dignity might repose, a motion was again made by Stevens that Richard Wilson, Esquire, should be called on to act as secretary, and in a moment, Smith, looking out from the black, swollen eye which George's blow had given, said—

"I second the motion."

In an instant Dick was on his feet, and many of them, thinking that he was eager to jump at the honor tendered him, began to cheer him. As soon as this mark of *respect* was hushed, he said:

"Gentlemen, I gave you notice night before last, that you could expect no assistance from me."

Then the difficulty was to find a man whose hand was steady enough to make out an intelligible copy of their proceedings for the printer; for they intended that the *whole world* should be filled with the fame of that jubilee.

This meeting was almost the counterpart of one held for the same purpose in the city of New York, less than a year since, and there was about the same difficulty in getting a respectable organization in the one case as in the other. Of this meeting at B——, however, it was never said, when their printed proceedings appeared, that they had many names which belonged to no one in particular. In most of their features these two meetings are so nearly allied, that one familiar with the meeting at B—— would say, that the rumsellers in Gotham must have had a copy of its proceedings, and that they only departed from the form when they were using names to their published proceedings.

The *cow story* had been heard by all who were in the court-house, and George Handy, in the Judge's cloth, was there to speak and answer questions for himself. Judge L—— was called on, and immediately spread himself, preparatory to his speech; and without looking to see whether any but the *jury* were there, he commenced, by saying:

"Ladies and gentlemen, I regret the necessity which has called me to appear before you at this time, for nothing but imperative necessity could have induced me to do so. Innovations in religion, morals and law, are everywhere to be reprobated, and good citizens should set their faces against them. Innovations on the *natural rights* of individuals and *constitutional* infractions are especially to be deprecated; and it is to consider innovation in reference to these two last named points that we are met here at this time.

"The liquor traffic, at this day, seems to be something against which a certain portion of the community are conspiring and arraying themselves, with malice *afore thought*, which is the evidence of depraved mind, regardless of the natural, and I may add, constitutional *rights* of others. Rights, my friends, are *everlasting things!* Law is the defence of the weak against the strong, and lest it should be made worse, ought to abide as it is, and no one ought to be guilty of the heinous crime of interfering with constitutions! *God save the commonwealth from those wolves who would devour it!*"

Here Smith gave a hearty cheer.

"Gentlemen, let me direct your attention to my venerable friend, the president of this assembly. Look at him! His locks are whitened now by the frosts of many years; and the fruit which the grave is claiming is nearly ripe, and ready to fall. He came into this community poor, when most of you were children. He did not remain poor. His natural energy and noble-heartedness moved him forward. In a few years after, he established a distillery in your vicinity, and while he has enriched himself, he has also helped to enrich the county. Who purchased your barley, your rye and corn? Where were you always sure to find a market for what you had to spare? Who gave you the means by which you were enabled to clothe and educate your children? Gentlemen, a grateful heart is pleasing to God. Remember that, and remember too, that ingratitude always meets its reward. Then I would have you use your influence to spare the feelings of that old man, who is left to us from the past, and who is soon to go the way of all flesh, and be seen no more in your community.

"I said, gentlemen, that natural rights were everlasting—I believe the technical term is *inalienable*—and that is stranger yet. *A natural right* means that which an individual has a right to do, under all *circumstances*, *independent* of any *thing* or *person to the contrary notwithstanding!* Now, on this principle—for you cannot help but see how broad it is—my friend in the chair has *right enough and room enough* to carry on his business to any extent that he pleases, and what is right for him is right for all.

"And now, gentlemen, for the retailers of our drams I claim the same privileges, and I insist that they are entitled to them! What! When a gentleman enters their house and calls for a meal of victuals, is he to be refused? Is he to be told, You can't be accommodated, sir? Then take away his privilege to sell *spirits*, and this is the very thing you must expect—the very thing you will meet; and hungry as you may be, you can have nothing! Why, gentlemen, *tavern-keeping* would not be worth a pin, if the right to sell liquor were taken away, and the *best houses* in the land would close their doors; then I guess you would see, to your cost and sorrow too, what kind of entertainment these *constitutional vampyres* would give you.

"I am advised, gentlemen, that a travelling lecturer, without either character or talents, who entertained a few people for half an hour, yesterday, at the church, said, in the course of his incoherent remarks, that we have no right to sell rum; that it was even worse than assassination, and that they had as good a right to sell *poison*, knowing it to be intended for self-destruction. And further, that those who favored it—and I suppose he meant myself—were no better than the rumsellers! I wish I had been there. I would have told him that rumsellers could make the widow's heart glad, and that they and their friends could give to those whom *Providence* had afflicted—as in the person of George Handy—a respectable appearance. Yet we are told they are bad men! and I am a bad man! But for what, unless it be for our kindness to the poor, and our money?"

Many persons were remarking very unusual excitement in the countenance of George Handy. It seemed as if reason was struggling with insanity for its old habitation. The evidence of this excitement became more and more perceptible as the Judge proceeded; and just as he uttered the words, "Smith is not chargeable with George Handy's misfortunes," George rose, and, with an effort in which he seemed struggling to reclaim reason, he said,—

"Am I in hell? If not, where am I? Judge L——," he continued, "do not *criminate* Providence! Do not say that Smith's mercy was more than the mercy of God!—*for it is a lie*, and you know it. It is true that I am dressed in your cast-off clothes; but still, with the little light which the murderous spirit of Smith has left me, I will bear witness against every word you have said. I know that it is false! I have proved that it is false; and while you are standing here to defend the rumseller, you are *worse* than he is. I will soon be where you cannot see me, but while I am able I will daily walk these streets, to torment yourself and your *clan*, and warn others against your wickedness."

Here poor George, with a convulsive shudder, sank again into his seat. Every one was surprised, for no one in several years had heard from him a coherent sentence.

"This," said the Judge, "is the doings of that fellow who was here yesterday. Why, they are even making madness itself more mad!"

"Judge L——," said the lawyer, who was not able to stand this any longer, "whence did you derive your legal opinions?"

"None of your business," said he, before he had time to see from whose mouth the question had come. Turning his head, and seeing the commanding figure of the lawyer, drawn up to its full length, he quailed for a moment, and then said, "Why did you ask me that question?"

"Because I thought you might recover damages," said the lawyer.

"What do you mean," said the Judge, a good deal confounded.

"I mean that the man who taught you the definition and principles of law which you have advanced, ought to be indicted for ignorance, and yourself ought to be in the same condemnation. You have taken the liberty to be very ungentlemanly towards myself, when you thought I was not present. I am here, and I will try to hear you to the end—go on, Judge."

This was the winding up of the Judge's speech. For the life of him, although he labored excessively, he couldn't get out another word. He knew that Dick's preceptor, and others of equal intelligence were present, who could detect his mingling of ignorance and duplicity, but for these he did not care. But when called to account by the "big lawyer," disappointment and anger drove him to his seat.

Here the very venerable chairman—the man who was poor and had become rich—the man whose head was white for the harvest of death—the man who had been such a signal *blessing* to that community—the man who would soon be seen no more amongst them—this very venerable man rose and said,—

"This is what I expected—nothing better could be expected. Here the judge of the court has been interrupted while explaining law to his friends, and he can't go on at all. These are gentlemen indeed! It would be a favor if all who are in the house, and who ain't with *us*, would leave," and down the old man went into his chair.

"We will accommodate you," said the lawyer, "and you will be welcome to what is left."

There was a demonstration at once towards the door, and the venerable president, fearing that himself and the Judge, who was yet choking on his speech, were to be left alone, called out, saying, "I did not mean that all should go—the meeting is not closed." This, however, did not stop those who were under way; and very soon everything which would have been desirable in almost any other place than a rum meeting, was safely out of the house; and everything that was left, except in number, was, for all the world, a *fac simile* of its great *antitype* in Gotham; and it could not well have been otherwise, for the cry of both was, "*give me rum or I die.*"

It would be vain to attempt to describe the appearance of what was left in the house. "Now," said Judge L——, "we are alone, and we will have leave to transact our business in a peaceable and orderly manner, as good citizens should do."

"Ah!" said Stevens, "the *cow* didn't do us much good,"—"Mr. George Handy, either," said the Judge; and Smith declared he wouldn't pay one cent towards the cow, and that after that, drunkard's widows might take care of themselves, for all that he would do to help them."

The *venerable* distiller rose again, and began to set forth in as plaintive a style as he could command, the great service which he had rendered to that community, and then dwelt at some length on the ingratitude of a large portion of those who, now in his old age, had turned against him, and were for driving him out of his stewardship.

The poor old man seemed to think that Judge L——'s definition of *natural rights* was true to the very letter; and that God had given to him a special right to entail misery upon his creatures until his last breath.

As might be expected, when the restraint of a decent audience had been removed, confusion soon introduced itself; and however much they may have intended to accomplish, nothing more was done, and in the midst of angry words and pugilistic gesticulations, the *thirsty* crowd retired to the quarters of the different rumsellers; and the wrecks of this splendid pageant for several days after, were visible in the gutters of B——.

The views then entertained by this old man of his "divine right" to sell rum, still exist in the minds of many at the present day; and the idea that any legal restraints are to be imposed upon the business, is looked upon by them as the most odious tyranny. Against this they therefore combine; and especially close and earnest is this combination against the *only effectual remedy* that has ever been suggested for the evils of rumselling—against THE MAINE LAW. It is—we will not say amusing—it is humiliating, to see the candidate for official place quake with fear before the dreaded influence of this combination, and seek, by every means in his power, to secure it in his behalf. Nay, more: to see grave legislators, when called upon to vote upon the question of enacting the Maine Law, to give a faint aye or nay, and to attempt to pacify the rum interest by flimsy apologies. This, however, will never satisfy the friends of the law. They think they see in this what has often been vainly sought for in various other ways—something that will *effectually* put an end to the traffic in rum, and of course remove the temptations which are now enticing the young at every corner. This idea is possessing the public mind with the earnestness of complete conviction, and the happy effects of the Maine Law, wherever it has been tried, tend forcibly to rivet and extend this conviction. It is believed, therefore, that this pervading public sentiment will soon be crystalized into the permanent form of efficient public law.

CHAPTER XI.

THE PARTY.—THE SNARE.—THE ESCAPE.

"I know a breast which once was light,
  Whose patient sufferings need my care;
I know a heart which once was bright,
  But drooping hopes have nestled there;
Then while tear-drops nightly steal
  From wounded hearts that I should heal,
Though boon companions you should be,
  O! comrades, fill no glass for me!"

IN the breast of Dick Wilson one peculiar, lovely hope rose above every other, and melted in warm and confiding tenderness amidst the still dear ruins of the wreck which he was endeavoring to raise. On no occasion did the image of his home pass entirely from his mind. To him it was an ever-abiding, present reality; and the joys of the stranger's heart had not the mystic power to drive sadness from his.

He was conscious of his poverty, and he knew but too well that others must be equally conscious of it. Dick's wardrobe was getting scanty, indeed; and this was all the more annoying from the fact that he did not know how it was to be replenished.

Before this startling reality he quailed, as he was sitting alone, taking a cautious survey of his worn garments, and seemingly trying to ascertain how long they would probably hold together. He was looking first at the elbow of his coat, then at the knees of his pantaloons, then at his hat and boots, and patched linen, and ejaculated, "Yes, these relics of better times are all going together—they will soon be done. I am not used to this,—I have given away better clothes than these, often; and I have no means to replenish them. But I am glad that my mother and Eliza do not know it, since for their sakes I would be willing to be even more stinted than I am; and to see them smile again as they once smiled, before the rumseller came to our *Eden*, I would endure anything that was tolerable."

In the midst of these unpleasant thoughts the stagecoach from P—— drove up to the office opposite his window. "Ah!" said he, "I shall perhaps get a letter from mother to-day, and if I do I shall feel much better. If it were not for such letters, I could not keep up as well as I do; but when I know how patiently they are all suffering, I ought not to repine."

He could hear from his place all the noise and confusion which usually awaited the arrival of the stage at B——, and he overheard the landlord who kept the hotel, saying, "This trunk is for Dick Wilson," and in the next breath he heard the surly reply of a young man who was standing by,—

"Well, the Lord knows if there is anything in it in

the shape of money or clothing, it will be a 'God-send' to him, for he is almost naked. Why, he hasn't a thing on his back that isn't thread-bare; and if he don't recruit very soon, he will lose all influence in this community, and then he'll be as good as dead."

Dick heard the sharp voice of Mr. Jacobs the landlord, quickly replying to this evidence of littleness, by saying,—

"Well, Horace, the Lord knows another thing just as well as he knows that, and this whole community know it, and you seem to be the only one who does not know it. If you could exchange some of your fine clothes and money for what brains Dick Wilson could spare, and *still be rich*, I tell you it would be a *precious* God-send to you; but your case is hopeless! You are living here and sporting upon money which I am told has been acquired in every way but an honest one, and now you rise up and lay claim to *censorship*, and talk about influence! You had better go down to the 'Old Stone House,' *famed* all over the State for its debauchery, and then talk about *influence* as it was about twenty years ago; and Black Jim, who lives there now, if he knew the whole history, wouldn't go *partners* with you in your position or influence. Dick Wilson is moving himself forward with commendable energy, in despite of poverty, to make his way to competency, and you are moving towards the poor-house; and that is the appropriate place for you. Your influence indeed! Good Heavens! what a precious thing it must be in your estimation! I would just as soon have '*Black Jim's*' influence as yours, for it is really greater, and will be more enduring."

Of this conversation Dick had not lost a single word; and he knew the person very well by whom it was commenced, so that such expressions, although not intended for his ears, were not wholly unanticipated by him.

He stepped to the door at once and inquired of Mr. Jacobs, who was still standing by the stage, if his name had not been mentioned.

"Yes, Mr. Wilson," said Mr. Jacobs, his face slightly coloring as he spoke, "here is a trunk for you, from P——, and I have just been having a word with that young *rowdy*, who is marching off, in reference to it."

"Yes," said Dick, smiling gratefully, "I heard you, and I guess he thought you severe."

"I don't care what he thought, Mr. Wilson," replied he, "such good-for-nothing fellows deserve severity."

"Well," said Dick, "I thank you—am glad I have found that fellow out."

"Yes, Mr. Wilson, if you have had any confidence in him, it *is* a good thing that you have found him out, for he is intemperate in his habits and hypocritical in his conduct. Mr. Wilson, my term in this house expires in the spring, and then I am going to look out for some more honorable employment than selling rum. I have some respect for myself—some regard for my fellow men, and more than all, for my family; and I will no longer compromise these interests by remaining in this business. Here is your trunk, Mr. Wilson," and turning to a black man who stood beside him, he said, "Here, Sam, take this trunk to Mr. Wilson's boarding-house immediately."

Dick thanked him kindly, and then turned into the office, preparatory to following his unknown treasure. He was soon ready, and just as it was placed upon the wheel-barrow, he passed from the door and kept pace with it. As might be expected, Dick's mind was on the trunk, and everything disconnected with it just then was an abstraction. At last Sam, puffing under the rays of a burning sun, said:

"Massa Wilson, I guess dis yer trunk am somewhat full. It's a mighty good load for one, I tell you. I tink Missus must sent you lots ob money dis time, and more good tings, too. My gracious! massa, de sun come down hot on dis nigger's back—I tell you, massa. Mighty rickety wheel-barrow dis is!"

Dick understood the point of this philosophizing, and when Sam had carried the trunk into his room, he handed him a quarter, at the sight of which Sam's eyes expanded considerably, and he said:

"God bless you, Massa Wilson. Sam remember you for dis yer kindness. I wish, massa, you'd git a trunk ebery day."

Dick had to break the lock, and this he was not long in doing; and soon the contents of the trunk were before him. His heart was glad as he beheld the elements of a princely wardrobe, in his own quarters, and himself the owner, with more than a sufficient sum of money to defray all the expenses necessary to fit it to his person. But the joy was only momentary; for it was interrupted by the thought that the value of these things would have been better bestowed if they had been given to his mother.

"This," said he, "if it had been given in some other shape to my mother and sister, would have been better bestowed, and although my wants are pinching enough, still I should have preferred it."

While such reflections as these were passing through his mind, his eye caught sight of a slip of paper, which he thought must have dropped from the trunk, and might perhaps be an explanation, as there is never anything connected with the charitable gift which is unnecessary. As soon as he opened it—for it proved to be more than a *slip*—he said, in delight:

"From Eliza! Then they know all about this. Let me read it:

"'*Dear Dick:* A very kind friend has sent you this handsome present. I am not at liberty to mention the name, as I would like to do; but I may add that we have all been remembered together. We have shared largely in the same liberality. I will tell you all about it when we get into one family again, as I hope we shall before long. Dick, we pray for you daily. Keep up, my poor brother. We are all well. We visit at Mrs. Livingston's to-morrow. Write immediately. Good-bye. Eliza.' "

Joy, in its fulness, rushed into his heart again, and he felt happy; for if he did not know the name of the donor, he felt that it was a gift of pure benevolence —a benevolence which looked not for a reward from man, but the aim of which was higher and holier than an earthly reward.

As he was passing back to the office, he found Sam mounted like a prince on a hitching post, at the door of the hotel, entertaining a half dozen of his sable brethren with his philosophizing propensities, for he was what is called a 'cute nigger,' and nothing escaped his observation; and to his mind there was something wrong about everything in which he had not a share. As Dick was passing by, Sam, with a good deal of impertinence, said:

"Massa Wilson, you found de trunk all right side up, did you?"

"Oh, yes, Sam," said Dick, cheerfully.

"Well, Massa Wilson," said Sam, "you wouldn't find it in dis way if any nigger but myself had toted it down thar on that broken-backed barrow. It takes dis nigger to do smart tings. When you gits a trunk agin, jist call on Sam. He's allers about."

"Yes, I will call on you, Sam." But Dick thought that the repetition of such an event was probably a good way off.

A few days after this, he was sitting alone in the office, very busily engaged in making out and arranging some papers for Squire B——, which were intended for the Supreme Court, and just as he had finished, enveloped and marked them, and was about to put them into the proper 'pigeon-hole,' a young colored boy entered the office, making the inquiry—

"Is dis whar Massa Dick Wilson be?"

"Yes, my boy," said Dick, "I suppose I am the person for whom you are inquiring; but you ought not to say *Massa* Wilson. You ought to say *Mister* Wilson. We have no such titles in this latitude."

"Yes, Massa Wilson, but den you got de ting itself, and Sanco can't see for why you no hab de name too. I tell you, Massa, Judge L—— be no more *massa* at de *soufe* dan he be at de *norfe*. I'll be bound he *be* massa wharever him can cotch a nigger."

"You live with Judge L——, do you, Sanco?" inquired Dick.

"I stays dar, Massa Wilson. Nobody lib at his house dese times but Miss Lucy, from New York, and Horace Stevens. All de rest only stay now!"

"What do you want with me, Sanco?"

"My gracious! massa, you 's so kind. I most forgot dis yer note. Here it is. It's berry sweet, I guess. Most de whole ob dem fussed about it. Look out, massa! Missus from New York writ dat note, and a mighty sight of fun dey 's had ober it too! Dey say some tings, massa. Dey seem to tink Sanco got no ears, 'cause he 's got a black skin. But mercy! Sanco mustn't for de life ob him say, or Judge L—— skin dis yer nigger 'live! Dat ain't all gold, massa, what shines—dat's a fact, it ain't—'cause den niggers' eyes be gold in de night: in fact, den most de whole nigger be gold all de time. 'Member dis, massa. Sanco says look out! Dis *mean something*, massa."

Although this little colored boy had awakened a strong current of curiosity in the mind of Dick, yet he was too honorable to attempt to wrest any secrets from him. The peculiar emphasis of the bearer, as well as his meaning hints, were the evidences that he had matters of importance which he would like to communicate, but that the fear of the lash prevented him from approaching nearer than an indistinct hint or a meaning emphasis. Dick might have drawn from him the whole matter—he might have opened his communicative heart and taken from it its treasured secrecy—for there is no power before which this race become so entirely impotent over their own hearts as by kindness—and Dick had the very kind of nature by which he could have taken everything from it. He, however, had a sense of honor, which prevented him from doing many things, merely because he *could* do them, irrespective of the rights and feelings of others. To him, if that heart was crowned with a *woolly head*, it was just as sacred as if God had given it a covering more indicative of nobility.

He opened the note at once, and he could not help admiring the nice mechanical beauty of the hand in which it was written. It was from Judge L——'s family, sure enough, and contained for him an invitation to attend, in a few evenings, a party at Judge L——'s, which was designed to be complimentary to Miss Lucy S——, the reputed *belle* from New York.

Dick thought that the expression of consideration which the note contained for himself, was over-wrought, and this, in connection with the fact that Horace Stevens had something to do with it, to his mind, made it altogether a suspicious affair, calling upon him to treasure the simple hints of Sanco.

From all he had seen, and from what he had overheard from Horace Stevens a few days before, he concluded that this was a trap set for some purpose; but what that purpose could be, unless it was what Mrs. Watson had told him, he could not divine.

"Well," said he, "whatever may be the object, I have the advantage this time; for I can stay or go, just as I choose. My clothes will be finished to-morrow. If this invitation had come a week earlier, why then I couldn't have done just as I chose, unless I had chosen to stay away, or go with these clothes: and that I shouldn't very likely have done. I can now go, and make a respectable appearance, too, and perhaps by a violent effort I may be able to keep up my *caste* with Horace Stevens, and the precious knighthood which he inherits from the old stone house and the *drover's saddle-bags*."

Dick felt that in the very step which he was about to take, or refuse to take, there might be consequences of more importance than from his knowledge there was reason to expect. Suspicions are hardly ever awakened prematurely, in the hearts of those who are naturally confiding and unsuspicious; but when once they are awakened, it is a difficult matter to allay them.

He knew something of Judge L——'s character, and the influences by which he was surrounded; and concluded to be governed in this matter by whatever advice he might get from Mr. Watson's family in reference to it, for he was assured that they were his friends.

As soon as it was convenient to do so, Dick entered Mr. Watson's house, and was met at the door by Mrs. Watson, who immediately asked the question. "Richard, are you going to the party at Judge L——'s?"

Dick saw through her mischievous smile, and replied,

"With your permission, Mrs. Watson."

"That's a good boy," said Mrs. Watson, smiling, and then assuming her ususal demeanor, which was pleasant, she said, "you have an invitation, Richard?"

"Verily I have," said he, taking it from his pocket, "here it is."

Mrs. Watson looked at it a moment, and then remarked, "They have taken more pains with yours than they did with mine."

"Ain't they written in the same style?" inquired Dick.

"No, I guess they ain't, Richard, nor by the same hand either—they want you more than they do me. However, I shall go, and it will be purely on your account. I suppose you have made up your mind to go?"

"I don't know that I have, Mrs. Watson. I am afraid, from all that I can get hold of, that there is treachery in this."

"There is no doubt of it, Richard, and it will only become visible as they reveal it. If Judge L—— has had anything to do with it, you may depend it is a complicated affair. But go, Richard, by all means. Look yourself, just as if you suspected nothing, and yet be watchful of everything, and you will in this way more than half conquer those who are engaged in this business."

"Is Mr. Watson going?"

"Yes, certainly; and that too on your account."

"Then, Mrs. Watson, I will go; and I want you to help me to watch everything that may be on foot concerning us. Have they asked Mr. S——?"

"Oh dear me—I guess not. He is too hard on the rumsellers for that, and they would not have asked myself and husband, only in hope that it might induce you to go. If they didn't want me, they will be disappointed, for I will go. I have some curiosity to see what a party at Judge L——'s looks like."

The evening at length came, and was very pleasant and beautiful. The village seemed to be in commotion, for parties were things which only occurred occasionally, and not often enough to keep one in their ways; but a party at Judge L——'s! why, it was everybody's wonder. Such a thing had never before been known.

On this evening, Dick saw again, in all the vividness of a life-like dream, his princely home, with an unstinted elegance, and in the midst of this vision, as he had often seen it in reality, he saw moving the fine form of his father, and close by his side two lovely sisters, and by a table a mother, in matronly pride, with the infant Harry in her arms, wrapt in the fulness of her domestic joys.

The circumstances, no doubt, had much to do with the frame-work of this fragile fabric, which soon was to be swept away into the land shadowed by dreams. But if the circumstances could awaken these things, which were so much like a reality, it was only by contrast. From such contemplations Dick Wilson was awakened to enter a house which was not naturally great, but around which circumstances, for the time, had been pleased to throw a fictitious greatness. It was to such a place that he was called, exhorted, and persuaded, and yet, astonishing as it was, it was at the house of Judge L——. The fact is, there were a great many positions which would have suited the Judge's abilities much better than the one of which he then appeared to have possession. He was a good judge of a horse, an excellent judge of brandy, and a most unscrupulous miser, and an intimate and confidential friend of the liquor-dealers, for whose interest and his own he would make the law and the evidence bend at any time; and they said, with heart and soul, "*he is a great man—he is our helper in the time of need.*"

Dick Wilson was arrayed in new habiliments, and his appearance was neat and gentlemanly. He was very tall, rather slender, and as straight as an arrow; and when he wished to do so, he could be as dignified as a prince.

"Now," said he to himself, "Sanco, Massa Dick Wilson is ready to be off, and to look out too, and thank fortune he has some good friends to help him."

One half-hour in the midst of that throng—which

was anything but respectable—found Dick calm and self-possessed. He found a number of his real friends there, who did everything in their power to make him enjoy himself;—there were some there also who had made a profession of friendship for him, but he had read their duplicity, and on that occasion was perfectly willing that they should come to a knowledge of it.

He had determined, before going, that under no circumstances, for a single moment, would he be tempted to relax his vigilance; and from certain things which had already transpired, his resolution was rather strengthened than otherwise.

He was just then overhearing, from a group who were not far from him, that which sent a shock of sadness through his heart.

"Horace," said one, "do you know where Dick Wilson got those fine clothes that he has on this evening? Why, he is as poor as a church-mouse."

"I guess they came from P——, in the stage the other day. I saw a trunk taken out, marked for him, and if it hadn't been for that impertinent fellow at the stage-office, I should have known all about it there."

"What did he say?"

"Oh, he said a good deal; he is a great friend of Wilson. It is generally understood here, that his family is subsisting on charity in P——; and I think, after all, that there is a hoax about this. I think Mr.

Watson has furnished these things for him, and you see, with all their gravity, they are here to-night; and I suppose they only came to see how their book-keeper would act, and what kind of appearance he would make in the presence of gentlemen and ladies; but we will *tame him* before he gets away. The Judge is up to these things, and a single swallow of *that wine* will set him over."

Not a syllable of that conversation escaped Dick's ear, and in that group he saw the beautiful belle of the evening, Miss Lucy S——, enjoying, with the appetite of a voluptuary, the perfidious conversation of those young men; and yet not a muscle of her face gave evidence of agitation.

Directly, Mrs. Watson passed near him, and a meaning look, all she could do, was rightly interpreted by Dick, and he was on his guard in a moment.

Just behind Mrs. Watson came Horace Stevens and the young 'belle' before referred to, and after an introduction, she entered into conversation with Dick, and the exceeding gentility of his manners nearly threw her off her guard; for it seemed at one time that she did intend to be merciful, but getting over this, she said, "I believe, Mr. Wilson, you are from P——."

"That is my native place, Miss S——," replied Dick.

"Well, Mr. Wilson, I do think it is a charming

place, and I should like very much to live there. I have been trying to get Pa to go there to reside, but I cannot. He is so much attached to his old ways, that I cannot persuade him to change them."

"P—— is certainly a beautiful place, Miss S—— and it has many delightful and thrilling revolutionary incidents connected with it."

"Don't you think, Mr. Wilson, that for my happiness Pa ought to move there?"

"Well, I declare, Miss S——," said Dick, "I cannot tell; but as a general rule, I think it is safest to give the judgment of age and experience the preference in everything which is not manifestly wrong. I have learned, although I am young, that we cannot truly paint our future history, or tell by what circumstances it may be influenced."

"Pray, Mr. Wilson, have you some experience in disappointments?"

"I have, Miss," replied Dick, with great tenderness; "this is the only thing in which I am rich!"

"Indeed! Then if Mr. Wilson has no objection, his experience would be a matter of interest to me, perhaps to the company—please go on, Mr. Wilson."

"It would be very painful to me if I did so," replied Dick.

"Then, Mr. Wilson, you will not be offended if I guess, will you?"

"Not at all."

"You have been disappointed?"

"Yes, bitterly."

"Of a tender kind, I suppose?"

"Very tender indeed."

"You are not poor, are you?"

"As much so as I well can be."

"Not an object of *charity?*"

Dick was silent, while his face glowed with a momentary indignation.

"Come, Mr. Wilson, do not suffer yourself to be offended."

"I am not offended," he answered, "and I do not think it will be possible to excite me this evening."

"Ah! you have come prepared then, Mr. Wilson?"

"I *have*," added Dick, with emphasis. With this she rose hastily, with a scornful air, and advanced towards the part of the room in which Judge L—— and Horace Stevens, and a few of the same class had placed themselves, to watch her success.

It was very evident to Dick, who, from his position, could observe those plainly towards whom she was advancing, that already she was telegraphing with her looks the success, as she fancied, which had attended the onset.

What Dick's thoughts were just now, we do not know; but we know what it would have been natural enough for him to have said and thought. If he did not show his feelings, still they were aroused, and they were almost forced to overleap the enclosure in which he wished to keep them, until he could get into his own room.

Dick looked up, and behold she was coming again, under the escort of Judge L—— and Horace Stevens; a force which, except in bulk, was little increased.

"Mr. Wilson," said the Judge, with an exceeding effort at dignity, "Miss S—— thinks that you are somewhat out of temper, and she does not like the manner in which you broke off a conversation which was interesting to her, and I have volunteered my services as an umpire in the matter. Mr. Stevens can argue the case on the side of Miss Lucy, and I will decide."

"I can't have anything to do with Mr. Stevens, Judge L——," replied Dick.

"Why not, Mr. Wilson?"

"Because I have the best evidence that he is not a gentleman."

"That, Mr. Wilson, is a severe charge," said Judge L——, "to make against one of my guests, one of the most respectable young men in the place."

"I am prepared at any suitable time to make it good," replied Dick.

During this brief conversation, Horace Stevens

showed clearly the evidences of a coward, who had courage enough to do an act of meanness, when concealed from view; but not the nerve to meet a manly opponent. He was silent.

"Judge L——," said Dick, "if I have permitted myself to be discourteous in your house, without a sufficient reason for doing so, I am willing to make every reasonable apology."

"That is fair," said a gruff voice, which none of the parties could distinguish.

"Ah, Mr. Wilson," rejoined the Judge, "you say *reasonable*, and that is a very ambiguous term; for it means almost anything which one may choose to make of it."

"I used it, Judge," replied Dick, "in the sense in which it is understood by honorable persons. I am no trickster."

"And *I* am no *trickster*, Mr. Wilson. Now just apologize. Mind, *it's a lady* you are settling with, and just say that you are sorry for your impudence."

"Apologize!—make myself a fool and a puppet!—put myself in a position where I will despise myself! I can't do that, and it is vain for you to ask any such thing of me. Judge L——, you have given this matter an importance which does not belong to it, in your own house. Will you now be kind enough to state this matter clearly. I do not feel willing that a single person should leave this house, under the impression that my conduct has been unbecoming. I know what becomes a gentleman, here and elsewhere."

"Not so loud, Mr. Wilson, we do not wish to be overheard."

"Judge L——, this matter is no secret in your house, it was understood before I came here, and it was nearly the first thing I heard on entering."

"You are mistaken."

"I am not mistaken, sir."

"Did Sanco say anything to you, Mr. Wilson, when he handed you the note," inquired Miss Lucy.

"Nothing more than was necessary in discharging his errand faithfully."

"Did you ask him any questions?" said Horace Stevens.

"Judge L——," replied Dick, casting a look of contempt into the eye of Stevens, "if you will ask that question I will answer it."

Will you answer me, Mr. Wilson," said Miss Lucy.

"Certainly, Miss, I will with pleasure."

"Did you quiz Sanco in reference to that note?"

"I did not," said Dick indignantly.

"Well, Mr. Wilson," said Judge L——, "Miss Lucy has said that you treated her *cavalierly*."

"Of that she must retain the liberty of forming her own opinion," said Dick.

"Come, Mr. Wilson, just say that you are sorry,

and then you and Mr. Stevens may right your matter as you will."

"I am not sorry, sir, and as for that fellow, I can settle with him whenever he may desire to do so."

Here the matter ended for the moment, as the company were invited to the refreshment room.

CHAPTER XII.

THE TEMPTER FOILED.

> "Then by a mother's sacred tear,
> By all that memory should revere,
> Though boon companions you may be,
> Ah! comrades, fill no glass for me!"

AGAIN Judge L—— approached, Dick and said, "Mr. Wilson, just say that you are sorry for what you have said, and this will right the whole matter, and it will be dropped at once."

"Well, Judge," replied Dick, "when I am sorry I will so express myself. At present I cannot belie my own feelings."

"Ah! yes," said the Judge, "it's all nonsense any how; but you are a tough stick—just like your preceptor; but then, Mr. Wilson, you ain't too old to bend yet. Will you walk with us to the other end of the parlor?"

"Certainly, Judge," replied Dick, with true courtesy.

Here the *trio*, of which Horace Stevens was one, held their way across the parlor like a triumphal cavalcade, with their fancied captive behind them. Mrs.

Watson, who was on this occasion one of Dick's advanced guards, understood the whole matter, and knew precisely what was going on; and she knew too that her presence was not wanted there. It made no difference however; she knew their plan, and meant to subvert it.

At length the company halted in front of an old-fashioned, stinted-looking side board, which was ornamented according to no style, ancient or modern; but according to the peculiar taste of the man who gave George Handy a suit of clothes, and then *presided* at the *rum meeting!*

Arranged on the side board in a convenient position were a few quart bottles, which were naturally as green as a cucumber-bed, with one elegant decanter, which had been presented to the Judge by a member of Congress. The company were standing with their backs to the side-board when the Judge, with an assumed military air, stepped before them and said—

"Ladies and gentlemen, there has been quite an unpleasant debate between Mr. Wilson and Miss S——, and I have been laboring to bring about a settlement; but I am sorry to say that I find Mr. Wilson to be really *stubborn*, for he will make no concessions."

"What is the charge?" exclaimed several of those who knew just as well as the Judge, what was going on.

"Miss Lucy says," replied the Judge, "that Mr.

Wilson has treated her *cavalierly*," and then drawing himself up with a good deal of dignity, he said, "What shall be the penalty?"

"That will depend upon the nature of the offence," said a gruff voice, which came from another part of the room. This was Dick's preceptor, and he had been sitting in the same position all the evening, apparently much interested with the pages of an old book, over which he seemed to be poring; and as the Judge repeated the question again, he called out, "Explain, explain, if you please, Judge; I can't vote on this case until it is fairly defined;" and he gave himself again to the book.

"Squire B——, there is nothing serious about this matter—it's all a joke, I assure you," said the Judge.

"Then," said Squire B——, raising his eyes and throwing a glance at Judge L——, the meaning of which he understood; "you ought not to make of it a serious matter."

"Oh! Squire," replied the Judge, "it's really nothing but a joke."

"I am not sure of that," continued Squire B——, "and if you did not design treating Mr. Wilson as a gentleman, you ought not to have asked him to your house."

"Don't you believe me, sir?" inquired the Judge, as if such a thing would be strange to him.

"I do sometimes, sir," replied Squire B——, "but I

am under no obligations to believe what is not sustained by evidence."

All this time Dick stood there mute and motionless as a statue. His forehead was pale, his cheeks were slightly crimsoned, and his lips were rigidly compressed, as if he was striving to smother the indignation which was burning in his heart. He remembered the *rum-meeting*, at which he had refused to disgrace himself by becoming its advocate; and he was looking for the vengeance of him whom he had thus mortally offended. But, in the face of this, he stood the picture of earthly nobleness, looking scorn and defiance at Judge L——.

After the Judge had recovered from the entanglements into which Dick's preceptor had thrown him, he called out again, "What shall be the penalty?" and was instantly replied to by one of the board, "A glass of *wine* with Miss Lucy."

At this moment, by what was doubtless a pre-concerted arrangement, two young *ladies* and two young *gentlemen—they were called so* by a portion of the community—presented themselves before the company with a supply of cake and wine.

"By my word," said the Judge, looking meaningly at Horace Stevens, "that is precisely what we wanted, and yet this way of settling a difficulty did not occur to me at all."

"That is *remarkable*," said Squire B——.

"What is remarkable, sir?" said the Judge, impatiently.

"No consequence at all," said Squire B——.

"This is it, precisely, Mr. Wilson," said the Judge, taking a tumbler in his hand and holding it before Dick, and then adding, "now oblige me, Mr. Wilson, by drinking to the health and happiness of Miss Lucy."

"I have no objection, Judge," said Dick, "to make friends if we are enemies, in a rational manner; but as to drinking friends, I will not do it—I will not run any risks. I have been sufficiently warned in and out of your house."

"You do not think, Mr. Wilson, that I have drugged it?"

"I don't know as to *that*, Judge, but I do know that to render it poisonous drugging is unnecessary."

"Well," said the Judge, "Miss Lucy, you must settle this difficulty yourself."

"It can't be settled by you, Judge, in this or any other way."

The tumblers were given to Miss Lucy, and turning to Dick, she said—"Mr. Wilson, I am sorry that without the least provocation you have permitted your temper to become ruffled this evening; and by doing so, you have cast an unpleasant gloom over all the company. Now, Mr. Wilson, take this glass, and let us drink to each other's future happiness, and

J

then it will go merrily around, and all will be smooth again."

"I hope, Miss," replied Dick, in a very gentlemanly, yet very firm manner, "that if the pleasure of the company has been for one moment interrupted, that you will not insinuate that I am in the least degree accountable for it. I will drink no wine this night, and I beseech you to desist from further offers of this kind."

"Are you a temperance man?" inquired Miss Lucy.

"Yes, I am," said Dick, "both from principle and necessity."

"Well, so far as principle is concerned, I guess we are all about in the same fix; but we don't know anything about necessity."

"You may know something about it," said Dick.

"Oh!" continued she, "a great many things may be. I suppose Parson Smith is trying to work you into a teetotaler. Have you any other objections beside your necessity and Parson Smith?"

"Yes, Miss," said Dick, "I have a poor mother;" and then, for the first time, the tears came to his eyes.

"Any other reason, Mr. Wilson?"

"I have a dear sister, beautiful in *heart* and *form*, who would tremble if she were here now; and I have a little brother; and these, in my heart, have a richness which the wine-cup would dissipate; for so it was with my father."

"What more?" said Miss S——.

"They are poor; and I am their dependence—their hope—the object of their daily prayers—and the only one to whom they can look for protection; and I must not, will not be tempted, while I am in my right mind." He then returned to his seat.

To all appearance the party went on pleasantly; but every one who knew Judge L—— saw disappointment in his countenance; and the general opinion of those who could only conjecture, was, that this gathering was got up with the view of entrapping Dick, to reward him for his refusal to take part in the rum-meeting.

"Mr. Wilson," said a gentleman, by the side of whom Dick had seated himself, "you managed to run the *gauntlet* pretty well."

"It was very difficult for me to do so," said Dick, and then continued—"If it had been Judge L—— alone, I could have got along finely; but to thrust a young lady into the work, was very mean in him; but then I fancy their profits are small this time."

"You can't tell, Mr. Wilson, what the profits are. Judge L—— is a strange man, and no one can tell where he makes or loses. He is one of those men who can forget a kindness very soon, but who never forgets an insult."

"Do you think I insulted him?" said Dick.

"He will so interpret it. He defines everything by

his feelings, and nothing by his judgment; and he can carry the appearance of friendship, until the very moment when he is ready for vengeance. It would have been better for you, my young friend, to have *tasted* that wine; for it would have made your situation much safer, inasmuch as you would not have incurred his hate."

"I think that was secured before this evening," said Dick.

"Mr. Wilson, I am far from being in favor of intemperance—indeed, I am an out-and-out temperance man from principle; but in *this* case, I really think that a few drops—not enough to hurt a child—while it would have done you no harm, would at all events have secured you the sympathy of most of the company; and for the present it would have appeased Judge L——."

"Your philosophy," said Dick, "will only hold good as a trap; for the theory of drops, if you will observe, is the silent yet potent cause of much mis chief. You have seen accounts of those sliding glaciers, and dashing snow slides of the Alps and Pyrenees, with the havoc they have made, as they leaped from crag to crag, overtaking the swift-footed chamois in their descending fury. There was a time, sir, when that mighty avalanche was but a snow flake; yet the aggregation of these is found sufficient to overwhelm with ruin, the pleasant valley which lay beneath them.

Mark the path along which the avalanche has gone, and it will occur to you in a moment, that there was a time when it was fair and beautiful—when it was rejoicing in the peaceful possession of whatever God had given to adorn its being. It is not so now, and why? A single drop fell upon that rocky bosom, and was frozen into ice. It remained. Another and another came, and remained; and then the gently rippling stream—and all the while the frost was fixing them to its bosom. At length the deep foundations of the rock gave way, and precipitated a tempest of ruin into the valley beneath—a melancholy emblem of the desolation wrought by intemperance. I am very well satisfied that the avalanche, which by the succession of drops is formed in nature, is a very faint type of the desolating character of the avalanche which the single drop you recommended may form; and which in its falling—for that is almost inevitable—will necessarily tear and drag out every root, flower and twig which may be there—yes, *everything* with which God has adorned and dignified intelligent beings—and in its course it will desolate the last green spot which misfortune still cherishes. I think, sir, your philosophy of drops only leads to quarts and gallons—to the open door of infamy, disgrace and ruin."

"Oh yes, Mr. Wilson, I understand you; but my philosophy is, that men ought to govern themselves.

They ought not to permit themselves to get beyond proper bounds in any indulgence! I am a temperance man from *principle*, and not from *slavery*. I believe in men taking things when they need them, and letting them alone when they do not need them."

"Every one cannot do this," replied Dick, "and those who are not absolutely certain that they have strength of resolution to do so, had better resist it entirely. The celebrated Dr. Rush, of Philadelphia, would not even administer it as medicine—not because it might not be instrumental in removing some diseases; but from the fear that it might implant a deeper and more deadly one; and he gave as a reason for doing so, that he did not want a single one, in the day of God's judgment, to rise up and charge him with having made him a drunkard! And now let me ask you, sir, will they stand in that *same audience* who do not administer it as medicine, but for gain to themselves—those who *never* cure, but *always* kill! The professional rumseller! what will he do there, as he rises in the midst of the ruin he has made upon the earth?"

"Oh, yes; I see now, Mr. Wilson. It's very plain. I might have seen it sooner—that you have got the same absurd notions into your head, which are absolutely crazing some people. Mr. S. our minister, is getting the very same notions, and I am sorry for you both, for it will prevent your success here."

"These notions," replied Dick, "did not *craze* George Handy; and it would be a fine thing for the community if Mr. Smith, the rumseller, could get the same notions."

"Well, Mr. Wilson, if *Parson* S. don't keep quiet, he can't stay here long—*he is the people's servant.*"

"But not the rumseller's," said Dick, and then continued—"What objection have you to Mr. S.?"

"He don't preach the gospel, sir."

"Your understanding of the gospel and his may be very different. Mr. S. is a fine scholar, and makes it his study; and it is fairly to be presumed that he understands it."

"You are mistaken, Mr. Wilson. I guess I know what is gospel just as well as Parson S., and I have just sent for a commentary, that will give me light on the Bible."

"What work is that, sir?"

"It's called *Cæsar's Commentary*, and I suppose it's a first rate exposition of what gospel is!"

"I apprehend," said Dick, smiling at the man's unusual intelligence, "that you will not find much gospel there."

"Have you read it, Mr. Wilson?"

"Yes, sir."

"Of what subjects does he treat most particularly?"

"Of his wars, the countries through which he passed, the difficulties he encountered, and his victories, as well as many things about the ancient Roman commonwealth."

"Has he no gospel in his book?"

"Not a bit, sir, that I could see."

"Wasn't he an old Roman Catholic Father?"

"No, sir, he was an old Roman General, and not so very old either—I should think not so old as yourself."

"Good Lord! Mr. Wilson, if you don't astonish me. Some one told me a very different thing; but then Mr. S—— don't preach the gospel, any how, for he is eternally at the *rumsellers.* Why, Mr. Wilson, I heard him say myself, from the pulpit, that sooner than see his daughter the wife of a drunkard, he would rejoice to see her in the coffin! Did you ever hear such a wicked expression?"

"I am not able to see anything so horrid in that," replied Dick, "for I suppose he only meant that he would rather see his daughter breathe her last in his presence, and amidst the associations of his own home, than to have her a drunkard's wife, at the mercy of the rumsellers, as poor Handy's was, and then die at last at their hands, as his did, leaving a child to attract the finger of scorn. I have a sister, and rather than see her situated thus, I should prefer to bear her to the tomb."

This gentleman, whose *intelligence* has been seen, had been put in nomination by the rumsellers of

B—— and their friends, for the legislature; and, unfortunately for the cause of temperance and good society, he had been elected. He was regarded by many as being the counterpart of the Irishman's *cow-bell*—"*a long-tongued, empty-headed thing*,"—and withal, he fancied himself fit for greater honors than this. In fact, he was just the kind of man who could serve the rumsellers with fidelity.

Mr. Watson, who was overhearing all this conversation, and admiring Dick's firmness, at last said to this gentleman,—

"Mr. Anderson, if a law prohibiting the sale of intoxicating drink should come before the legislature, which way would you throw your influence?"

Mr. A. looked very much as if he was trying to satisfy his own mind as to which side would pay the best price, or give the surest promises of a re-election, and then said,—"That would depend entirely upon circumstances."

"What circumstances?" said Mr. Watson.

"Well, sir, the *shape* and the *party* which brought it up. If it came up in a way that would stop the business entirely, I would vote against it. I think I should—I don't know. And if it was brought up by the opposite party in politics, why then I am sure I would."

"If you brought it up yourself, how would you vote then?"

"There is no danger of that, sir; I'll never start such an unpopular thing as that."

"Suppose, Mr. Anderson, your constituents should unequivocally express it as being the wish of a majority of them, that you should do so, what would you do then?"

"I don't know what I should do," he replied.

Mr. Watson could get nothing out of Mr. Anderson except, *I don't know, it depends on circumstances*, &c., and gave him over again to Dick.

"I am told, Mr. Wilson," said Mr. Anderson, "that you think of opening an office in this place, after your admission. Now, let me give you some advice which may be for your good, as young men don't always know what is best for them. I would advise you, when you are called on again, as you were by Judge L—— and Mr. Stevens, to deliver an address—*to do so*. You will lose nothing by it; and if you were to make a speech in favor of rumsellers, that would not compel you to drink their rum. At such a time as this, Mr. Wilson, you ought not to refuse the *civilities* of the house; but you ought to eat and drink such things as are set before you, asking no questions for politeness' sake. Now that is gospel. Just see, if you had tasted that wine to-night, how pleasantly everything would have gone off. When a friend meets you in the street, and asks you to walk into a hotel and take something, why, do so! it won't hurt you, and it will greatly increase your popularity, and, by-the-bye, what's best of all, it will increase your chances in political life. Ah! Mr. Wilson, you are not through yet. There comes the Judge and Horace Stevens."

Dick turned his head and saw them by his side.

"Mr. Wilson," said Judge L——, "we have called to give you another opportunity to make an apology to Miss S——, before the company quits the house."

Dick was silent.

"Yes, Mr. Wilson, you must apologize or——"

"Or what?"

"I will consider you as intentionally insulting myself and guests."

"Judge L——, let me tell you now, that I did not intend to insult either yourself or your guests; and with this explanation, you are at liberty to draw such conclusions as you may choose. I have not been sleeping since I came here, neither have my ears been closed; and I now tell yourself and Horace Stevens, that your low trickery—your stealthy whispers, and your drugged wine-cups, have all been understood. I was hardly seated, before it was evident to me that I had been brought here to be insulted, and only because I refused to occupy a position at your rum-meeting, which, as Squire B—— said in your hearing, would have made me falsify my own convictions, and play the hypocrite. I have heard Horace Stevens and this same Miss S—— speculating on my poverty in your hearing, and with your approbation; and now let me tell you, that I believe this whole matter has been planned by yourself. A man in your position ought to be ashamed to be so wedded to the rum interest as you are,—you ought to have more forbearance than merely for the sake of gratifying them, to wreak your vengeance on one who has already been so deeply afflicted by it. I am poor, Judge L——, but I have never asked a favor of you yet. I came to your village to do what *your friends* prevented me from doing under more favorable circumstances. I am poor,—yes, as it has been said in your house to-night—'*a book-keeper.*' I am willing to do anything that is honorable for the sake of those whom I love. But, Judge L——, if I am poor, you cannot shake me. I despise your meanness, and now I leave your house to enter it no more."

Dick walked quietly out of the room in which the unjust judge would have offered him up freely as a victim, although helplessness was clinging to him for protection.

What boots it to the rumsellers and their votaries who falls? What do they care whose heart is broken? What value do they set upon tears which are scalding the cheeks of the widow and her orphans? Ah! yes, and what do they care for the partial restraints which the law now imposes upon their business? For these things to them are nothing; and partial legislation has proved itself to be what the pruning hook is to the hedge—*it gives it room to expand and to flourish! Let the axe be laid at the root of the tree*, and then they will unbosom their instruments of death, and give up their power to afflict mankind!

CHAPTER XIII.

THE MAINE LAW.—LEGISLATIVE JUGGLING.

"Is this, O life, is this thy boasted prime?
And does thy spring no happier prospect yield?
Why gilds the vernal sun thy gaudy clime,
When nipping mildews waste the flowery field?"

On a bright afternoon in the winter of 185—, a company of gentlemen were seen emerging from a carriage, at the door of one of the first hotels in the capital at ———. In almost any other place than in the capital of one of the largest and most influential states of the Union, their appearance would have attracted a large share of the popular curiosity; and even as it was, they did not entirely escape notice. So far as the appearance was concerned, it pointed them out as being men of wealth; and this of course procured for them the extra civilities and accommodations of the house.

In the parlor of this house, and before a cheerful fire, these gentlemen seemed to be enjoying themselves. After some private conversation with each other, in which each seemed to be deeply interested, one of them rose and left the room, and almost immediately returned, carrying in his hand a list of the members of the Legislature.

"Ah!" said one, "give us you yet for an emergency. Henderson, we can't fail when you lead."

"Money will do anything," replied Mr. Henderson.

"Well," said another, "if money will do anything, we can accomplish our object here very soon. We have, you know, the privilege from those who sent us here to try its virtue to any extent."

"It is true," said Mr. Henderson, "that those who sent us here have given us the privilege of using their money freely. Necessity has made them remarkably generous just now; but still, for our own interests, we must move cautiously. We must not forget, gentlemen, that there are some who are always looking for emergencies in the affairs of others, that they may turn them to their own advantage. We must keep cool, and so far as possible, we must keep our anxiety to ourselves."

In this company there was one whose appearance contrasted strangely with his companions. They were men in the prime and vigor of life; but he was a man of seventy years, and of venerable appearance. But if he contrasted strangely with his companions, his appearance and his years did more so with his mission.

"It will be important for us," said the old gentleman, "to meet the members privately at their rooms, that no suspicion of our business may be excited. I have had much experience in legislative lobbying, and have always found this to be decidedly the best course. We must meet each night to compare notes of the day's success, and to prepare our future plans. This meeting must be held at a late hour, for most of our work is to be done after the adjournment of the House. We can then have the undivided attention of those whose influence we hope to secure; and the members at this time are also much more *approachable*, being *mellowed* by the influences which we know full well how to employ. We must be more circumspect than were our friends at their late meeting in New York. In their excitement they committed many egregious blunders—blunders, the effect of which it will cost us much labor to repair."

"I am very sorry," said Mr. Henderson, "that we were foolish enough to sanction the proceedings of that ridiculous meeting, whose representatives in fact we are."

"To what item in the proceedings do you refer particularly?" said one.

"Proscribing the leading journal in the city. That, you may rely upon it, was a short-sighted piece of business, and it did us more harm at home, and it will do us more harm all over the State, than anything that we did there. This foolish, ill-advised act has given the editor a double power to operate against us; and you are aware that we can get no counterbalancing editorial aid. I am heartily sorry that we sanctioned any such proceeding as that."

"Yes," was the general rejoinder, "that was a great mistake; but after all, in such a promiscuous gathering, it is well that nothing worse was done."

"You may well say promiscuous," said Mr. Henderson, "for such a gathering I never saw before; and it would be an important matter that would lead me into such a *bedlam* again. Really, gentlemen, there are features in our mission which are not over and above creditable; but we must hide them if we can."

"Come, come," said the old man, "we must not spend our time in this way—let us sit up to the table and examine this list, that we may know at once where and with whom our business is to be transacted."

One of them took the diagram of the seats of members and commenced a careful examination, and occasionally marking a name with his pencil. When he reached the end he looked up with an air of satisfaction and said, "I think I have the matter arranged now, in a manner that will point out to us at once in what quarter our business lies."

"Let me see the list," said Henderson; and then after a moment's examination he said, with apparent dissatisfaction, "This won't do at all."

"Why not?" said the gentleman who had pointed out, as he thought, so distinctly the whole course.

"Because," said he, "you have the names of persons here whom we could neither flatter nor bribe into our service."

"Let me look at it," said the old gentleman; and after eyeing it closely for some time, he continued: "This will never do. There are names here that we can't get. We might as well try to enlist in our favor Neal Dow, or White, or Snow, or any of that class. It will not do for us, gentlemen, to make a single mistake in this matter; and as we are strangers here, if we are not exceedingly careful, we will be very apt to disclose our plans to some who are our enemies, and be quite certain of defeat."

At this juncture there was some beating about and changing of plans, and it was finally thought best, in order to understand fully the complexion of the Legislature, to hold an evening's consultation with a member, whom they well knew to be favorable to their plans.

They accordingly met him in the evening, and were pleased to find him a man of imposing personal appearance, surrounded with the evidence of ease and extravagance, and withal an air of calmness, which made their approach comparatively easy. They at once introduced themselves as the agents of the liquor interests in their great city.

"Ah! yes," replied the legislator, "I believe I have had some correspondence with some gentlemen of your city on this subject; and to be candid with you, gentlemen, I am afraid there is little hope for the rum traffic. My opinion is, that before the adjournment of the present Legislature, this whole matter will go by the board. I don't believe that anything can save it; and those who value their reputation more than their money, must keep their hands out of it, or they also will go overboard."

"What grounds have you for thinking so?" said the old gentleman.

"I will tell you, sir," was the reply, "and then you will be able to decide for yourself whether I am correct or not in my opinion. You are probably aware that you have not at this moment, nor can you enlist into your service any respectable public journal. They are all on the other side, or neutral, and represent not only the wishes but the will of the people, which is manifestly against you and the whole liquor traffic, and in favor of its being made, by stringent legislation, a *penal offence.* There are at this moment petitions to this effect in the Capitol, containing nearly four hundred thousand names; and they present a most striking fact, which is this: these petitions represent the orderly and respectable portion of the community; and these evident demonstrations of the people's *will* in the matter cannot be lightly considered or turned aside. Now, as to their right to make known their will in this way, there can be no question, nor as to the great force of their arguments. There are about twenty-five thousand drunkards in this State alone, who, in connection with the business in its wholesale and retail character, costs the State annually millions upon millions of money—a fact we cannot gainsay; and when dollars and cents are swollen into immense amounts, that is an argument which the people can understand; and if we add to this the poverty and suffering, the vice and crime which the friends of temperance represent as flowing from the rum traffic, you can readily see what we have to contend against. I don't know what may be the popular feeling of your city in reference to this matter, but certainly, gentlemen, if you have any friends there, they ought to speak out—NOW is the time for them to do so. If you remain here a few days, you will soon understand the feeling of the State upon this subject, for the name of *Maine* is as familiar and as popular here in these days, as the name of Tippecanoe was twelve years since. In fact, everything is cut and squared according to the proportions of the 'Maine law.' The practical workings of that law, in the State of Maine, have so far been highly favorable to temperance. In that State the expressed will of the people was carried out, and the traffic in rum was placed upon the statute by the side of *other crimes*, and the rumseller by the side of *other criminals.* The aggregate expenses of the State have in a few months decreased in an unexampled ratio, and the decrease in expenditure has not been the only advantage derived from it. It has been confidently asserted on the floor of the House, that everywhere throughout that State it has diminished greatly the consumption of intoxicating drinks, and the evils inseparable from that consumption have of course ceased. You can see the advantage they have over us in this contest. Millions of money are foolishly expended in this State—our asylums are crowded—our prisons filled to overflowing—and victims for the scaffold, their number is frightful.

"The Maine law has produced a different result. It is conclusively shown to have diminished taxation, crime, pauperism, and misery, and to have introduced hope and happiness into thousands of desponding hearts and desolated homes. If it were not for this standing demonstration, you might hope to succeed; but as it is, it lies in your way, and will be there whichever way you turn."

"Can't we double the *cape of Maine*," said Mr. Henderson, smiling, "and get 'round by some kind of legislative strategy?"

"I should rather attempt," replied the legislator, "to double Cape Horn in a skiff. I tell you, gentlemen, it will take steady sailing and a practised helmsman to go through such a sea as this; and I am not aware of any kind of legislative manœuvering by which your interests could possibly be secured. Do you know, gentlemen, with any kind of certainty, how Pennsylvania will decide upon this question?"

"It will be very close," replied Mr. Henderson,—"*one or two votes** either way may decide the matter. We are in constant communication with Philadelphia, and are assured that nothing by which they can hope to influence the Legislature will be left undone. It is, however, very uncertain."

"That is just what I supposed. The people are waking up everywhere; and so far as Pennsylvania is concerned—in view of *expenditure, drunkards, crime, and poverty*—she is not a whit behind this State; but as yet I believe she has not disgraced any spot within her dominions by the appropriation of it *to a mass rum-meeting!* How does the matter stand with Massachusetts?"

"Massachusetts and Rhode Island," replied the old gentleman, "are about as good as gone. The Bostonian rum-manufacturers and dealers do not appear to manage well; they are too saving of their money; and I am convinced that the time has now come when nothing but money can save us."

The mention of money only enabled the legislator to see new difficulties in the case, and he continued—

"Now, gentlemen, if you are not willing that the wish of the people should be carried out, by the enact-

* The passage of the "Maine Law" bill (so called), was defeated in the Pennsylvania Legislature by *two votes.*

ment of the 'Maine law' in this State, what would you be willing to give them in its stead?"

"Oh, good heavens!" said the venerable old man, "anything but the 'Maine law,' for that is the worst; and anything else will be better."

The old gentleman betrayed, contrary to his wish and that of Henderson, the great anxiety which they had upon this subject, and he exclaimed again,—

"Give them?—we will give them the old, the new, and *all* the excise laws linked together! Anything under the heavens but the 'Maine law,' for there is no getting around that."

"They make a strong plea on this count, gentlemen; for they say, publicly and privately, in and out of the House, that you have violated every pledge you ever made; and that, in spite of all they could do, you have overreached and abused them."

"That is what we still desire to do," said Mr. H.; and added—"There never has been an excise law framed yet, by any Legislature, which could not be evaded; and that accounts for the liberality of my aged friend, in offering anything else than the 'Maine law.' If the spirit of existing excise laws could be carried out, they would destroy rumselling; but the administrators of the law easily evade its provisions, and here is where all *excise laws* lose their spirit and force, and if the thing can rest here, we shall be satisfied. There are many excise boards in this State, from whom the privilege to traffic in rum can be obtained for a small price. The promise of a vote, or of influence at a coming election, will sway them. For a liberal fee, I would show the way to get around any excise law that any Legislature might make, short of the 'Maine law,' and then, I must confess, that my skill as a pilot ends."

"Yes, Mr. H.," replied the legislator, "you understand the matter; and I have no doubt that more than one half of the rum sold in the State is sold fraudulently.

"You are right, sir," continued the legislator, "but then, in order to secure your success, you would, in the first place, at your town elections, secure a rum excise board; and this matter is generally quite easily accomplished.

"The excise boards in this State have proved utter ly insufficient. In many instances the rumselling influence has created them, and then the rumsellers, high and low, have used them at their pleasure; and just where rum-drinking was a special curse, there they permitted it to be poured out freely, and by men too of abandoned characters.

"Instead, therefore, of any improvements, the advocates of the 'Maine law' say that matters are growing worse—that those who are engaged in the traffic are pushing it on with more recklessness and success than ever before; and that they have no reason to hope that it will ever be better, while the law vests its control in the hands of those whose governing principle is self-interest. You know, gentlemen, that for the most part, all the excise laws of this State have been so tortured in the hands of those to whom their execution has been entrusted, that they have become a mere farce—a world-wide burlesque!

"It is so, also, in States where licenses are granted by a different process. Take Pennsylvania, for example: In that State, licenses are granted in open Court, on an application to which twelve respectable signatures are appended, setting forth the good moral character of the applicant, his reputation for temperance and sobriety, together with the absolute necessity, that in a particular location it is *necessary* for the well-being of the community, that rum be sold!

"One would think that in Pennsylvania the business was pretty well guarded, inasmuch as this privilege is vested in the judgment of twelve respectable citizens—neighbors of the applicant, who are supposed to know that what they certify of him *is true.* Facts, however, prove that there is no safety even with this security. They show that even good citizens may be influenced and warped to such an extent by surrounding circumstances, that they have not the courage to say that they cannot in any way *abet* in the traffic! With all the precaution which hedges about even the incipient steps of procuring license to sell rum in

Pennsylvania, many unprincipled men—men of depraved moral character, can get twelve citizens to vouch for them, and the courts seldom take the trouble to inquire into the matter, and are permitted to establish themselves according to law, to violate it every day of their lives!

"In a large, influential, and wealthy district in Pennsylvania, the people were taken by surprise when the presiding Judge,* who had just been elected to the bench, in charging the grand jury, alluded to the deception practised upon courts by false representations, and announced it as his purpose, when he had the least suspicion in reference to applicants, to bring their vouchers into court, and see if they would say the same thing under the solemnity of an oath. This was taking the matter at once by the ears, and is a noble example which those in like circumstances might imitate; and they would do themselves no injury by following the precedent. Courts seem almost entirely to forget the importance of this matter to the individual and general interests of the commonwealth. If a deed for twenty-five acres of mountain land is brought into court as evidence in any case, it is closely examined. The same thing is true in reference to a will or a deposition; but an application for a tavern license—the granting of which is, in many cases, the greatest affliction under which a community could suffer—very

*Hon. William B. McClure of Pittsburgh.

often when the paper is closed, the court could not mention two of the appended names, on the integrity or veracity of which they have granted the license; and the same loose administration of the law which governs the rum traffic here governs it there, and renders it almost a nullity. I must confess, gentlemen, that the more I look into this subject, the greater the difficulties become. Arrayed against us are the women and children, and they are lifting up a voice which will make itself heard. You might just as well try to stifle the thunders of Niagara as to hush the plaintive wail which they are sending up to legislative halls. It is becoming louder and louder, and soon their united voices will be against you, and then you might as well try to stand upon the heavings of an earthquake, as to attempt to oppose *their* influence. They no not spend their strength for money or for popularity. It is in one mighty plea for mercy!"

"Ah! yes," said the old man, "but it is a morbid public sentiment which permits them to take their position on this ground, in reference to the 'Maine law.'"

"They are the sufferers," replied the law-maker, "and ought to be heard. It is equally a duty and pleasure with them to effect those reforms which the law permits, and if there be any work on earth in which they have a right to take part, it is this, unquestionably."

"What is the complexion of the Legislature on this question?" inquired Mr. Henderson.

"That I cannot tell, sir; but if they follow the wishes of their constituents, they are fairly against you."

"Well," said he, addressing his brethren, "we may as well give it up, and return home in the morning, for if matters stand in this way, the case is hopeless."

This legislator was a shrewd man, and he understood well that the philosophy of getting a handsome fee was to represent the difficulties in the case as great as possible, and he let them go, being assured in his own mind, that they would call again in the morning.

So far as he had gone on one side, his representations were true to the life, and would have produced a fine effect if he had possessed the courage to have shaken off the rumseller's influence and money, and advanced them independently in his place. But this, unfortunately for himself and his constituents, he had not the magnanimity to do.

They met in caucus again that night, and were disappointed.

"Perhaps," said the old gentleman, "we missed our man after all, but if the case stands as he said, it is rather dark for us; and he seems to understand himself pretty well."

"Yes, so he does," replied Mr. Henderson, "remarkably well, but no better than I understand him, and I am just as sure of his influence as if I saw it operating already. We must move very cautiously. All he will do will be done behind the door; that man will never come to the light in this matter—mark that!"

After repeated consultations with this gentleman and other legislative dignitaries, these commissioners of the rumsellers returned home, fully assured that the 'Maine law' would find all kinds of under-handed obstacles to contend with.

This proved to be true, for a system of patching upon it embarrassing amendments killed it, and the *wish* of the people in the matter was overruled by the influence of a few princely liquor dealers. The same thing will be tried again and again, and only the uncompromising vigilance of the people can prevent a recurrence of the same result. The rumselling influence will do everything to clog the wheels of legislation on this subject—they will leave nothing undone. They will compass sea and land to keep the privilege of selling rum; and the only way in which this tide of perfidy can be arrested, is for the people to see to it, that those whom they select to frame their laws, shall be men whose sympathies are on the side of right, and who in the discharge of the sacred duties of law-makers shall be governed by the honest convictions of their judgment, and not by fear of the apprehended frown of the maker, seller or drinker of rum.

CHAPTER XIV.

THE DROVER'S GRAVE.—"MURDER WILL OUT."

"Remember Heaven has an *avenging* rod;
To smite the poor is treason against God!"

THE signal triumph of Dick Wilson at the house of Judge L—— over the temptations by which he was beset, soon became generally known, to the great annoyance of the Judge and those who were associated with him. Dick's course was generally approved by the inhabitants of the village, even by those whose characters were the reverse of his own; for consistency and firmness in the right always commands the respect even of the vile. To some, however, it seemed to be strange and unnatural that a young man and a lawyer in prospect should be so unsocial in his habits as thus to refuse the civilities of a neighbor's house. Others did not see fit to call the offer of wine by that courteous name, and admired the courage which had so signally resisted the wiles and enticements of that night. As a consequence of this noble resistance, every family in the village who prized virtue, valued peace, cherished love, or feared God, took occasion to speak in his praise, and did not say to their sons or daughters, "You had better not associate with Mr. Wilson until you know more about his character."

One single exhibition of true nobleness, as it gushes forth freely and warmly from the heart, untrammelled by artificial laws, will do more to beget the abiding confidence of other hearts than all the blandishments of artifice and duplicity which the most practiced may employ.

Everyone now, with the exception of the rum-sellers and their adherents, were gratified with this exhibition of Dick's character. Those who had heretofore been indifferent, not knowing but he might turn out as the majority of young men there had hitherto done, after they saw him shake the viper into the fire, instinctively turned to regard him as the nucleus about which large prospects of future usefulness were gathering, and which promised to do much in wiping reproach from their village and securing the interests of their children from the poluting social influences which had too long held sway among them. It was generally understood that Dick intended locating himself in their midst, and that immediately after his admission to the bar, through the persuasion of Mr. Watson and others, to bring the wreck of his family there to reside. To many this was cheering intelligence. They thought he had passed successfully the most dangerous temptation which was likely to beset him, and they would freely exchange the entire rum interest of the village for the mother and sister and brother of that Spartan youth. To the plainest question, however, there are usually two sides, on each of which will be found arrayed those of opposite opinions, interests and tastes. It was so here, with the exception of Jacobs, who seemed to occupy rather anomalous ground, being strictly identified neither with the rum interest nor its opponents. With this exception, the question of Dick's permanent residence among them was looked upon by his friends with hope, and by his enemies with fear and disfavor. His refusal to speak at their rum meeting, to act as secretary for them, and last of all, to drink at the house of Judge L——, had fixed the hate of the latter, and they lost no opportuity to show it, and the combined influences of the bar-room and the gambling-cellar were resorted to, in order to prejudice his interests.

Persecution has often a sickening effect upon the heart; yet it is sometimes overbalanced by its salutary consequences. Its effects are much like those of the crucible; it distinguishes between the false and the true, pointing out those in whom confidence may be safely reposed, as well as those who are unworthy of it.

The man who by long acquaintance has familiarized himself with the scenes attendant upon the rum traffic —with the want, the misery, the suffering, the horror that are daily before him whose daily bread is purchased with widows' sighs and orphans' tears,—such a man, if not fully prepared for "treason and murder," is emphatically ripe for "strategy and spoils." Human sympathy or respect for the common rights of his fellows, have no place in his bosom. If men or measures come in conflict with his vocation, he is equally unscrupulous of the merit of the one or the justice of the other. His time, his talents, his means, and all the arts which ingenuity and depravity can suggest, are industriously employed to maintain himself and to circumvent those who would rid society of his pestilent influence.

Mr. Stevens, the superannuated rumseller and knight of the "old stone house," was the ostensible leader of Dick's enemies, and he was often heard to swear that he should never locate among them. The threats of this poor old man, however, who had been worn out in the service of rum and the crimes which grow out of it, did not intimidate Dick in the least, but rather tended to arouse him to new exertion. It was evident that his hopes were becoming brighter as the time of his admission to the legal bar drew nearer.

Perhaps you know, reader, the strange power which the anticipation of future happiness has over the soul —how it can people the most bleak and desolate path in life with new and beautiful creatures, which are so near akin to reality that the heart loves to dwell upon them, and around them its affections linger peacefully. Such were the feelings with which Mrs. Wilson and Eliza were awaiting the admission of the son and brother to the bar, and such were the feelings and the hopes which he was straining every nerve to meet, and for the accomplishment of which he had toiled for many years. Their happiness was the light and life of his existence—the centre about which all his hopes clustered. Amongst those who were lovely, to him they were the loveliest, and every image which his imagination could paint was imperfect without them.

One day, while Dick was standing at the door of the office, he observed a stranger alighting from a gig in front of Mr. Jacobs' hotel; and as Sam was about to drive the horse to the stable, he heard the gentleman say that he should probably remain a few days, and wished to have good care taken of the horse. He was apparently thirty-five years of age, with form and features finely developed. For several days he was seen passing through the streets, and was not known to have spoken to any one but Mr. Jacobs since he entered the village. It was supposed at first that he was a collecting merchant from Philadelphia, but that opinion soon passed away, and his business for the time was unknown. On the third day after his arrival, Mr. Jacobs met Dick in the street, and spoke of the singularity of his guest, and remarked, at the same time, that although he appeared to have no business, yet his opinion was that he had some very important business.

"Do you know his name, Mr. Jacobs?" inquired Dick.

"Yes; his name is Gilmore."

"Where is he from?"

"From one of the back counties of the State."

"Have you any idea of the nature of his business?"

"I have, but I cannot name it."

"What has brought Stevens and Judge L—— about here so much for two or three days?"

"I don't know; but it seems to me that gentleman's presence troubles them. Stevens asked me his name yesterday, and when I told him it was Gilmore, he turned as white as a cloth, and I have not seen him about since. If I am not mistaken, Wilson, this man will reveal his business to some one before he leaves."

There was nothing in this to excite Dick's curiosity; for, as yet, he had nothing on which he could base an interesting conjecture; and he was not so much accustomed to attend to the concerns of others, as many were by whom he was surrounded.

In the early part of the evening, Mr. Jacobs called on Dick, informing him that the stranger wished to see him.

"How does he come to want me?" inquired Dick.

"He stated to me confidentially, Mr. Wilson, that he had business of importance, which required the assistance of a lawyer, and wished me to recommend him to the best one in the village, and I referred him to you."

"I am certainly much obliged to you, Mr. Jacobs," replied Dick, "but did you tell him that I was not yet admitted?"

"I did, Mr. Wilson, and also told him when you would be admitted."

Dick immediately started, wondering what this unexplained thing could mean. As he entered Mr. Jacobs' bar-room, he observed Stevens amongst others, and he passed on to the parlor, where he was introduced to the stranger. After a few moments' conversation, in which it plainly appeared that the stranger was a gentleman, he asked Mr. Wilson to accompany him to his room, which he did, and when seated, he said,—

"Mr. Wilson, do you know the construction of this house?"

"I do know something about it," said Dick.

"Is there any danger that we will be overheard?"

"I think there is not, sir."

"My business," said the gentleman, "is very important, and if it were known, all my hopes and plans in finding my father's grave, would be frustrated."

"Did you say *finding your father's grave?*"

"Yes, Mr. Wilson, I have reason to suppose that the remains of my father are in this vicinity. I have been for two weeks in a neighboring village, and I have learned enough there to assure me that there can be no doubt about it; but the difficulty will be to find sufficient evidence to point out the grave and the murderer of my father."

"How long is it, sir," said Dick, "since your father disappeared?"

"About twenty-five years."

"What was his business?"

"He was engaged in driving cattle, sir."

"Ah! a drover, a drover?" said Dick, abstractedly.

"Do you know a man named Stevens, in this village, Mr. Wilson?" said the stranger.

"Yes sir, very well."

"What is his character?"

"Bad enough, sir. I hardly think it could be worse."

"Do you know anything of his having kept a public house here at one time?"

"I have understood that he did, sir, and I have understood that a drover disappeared from his house under very suspicious circumstances."

"Yes sir," replied the stranger, "I have no doubt but he knows very well where my father is sleeping."

"Have you evidence in reference to your father, that will show clearly that he was really here?"

"Oh yes, sir, that can be substantiated; and also that he had five thousand dollars in money."

"Well," said Dick, "I have no doubt but Stevens

has your father's money; but the difficulty will be to get at it. He has a few friends here, and they will do everything in their power to aid in concealment. I believe that Stevens suspects you now. I know of no other way in which to account for his strange conduct since your appearance here. I think the best way to develop the matter, would be to create a little suspicion; and if you should think this best, it must be done with great care. I would advise you to go to Judge L——, who is one of Stevens' warmest friends, and just open the matter to him as you did to me, and if he knows anything about it—and I should not be surprised if he did—he will be putting Stevens on his guard at once, and something, if they are well watched, may leak out. You must be careful not to let Judge L—— know that you have said a word to me on the subject."

The stranger thought that this might be the best way, and after a good deal of conversation in reference to the plan to be pursued, he stated to Dick, that he would then pay him one hundred dollars, and in the event of his success, he would pay him a thousand beside.

The stranger then asked him if Mr. Jacobs might be let into the secret with safety, and was informed that he could, and that he might be of service; and when the thing was made known to him, he at once agreed to find a person, who for a few days would watch every movement that Stevens and Judge L—— would make.

The next morning, as early as it was proper to do so, the stranger called upon Judge L——, and disclosed his business to him. As might have been expected, he defended Stevens, and assured the stranger that there were few men who would be so unlikely to do an act of that kind as he.

"I have been acquainted with him for many years," said the Judge, "and I ought to know him very well, and I think I do. Now, my dear sir, let me tell you, that if you breathe such a suspicion to any other individual in this community, you will be in danger of your life. There is a young man here, named Wilson, who is a warm friend of Mr. Stevens, and if it was known to him that you had any such suspicion, he would excite a mob against you at once."

He had been sufficiently apprised of the relation existing between Mr. Stevens and Judge L——, and only replied to him, that he had gone too far already to stop, adding—

"I am not much afraid of mobs or decrepid rumsellers; and I have but little confidence in their friends."

Immediately after he left the house, Judge L—— was in the street, and soon black Felix was seen hovering in his rear. The Judge seemed to understand his business, and so did Felix; for he also had something important to accomplish. At length the Judge came up with Stevens, and Felix passed them just as they had designated a place where in an hour after they had appointed to meet. Smith's tavern was one of those old dilapidated affairs which had grown with the times, until twenty additions had been made to it. In such a place as this, secrets were not very safe, and especially as every one of the partitions in the house was abundantly supplied with knot-holes. Felix was shrewd, and he made his appointment with himself at the same time, in an adjoining room, which Smith had used to store away those whom he did not wish to be seen about his premises. Into this place, half an hour earlier than the appointment, Felix, without any difficulty, found his way, and patiently awaited the arrival of those in whom, just then, he was wonderfully interested. At length they came, and the first thing he heard was,—

"Stevens, fill that glass up. You must not take this matter to heart, you are in no danger. Heavens on earth! they can't find evidence to convict you now. Drink and be merry, and let the drover's son go to the devil."

"Do you think," said Stevens, "that there is any possible danger of this matter getting out?"

"It can't possibly get out," returned the Judge, "unless either you or myself reveal it; for no other living soul knows the facts concerning the drover's disappearance."

"It was a devilish good thing for me," said Stevens, "that he went to you for advice; but I suspect Wilson knows something about the matter."

"I don't think he does," said the Judge; "I was apprehensive that he might call on him, and I warned him against doing so, assuring him that Wilson was one of your best friends."

As they became warmer over Smith's whiskey, they talked with less reason, until they had made a full revelation of the important facts in the case. As they were about ready to leave, Stevens said,—

"I believe Dick Wilson has been consulted in this matter before you were. I saw Jacobs taking him into his parlor last night. I wish to the Lord, Judge, we were rid of that fellow."

"Is there any danger, Stevens, that the grave can be discovered?"

"Oh no, Judge; I am not afraid of that—the lot will never, in all probability, be occupied, and there is a pile of stones resting on it now, which look as if they had been always there."

"It will be best, as soon as possible, to find out whether or not Wilson knows anything of the matter."

"How am I to do this?"

"Go and call on him at the office."

"Will you go with me?"

"No; if I did he would suspect us at once; but go

yourself, and I will go bail that he will be civil as long as you are."

After drinking again, these worthies started into the street, apparently unconscious that they had been unravelling a chain of facts, pointing to a grave which for twenty-five years had been concealed, and pointing out, too, the guilty individual. Felix at once carried the result of his *eaves-dropping* to Dick, who communicated it to the stranger. The matter was now plain enough, and after arrangements of a private nature, for future proceedings in the matter, the stranger visited the stone pile, under which, in all probability, his father's remains were reposing, and left the village. This was a strange matter to Dick, and he did not know how to interpret it; but evidently it had placed his enemies in his power, and this at least was an advantage to one in his situation. His fee, like his heart, was at once divided between himself and his mother; and this signal success always made him look forward with greater earnestness than ever to his admission to the bar. His intention was, that the case should be thoroughly sifted, and that the horrid crime should be brought to light.

CHAPTER XV.

THE GUILTY TREMBLE.—DICK'S PROSPECTS.

"Whose daring revels shock the sight,
When vice and infamy combine,
When drunkenness and crime unite,
And every sense is steeped in wine."

THE case of Mr. Gilmore, the drover, and the singular revelations which had so recently been made in reference to it, seemed to excite Dick Wilson intensely. It was not, however, the hope of bringing speedy vengeance upon the aged criminal; nor yet was he moved to it by the hope of personal gain. The stranger had deeply enlisted his sympathy, and this, in connection with the yet fresh recollections of his own father, who had perished at the hands of those who were as guilty as Stevens, moved him to press forward in an investigation of the matter. For several days and nights he had been unusually busy in running over the pages of musty-looking volumes. After considerable research, without finding much that was applicable to the case in hand, an old book, containing many of the reports of English trials, seemed at last to have gained complete mastery over him.

The reader, even under ordinary circumstances, can find subjects of deep interest in these reviews of legal lore, for with much native courage and true heroism of soul, they present also the dark spots in human character. In the persons of Emmet, and McNevins, and the Sheerers, the great State prisoners of the rebellion, arraigned at the bar of English authority, they present a galaxy of noble names, whose melancholy history, whose premature fall by civil tyranny, will be cherished and reserved for all time. Then, after the lapse of years, in the person of Warren Hastings, is brought vividly before the mind the princely prisoner and the power of those splendid intellects by whom he was impeached. There, too, we may look into the English prison, contemplate the griefs of Lord William Russell, and see him on the eve of his execution, without stain upon his character, parting with his family, and commending them to God. There, too, is the exhibition of crime, in all its grades and with all its aspects of wickedness, clearly and forcibly presented to the mind, revealing the fact that the eye of God had looked upon the scene, and had kept here and there an open view in the history of the murderer.

It was this latter class of recorded facts which had the power to rivet Dick's attention to the page, and after going through with the record of the one which had arrested his attention, he said—" This is remarkable: here is almost a similar case," and added, as he commenced pacing the floor—"Both these cases had their origin in rum, and it seems as if God had in both cases forced rum to become the revelator of its own dangerous character and hidden wickedness. God only knows how long the heart-broken widow may have watched for the coming back of her husband; and when month after month and year after year had passed slowly and sorrowfully away, with a hope wrapped up in its own life-feeding sources, she still looked for his return—the return of one who for twenty-five years has been sleeping within two hundred yards from where I am now sitting, and who will never again re-enter that home. The widow is dead, and now the son, guided by the uncertain and disconnected reports which reached the far-off home, has come in search of the father's grave; and almost miraculously, by the singular coincidence of rum betraying itself, the facts have been revealed, and his feet have pressed the soil which for a quarter of a century has rested upon the cold bosom of his father."

While Dick was musing upon this strange affair, a person who was not wholly unexpected, entered the office. It was Mr. Stevens, whose coming, by the report of Felix, the *eaves-dropper*, was almost certain. He entered the office with his usual lordly air, and with his accustomed duplicity inquired for Squire B——. Dick, in quite as cool a manner, informed him that he was absent, and had been for several days. It was evident enough that from some cause or other he was very uneasy. He was generally pretty well "primed," and there were times when brandy couldn't stagger him.

"I am very sorry, Mr. Wilson," said he, quite courteously, "that Squire B—— is not at home—very sorry indeed. My business is of a pressing nature, and requires immediate attention."

"Perhaps," replied Dick, "I may be able to attend to it for you. Squire B—— left his business in my care until he should return, and if it is business that I can do, I will attend to it for you."

"Ah! yes, I dare say you would; but you couldn't attend to it, Mr. Wilson. It is very important, as well as strictly confidential. You couldn't do it."

"Very well," replied Dick, "then it will be best for you to defer it until he returns, as he gave me no directions about any confidential business."

"When will he be home, Mr. Wilson?"

"To-morrow," replied Dick; "and as soon as he comes, I will inform him of your anxiety."

"Yes," continued Mr. Stevens, "I think it would be best to wait until he returns. Important matters, you know, ought always to be intrusted to old heads, for they are better at keeping secrets, when it is necessary to do so."

"Certainly," replied Dick, "it is right that men of

experience should have the preference; but then I don't know that experience is much assistance in keeping secrets. You are aware of the fact, no doubt, that in some way or other, secrets always get out, and the more important they are, the surer are they to find a leak somewhere, and sometimes those whose interests are most intimately involved cannot keep them."

"That ain't the way with me, Mr. Wilson. I can keep a secret—I tell you I can."

"That may be, you may be an exception; but the general law of secrets is, that they have the power of self-transmission. I have been engaged this morning in looking over the reports of English law trials, and particularly those which were of a criminal character, and I am convinced that I might have taken a very strong position, and have said that there were secrets, the disclosure of which would subject the possessor to the most severe penalties of the law, and that notwithstanding they would betray themselves."

"Now, Mr. Wilson, no man need tell me that I couldn't keep a secret. When I want to keep a secret, I tell you that I can do it."

"Here is the case," said Dick, "and if you will spend the time to read it, I think you will agree with me."

The old man took the book into his hand, and then took off his spectacles, and wiping them with a flourish of dignity, replaced them. He straightened himself in his chair, threw one leg over another, and resting his elbow upon his favorite gold-headed cane, commenced the perusal of the singular case.

In the meanwhile Dick had placed himself in a position where he could see the movement of every muscle in his face. Presently he saw the nervous agitation—the relaxing and contracting of the muscles —the involuntary shudder. His cane fell to the floor, his look of dignity disappeared, and his whole countenance was the aspect of guilt, without a single thing expressive of remorse. At length he finished, and laying down the book, he addressed Dick:

"This must have been a hardened villain, but then you know they have very bad men in England. I have never been there, but I have always heard this, and from this account I should think it was true. Have you ever heard of a case of this kind, Mr. Wilson?"

"I have heard of a great many instances, Mr. Stevens, where murderers to all appearance had succeeded in covering up their tracks; but I must confess that I have never heard of but one case, for which this in all its leading features, as well as in most of its particulars, seems to be a parallel."

"Was that in England?"

"Oh no, sir; it was in this country—purely an American tragedy."

"Indeed! do you say so? I didn't think there

were such bad men in America. In what State was it?"

"In the State in which we are residing, sir."

"Was the man who committed the murder a tavern keeper?"

"Yes sir, he was at the time he committed the crime, and I believe he continued for several years after to sell rum."

"Was the man whom he murdered a drover?"

"Yes sir, he was, and I believe he came from one of the back counties of this State."

"Well, of course, Mr. Wilson, he has been executed, hasn't he?"

"Not yet, sir; the matter has never been made public, and there are circumstances in the way of the prosecution of the case just now."

"Ah! Mr. Wilson, I suppose the *evidence is wanting*."

"No sir; there is no lack of evidence."

"How many witnesses are there?"

"Only one that could be relied on."

"How did the thing get out?"

"The *walls* communicated it."

"Well, Mr. Wilson, but the *walls* couldn't tell it.

'Mr. Stevens," said Dick, while he looked into the eyes of the guilty man, "I will tell you how it was made known: the principal and the witness were closeted together to confer upon the plan by which detection might be avoided, and also to consult on the ruin of *another*, and while they were there making merry over the whiskey which was furnished for the occasion, they betrayed themselves."

"You say, Mr. Wilson, they were planning the ruin of another."

"Yes sir, they were trying to drive a young man to drinking as the surest way to effect his ruin."

"When did this happen?"

"I am not at liberty to tell you, but the time may come when all restriction shall be taken away, and then I will consider it my duty to tell you."

"Well, thank God," said Mr. Stevens, "I never murdered any person. I used to keep a tavern here at one time, and there were some good-for-nothing fellows who were always in the habit of lying about my house, drinking, and who died there at last—two or three I think in my bar-room; but nobody would think of calling that murder—they wouldn't in these days, anyhow."

"They ought to have called it by its right name," said Dick, promptly, "for certainly, Mr. Stevens, those who kill with rum, *for a price*, are just as guilty as those who use a less painful mode, and they should be made just as amenable to law. I have no doubt the time will come, in the progress of civilization, when the man who kills outright, and he who slowly kills by rum, will expiate their guilt together."

"Good Heavens!" exclaimed Mr. Stevens, affecting great surprise; "young man, you make a wide sweep."

"No wider," replied Dick, "than the principles of justice make; and this is, or ought to be, the foundation of all law."

"But don't you see," said Mr. Stevens, with a good deal of vehemence, "that you involve a very large class of persons, many of whom are wealthy and respectable."

"Mr. Stevens, I have nothing to do with involving them—they involve themselves. They do it intelligently and deliberately, in the face of the multiplied evidence of its criminality, and they carry on their work when they know certainly that they are accomplishing the ruin of those with whom they are bartering. Wealth ought not to be permitted to rise superior to law, and no business ought to be tolerated in a civilized community, the effect of which is an unmitigated curse."

"Didn't you say, Mr. Wilson, that nothing was yet known, except by very few, of the case you mentioned?"

"Perhaps I did, sir; but I ought to have said, that suspicion had always rested on the individual; but that until very recently no sufficient evidence could be reached."

"There is such a witness now—are you sure of this?"

"Oh yes, sir; I have it from his own mouth."

"Do you think an individual ought to be punished for a crime committed twenty-five years since?"

"Certainly I do, Mr. Stevens. It is said that it is never too late to repent, and of course it is never too late to afford to such individuals an opportunity to do what, under other circumstances, they would probably never do. It appears to me that one example of this kind would have a better effect upon the public mind than a great many examples of a different character."

"Have you seen Judge L—— lately, Mr. Wilson?"

"I have not. I have no confidence in him, and I shun him rather than seek his presence. He is the only man of whom I ever felt any real dread."

"I think he is your friend, and you could very easily make him a warm friend."

"Mr. Stevens, you know better than that. You know that I could not have a more bitter enemy. You know that it would be a matter of delight to him if he could ruin me. I hope you will not attempt to deceive me in this manner."

"I understand you intend stopping here to commence the law."

"That is my intention, sir; and I am now making arrangements with that view."

"I dare say you will find it very pleasant when your family come here to reside."

"I hope to find it so, sir, and I am looking forward to that event with a great deal of pleasure."

After muttering some apology for intrusion upon time, &c., the old man left the office; but Dick was assured from his uneasy manner that he would be back again before long.

He had come, according to arrangement with Judge L——, in Smith's back-room, to sound Dick, in order that he might ascertain whether or not Mr. Gilmore's business had been made known to him. This he had not been able to determine; but the singularity of the coincidence, and the particulars of the case to which Dick had cited him, were so much like the one in which he was the chief actor, that guilt was plainly visible both in his countenance and actions.

He intimated his own friendship, and proclaimed that of Judge L—— for this young man, when it was known to all, that they were seeking his destruction, and the only reason for it was, that at their command he had refused to destroy himself. Dick, after some reflection, resolved that if he came back again, he would at once free his mind from any doubt on the subject, by confronting the criminal with the evidence of his guilt. He said to himself—"There can be no harm in doing so. Felix is trusty, and Stevens is just what his countenance betokens—a *human fiend*. He has lived and wallowed in the filth of *drunkard-making*, until humanity has departed from his constitution. He has committed every sort of crime, including the blackest; and this solitary instance of murder, while it is the *only one* of which the law takes cognizance, is far from being alone. The one was against the *law*, because the weapon was not licensed. The rest were according to *law*, because the instrument was legalized for a stipulated price. Amazing inconsistency!" thought Dick, "that legislation has been so blind upon this subject, as to privilege *one class* where *anothor* has been proscribed; and especially when the latter is infinitely the worst, for there is hardly a crime that can be mentioned, which does not come forth as spontaneously from legalized rumselling as vegetation comes from the earth."

In the village of B—— this fact was often demonstrated. The wrecks of many families who had been happy, were still there, and their children either beggars or thieves.

Dick had been busily engaged in reviewing his studies, preparatory to examination and admission. The visit of Mr. Gilmore had to some extent interrupted him; yet after his departure, he seemed to apply himself with greater interest than ever. Mr. Watson, with several other friends, who were acquainted with his circumstances, and who had urged him to locate there, offered him every facility in their power in making arrangements for the comfortable removal of his family. In all the arrangements which were made,

Mr. Watson took a leading part. Without Dick's knowledge, he had been for some time engaged in fitting up one of his own houses for the family. It was a beautiful location—one which Dick had often seen, and where he imagined that himself and his dear ones might be happy. He had never said a word to Mr. Watson about it, yet he had often half made up his mind that he would do so.

One afternoon Mr. Watson's little boy came into the office, with a request that Dick should come and take tea with them that evening, and as the little fellow was leaving, he said:

"Mr. Wilson, what shall I tell mother?"

"Tell her I will be there, Charley," was the reply.

In a very short time Mr. Stevens returned, and in a more abstracted manner than in the morning, repeated the same question, inquiring for Squire B——. Dick informed him, as in the morning, that he was not at home.

"Ah!" said he, "I believe you did tell me so. That was a most remarkable case you spoke of this morning, and I would like very much to know the particulars of it. I don't know what makes me feel so much interest in this matter."

"It is not strange," said Dick, "that you should feel interested. It is rather natural. Two cases of this kind so nearly alike are enough, under *ordinary* circumstances, to stir up one's curiosity."

"That's a fact, Mr. Wilson. My curiosity has always been very great, and I never knew what to call it before. Curiosity!—that's it exactly, and I feel better satisfied now. This curiosity is a powerful thing, when it is once awakened by such awful things. I will be obliged to you, if you will tell me some of the particulars of this case."

"If you will walk out with me," said Dick, "I will tell you enough to satisfy you that I am in earnest."

Mr. Stevens readily consented to do so, and off they went. Dick took it upon himself to lead in the walk, and directed their steps by a circuitous route to the *stone pile.* Just as they came alongside of it, Mr. Stevens said, with signs of impatience:

"Mr. Wilson, don't forget your promise, for I shall be offended if you do not satisfy me."

"Let us set down here," said Dick.

"I would rather not," was the reply.

"Why not?" quickly inquired Dick.

"It is unpleasant."

"What makes it unpleasant?"

"I don't know."

"Have you ever been here before?"

"Many a time," was the trembling reply.

"Have you been here on any *particular occasion* for a *particular purpose?*"

"Not that I can recollect."

"Your memory must be treacherous indeed. Does

not the father of Mr. Gilmore lie beneath this pile of stones? You surely cannot have forgotten the night on which you bore that lifeless body to this spot, and here interred it."

Mr. Stevens attempted to speak, but he could not articulate a single word, and Dick continued:

"You have, without cause, sought my destruction, and here now, poor old man, you stand trembling before me, in the presence of the rude sepulchre which contains the evidence of your guilt. I know the whole of this matter. Are you satisfied? Say, are you *satisfied?* Aged criminal! your sins have found you out."

Dick at once directed his steps to Mr. Watson's house, having left the guilty man standing in horror near the grave. As he entered, his excitement was at once apparent to Mr. and Mrs. Watson, and they interrogated him as to the cause. He revealed the whole matter to them; as well as his arrangements which were made with Mr. Gilmore's son in reference to the prosecution of the case. Mr. Watson expressed his regret that anything in reference to the matter had been made public until after his admission, adding, that if Felix could be bought in one case, he could also in another, and that if Judge L—— and Stevens together could ascertain who the witness was, that it would be impossible to get at the facts.

After tea, Mr. and Mrs. Watson asked Dick to walk

out with them. They led the way and soon arrived at the very house which, before any other in the village, Dick would have selected as his residence. As they entered, he saw that everything was in readiness for the reception of a family. It was plainly yet pleasantly furnished throughout, and Dick thought even without an inhabitant, it had still an air of cheerfulness about it. After they had examined the house through, and Dick had expressed himself freely in reference to its pleasant appearance, Mr. Watson said:

"It is a pleasure to me to inform you, Mr. Wilson, that this house has been fitted up for yourself, and it will afford myself and family much pleasure to see you and your mother, your sister and brother, after the severity of the trials through which you have passed, once more in the enjoyment of peace and happiness."

"Richard," said Mrs. Watson, "I think you will yet see pleasant days, and I would now advise you to lay off that melancholy expression of countenance. Your mother ought not to see it, for it will represent to her a canker at the root, and may bring unnecessary sadness to her heart."

"Ah!" said Dick, with a painful smile, "the extreme of ambition and the extreme of poverty, with an absolute dependence on the kindness of others, is hard to endure. But I will try to wear it off, and I will struggle to show you that I appreciate your kindness."

CHAPTER XVI.

THE PLOT.—THE VICTIM.

" What dire necessities on every hand,
Our art, our strength, our fortitude require !
Of foes incessant, what a numerous band
Against this little throb of life conspire !"

As Mr. Watson had suggested, Dick had acted very much against his own interest and the ends of justice, in making any revelation whatever to Mr. Stevens. The matter, with the manner of its discovery, soon became public, and, worst of all, Felix was gone, and no one could give any account of him. There was no doubt in the minds of the better portion of the community in reference to the correctness of the report, and if there had been, the sudden disappearance of Felix would at once have removed it. This was a singular advantage gained over Dick by Mr. Stevens and his friends, and although Mr. Jacobs, who was himself a rumseller, declared that Felix had communicated these things as facts, the cry of slander was notwithstanding raised against him.

After the disappearance of Felix, Dick at once wrote to Mr. Gilmore, informing him of the fact, and requesting him to come on immediately, that the grave might be opened. While this, if the body were found there, would relieve Dick in the mind of every one from the suspicion of slander, it would not necessarily convict Mr. Stevens of the crime of which he was no no doubt guilty. In the meantime the influence of Mr. Stevens and Judge L—— and their friends was made to bear upon him with as much severity as possible, and every opportunity was improved to injure his feelings and prejudice his interests. Even the venerable distiller, who had presided at the rum meeting, and who had been such a signal blessing to that community, by affording them a market in which the *necessaries* and the *happiness* of life might be exchanged for rum—he too was awake, and ready in any but a legal way, to wipe this suspicion from the craft.

It was now observed that Mr. Stevens strutted the streets more pompously than ever before, and as often as possible took occasion to pass the office of Squire B——, not neglecting to cast a threatening look at Dick when he met him.

In a short time Mr. Gilmore arrived, and arrangements were at once made to open the grave. Many persons were collected to witness the result, and every one present trembled with intense anxiety. Stevens was present and stood as near the spot as he could possibly get.

"These stones," said the old grave-digger, as he

commenced his work, "have not laid here as they now are for the twentieth part of twenty-five years."

This at once created the suspicion, that if it was in fact a grave, some person had recently disturbed it, and if so, its occupant had undoubtedly been removed. The stones were soon cleared away, and the work, to all appearance, ready to be commenced in earnest. It was now a matter of surprise to many that the old man hesitated to commence his work, and some one in the crowd called out—

"Jacob, why don't you commence digging?"

"It's no use," he replied shaking his head, "for this here spot has been worked on very lately," and picking up from the earth something that attracted his notice, two or three rusty buttons were shown, and it was manifest enough that this relic had not been long exposed to the action of the atmosphere. Jacob at once handed the buttons to Mr. Gilmore, and said:

"I will go down to the bottom, if you say so; but whatever may have been here, it is now gone, and we will not find what might have been found a few weeks since."

Some thought it was best to give up the search, and others, encouraged by what was already found, advised to the prosecution of it. The grave-digger persevered until he had got to the depth of two feet, which proved to be the bottom of a hastily made grave.

"Now," said he, "I am down at the bottom."

"What do you think?" said Mr. Gilmore. "Has this been the grave of a human being?"

"Oh, there is no doubt of it," said Jacob.

"Have you ever opened a grave before?"

"Yes sir, many a time."

"What has been their appearance usually?"

"Just what you see here, sir."

"How long do you think it has been since this grave was opened?"

"Not over a month, sir, and I should hardly think as long as that. You see it has been nicely done; and before I commenced lifting a stone," said Jacob, "I knew what had been done here; and when the stones were removed, I found that the surface had been thickly covered with fresh grass seed, which has not yet began to sprout. There has been foul play here. I don't know who did it; but there has been a dead body put here, and it's very likely that the same hands that put it here have taken it away."

At this moment Mr. Gilmore advanced to where Mr. Stevens and Judge L.—— were standing, and said in the hearing of all present:

"Mr. Stevens, I have come from a distance to find the remains of my father, who, I have no doubt, fell by your hand. You have managed to buy and send away the only witness by whom this fact could have been established, and then, to elude detection, you have rifled the grave, and stolen the evidence of your crime to some other hiding place. Before I left here, I was fully aware of your guilt. I called upon Judge L——, your friend, who is standing by your side, and who knows that you are guilty, and he warned me against Mr. Wilson, as being your bosom friend, and persevered in proclaiming your innocence; and yet on the same day he was closeted with you, and giving you counsel how to conceal your guilt. I am as well satisfied of your guilt as if I had found the remains of my father in this grave."

Mr. Gilmore consulted nearly all the negroes in the place in reference to Felix; but even the philosophic Sam could give no intelligent account of him, farther than that he had seen him ride out of town on one of Mr. Stevens' fast horses. After several unavailing attempts to get a clue to the whereabouts of Felix, Mr. Gilmore resolved to give up the search and go home. He saw the embarrassing position in which Dick was placed, and heard, during his sojourn in the village, threats of prosecution for slander. In view of these things, and to raise the spirits of this young man, he assured and re-assured him of his entire confidence in him, and intimated the possibility of something yet being known which might set the matter right. He assured him that so far as a prosecution was concerned, there was not the least probability of anything of the kind, and if it should 'take place, said he, "I will stand between you and your enemies."

The time when Dick expected to be admitted was near at hand, and this matter had so confounded him that he was far from being in tune for it. Gradually, however, as it approached, he seemed to recover from the mortification which the placing himself so completely in the power of these reckless men, had produced.

The day at length came, on which he expected to be admitted to the bar, and commence an active existence. On the Saturday previous, he had received a letter from his mother, and also one from Mrs. Livingston. These letters were full of kindness, and both congratulated him upon the noble manner in which he had contended with poverty. The one from his mother was peculiarly dear to him, for in it he saw how entirely and how confidingly the little household were leaning upon him. It expressed the joy which they felt when his last letter informed them of the kindness of Mr. Watson in providing for their comfort, and assured him of the comfort and happiness which a re-union of those domestic ties, which had been so rudely severed, would bring to their hearts. The expression of love, the spirit by which home ought ever to be consecrated, was breathed in every line and embodied in every word; and then he saw the insignificance of his persecutors, some of whom seemed to be like hungry wolves, waiting for their prey.

In the village of B——, the admission of an individual to the bar was by no means an every-day occurrence, and hence an event of that kind was looked for with a good deal of curiosity, and in this instance it was more than usually intense.

At length the old court-house bell was rung, and the house was soon filled up, and just as the crier had finished the sentence, "God save the commonwealth!" Dick and his preceptor entered together. After seating himself by the counsel-board, and exchanging meaning glances with several of his friends who made out to catch his eye, he turned to survey the gathering, which was unusually large. The first person who attracted his attention was Horace Stevens. He felt himself to be prepared for all the legal and honorable requirements of that day. He regarded himself as about taking a position in society which would afford him an opportunity to show himself worthy of the confidence which had been reposed in him.

After the tedious charge to the grand jury—in which rumselling was not hinted at—they retired to analyze the criminality of the county, and find something for lawyers to do. Squire B—— rose and addressed himself to the court in the most respectful terms, requesting that a committee might be appointed to examine Mr. Wilson, and suggested that if the court had no objection, he would prefer, for his own part, a public examination. He stated farther, that there was a very unusual number of persons present, and he presumed they had come with the expectation of hearing the examination. Judge L——, who was of course on the bench, had not the reputation of being very accommodating, either in or out of court, and on this occasion anything that would tend to increase the popularity of Dick, of course would not be granted. In reply to the motion and suggestion of Squire B——, he remarked that the time of court was very precious, and could not be spent in flattering vanity.

"I will appoint a committee," said he, "to examine this young man, and they can retire to some private place during the adjournment of the court at noon; but I cannot, and I will not, take up the time of the court with this matter."

A committee was accordingly appointed; but Squire B—— was not one of the number. He had no more reason to expect favors of the Judge than Dick had, for he had watched and divulged his low trickery as often as he had had an opportunity of doing so. When the committee were appointed, he remarked to a lawyer by his side,—

"This matter is going to make trouble, you may rely upon that."

When the hour for a recess arrived, Squire B——

invited the committee to his office, to perform the duty assigned them. After a close and protracted examination had been made, every member of the committee concurred in expressing the opinion, that it was one of the most satisfactory examinations at which they had ever been present.

As soon as the bell was rung for the afternoon session of the court, the house was again crowded, and the court being formally opened, the chairman of the committee—who was from an adjoining county—rose and asked the court to hear a report of the examination of Mr. Wilson. This report was introduced with much feeling, and so far as a large part of the audience were concerned, with great effect. The whole thing was of the most flattering character.

Squire B—— rose slowly, and made a motion to the effect that Richard Wilson be admitted as an attorney, to practice in the several courts of the county. This was a moment of excitement with Dick. The excitement, however, was that of hope unmingled with fear. The dark future which hung over him was unknown. Could he then have withdrawn the veil, and see what was soon to be but too clearly revealed, he might, with Byron, when standing upon the highest crags of the Alpine mountains—poised midway between the heavens and the earth—have breathed out from his hopeless heart, into the ear of the furious storm-god, as he was passing in the angry chariot of the thunder clouds—"Tell me, ye storms, are YE like those within the HUMAN BREAST?"

For a moment after the motion was made by Squire B——, Judge L—— seemed to be very much perplexed; but it was evident enough that he had been drawing quite liberally on the assistance of *rum*, to aid him in carrying out his purpose.

"Gentlemen," said he, "I have heard your application for the admission of Mr. Wilson, and from your reputation as jurists, I have no doubt that your report is correct. I regret exceedingly that there are insuperable difficulties in the way of granting this application at this time. It may not be known to you, gentlemen, that Mr. Wilson lacks yet several months of the time which the law prescribes as being necessary for one of his age, to be spent in the study of law prior to admission. The court feel the importance, gentlemen, of adhering strictly to the law, and you will see the necessity of doing so, when you consider the dangers to which the standing and respectability of the bar is liable; and these, at the sacrifice of every personal feeling, the court is determined to preserve in their purity. The court find it necessary, therefore, to hold this application under consideration until the next regular term, at which time, if Mr. Wilson pursues his studies diligently, he may possibly be admitted."

A single glance at Dick would have told you that

hope in his heart was crushed—it would have pointed to the dying fires which had warmed him up and kept him alive in the days of his toil, in preparing for that hour. For a moment he looked wildly around that densely-peopled court-room, and in the eyes of several he saw that the smile of vicious triumph was already kindled. He cast no look towards his friends, for while he thanked them for their former kindness, he felt that he needed their kindness no longer.

For a moment he rested his head upon the counsel board, and when he raised it again his features were calm—all evidence of feeling was gone, and all that could be seen of his broken heart, with its crushed and bleeding affections, was a solitary tear. Like himself, it was alone—and soon that evidence of agony, so emblematic of himself, disappeared. Here the crier was ordered to adjourn the court. In the midst of the silence and astonishment of the moment, Squire B—— rose, and fixing his eye on Judge L——, until it seemed as if it would pierce his very soul, he commenced,—

"May it please the court, this is one of the most flagrant pieces of villainy that has ever been concocted and carried out in a civilized community. How cool! No doubt, days and nights of concert with *others*, have been spent in perfecting this plot. It affects to be the promptings of kindness—the respectability of the bar! What does your honor care about character?—about respectability? What appreciation have you of kindness?"

Here Judge L. informed Squire B—— that he would have him committed, if he pursued these remarks. Said Squire B——,

"You cannot find an officer who is mean and base enough to execute your command. What attachment have you to honor?—None. Here is Mr. Wilson, a young gentleman of fine abilities, and enviable acquirements, thoroughly prepared to practice in any court. He has not been trained at that bar, sir, whose foul practices you understand best, and in the minutia of which you are deeply read and wonderfully skilled —but at the bar, sir, where honorable men like himself contend with each other for justice. Here upon the threshold you intercept his progress. The withering pestilence of the rumseller, let loose in its fury, wasted and scattered the opulence of his city home, and sent him forth penniless and alone, to search for a place in which, by his own industry, he might finish his profession and find a home, to which he might remove those who are dependent upon him. Tell me, then, if up to this moment he has not nobly acquitted himself? Chance brought him here. Will you tell me who has been injured by his coming? Those who affect to have been injured by him, had reached the *acme* of wickedness before he came. He has injured none, and those with whom he has associated must regard themselves as being richer in the true ornaments of life, than before they enjoyed his society. Now, sir, when he has passed through the trying ordeal of poverty—where he has proved himself not only equal, but superior to the disastrous circumstances by which he has been surrounded, and with the tenderest relations of earth clinging to him for protection and shelter—you have chosen to mete out to him a furious vengeance."

The stillness of this moment was suddenly broken, and every eye was turned towards the door. Dick's cup was more than full—it was running over; and unobserved by Squire B——, he had risen from his seat, and was advancing towards the door.

"There, may it please the court," continued Squire B——, "there goes your victim! he is bearing out of this court-room, which you have rendered infamous, his broken heart."

Dick had paused, and was leaning his elbow on the prisoner's box, apparently indifferent to all that was passing, when he seemed to be suddenly aroused as from a dream.

"Judge L——," continued Squire B—— "has he ever done you a wrong which was not an *hundred times* provoked by yourself? No! You know that he has not. You know that you have followed him with cruelty, almost since you first saw him. You have been confederate with the rumseller to destroy him. *I know* that you have disgraced your position by compromising the principles of justice with a miserable client, in a crime of twenty-five years' standing. I know very well, sir, the history which for a quarter of a century has loomed in ghost-like terror about the old '*stone house.*' Judge L——, enter it upon the record, that your infamous spirit has finally *triumphed* over the young and unoffending!"

Amidst the intense confusion which prevailed, Dick had left the house, and every one who was not compelled to remain soon followed his example. Every one who had been taught to prize virtue, left with a sad heart; and Mr. and Mrs. Watson, as they turned towards their home, were deeply impressed with the treacherous character of the Judge, and feared the consequences, which they apprehended might follow.

"Poor fellow," said Mr. Watson to his wife, as they passed along, "I am afraid that even his generous nature, backed by all his love of home and the fair prospects before him, will be insufficient to withstand the crushing blow. Though he has withstood manfully all the other temptations which have been almost constantly before him, I am really fearful that this bitter disappointment will unman him. Before the death of his father, you know, he drank freely; and he has often told me that he has had to struggle hard here, to resist the importunities of his own appetite for strong drink. I had supposed the danger past, and that, young as he was, once established in business, with his family around him, the influence of a pernicious early habit would be entirely overcome. But this, coming to him so suddenly, so severely, I fear will be too much for him. I tremble for the consequences."

And well he might, for nothing is more clearly established than that the love of strong drink, when once formed, lives while the heart beats. To resist it requires a life-long struggle. Years of abstinence may have been practiced, yet a single draught of the maddening poison fires the appetite to resistless intensity, and the victim falls powerless in the hands of the destroyer. This view of the case shows clearly the danger constantly attending the use of alcoholic drinks. To *use* them is to form a *relish* for them. To *love* strong drink, though we may now avoid intoxication, is among the most perilous positions in which we can be placed. We *may* escape with only a shortening of life, and the rendering of it comparatively miserable. We *may* not become drunkards, yet the chances are against us. If our lives are prosperous and fair—if nothing occurs to tax peculiarly our fortitude, or our energy, we may float on, being considered as only moderate drinkers. But if storms assail us, then it is that our rotten sails and rickety hulks are tried; and if we have been *moderate* drinkers before, we become drunkards now, and at the very time when the duties and responsibilities of life press upon us; and when we should assert our manliness, by meeting and discharging them, we falter and fall.

Dick's footsteps were soon heard at the door, and Mr. Watson rose to meet him. He saw at once the strange calmness which the chilling events of the day had printed upon his brow; and there was a wildness in his expression which told but too plainly the conflicts of emotion with which he was oppressed.

"Mr. Watson," said he, "I have come to ask a favor of you. You have been to me more than a father since I came to your door, a stranger, seeking the means to obtain my daily bread. I can never repay you, or your dear lady, for your kindness, your many favors to me. I wish you, if you will, to mail this letter in the morning to my dear mother. It will acquaint her of my misfortune, and of my determination to leave this place."

"But you will not leave us?" said Mr. Watson.

"Yes, Mr. Watson, I must. My business here is over. There is nothing to keep me longer. My hopes are all wasted by cruel malice and hate. Oh! my dear friends, do not think me indifferent to you. Whatever betides me, you will ever be gratefully remembered."

"Where do you intend to go, Richard?"

"God only knows, Mrs. Watson. I am determined

to leave this place, and where I shall finally stop, this whirling brain has not yet decided."

"But, Richard," said Mrs. Watson, "think of your mother—your sister—your helpless brother!"

"Ah!" said Dick, "those are precious names to me. They have hitherto held me up against discouragements. The letter will explain the matter. It will tell them that I have kept the field resolutely as long as hope remained, and when that died, I fled from the field of my disappointment, and whither, time only can tell."

Then turning to Mr. and Mrs. Watson, and extending his hands he said,—

"Good-bye, my dear friends. You may, or you may not, see me again. I shall struggle to show myself worthy the confidence you have reposed in me, but on some other field than this," and turning, he walked rapidly away.

CHAPTER XVII.

DUTY AND PLEASURE.

"Onward, onward may we press,
Through the paths of duty:
Virtue is true happiness,
Excellence is beauty.
Minds are of celestial birth,
Make we then a heaven of earth."

It was well known in the village of B—— that Dick Wilson had left, and many a heart had sorrowed over his misfortunes as they contemplated the probable consequences, for which they knew the rumseller was responsible.

Months had passed, and no reliable tidings of Dick Wilson had come back to the village from which he had so suddenly departed. Mr. and Mrs. Watson thought and spoke much of him, and their children often asked the question, "Mother, where is Richard?" and invariably in answer to these interrogations, which were prompted by their childish love, she would take the occasion to warn them against those unfeeling men, who were capable of blotting out the light, the loves, and the hopes of life; and for these things they could not fail to honor that mother's memory. Mr.

S——, the minister, was still there, and likely to remain, notwithstanding the bitterest opposition.

* * * * * *

A traveller is on the cars, and his attention is directed to a group who are sitting near by him. The first object is a woman habited in the weeds of mourning, and her appearance indicated that she had not reached the middle of life. She sat quiet and thoughtful in the midst of a mourning band, who seemed to regard her as their only protection. The lines of care were deeply traced upon her brow, and upon her cheeks, too, are the deep furrows, which look as if the tearful flood of years had held there its uninterrupted way. With her, sadness seemed to be doing a rapid work, and reason to be tottering on its throne. She turned her eye from the strangers by whom she was surrounded, with a sweet familiarity towards heaven. It was plain that she knew the way thither, and that often in thought she had been *there* before. Her lips moved reverently, and an unearthly serenity gilded for a moment her countenance, and then, with a full, rich smile, which looked all the brighter as it contrasted with the gloom of her mourning apparel, she cast a glance of love upon her charge, and tried to be calm.

"Who can this be?" inquired the traveller; and then, as if lost for an answer, he said, "Well, whoever she may be, she is deeply marked by sorrow.

There surely was a time when her heart was not sad, when no cloud of grief shaded her brow, and when those tears flowed not. These could not have been tears of joy; for they leave no traces: they wear no furrows. It is theirs to tinge the cheek of beauty with a deeper hue of gladness, and add lustre to the eye which they have moistened. She is a widow, no doubt, and he upon whom she bestowed the virgin affections of her heart—upon whom she was leaning for support and trusting for defence in the wilderness of life—is gone. But where? To the grave, perhaps, and she is alone, save with her little band, for whom only her heart seems anxious to beat on. He, the husband, in the spring-time of existence, may have forgotten his solemn vows. He saw his first-born infant, and in an ecstasy of pleasure, he may have sworn over it that he would be faithful to those solemn engagements, and yet it may be that he turned from the path of safety and domestic happiness, not willingly, but under the influence of strong temptation."

The traveller resolved to satisfy himself, and learn from her own lips the history of her griefs, and to his sympathizing inquiries, she replied,—

"I am a drunkard's widow, and these poor children are a drunkard's orphans."

At this moment the traveller heard the mention of a name, in which he was deeply interested. He turned himself hastily toward that part of the car in which some one, he was sure, had spoken that name. There was a company of young persons of both sexes, and the very opposite of the quiet one from whom he had just turned. Their spirits seemed to be elastic and cheerful as the air they were breathing, and as their merry laugh rang out from the yet unchecked fountain of joy in their hearts, no cloud of permanent sadness rested on a single countenance in that gay throng. Sorrow had left no traces there: no withered beams of hope were strewing their paths. These happy ones were returning to their homes amidst the associations of city life, after enjoying themselves for a short time amidst the rusticity of rural scenes, and, as was natural enough, they were amusing themselves in the recapitulating of new sights and sayings. But among them was one who, if she had not gazed so minutely or so reverently upon the majestic scenery by which their rural rambles were skirted, had, notwithstanding, looked upon that which had been and was still more majestic and sublime in its being. She had seen a desolated heart, and she had sympathized with forlorn and neglected merit.

"Well, Kate," said one of the company, addressing a girl of queen-like beauty and dignity, "your taste must run in an odd channel. Oh! you don't know what you have missed by your strange preference for that poor family—the widow and her sun-burned daughter. I dare say you lavished your pocket-money very freely upon them. Ah, ha! my girl, what will your mother say to this?"

"Lucy," said Kate, "I am never afraid to account to my mother, and this time I shall do it with more pleasure than I ever did."

"Oh yes, I suppose your mother will praise you. I remember now—her maxim is that *religion* and *charity* go together. I declare, Kate, if a person can't be religious without bearing its burdens, it's bad enough."

"Religion don't ask you to bear its burdens, Lucy; it comes to bear yours. My mother will praise me, that's true; and I love her all the better because she has taught me to be kind to the suffering. I have given away no money, but if it had been needed, I should have done so with a singular satisfaction. I have sympathized with that family, and although you may laugh, I am proud to own it; and for so doing I have been repaid in many ways which, I hope, will benefit me through life. I regret very much that each of you did not accompany me with your sympathies to the house of that heart-broken woman. You have lost much—more than you are aware of."

"Why, dear me, Kate! we couldn't go there at all. I am surprised that you should think of such a thing. Our education is all against that. We would have given you our charity to have carried with you to that family."

"Ah! they are cheerless enough now, without being frozen by those charities which are unaccompanied by the heart."

"Oh! we didn't mean to freeze them, but to tell you what we would have been willing to do, if you had made the request. We are not misers; but as for going to such low places as that, we can't do it; and what's more, our parents would not permit us to do so. We thought it strange enough that you went, but then we referred it all to the singular sentimentalism which has been coming over you ever since you took that little ragged class of vagrants, whom your father tamed, and brought into the Sunday-school. I suppose it's all right, but we can't do it. We ain't low enough to teach little vagrants!"

"Lucy, I beseech you do not use that word *vagrant*, for there is something about it so unnatural and chilling, and so very cruel, when applied to children, who, in many instances, if they are almost anything that is bad, are so from the force of circumstances. Those children, who you are pleased to call vagrants, are indeed very poor. Some of them have poor mothers, but unfortunately all of them have fathers who are intemperate. I have been at their homes, and I know what their miseries are. I am willing to admit that there are cases when that term of reproach may have an application, but it never will apply to the child. It ought to be stricken from the catalogue of reproach, and some other word, one that has a winning spirit, instituted in its place. Better call them *victims*."

"Whose victims?"

"The rumseller's. Suppose those children had overheard you, pointing them out by that cold word—would its tendency have been to make them better or worse? I love those children—not because they are the children of intemperate fathers—but because they are human beings, whose destiny must be shaped for good or for evil. The diamond, although it may be unsightly when taken from its bed, yet when it has passed through a refining process, it may vie with the sun. So with these children. If they are poor, and comparatively uncared for now, by sympathetic care they may be prepared for usefulness here, and happiness hereafter. Do not, therefore, use the word vagrant, when you speak of children, and be careful how you apply it when you speak of the young or of the old, however far they may be advanced in crime. Oh, remember that poverty is not without its feeling instinct—nor is misery without its sensitive spirit."

"Well, Kate, I will give you my word it won't be used again. You seem to have a special respect for poverty and low life, and it amounts almost to making heroes out of your little 'victims.' I never yet have crossed the threshold of poverty, and that may be the reason why I do not look at the matter as you do."

"Poverty," replied Kate, "is by no means rare, and

you may yet be forced to cross its threshold in entering your own home. We cannot tell what is before us. Poverty, when virtue clusters about it as a defence, is able to stand in the evil day ; but when it has combined with vice and shame, it has no defence ; but yet, even this kind is not hopeless—it may be restored. Kindness may revolutionize the soul, and win it back to the ways of peace."

"Ha, ha! indeed, you are getting sentimental. Your visits amongst the hills have wonderfully affected you. But, Kate, you may do as you please, you cannot make me mingle with this kind of low life. It's a pity these low people can't make out to get along with their own society. It's good enough for them, and they ought to be contented. It's out of the question for them ever to be respectable. I presume they were always just so."

"I am surprised to hear you talk in this way. Why, the rumseller can make almost anything bad. He can change an industrious into an idle man—an honorable into a dishonorable one—an affectionate father and husband into a fiend. Yes, he can turn a domestic paradise into something as rayless and as cheerless as Egyptian night."

"Well, now, Kate, this is strange. Just look at it. You know, as well as I do, that these drunkards are low people, and that they can never rise—it is their nature to be just what they are. If rumsellers were doing the harm that you talk about, do you think that intelligent people would sustain them?—I guess not."

"I admit, Lucy, that it is strange; but far the worst is, that it is true. If intelligent Christian people had that jealous fear for the peace and safety of their own homes, which one would think they would have—if the peace and happiness of their sons and their daughters, which is precious above every price, and which is daily menaced by this monster cruelty—they would shake it, with the mighty energy of a giant's grasp, to the earth. Oh, but it does seem as if a mercy-loving God would soon awake to full vigor, the slumbering instinct of humanity. It does seem as if it must awake before long, to avenge the widow and the orphan. I am well persuaded that it is only because people do not more familiarize themselves with the homes—the wants and the miseries of the drunkard's family—that they are so slow to move on this subject."

"Kate, this would be a nice work for genteel people—to be caught in the alleys, and garrets, and cellars of those miserable places. I am utterly astonished that you should think of such a thing. You are an exception to everything. You are good—better than you ought to be."

"Thank you, Lucy; but I think God made genteel people to be more than the slaves of fashion—for more than to bend their necks to receive and wear its yoke.

If this is all they feel to be their duty in life, then they will come down to the grave with not a single duty of life discharged. You may laugh now; but you would weep if your brother were a drunkard."

"Oh, Kate, there is no danger of that: that's impossible."

"I admit, that it is improbable, but I cannot admit that is impossible. I have heard of many, and especially of one, who, so far as natural nobleness could make him such, was as good as any brother, and, until cursed by the rumseller, was as noble a son as any one over whose destiny a mother's heart ever yearned."

"Pray, Kate, who was this paragon of excellence?"

"He was a widow's son."

"Ah! I see: poverty made him noble."

"You are mistaken. Wealth made him unsuspicious."

"Where does he live?"

"God only knows, if now he lives at all."

"Well, what is his name? You can tell that."

"Not now."

"Why not?"

"With the name there are other things you must know."

"Why must I know them?"

"Because you are connected with them, and you are a part of the scene."

"Where did you learn all this?"

"From the lips of that poor widow."

"Oh, fie! Kate, you are a good girl; but if that poor widow and a strayed or stolen son are the heroes, I guess it ain't very interesting."

"Oh, yes," replied Kate, pleasantly, yet earnestly, "you would like to hear it."

"Well, what is that widow's name?"

"I did not intend to tell you, but I will. Her name is Wilson."

"Wilson? Wilson? Has she lived there long?"

"I believe not."

"That name seems to be familiar."

"Yes, I presume it is. Do you remember spending several months in the village of B——? You know the portrait which is hanging in our parlor? You have often admired it, and several times you said that it reminded you very much of one you had seen. You were right: it was Richard Wilson's."

She who had been the reputed "belle" in the village of B——, started in astonishment, and the deep anxiety in her countenance made it a matter of general interest, and Kate was besieged with requests that she would relate the widow's history, which she agreed to do, if at an appointed time they would meet her at home.

They reached the depot, and the passengers were hurrying to their respective homes. The grief of one can reach the heart of another, and tinge with sadness even the glowing cheek of beauty; but when it does, it makes that cheek look all the lovelier. This the traveller saw in the beautiful demonstration before him; for in every feature of that beautiful girl, gentleness, love and dignity were surpassingly developed. There she had stood in the midst of that smiling, fickle band, the only one of their number who could defend, with heroic magnanimity, the poor and unfortunate—laying the blame where of right it belonged, at the door of the rumseller.

Oh! that the youth of America—those whose banners, ornamented by the hands of their gentle sisters, and followed by their prayers, have often danced proudly on the battle-field, and waved defiance in the face of the maddening charge—were all like this young heroine of virtue!

CHAPTER XVIII.

KATE HAMILTON AND MRS. WILSON.

"O ye, to pleasure who resign the day,
As loose in Luxury's clasping arms you lie,
O yet let Pity in your breast bear sway,
And learn to melt at Misery's moving cry."

"Well, girls," said Kate Hamilton, when her auditors had assembled at her father's house, "you seem to think that wealth and respectability are proof against those changes of condition which often result from the rum traffic."

"Ah!" said Mr. Hamilton, "that's a great mistake, as in my limited experience I have already known more than a dozen wealthy and worthy families who have been reduced to beggary and rendered miserable by intemperance."

Here it was evident enough that Kate's auditors were fearful, lest Mr. Hamilton should rise above the commonplace morals to which they were accustomed, and give the matter a seriousness which they thought would lessen its interest. Kate had already informed her parents of all she had seen or heard from the widow; and in their own domestic circle, in a feeling and Christian manner, they had canvassed the subject.

"Now," said Kate, "if you still entertain the opinion you did, I think I can convince you that you are wrong, and that reverses have a foundation in fact deeper than they usually have in the wildest fiction."

"Kate," said the young lady who had been foremost in the conversation on the cars, "do you know who that portrait represents?"

"I have heard of him."

"Have you ever seen him?"

"I have not."

"How did that portrait come into your possession?"

"Frank brought it home with him from college."

"Did he never tell you whom it represented?"

"Yes. Dick Wilson is the original."

"Kate, you are jesting. Are you sure, that the portrait represents Dick Wilson?"

"Yes, I am sure of it. He was a most intimate friend of my brother's, and in looking over Frank's old letters a day or two since, I found several from him. Did you ever know a person of that name?"

"Fate," said Lucy, "has brought me here this evening, to rehearse to me a lesson I was trying to forget. Go on, Kate."

"These things," said Mrs. Hamilton, "are hard to banish. The thorns which we pluck with our own hands, and place in our own beds, will surely pierce us, and often with many sorrows."

"Fate is a hard master," said Lucy, as she looked intently into the unruffled countenance, which brought

20

back the thronging recollections of the past, and from which she seemed to hear, in a gentle whisper which spoke to her heart, "I have a mother," and then, as on that fearful day in the court-house of B——, it seemed to be rushing from her presence in the wild frenzy of despair. For a few moments she seemed to be deeply absorbed in reflection, in which, no doubt, the past history of the individual pictured before her was rising in its sad realities, and she faintly ejaculated, "Where is he? Where is he?"

"On the sunny plains of Mexico," said Kate, "he sleeps a quiet sleep in a soldier's grave, where the din of battle and the wail of the dying chanted his requiem. Ah! but say not 'fate,' for it is a cheerless word, and here it is wholly inapplicable. Fate, mingling in our misfortunes, would encircle them with additional terrors, and so continue, until even *despair* would be welcome to the heart. Say, Providence: there is something sweet and inspiring in the vastness, the intelligence and goodness expressed by that word."

"You say he sleeps?"

"Aye, the long sleep, dear girl, which is broken only by the resurrection. But I will tell you all in its connection."

"Go on, Kate. Oh! if once again I could see that face as on the fatal night when first I saw it. Then beauty and dignity covered it, and then I, a foolish girl, was willing to contract for its ruin, and for the breaking of those hearts to whom misfortune had endeared it. There is a madness in the wine cup which, until now, I never saw."

We feel, but cannot explain, the laws of association by which we are surrounded—the nicety with which they are woven into the very constitution of our being; and yet we know that by this connection the simplest agency may awake in our recollections—in our very souls—those events which in joy or sorrow rise up before us again; and they have a whispering voice which has power to chain and hold in captivity even the stern energies of a mind which ordinarily is not easily moved.

Oh yes, grief-smitten mother! in your premature widowhood you have felt, seen, known, that there is a fearful meaning in the feeblest memento. Even the wail of your infant child can call up those overwhelming recollections which remind you of the bright days of your home—days which were darkened by the coming of the rumseller, to riot without mercy on the affections of that home.

"Now, girls," said Kate Hamilton, "why or how it was that I strayed from your society during our recent visit I cannot tell; and neither can I tell why it was that my attention was directed to that family. But one thing is certain—we don't always direct our own steps. The old grave yard lying just opposite the house, with its antique appearance, attracted my curiosity, and I entered it. After passing through it, I seated myself on a beautiful grassy knoll, whose sweet appearance during a century had kept at bay the grave-digger's spade. The door of that humble dwelling was wide open, and I was sure that it was the abode of poverty. Occasionally I caught a glimpse of the inmates; but after all, the grave yard was my study, and I was unwilling to be interrupted. I was rising to depart, better, I hope, than when I entered, when my attention was arrested by what to me, at that moment, seemed to be the finest music to which I had ever listened. The singers were trilling, with a mournful cadence, in which feeling and musical precision were blended into the sweetest harmony, a precious old song, to which I am passionately attached, and I listened as if listening to the music of seraphims, while they sung, with a rich, clear melody, the words,

> "Oh, come, come with me to the old kirk yard,
> For I well know the spot, through the old green sward;
> Friends slumber there we were wont to regard,
> And we'll trace out their names in the old kirk yard."

An indescribable sensation came over me, and as they concluded, I said involuntarily to myself—'Here I am, amidst the rural scenery of nature, where I expected to hear no music but that which is breathed from nature's own lungs, and yet here I have heard almost the perfection of that rare accomplishment.' I knew very well that nature educated in some degree her own children—that her high mountains and dashing cataracts could give to her rural offspring the fervid inspiration as well as the rich, mellow voices to which I was then listening—but I knew that nature could never give that elegant precision. I arose from the beautiful spot where I had seated myself, in the resting-place of the dead, and crossed over the street to the door. Oh, if you had seen that group! The door was still open, and I could see them plainly; and what a contrast there was between those pale cheeks and those rich voices! There sat three persons—a mother, a daughter, and a little boy—grouped together in the informal order of true affection; and it seemed as if they were trying to console each other to the last. They were sad indeed, but intelligence and dignity were in their sadness. They were pale, but there was beauty in their paleness. They were poor, but there was an evident nobility in their poverty. And last of all—any one might have read in the calm expression of their countenances, that in *enduring* riches they were princely. As I stood before the door they invited me to enter, without any appearance of confusion; and as I did so, the young girl immediately handed me a chair. After seating myself, I asked to be excused for the informal manner in which I had made my appearance, and then told them how passionately I was attached to the song which they had been singing.

"'We are glad to see you,' said she, who proved to be the mother of the two by her side. 'That old song is very precious to us; and yet we seldom sing it—only when we would hold fellowship with those whom it vividly pictures to our mind, as when in the bloom of youth and in the strength of manhood.'

"I asked them to sing 'The Old Kirk Yard' again, and they cheerfully complied with my request. When they had finished it, and wiped the tears from their cheeks, the little boy, with a pleasant, playful smile, approached me. There was something remarkable in that boy's countenance. It seemed as if I had been acquainted with it for years, and yet I was sure that I had never seen it before. Placing his hand in mine, he said,

"'Will you please, Miss, to tell your name? You don't live about here, do you?'

"I told him that my name was Kate Hamilton, and said, 'Now you will tell me your name, wont you?'

"'Yes, Miss,' said he; 'my name is Harry Wilson.'

"I then asked the lady if she had resided long in the place, to which she replied that they had been there but a short time, and that the city of —— was their native place.

"'Oh no!' she continued, 'we are almost as much strangers here as you are yourself. Myself and my poor children came here recently, and are comparatively strangers. We were forced to turn our backs upon our *home.* Yes, yes!' she continued, in a paroxysm of grief, 'the city of —— is our native place—my own, and the birth-place of my children. It will remain so forever; but, alas! we may not hope that it will ever again be our home. All is lost—all that endeared it to us is gone! Our home, with its cherished objects, has been swept away forever. Other feet are moving, and other hearts are happy, at this moment, where ours once trod, and where our hearts were happy; but that was before the spoiler came. Other voices are ringing in merriment through halls which once were familiar with ours, and other children are prattling in the same nursery where these poor children once played; and, oh! may they never feel in those same halls the bitterness which we inherit! By what fearful temptations is poor human nature continually surrounded, and especially in fashionable life! The rich may often do what the poor dare not; but this is a fearful evidence that their path is doubly perilous, and that it is as much subjected to the inroads of the rumseller as in the path of the poor. Miss Hamilton, *he* has ruined *us!* When I look at my poor children, what must I think of him? When my heart turns to the grave yard, can I bless him? When I go forth in thought to search for the grave of my lost one, can I have words of kindness for him? No, no! I cannot; but I will not curse him. I will leave him in the hands of that God from whose judgment he cannot escape. These children, four years since, had before them the prospect of ample wealth, and claimed a place in the best society. I say the best, for so it is called; but it's often greatly misnamed. Their morning was as bright as it could have been; but it has been quickly succeeded by a dark day of gloom and affliction. What are they now? They are young—they are innocent—they are uncomplaining. A murmur is scarcely heard from them. They are poor, and to a great extent they are uncared for by any save myself. I have this picture continually before me. I can close my eyes, but I cannot shut my heart. I see them shut out from society; and then I see the fearful consequences which necessarily follow—the scoffs and the insults of the rude and the low-bred, mingled with the chilling indifference of the proud. I see them pouring out their griefs and their tears in secret places, where none but the eye of God can see them; and when I see this, how painfully appears before me the contrast and the cause. Oh, yes! my young friend, when I see all this, as it comes unbidden to my mind, with the appalling visage of some dark spectre, bearing misery to the hearts of those dear ones of mine, whom a gracious God has yet spared to me, it almost drives me to madness. When I see and feel this, I cannot help concluding that the rumseller's business is humanity's bitterest curse; that he who pleads for it is doing a flagrant wrong to his kind. I know not how soon this fragile form of mine may bend to the earth before the rude storm, whose fury has loosened my hold on life. My children may yet become the inmates of the poor-house, but while I live I shall labor to prevent it.

"'Our circumstances,' she continued, 'have been very different from what they are now. My husband was a wealthy merchant in the city of ——. He had a generous disposition, and we had all of earthly comfort that our hearts could desire. We had joy, happiness, friends. We supposed that these things would outlive ourselves, and be a portion for our children. He was richly endowed with all the social qualities of life, and his manners were winning in the highest degree. He loved his family as he did his life. Our style of living was fashionable. In this respect, I can truly say, that it amounted to folly; but then we could not avoid it: for our circumstances, together with our position in fashionable life, fastened it upon us, and for myself, I endured rather than enjoyed it. We suffered this cruel species of slavery, because we could not break the chain. But it is broken now—broken by its own rottenness, and just when it had succeeded in paralyzing those energies which should have been free to meet and struggle with adversity. Our side-board—ah! yes, here was our fatal mistake—was always richly furnished with sparkling decanters, to which the friend was always made welcome, because we thought there was *no harm* in it, and *no danger* to be apprehended from it! It seemed to bring cheer to their hearts, and wit and sprightliness to the conversation of our guests; and many who have forgotten the name of Mary Wilson, will have difficulty in forgetting the kindness with which their coming was always greeted at our house. In all this we saw no danger. Our children were growing up around us, and our domestic happiness was completed by their childish love. It was *fashion's* voice, and we obeyed the call; for it promised to screen us from the evil hour, if, peradventure, it should ever come. We never thought that this stream would overflow its banks—we never dreamed that that side-board in our own house was opening a path to the *bar* of the rumseller. There was one, however, who saw the danger, but who, from fear of offending, did not mention it until it became apparent to myself. One day a person entered our parlor and inquired for my husband. He was an old minister, whose locks had been whitened by age, and who was an intimate friend of our family. My husband and myself had every confidence in him, and were always glad to see him entering our house, for we knew that our good was the object he sought to promote. My husband was at home, but at first refused to come into the parlor. I expostulated with him, and entreated him by the proverbial civilities of his house to come in at once. I could not at first understand why he was so reluctant to see this good old man; but directly the truth flashed upon my mind, and I said,—

"'Come, Richard, he will do you no harm. His visits are always cheering,' and taking him by the hand, we entered the parlor together, and my husband welcomed him with genuine cordiality. In the society of that old man, no one could have kept back the acknowledgment that his presence rendered the very atmosphere more sacred. On this occasion he was familiar and affable as usual, and yet, although he had not named the purpose of his coming, it was evident that a sense of duty had directed his steps to our door. For some moments he seemed to be engaged in a struggle with his own feelings. It seemed as if he were looking deeply into his own heart, in which a sense of paramount duty was struggling with the very natural fear of offending. He began:

"'Mr. Wilson,' said he, 'it is now a little more than nine-and-thirty years since a pious mother, now in heaven, I have no doubt, committed you with her dying breath to God, and left you motherless in the world. You have grown up to manhood, and you are surrounded by a young family. You have been blessed with all the comforts that the world can give; and yet I am fearful that you will find it to be after all a broken staff. I have often prayed that the prayers of your mother might be answered; but my hopes are every day declining. Wealth and fashion are fearful obstacles in the way of a faithful discharge of duty. It has been so with me on many occasions. I have come to your house before on the same errand which has brought me here to-day, and I have gone away again cast down and discouraged—almost resolved to let you go. But why should I fear to approach this subject, or conclude that it will be thanklessly received? If I had overheard a band of incendiaries covenanting amongst themselves, that at the solemn and lonely hour of midnight they would fire your dwelling, I surely would hasten to you with the tidings, and you would thank me for it, too. Or if I had heard the low, stealthy whispers of an assassin band, fixing the hour of your destruction, would I not hasten to you to warn you of your danger? and would you not thank me for it? Or if I knew that in your absence your wife and your children were to be hurried out of this house and launched into the jaws of an unrelenting poverty, would I not, for the love I bear to yourself, your wife and your young children, hasten to your door, break in upon your quiet slumbers, and bid you to be watchful?—and you would thank me for it too. Mr. Wilson, I see all this, and more than all this, looming in terror about your door. I see ruin, misery, and death flocking to your threshold, to blight its joys. I see your wife and children, unless there is a rapid change, taking a last, a wild glance at all that is left there to love, then turning from these halls, to enter them no more. I see them on their way to your yet fresh grave, to consecrate it with tears.'

"'What reason have you,' said my husband, 'for those alarming conjectures? I apprehend no such danger as that of which you speak. I know no cause for alarm.'

"'I know,' said he, 'that the wine-cup is obtaining the mastery over you; there is, therefore, most imminent danger.'

"'I do not think it is,' replied my husband.

"'Ah! Mr. Wilson, that increases the danger. You do not see it yourself; if you did, you might avoid it.'

"'Well, it is strange, sir,' said my husband, 'if such is the fact, that I should not know it. I think I am safe enough, however.'

"'Well, I am sorry that you think so. I wish it were true; but a long experience has taught me that with perseverance in this way, ruin—the ruin of everything—is inevitable. I am sure the wine-cup is becoming your master. I do not see the evidence of this in your domestic circle; nor do I see it so much upon your cheek, as I do in the grass-grown path of your former life—a path in which you were wont to travel in the discharge of high and sacred obligations. This path is closing, and I see a fresh path, which is every day widening and deepening, from your door-stone to the place of sin and death; and there I see you sitting with apparent satisfaction, in the rumseller's den. Ah! my friend, he is skilled in his business. He knows every turn in the road along which yourself and your possessions are coming into his power. I have not seen you engaging in the revels which are usual in many of those places; but you have argued in favor of the liberty to sell rum. Your temperament, Mr. Wilson, is of the kind which will move you fast in whatever direction you take. You are unsuspecting, and hence direful consequences will come to you unexpectedly, and before you are aware of it. Forsake your course quickly, as you love your own soul—your own peace—as you love your family, as you love everything that is dear upon the earth, or sacred in heaven. Forsake it, and return again to duty, to peace and hope. As you have been in the bar-room from time to time, have you not frequently met with those who were habitually there, wasting themselves and squandering the little for which penury was pleading at home? Beware of these associations, Mr. Wilson, for they will ruin you. Beware of your own conduct, too, for you may ruin hundreds. Your position gives you influence to do harm as well as good. You may ruin your own family, and you may wound a thousand hearts, and cause them to bleed through the whole journey of life.'

"After engaging in a fervent prayer, the echoes of which are yet alive in my heart, he rose to leave; but on reaching the door, to which my husband had accompanied him, he suddenly halted, and taking him by the hand, said:

"'Now, Mr. Wilson, I beseech you, by the memories of those who are sleeping on the shores of the Delaware; I beseech you by the loves and the hopes of the living; I beseech you as a husband, father, friend; I beseech you by everything, present and future, and by all that pertains to the endearing relations of life; for the sake of crushed and bleeding humanity; for the sake of your own present and eternal interests, and in view of your dying hour—turn yourself and your influence against the rumseller.'

"After he had gone, my husband sat down for a moment, as if appalled by what had passed. There was no evidence of passion in his countenance, and rising in an agitated manner, he commenced pacing the room. Suddenly he came up to me, and taking me by the hand, said:

"'Mary, can you tell me what Mr. J—— means? I was not prepared for such a shock as this. It is both sudden and strange. Surely he does not think that I am a *drunkard!* Then what under the heavens does it mean? Do you think any of the children overheard the conversation? If they did, you must right it in some way.'

"'You can do this, Richard,' I replied, 'better than I can, and without speaking a single word to them.'

"'How, Mary?' he immediately inquired.

"'Ah! my husband,' I continued, 'can't you tell how? Go a little into the past history of our home, and see if you cannot get my meaning. I have never chided nor reproved you harshly, and I never will; but still I am not blind.'

"'Mary what do you mean?—for heaven's sake tell me and I will do anything that is not absolutely impossible.'

"'Richard,' I replied, 'do you remember the pride and pleasure you once took in spending your evenings in the society of your family? Do you remember how often you have quoted to me those beautiful lines—

> "Home! who can tell
> The touching power of that most sacred word,
> Save he who feels and weeps that he has none?"

"'Yes, Mary, I do remember, and they are dear to me now.'

"'Are they as dear as they once were; or are beauty and loveliness passing from the cheeks of those dear children?'

"'Mary,' said he, while the tears rolled down his cheeks, 'they are dear to me—they are a part of my being. You do not think that these children could lose their place in my affections?'

"'But, my husband,' I replied, 'others have the power to rob us of your society.'

"'Oh! Mary, it is my business that is pressing me —necessity compels me to be absent from you.'

"'Richard, is it not the necessity of which our friend has spoken.'

"'Do you think he could have seen me there?'

"'Where?' I inquired.

"'No matter,' said he, 'I was wandering.'

"'Do tell me, Richard, where you meant?'

"'Yes, Mary, I may as well tell you—*I mean the rumsellers*—and you have as good a right to know as any one else.'

"'Ah! that is what I feared,' I replied. 'That has troubled me. The rumseller's work! Let heaven name it properly; for as yet it has not a name which denotes its dark character. I have seen its fruits in the face of age and childhood, as they have come to our door for charity, and I thank God that I have always tried to sympathize with them; for the day may come when we may need the sympathy of others! Oh! Richard won't you promise me that you will forsake those unworthy associates, and that you will turn your influence against them at once? Won't you join with the humane in prayer to God against this business, which is rife with every misfortune.'

"'Yes Mary,' said he, 'I will promise you that I will at once forsake these men, and these places. I know what they are better than you do. You have only seen the product of their labor—I have seen the machinery in its terrible operation. I promise you, and I call God to witness, that I will forsake them. I never knew what misery was, until I became familiar with it at these haunts.'

"'At the sound of these words, my heart leaped for joy, and I thanked God fervently for having sent his servant on that day to our house. Again the holy lamp of life was lighted, and burned brightly in my soul, because I thought it was burning with like brilliancy in the bosom of my husband. Alas! how little after all did we know of the rumseller's power! I did not think that it could throw itself into the domestic circle, and lead out its reluctant victim to the slaughter! It has done it. The *law*, the boast of civilization, sanctions it. I am its witness—these children are seals set to its truth.'"

CHAPTER XIX.

WHAT RUM DOES.

"Fly from the wine cup,
Though pleasure may swim
In the bright rosy bubbles
That float round the brim.
Far down 'neath the depths
Of the read wine that flows,
Lurks the Syren that lures
To the vortex of woes."

"'IF I had known,' continued Mrs. Wilson, 'what a fearful power the rumseller swayed over his victim, I could hardly have cherished a single hope for my husband's safety. Such knowledge, however, at that time, was impossible; for then I could not suspect a human being of such absolute cruelty. If I had then understood that its charm was *serpent-like* in its character, and that it never removed its eye from its prey until its victim entered its jaws—then I should have resigned my husband to his inevitable destiny, and given myself to preparation for the worst. For a time I was happy again—happy in the presence of my husband, as when mutually we smiled upon our first-born. Our children seemed happier—everything appeared more lovely, and to me it seemed as if the fast wilting leaves of hope had suddenly ceased to wither, and had arrayed themselves once more in freshness and in beauty. Oh! what a broad, deep, and sacred foundation does that hope, which concentrates in the well-being of a loved one, lay in the soul, and how does the full tides of interest and affection love to sport at its base, and rejoice in its success. One morning, as my husband was leaving the breakfast table, *in better* spirits and with a more cheerful manner than he had manifested in many days, he called me aside and said,—

"'Mary, you look happier than you have done in months. Everything seems to be clad in new life. It is strange that I should not have seen this before. I never supposed that anything could hold such a spell over my being, as to darken my mind, and mutilate my hopes and my happiness at the same time. I feel, and have felt for days, as one who had been brought back from the grave, or as one who had been released from the grasp of uncompromising tyranny. Oh! the headaches and the heartaches of that path!—the gloom, the anticipations of a lingering death on earth; and then—oh yes! and then, the lingering death—which, in the far beyond, still linked to life, utterly refuses to die! Don't you think, Mary, it was a happy thing for us that God sent that old man to our house to alarm me—to warn me of danger?'

"'My heart was wild with glad emotion, and I

answered, yes, dear Richard, I think it was; and I am sure we can never be sufficiently thankful; for you were well-nigh hopelessly tangled in the meshes of the rumseller's net.'

"'There is no doubt about that, Mary,' said he, 'but you can know but little of its peril. Indeed, it is impossible for any one to know it, except those who have unconsciously fallen under its lash, and smarted from its stripes! But, you must pray for me; for as much as I love you, much as I idolize our dear children, and much as I value our domestic peace and happiness, I must tell you that it is difficult for me to keep my resolution, and realize the cherished wish of my heart. You may think this strange; but wherever I turn, I meet the temptation to forswear myself, and jeopardize every interest of my life. To get without the reach of it is impossible. In every street, and at every corner, start out those forces, before which a trembling resolution falters—*generally falls!* These temptations,—ah! here is the secret—before them everything gives way! Remove them and the poor drunkard will make and *keep* his resolution to live soberly; but until this is done, nine out of every ten will fall—fall hopelessly and forever!'

"'We had many conversations of this kind, and I hoped and believed, notwithstanding the danger by which my husband was surrounded, that he was safe! I thought our happiness secured. It was, after all, a dream; and why did I permit myself to hope? The rumseller! the rumseller! It is his to abrogate every oath which his marked victim may have taken before the altar of affection, in the heart of his beseeching wife and children! It is his to stand by till the last drop of blood has fallen to the ground; and then to exclaim, with inhuman indifference—"It is a pity that he ruined himself! He was indeed a clever fellow; but he would have rum!" Himself, indeed! Look at your victim! His blood has flowed out—his eye is closed—his heart is quiet! Did you not measure out to him the poison? Then, like Cain, you have slain your brother. This is the verdict rendered, not only by widows and orphans, but by humanity at large. Gradually I saw that the resolution of my husband was giving way before the temptations by which he was beset, and soon his time was given again to the society of the bar-room—the deadly upas from which I feared he could not escape. My hopes were almost dead, and I had well-nigh concluded that it would be useless to attempt his reformation. Ah! but thought I, that victim is my husband. Our mutual oaths went up together to heaven, and were recorded there, side by side; and now shall I give him up, and let him die as the brute dieth? The instincts of a wife, of a mother, forbid it. On one pleasant morning, when everything without was bright and beautiful, and when everything within my heart was sad and cheerless, I took him into the parlor, that we might be alone, and then said to him—'Richard, this is a lovely morning,' and in an abstracted manner he said,—

"'Yes, Mary, it is; but I must really go. I have some important business this morning, which is waiting for me, at the store.'

"'I understood it, and said—'Tell me, Richard, may I hope any longer?'

"'Mary,' he replied, 'it is useless for me to try. My resolution is broken, and it would avail me nothing if I should resolve again. You had better make up your mind to the worst; for, Mary, it will come. I cannot prevent it, and I fear it is not far off. They have too much power over me. I am too weak to stand against the temptation. There was a time when I could have done it; but that time is past, and I beseech you, let me go!'

"'How can I do this?' I inquired. For some moment she made no reply. He had placed his handkerchief to his face, and was weeping bitterly. His whole frame denoted intense agitation. Oh! Miss Hamilton, that was a fearful sight to look upon: to see the father and the husband bathed in tears and trembling in agony, dragged out from the loves of his own house by the witchery of rum. At length he said to me,—

"'I feel that I cannot recover myself. If any one,

two years since, had pointed to this fearful moment, I would have asked the question, "Am I a dog that I should do this thing?" But it is done, and now I cannot help it!'

"'You love me, Richard?' I replied.

"'Yes, Mary, as I ever did.'

"'And you love your children?'

"'Yes; poor children—I love them, but they will have but little cause either to love or respect my memory. What is to become of them? My character is ruined not only, but my estate also! Ah! you will soon know all. The prediction of our old friend is rapidly fulfilling. The storm has gathered, and is ready to break.'

"'Richard,' I continued, 'wont you resolve, and try again? Oh! if it be possible for you to escape, do not give yourself up to destruction. Your wife—your children—yourself! Oh, God! must all be lost! Won't you try again?'

"'My dear wife!' he replied, 'you know not how the strong man trembles, and how he writhes in utter hopelessness, when he has once become the slave that I am. I would do anything to be free again, but it is too late. Mary, make up your mind to let me go, and as soon as possible let the cold grave hide me, since for me there is no more peace, and I live only to disgrace you and our dear family.'

"'I hope, Miss Hamilton, that your heart will never

be rent by the influence of such a terrific moment. During that day, for the sake of my children, I assumed an air of composure; impressed, however, with a feeling that the worst would soon come. At this moment one of the servants came in, and announced the entrance of Mrs. Philips, one whom, of all others of my acquaintance, I least desired to see. She was a married lady, of middle age, to whom fortune had come suddenly, and she was one of the most envious spirits I ever knew. As soon as she recovered from her affected sympathy, and had satisfied herself with a survey of our parlor, she said,—

"'Mrs. Wilson, it is hard—very hard—absolutely cruel. You can't endure it—it's dreadful hard to suffer all this—it will kill you. It's a shame for people to take such advantages. I did not think, Mrs. Wilson, that there were such *mean*, *dishonest* people in this city. This fine house and furniture, and yourself and your sweet children! Has there been any one here yet, to look at your furniture? All these nice things must go, and I dare say they will go cheap. That's an elegant piano—pure rose-wood; and these carpets—in fact, everything is of the best quality. I would like to have some of these things. Ever since I heard of the advertisement, I have hardly slept a wink. I presume you would be just as willing that I should have some of them, as any one else. You would rather see them taken by your friends than by strangers.'

"'I was almost stupefied, and inquired what she meant.

"'Why, dear me, Mrs. Wilson, don't you know? Why, you are to be sold out of everything which the *law don't allow you*, in three weeks. Your husband is broke clear down; and everybody says that it will be impossible for him to recover. His store is closed, and has been for two days. I am told, and I suppose it is true enough, that in one gambling establishment in this city, he has been robbed, in the way of loaning to gamblers, of about one hundred thousand dollars, in the last year! This is all true, I assure you!'

"'I had been looking for trouble; I had made up my mind on that morning, that it was inevitable. But then, after all, I was not prepared for anything like this. If what I had just heard was indeed true, I knew how it had been brought about. My husband was not a gambler; of that I was certain. I knew that he was generous, and that perhaps when blinded by strong drink, he had been robbed of the means on which we were dependent for subsistence.

"'Mr. Wilson did not return that evening, as he usually did, to tea, and after waiting for several hours, I sent a servant out to look for him. I directed him first to go to the house of a rumseller, at which I knew my husband had been in the habit of spending much of his time. The servant soon returned, and I saw in a moment that something was wrong, and in answer to my question, he immediately informed me that he had seen Mr. Wilson in the bar-room of the house to which I had sent him, bleeding profusely. I lost no time, but with my servant, immediately hastened thither. The saloon, or bar-room, was filled with rowdies. Finding it impossible to press my way through the crowd, I entered a room on the opposite side of the hall. This was filled with persons of genteel and quiet appearance; they were strangers, and were engaged in conversation, and I overheard one saying, 'I think he has nearly killed him.' As soon as I could find words, I said to them,—

"'Gentlemen, can you tell me if there has been a person badly injured here to-night?'

"'Yes madam, there has,' replied a gentleman of strong, muscular appearance. This was the only moment of my life that I ever felt as if summary vengeance would be sweet. I asked the gentleman if he would have the kindness to ask the proprietor to walk into that room. I had seated myself facing the door, and when it was opened, I saw that the crowd had dispersed. In a moment the proprietor entered, and I at once asked him if my husband was in his house. He turned from me suddenly, as if intending to depart at once, without answering my question; and in my agony I cried out, 'Stop, villain! You cannot escape in this way.' He stopped, and collecting himself, said to me, with an air of superiority:

"'What business have you in this house, madam?'

"'I am in search of my husband,' I replied.

"'Who is your husband?'

"'Richard Wilson!'

"'He is not here, and has not been here to-night.'

"'Do you say, sir, that my husband has not been here?'

"'I do, madam.'

"'My husband has been here, sir, and is now in your house, either dead or alive—God only knows which. I will find him, sir. It is folly for you to attempt to deceive me. My servant saw him in your house this evening, with the marks of violence upon his person. If you have murdered him at last, I beseech you in the name of mercy, let me see his body, that I may give it a decent burial.'

"'Madam,' said he, 'if Richard Wilson is your husband, you cannot see him this evening. He has retired in a state of intoxication, and does not wish to see you.'

"'How do you know, sir, that he does not wish to see me?'

"'You can't see him, madam; and you may as well leave this house,' he replied, as he turned to leave the room.

"'Landlord,' cried a voice behind me, which I at once recognized as that of the person who had called him into the room, 'if you take another step, you do it at the peril of your life. Another step, and the record of your abominable crimes will meet you in the judgment. Stir not, sir; attempt not to leave this room, and know from one who has the power to command your craven spirit, that this lady shall see her husband, and instantly, too. God only knows in what situation she may find him. It may be dying, or already dead.'

"'With the true instinct of a spiritless coward, he brought volleys of oaths to his assistance, declaring that Mr. Wilson should not be seen.'

"'Then,' continued the gentleman in whose presence he was trembling, 'I understand that it is your determination, sir, that this lady cannot be permitted to see her husband.'

"'You understand me right, sir,' was the surly reply.

"'Well, sir,' said the gentleman, 'it is my determination that she shall see him, at once; no matter through what, or to what, it may lead;' and then turning to the company, not one of whom, during the conversation, had said a word, he said:

"'Gentlemen, for the most part, we are strangers to each other. I am not naturally quarrelsome, and yet I am not a coward. You have all seen in what a dastardly manner conjugal devotion has been set at defiance, and insulted by this wretch. You have seen the wife come here to find her husband. She has been refused to see him, though he may be dying under this roof. Gentlemen, here is a duty for us to perform; and whatever consequences may attend it, the man shall be found. Let us make this case our own, and suppose that our *wives* or our *sisters* were trying to gain admission to our sick or dying rooms, and were thus inhumanly and brutishly repulsed, would we not invoke the stranger's arm, to intefere for us?'

"'He took a lamp from the table, and advancing toward the trembling miscreant, he said, 'Take this light, sir.'

"'In an instant, every one in the room was on his feet, and it was evident enough that they were prepared to act with firmness and decision.

"'There can be but little doubt,' said the stranger, 'but this den has its keepers—those who will defend it, in order to hide from justice the evidence of their crimes. Let us, therefore, remember that duty is calling us to this encounter, and if we must fight—nay, if it be necessary to tear this infernal den to pieces, we will do it!'

"'Addressing the rumseller, he said:

"'Now, sir, lead us instantly to the place where you have concealed this lady's husband! Let nothing tempt you to lead us into an ambuscade, for in that case, you will be the first to fall.'

"'He took the lamp, and with a trembling step, he

proceeded. After passing up to the fifth and last story of the house, in a small room, which, from the fragments that were scattered through it, plainly indicated that it was occupied by the lowest class of servants, I found my husband—no light—no water—no friend near him, and literally clotted in his own blood! Here the rumseller placed the lamp on an old box which stood in the room, and appeared to be about leaving us.

"'Stop,' said the stranger, 'we are not done with you yet. Make no attempt to leave.'

"'He appeared to be entirely unconscious either that myself or others were by his side. I spoke to him, and asked him if he knew me. An expression of wildness passed over his features, and he spoke faintly, and yet so that all in the room could hear:

"'My God! Mary, is that you? Has it come to this? They have succeeded at last! Oh! for God's sake, take me from this place quickly. Do not let me die here! Take me home, that I may see once more those dear children, who are ruined!'

"'After speaking thus, he said:

"'Who are those men?'

"'I informed him they were gentlemen who had assisted me in finding him. He then said:

"'Well, I am lost! lost! lost!—but God bless them and their wives and children, and keep their feet from learning the bitter way in which I have trod.'

"'As reason returned, he fixed his eye upon the guilty rumseller, and said:

"'Your victim is in a dying state. There, sir, is my wife: you have robbed her of everything. My young children!—you have stolen the bread from their mouths, and hope and happiness from their hearts. God reward you!'

"'I must cover up the scenes by which this event was immediately succeeded. I cannot wring my heart and bleed it afresh by a narration of the fearful history of the few days which elapsed before the death of my husband, which was immediately followed by the death of a lovely daughter. A few hours after we had returned from the funeral, and while we were grouped together with a few friends in the parlor, who were endeavoring to console our desolate hearts, we were startled by the entrance of a civil officer, who informed us that all our personal property was under execution and was to be sold in a short time. This was new to my children, but at that moment they seemed to have been so entirely broken in spirits that the intelligence of this new calamity, by which they were to be beggared, did not seem to affect them. They looked at each other, and at me, but not a word was spoken. The officer, with whom I had no acquaintance, was still standing in the room, apparently waiting an answer from me, and I said to him.

"'I understand you, sir.'

"'Well, madam,' said he, 'it has been enjoined upon me by those for whose benefit your property has been levied upon, to take security for its safe delivery on the day of sale, or to remove it at once to the quarters of an auctioneer. This, madam, I cannot and will not do. I know how these afflictions have been brought upon you, and I know into whose pockets the proceeds of your property will go. I think it would be an act of justice and mercy to raze many of those places in this city to their foundations. Heaven forbid that I should add to your sufferings. I will neither remove your goods nor take security. I have no fear about them.'

"'I assured him that nothing should be removed, and he left. The day of sale arrived, and we saw article after article passing from our possession. This was severe. Those cherished things wasting and scattering in our presence, was almost beyond endurance; but the law allowed the rumseller to be paid for his work, and we knew they must go. It was late in the evening when the sale closed, and it was quite dark before the last articles were removed by the purchasers, so that it was necessary for us to remain in the house during the night. This was not our intention; for through the kindness of a trusty but poor old Scotchman, we had procured a very small house in a retired part of the city, to which it was our intention to have removed that day. This, however, we could not do, it being necessary for us to wait until all was over, to know what we might carry with us. To us, that was a bitter, gloomy night. Everything but the meager allowance of the law was gone, and I have often thought that those who are excusing themselves by saying that they can do nothing to stay this current of ruin, would, had they been present, have been awakened and enlightened, and moved to action. Through that long and cheerless night, while my children, overcome with grief, were sleeping soundly, often did I rise to look at them and weep over them. The next morning all that was left us of earthly goods was carried to our humble home, where, until within a few months, we have resided. Miss Hamilton, I have told you all that I can bear to tell you, and I hope you may find it of some service to you through life.'

"'Did you not say,' I inquired, 'that you had a son?

"'Yes,' replied Mrs. Wilson, 'I did.'

"'Where is he?'

"'That I do not know.'

"'What was his name?'

"'Richard.'

"'Have you ever heard him speak of Frank Hamilton?'

"'Oh, yes,' she replied, looking at me intently, 'very often. We were well aquainted with him. He spent a vacation once with poor Dick, and I was so much pleased with him and his friendship for my son, that

I presented him with an elegant portrait of him. Do you know Frank Hamilton?'

"'Very well, Mrs. Wilson.'

"'Are you a relation of his?' she quickly inquired.

"'I am his sister, Mrs. Wilson, and your son's portrait is suspended in our parlor.'

"'Is it possible? Where is your brother?'

"'He is in Mexico, and we are looking for him soon. Indeed, he may be now in New York. The war is over, and those broken regiments are on their way back to their homes!'

"'Ah, yes, Miss Hamilton,' she replied, 'but there are those who will not come back—those who will not return with coming regiments. No, no! the dead at Monterey will never come back. My poor son must remain there. It may be, that your brother has fallen in with him, and will know something of his end, and oh! what a pleasure it would bring to this desolate heart to see one who saw him there, and know from that one how it was.'

"'Is it possible, Mrs. Wilson,' I inquired, 'that your son has fallen in Mexico?'

"'I think there can be no doubt of it, although we only know it by report.'

"'Why did he leave you?'

"'Necessity, Miss Hamilton, compelled him to leave home to finish his studies. The wreck of our fortune left him entirely dependent on his own exertions.

My son went to a village about one hundred miles distant from the city, to complete his studies, preparatory to admission to the bar. In this new situation he sustained himself for a year with great credit, entirely by his own exertion. But ah! the rumseller and his friends were there, and how could he be safe? We knew the danger, and we prayed for him daily, that he might be kept from temptation. His letters were always cheering to us, and they became more so as he neared the time of his expected admission to the bar. It was our expectation to remove in a few days to the village of B——, where, through the persuasion of his friends, he had concluded to locate himself. All our arrangements were made, and the darkness which had rested upon our path was disappearing, when we received the following letter from poor Dick:

" '*My dear Mother, Sister, and Brother:*

" 'Farewell! Your hopes and mine are broken. My prospects yesterday were bright: they are now in ruins! I would like to see you once more—you all, for whom I have lived, and for whom I was willing to toil. I have been beset by a cruel and chilling conspiracy. I refused at the house of Judge L—— to drink wine with a *foolish girl.* For your sakes more than my own, I was unwilling to risk the peril. This morning I expected to have been admitted. My ex amination was passed. I was *refused* and *rejected* by the same Judge! I love you as I ever did. Good bye! Tell little Harry that he must fly from those who have ruined his father and his brother. Good-bye!'—

"'Since then we know nothing of him, only as we have heard by accident that a person of his name had fallen at the battle of Monterey. We have nearly ceased to hope. My husband has been taken away, and I suppose my son also. We have been robbed of everything, and we are only one of the hundreds of thousands who are writhing under the bitter infliction.'

"There," said Kate Hamilton, pointing to Dick Wilson's portrait, and with her eye fixed on Lucy, "that was cruel. You ought not to have tempted that noble young man. Ah! you cannot measure the consequence of that glass of wine with which you tempted him."

"Kate," said Lucy, "I will go at once to that widow, and make atonement."

"How will you atone? Can you give her back the son, full of vigor and hope, as when you saw him first? Can you open the grave and bring him up, manly and beautiful as he was on the last day you saw him in that peopled court-house? No, no; yours, I fear, were but a part of those influences which drove him from home and friends, and that led him to a distant clime, in which his life has been sacrificed. For this you cannot atone."

Lucy was silent for a moment and, then buried her face in her hands.

CHAPTER XX.

THE REFORMED RUMSELLER.

"Ah! who can tell how hard it is to climb
The steep where *wine's* red temple shines afar;
Ah! who can tell how many a soul sublime
Has felt the influence of that malignant star,
And waged with virtue an eternal war."

"I HAVE been in the business," said a reformed rumseller, "in the best, but never in the worst places, and I know what it is, and to what it tends, notwithstanding the eloquent pleadings of its apologists. I know what it is in the capitals of the largest States in the Union, and in the capital of the nation."

"Well, what do you think of it?" said a less than half persuaded philanthropist, who found it impossible to satisfy himself that rum was not among the necessaries of life.

"I think, sir," said he, "that it is degrading to him who is engaged in it, and that of all other employments, it is the most injurious to the community in which it is carried on."

"Do you think," inquired the hesitating philanthropist, "that there is any possibility of doing away with it?"

"Oh yes, sir; of this I have no doubt."

"In what way do you propose to do it?"

"By wise legislation, sir; and this is the only way in which it can be done."

"Well, well, sir—but hasn't our legislation been wise heretofore?"

"I think not, sir. The true, effective course would be to give it no quarter—to strike it from existence at once and forever."

"But can this be legally done?"

"I think so, clearly. We certainly have a right to suppress any traffic, any business, the *only* tendency of which is to injure the community; and as the selling of rum to be drank, has this effect and no other, the right of the people to protect themselves from its effects is, I think, beyond reasonable question. The stale cry of *illegality*, *unconstitutionality*, &c., has lost its force, and is no longer in the way of proper legal restrictions."

"Do you seriously think that legislators will risk the venture?—that they will be willing to go for so stringent a law as you propose, and run the hazard of losing the votes of all those who are opposed to the measure? If you do, you have greater confidence in their uprightness and courage than I have. The law you propose strikes at a business in which immense capital is now employed, both in the manufacture and sale of alcoholic drinks. Hundreds of thousands depend upon it for support. The great interest of agriculture furnishes the raw materials, and annually draws from it a large amount of its receipts. All this you propose at once to annihilate—a work, sir, which I think you will find easier to talk about than practically to execute."

"The time was when these objections influenced legislation, and were so controlling that the laws enacted were a nullity. That time has now passed. Three-fourths of the electors, in a large section of the Union, are decidedly in favor of the measure. They are also determined that those to whom they give their suffrages shall, on this question at least, no longer misrepresent them. They know their rights, and they also know their powers. They have deliberately, and yet decidedly, concluded to assert the one, and to exercise the other; and mere demagogues and time-servers will be driven into merited retirement, while their places will be supplied by men with whom principle will be paramount to policy. A few years since, in a certain State, while the school question was before the Legislature, there was quite an excitement. There were men whose constituents had spelled their tickets, '*kno skool*'! and everybody knew how they would go. It was said that they would echo the *kno skool* of their constituency; and so they did. But one of the most intelligent and prosperous districts in the State had sent to the Legislature a man who was utterly unlike themselves. At length the school law was taken up, and the fidelity of their representative was of course to be tested. At this time, one of his constituents, a very intelligent friend of the school law, happened to be on a visit to the capital, and his curiosity led him into the Legislature. He was just in time to hear one of the most eloquent speeches of the session, and was of course delighted with it. But when the vote was taken, he was much disappointed to find the representative from his own district vote '*kno skool.*' In answer to the question, how so intelligent a district as his happened to be represented by so stupid a blockhead as had just voted, he said that he was a rum-representative, sent up there to protect that interest; and that he should vote against popular instructions, was, after all, not so surprising. He said he was comparatively little known to the electors—had, by agreement with his rum-supporters, pledged himself to the friends of temperance, and received their votes, and was by this *ruse* elected by a large majority. This method of deceiving the electors cannot now be successfully practised. The trick is understood, and is guarded against."

"But how can you guard against this? Pledges, you say, are not regarded."

"There are men whose past lives and conduct furnish a certain guarantee that they will *act* as they *talk*. It's these that we shall elect."

"Then you do not believe in *political catechisms?*"

"I do not. The best assurance of fidelity, I repeat, is the recorded conduct of the men, of whom we have now an ample supply in all localities; and he that, at this day, is not publicly known as an uncompromising friend of temperance, should not be intrusted with the responsible duties of legislation. Elect such men —and that we shall, is now no longer doubtful—and the 'Maine law' follows as a matter of course."

"Why did you quit the rumselling business?"

"For three reasons, sir. The first was on account of my family. A bar-room is a bad place in which to educate a child, exposed, as it is, not only to the temptations of rum, and the filthy and loathsome conversations which rum produces, but the worst of all possible examples. In the second place, on my own account. I felt its demoralizing effect upon me, even while engaged in it, and so does every one similarly situated. I knew almost certainly that if my life were spared, I should be doomed to reap the consequences of rumselling—little respected by the good, and uncared for by any. In the third place, on account of the evil consequences which I saw resulting to others. I could never believe, hard as I tried, that money was to be gained, no matter by what means; yet it appears to me that this is the only maxim on which the rumseller can, at this day, justify himself. I once saw, in my own house, such a fearful exhibition of the evils of rumselling, that I quit it at once and forever. From my own bar was the rum given which sent a generous-souled young man onward in the path of degradation and misery."

"Did you do this yourself, sir?"

"No, sir; but I saw it immediately after it was done, and I never think of it without shuddering. About nine o'clock one evening, while keeping a public house in the village of B——, a young man, with whom I was well acquainted, entered my bar-room and seated himself quietly. Usually he was cheerful; but now he spoke to no one. In a short time a colored man came in with his trunk, and as it was placed on the floor, he said:

"'Ah, companion of my misfortune, we must go again, nor can we expect to keep together long. The severities of life will separate us.'

"I knew that his hopes were in ruins, and vainly endeavored to assist him in regathering them.

"'That, Mr. Jacobs, is impossible,' said he: 'it would be as easy to gather the chaff which has been driven off by the madness of the whirlwind. I have no hope.'

"I tried to ascertain what destination he had in view; but this was impossible: he did not seem to know. He took from his trunk a package of letters, then closing it, seated himself on the top of it. His feelings were intense, as he glanced over the letters in a hurried manner; and then, putting them together again, he ejaculated:

"'My mother! my mother! your cup of misery is full!'

"I left the room for a moment, and on returning, to my surprise, saw him standing at the bar, with a decanter in his hand. I would have prevented it, but at that moment half a dozen young men entered the bar-room. These were the persons who had prepared him for the rumseller—the persons who had driven him there, and for a moment they quailed before him.

"'Come, come, Mr. Wilson, said one of them whose name was Horace Stevens, don't take this matter too much at heart: it will all be right in a short time. I am glad to see you at the bar. I have more hope for you now than I ever had. We will drink together and be social. It's the life of the law to be social. Let us drink and make merry!'

"'Now, Mr. Wilson, give us a sentiment, and matters will all be right.'

"For an instant he looked into the faces of those who were determined to crown his ruin, and then looking into the glass, as if to measure its wasting curses, with a look of phrenzy, he drank! Oh, bitter draught! I had known his early fondness for drink, and the great struggle which he had had to resist the importunities of a pernicious appetite. Yet I had supposed him secure in his own firm purpose to resist. But when I saw him yield, I knew that all was lost! Henceforward, I feared, he would be a passive victim in the tempter's snare, for such is the usual, the almost invariable result. I felt that if there had been no rumseller to have taken or given the advantage to others, at that moment, that young man would have been comparatively safe. He would have recovered from his disappointment; the storm would have swept by, and his sun would have shone brightly again. But as it was, that sun rose no more. Rum perpetually eclipsed it!"

"Did you ever learn what became of this young man?"

"Yes sir; after wandering about from place to place for some time, he enlisted in the service for Mexico, and it has been reported that he was killed at the battle of Monterey. This, I think, was not true, as I have been creditably informed that he has since been seen in the United States."

"Did you hear anything about his situation?"

"Yes sir, and it was bad enough. He was a complete wreck."

"And this example, Mr. Jacobs, led you to quit the the business?"

"It did sir, and every honorable man who has any respect for himself, for his family, and the peace of the community, will, I hope, do the same thing soon;

and those who have no honor to move them, who care nothing for themselves, their families, or for the peace of the community, ought to be *forced* to give it up at once. Now, sir, this is what must be done by legislation. Heretofore the people have been unconsciously strengthening the hands of the rumseller. From them has he obtained his power to mock the pleas of the drunkard's wife and child. I think sir, if you will examine this matter carefully, that you will agree with me, that strong legislation only can correct it."

"Indeed, Mr. Jacobs, I think you are about right, and if legislation is the only thing that can correct it, we had better have it at once."

"Well, this is what we *intend* to have; but we shall meet opposition the most strenuous and untiring. While the friends of the measure are prompted to effort by a regard to the public welfare, its enemies are stimulated by the considerations of self-interest. The former can employ only the arguments of truth, and can appeal only to the intelligence and virtue of those whom they hope to move. The latter will, no doubt, as they have heretofore done, employ the most unscrupulous of means. Gold, their only idol, will be freely employed in the preliminary canvass, at the ballot-box and in the halls of legislation. But it will not now prevail. Men, 'above all price,' will occupy the seats too long held by the mere sycophant; and when the question comes up, 'Shall the Maine law pass?' those with strong nerves and stout hearts will be ready, with a firm and cheering 'aye,' which will dissipate all doubts, and gladden alike the heart of the philanthropist and the Christian."

CHAPTER XXI.

FLYING FROM TEMPTATION.

"Fly from the tempter—
From the brow of the brave
She has torn the gay wreath,
And made him a slave;
E'en the pride of the statesman,
The fame of the just,
The wine cup has humbled,
And trod in the dust."

THE conclusion of peace, after the surrender of the city of Mexico, was the signal to the American volunteer, that his work was done, and that again he might turn his battle-soiled frame towards home. Many anxious hearts were waiting impatiently for the return of those regiments, whose ranks had been thinned by disease and the Mexican lance. Some were waiting for the return of the living, and others to hear the fate of those who would return no more. It was soon understood that the shattered remains of the 11th regiment of infantry were expected that day to land in the city. This was believed to be reliable intelligence, and, in consequence, joyful was the countenances of those who expected to meet their friends, while others were agitated by mingled emotions of hope and fear. At last, and while crowds were thronging the landing, the noble vessel, bearing in her bosom the broken ranks of those who had perilled their lives in a foreign clime, drew near; and then were heard the questions—Where is my husband?—my brother?—my father?—my son?—and many were answered, *in the grave!* Mr. Hamilton and Kate were there; but not in the crowd. From their position they were able to see the soldiers as they left the vessel.

"Father," said she, "there are but a few more to come off—I am sure Frank is not there," and as the last of those veterans left the vessel, she added, with painful emotion—"No, Frank is not there." Mr. Hamilton replied, "No, my child, he is not."

Leaving the carriage in charge of the servant, he at once advanced to where the regiment was forming, and meeting a young man, whom he at once knew to be a non-commissioned officer, he eagerly inquired after his son. He was informed that he had been transferred to another regiment, and that he had already, or would in a few days, land at Pittsburgh, with the remnant of the first and second Pennsylvania regiments. He immediately returned and said to Kate,—

"Thank God, the boy is safe, and will be home in a few days."

"Yes," said Kate, fervently, "thank God—but,

father, poor Mrs. Wilson's son *comes not back!* He has fallen a victim—to that fell temptation, which by legal sanction fills the land, and by which so many are ruined."

"But, my dear child, this temptation will not, I am confident, much longer exist. The signs of the times encourage me to hope that the hour of deliverance is near at hand; and I have no doubt that twenty years hence the business of rumselling will be regarded with as much abhorrence as we now regard the foreign slave-trade. Yes, my daughter, the day is coming—and I thank God for it—when all, in every path of life, will forsake this business, and frown upon it with indignation; and when it is left to the protection of the *manufacturer*, the *vender*, and the *drinker*, it cannot sustain itself for an hour."

In a few days Frank Hamilton returned, and at his home all was joy and gladness. The father, and mother, and brother, and sister, with sweet cordiality, gave themselves up to the pleasurable emotions which filled their hearts. They were anxious, of course, to hear from the youthful soldier the history of the scenes through which he had passed—from the beach of Corpus Christi to the halls of the Montezumas; and he appeared as anxious to gratify them.

Frank was sitting opposite the fine portrait of Dick Wilson, which Kate had removed from the parlor into the family sitting-room. As his eye fell upon it, an involuntary sigh escaped from him, and the quick ear of Kate heard it; and it assured her that he knew something of the history of him whom it represented. Frank proceeded to tell them the most startling of those incidents which are inseparable from war, and of which he was a witness. When he had finished, the evening was far spent, and Kate inquired if he had heard anything of Dick Wilson.

"Why," replied Frank, "what has put that into your head?"

She then told him what she knew and had seen of the family, and he replied:

"Kate, I am glad you know where they are—I know all about poor Dick."

"Well, Frank, do tell us something about his death."

"His death?" replied Frank. "He is not dead!"

"His mother says he is."

"Then, Kate, he has died within a month, for I saw him embarking for the States."

"His mother heard that he was dead!"

"It is a mistake. I suppose he landed here a few days since with the 11th regiment of infantry, and it is probable that he is yet in the city, as I requested him particularly to wait until I should arrive. I gave him the street and number of our residence, and requested him to call—though I did not expect that he would do it."

"Is this possible, Frank?"

"It is certain; and I have no doubt but in a few days you will have the pleasure of seeing him in this house. Col. C——, from Virginia, became very much attached to him; and I understand the Colonel is lying sick at the Irving House, and the probability is, that Dick is still with him, as I do not think that, under any circumstances, he would leave him in that situation."

"Then," replied Kate, "you have heard of his misfortunes?"

"Oh yes, my sister, I know all about them—we have been much together, and I know them from his own lips. I hope he may yet be saved; for with the single exception of excessive drinking, he is as noble as he ever was. When in Mexico, surrounded by the influence of a partial civilization, he was but slightly tempted; but how he may withstand the allurements of a Christian land—his native country—I cannot say! Kate, it is a humiliating acknowledgment, that one who has formed a relish for intoxicating drinks is less tempted to indulge it among the rude and half barbarous Mexicans, than among the enlightened citizens of this Christian land."

"When did you fall in with him?" inquired Kate.

"As soon as I landed at Corpus Christi, I entered the commissary office, to look about me, and see if I could ascertain the nature and character of war. I felt somewhat home-sick; the novelty was worn off. I had seen enough to convince me that this was no pleasure-trip, if Government did pay the expenses. It was the first time that a foreign sun had ever thrown its light on my path. As I entered this office, I found a good many persons, whose countenances indicated as much anxiety as mine. They were seated in every kind of order—on drums, boxes of muskets, cavalry swords, provisions, &c. As soon as I seated myself, my whole attention was arrested by a single countenance, and I became more interested from the fact that he would always turn from my gaze. I was seated on a pile of cavalry swords, directly opposite to him, and for the purpose of better satisfying myself, and giving it at the same time the appearance of indifference, I took up one of those swords, and twisted and turned it, until an observer would have thought that I could tell all about the instrument, when I was hardly conscious that I had it in my hand. The gray roundabout and pants make a great difference in one's appearance; and yet I was certain that in that care-worn face there was left an expression still, of one whom before that I had seen and known.

"A lieutenant soon entered, and this young man rose to answer his call. I watched him closely, as his pen glided over the paper in preparing the order, and then heard the lieutenant say, 'Dick, you would make a fine lawyer;' to which he merely replied, 'Do you think so?' After this, he turned his face to the window, and so remained for a few moments, and when he again turned to the desk, I saw the evidence of tears, which he vainly attempted to conceal. A very little thing, Kate, will waken up in the heart the most tender recollections, and I knew that something had touched a deep chord in that young man's heart, by which, perhaps, the cheerless memories of disappointments were revived afresh; but until that moment, it did not occur to me that it might be Dick Wilson. I immediately left the office—for I found that it would be impossible for me to satisfy myself without addressing him. As I was leaving, and had got some distance from the office, I turned and looked back, and as I did so I saw him standing at the door, with his arms folded across his breast, and I concluded at once that he had come there to look after me. There was something very imposing in his appearance, and what I could not determine, while sitting face to face with him, was now clear enough to my mind, and I was sure that that was Dick Wilson. In the early part of the evening, I was dispatched to the commissary office, with an order for blankets. This was the very opportunity for which I was seeking, and I went to the office at once, and produced my order. He immediately wrote another order, and handed it to me, saying,

"'This, Mr. Hamilton, will procure them for you.'

"I was startled by that voice, and the familiarity

with which my name was called, and I said at once, 'Is this my old friend Dick Wilson.'

"'Yes, Frank,' he replied, 'this is all that misfortune and the rumseller has left. I have had a hard time since we parted.'

"'But, Dick, what brought you here?'

"'The same that will drive many another poor fellow here, and which will make him anxious to give away his life, has brought me here—I mean the RUMSELLER—the *licensed* pest of civilization!'

"He asked me if I could spend the evening with him; to which I readily assented. After making the necessary arrangements for the comfort of those in my charge, I returned to the office, and at his request, we directed our steps towards a retired place on the bank of the river. Yes, Kate, there I was, on the banks of the Rio Grande, arm in arm with as noble a heart as ever beat, and as we had often been in earlier days. How differently situated! Then his hopes were promising and his heart light. Now he was oppressed with sadness.

"'Here, Frank,' said he, 'is a spot to which I have been in the habit of resorting almost nightly; and there is something in its very loneliness which endears it to me.'

"We seated ourselves, and after a pause in which I saw that he was making an effort to control his feelings, he said,—

"'Frank, you did not expect to meet me here, in this situation."

"'Dick,' said I, 'what has led you to this step?'

"'Ah! Frank, I cannot lead you through the terrific process by which I have been moulded into what you see before you. You see how much I am changed; and while I cannot now help it, I am far from being insensible to the fearful fact.'

"He related to me the severe misfortunes of his family, as well as his difficulties with Judge L——, and his departure from the village of B——, and then continued,—

"'But, oh! Frank, I did not intend to fall. I was disappointed—broken down—cast to the very earth. I knew the strength of those hopes which were clinging to me; but in that hour, when, to me, my path seemed to be hopelessly dark, and the sun of my life seemed to have gone down to rise no more, I availed myself of the rumseller's *consolation!* Ah! yes, it was then, in an hour of mental unconsciousness, that I fell—I am afraid, *hopelessly* and *forever!* And, O God! in that delirious moment, what did I entail upon myself and weeping, heart-broken innocence, in the persons of those who were spared in the wreck of my home? Ah! yes, I am sure that if this temptation had not been in my path, that I could have survived the shock of that disappointment; but it was in my path, and I fell, as thousands have fallen. From the moment I tasted the poisoned chalice, I felt the beginning of certain ruin. Sometimes I had hope, but it was dim and indistinct. I knew not where to turn or whither to fly, and bade farewell to those whom every moment since I have loved better than my life. Since that time I have been a wanderer, without any object; nor could I picture to you the scenes and the sufferings through which I have passed. Often as I have seen the slave dragging out his weary life, have I wished that I had been born a slave! I have wished that the power of thought could be silenced within me, and that I might forget myself in the grave. After wandering about from place to place, and finding my health rapidly declining, it occurred to me that if I should leave the United States, I might, after all, recover. It was not without an effort that I expatriated myself. It was not because I did not love my native land, but because I felt that the *rumseller* had the power to mould my destiny as he pleased, and lead me through the broad streets of my native land to the base of his sacrificial altar! Oh! Frank, talk about slavery! The subjugation of the body is absolute tyranny; but it cannot compare with the absolute and cruel subjugation to which the rumseller reduces his victims. It stings sharper, deeper, than the driver's whip; for it strikes both the body and the mind, and with maddened fury drives them together into the cheerless vortex of desolation! I sometimes hope to withstand, in this half-civilized region, the few temptations which beset me; but at home they were so constant and so strong, I could not resist them. This is all that brought me here; but if I must die by his hand, I would rather be at home. I came here only to avoid a power sanctioned by *American law*, and which is the most despotic of any on earth. Five weeks ago I was standing on the wharf at New Orleans, looking with anxiety at a vessel which was preparing to leave for this place. I was without money and without friends, surrounded by strangers, and sixteen hundred miles from the place of my nativity. I knew not what to do; for in the streets of that city I had seen hundreds whose appearance showed them to be forlorn and friendless as myself, and most of whom, by their countenances, indicated that they were familiar with crime. At that moment I was trying to solve a fearful problem. I was deciding between two evils, which to me appeared of equal magnitude: whether to live and permit the rumseller to exercise his authority over me, or to commit suicide.'

"'Why, Dick,' said I, 'surely you did not think of that!'

"'Yes I did, Frank. You may think it strange, but I tell you, the *rumseller* can make one think and do almost anything. I found myself, before I was aware of it, at the door of the custom house, and still undetermined as to which would be the best for me. I was standing here, when a gentleman came to my side, who, for some moments, eyed me intently. To me, his gaze was exceedingly painful. I did not know but he might be a civil officer, who was in search of suspected persons, and perhaps was about to fix upon me, as one having the appearance of a criminal. I knew that I had the rumseller's *mark* upon me; and among strangers, I was aware that this mark was fatal. They generally think—but they misjudge when they do so—that the victim is as accomplished in wickedness as the destroyer. Even in my forlorn situation, I could not endure such a suspicion. I had slept in the open air, on the banks of the Ohio and the Mississippi. I had gone for days without food, and this I had endured; but to be suspected of crime, I could not endure it; and immediately inquired,—

"'Do you see anything about me, sir, to call for such close observation?'

"'If I am not mistaken,' he replied, 'your name is Wilson.'

"'That is my name, sir,' I answered, 'but where have you seen me?'

"'I saw you,' he replied, 'on the evening of the day on which your hopes were crushed. I never saw you before, nor since, until this moment; but I should have known you in any place, or under any circumstances. I see, Mr. Wilson, what your misfortunes are, and anything that I can do to alleviate them, will be done cheerfully. What do you want to do?'

"'I want,' I replied, 'first of all, to escape the temptations of the rumseller; for, until I can do this, it is in vain for me to attempt to do anything.'

"'I am sorry,' he replied, 'to see you under such influences.'

"'I told him that I believed that it was utterly impossible to escape them, and that I thought it would be my best plan to go to Mexico—that possibly I might be safer there.'

"'Then,' said he, 'as your constitution is evidently too feeble to go into the army, I think I can procure you a situation in the commissary office, at Corpus Christi.' After some conversation with a gentleman named Nicholson, the business was immediately arranged, and a passage secured for me on board of the vessel to which I had referred. Since that time, I have been here; and while under other circumstances it would afford me pleasure to see acquaintances, as it is, I have tried to avoid it.

"'I knew you, Frank, as soon as you entered the office, and saw, in a moment, that there was still something about me that you recognized; but I did not think that you would be able to identify me, until that young lieutenant called me Dick. Ah! my friend, you cannot tell what burning recollections your appearance aroused within me, and yet, if you had not recognized me, I think you would never have been conscious that, in a land of strangers, you had been in the same room with your *fallen friend!*'

"After we had conversed for some time about many things, I asked him if he had given up all hope of recovering himself, to which he replied:

"'Oh no! Frank, I hope not; I think if I can endure this climate for three years, that I may then return to the United States with safety, and if it were not for the *rumseller*, I should return to-morrow.'

"I found Dick kind, gentlemanly, and warm-hearted as ever. It was necessary for me, a few days after this interview, to proceed to Fort Brown, and we parted again, after I had obtained a promise from him to write to me often.

"About a month after this time, I received a letter from him, dated '*Charity Hospital, New Orleans*,' in which he informed me of his situation. He said that, finding himself unable to endure the climate, and being assured that he must die, he was anxious, if possible, to reach his mother, and die in her arms; but that on landing, it was necessary for him to be taken to the hospital, where he expected to die. He concluded by saying, 'Frank, if you live to return home, I have a dying request—search out my poor mother, and tell her all you know of me.'

"I think it was about six weeks after the date of this letter, that I was sent to Corpus Christi, on business; and just as I was about to leave, a gentleman said to me, 'You can tell *Rough and Ready* that there is a regiment of volunteers from Louisiana, under command of General Gaines, expected to land here to-day.'

"My return was not urgent, and I determined to wait and see them; and sure enough, in a few hours the vessels came in sight, and soon were near enough to distinguish the gray uniforms with which the decks seemed to be crowded. Here, to my surprise, I met Dick Wilson again. He was feeble, and hardly able to bear the weight of his musket. His spirits were low, and conversational powers, which were of the first order, seemed to have left him almost entirely. I did everything in my power, during that day and the next, to rouse him, but I found it impossible to do so. We parted again, hoping soon to be brought together by the concentration of all the troops in Mexico into one army. This, however, did not occur; and I soon learned that some illegality in the formation of the regiment, under Gen. Gaines, had caused it to be disbanded, and that many of the men who composed it had returned to New Orleans.

"Here, again, I lost all traces of Dick, and although I inquired often of those who were continually coming into the service, I could find no one who knew anything of him. I could not forget him; and while I sympathized with him, and wept over his condition,

I felt that his fall was inevitable. I knew the rumseller's power over his victim, when once he had succeeded in making a beginning; but, Kate, until I met Dick Wilson, I never fully realized his complete despotism! Here I had an opportunity to see it. I knew him before the rumseller had touched his constitution, his character, or his hopes. We had read Horace together—together we had admired the beauties of Longinus, and wept over the death of Socrates. In all the pleasures and duties of a student's life, we had been together, and but a few years—short and changeful—had passed away, since on the same platform we had received the parting benediction of the venerable president. Then he was everything that was noble; now he appeared to be hanging indifferently from the frowning precipice which overlooks the chasm of despair!

"When I met him first, at Corpus Christi, I had hope; but when I met him in the Louisiana regiment, I saw the unmistakable impressions of the rumseller's work, fostering a disease which was preying deeper than any other upon his constitution. I had given him up, and expected to see his face no more."

CHAPTER XXII.

THE LOST FOUND.

"Fly from the tempter,
Who has led thee astray
From the high aspirations
Of life's early day:
Ere the hopes of thy mother
Have faded in gloom,
And her gray hairs, dishonored,
Are laid in the tomb."

FRANK had related the circumstances under which, for the third time, he had met with Dick Wilson in Mexico, as well as the hopes which he still entertained for his safety.

"Do you really think," said the good Mrs. Hamilton, who was impatient with interest, "that he has landed here?"

"Oh, I am sure of it," said Frank. "I saw him embark for New York. I'll show you in the morning—mind if I don't, mother."

"God be praised!" said the tender-hearted old lady. "We may be able to restore him to his heart-broken mother yet, and this will be like giving life to the dead. My son, if you find him in the morning, you must bring him home with you. Have his trunk brought directly here."

"His trunk!" replied Frank. "You mean his knapsack."

"Well, Frank, bring all he has, be it much or little, and we will induce him to remain with us as long as possible, and we will try every way to strengthen his good resolution."

The hour was late, and Frank found it impossible to answer satisfactorily half the inquiries of Kate, and in a pleasant way he said to her:

"I would advise you to exercise your usual caution, and not to fall in love with Dick before you see him. You may be wonderfully disappointed. And pointing to the portrait, he said: "You must not base your judgment on that, for he is greatly changed."

In the morning, Mrs. Hamilton, Kate and Frank were all in a hurry; and even Mr. Hamilton, who was remarkable for regularity, betrayed some slight wandering from his usual course. When the time for family prayer arrived, Mr. Hamilton offered up a fervent petition in Dick's behalf, and prayed that the same God who had restored the long lost Joseph to his father, would also restore this young man to his widowed mother.

"Now," said Mrs. Hamilton to Frank, as they were seated at the breakfast table, "do you think you can find him this morning?"

"I think I can, mother, if he is in the city. He may have gone to Virginia with Col. C——; but I do not think that he has yet been able to leave. I am glad, mother, that you are so much interested in him, for it too often falls to the lot of those who are unfortunate, that they meet only indifference and inattention."

"I am interested, my son, to save, if it be possible, Richard Wilson. The mother, the brother, and the sister, who are now weeping for him, did not willingly surrender him to the rumseller. If we can now restore him safe to his dear ones, it will be doing a work for God and humanity. That is what we live for, and no nobler end can we hope to attain."

After breakfast, Frank was soon in the street, making his way towards the Irving House, where, he had heard, Col. C—— had taken rooms, and where he expected to find Dick, if he was still in the city.

"Who knows," thought he to himself, "what may be the result of all this? I thank my parents that they loved me and watched for me more than for the vanities of life. What I am, I owe chiefly to their judicious care. In three years I have met Dick Wilson in almost all imaginable situations of suffering, and far from home. We have sat down together to talk about the past, and then he spoke with a mournful eloquence of its melancholy recollections. I have heard him say, while sitting under the shade of the same ancient elms where Cortez is said to have offered his human sacrifices, that the rumseller had so transformed him, that he felt more at home on the soil which had drunk the blood of thousands of semi-barbarians, at the hand of the Spanish robber, than he did in his native land."

With such thoughts as these revolving in his mind, Frank Hamilton entered the Irving House, and going at once to the register, found the names of Col. C—— and Richard Wilson registered together. This was a matter of rejoicing to him, and he hastened at once to their room. As he entered, Dick rose to greet him, and Col. C—— could not help admiring the pure friendship which these young men manifested for each other. Frank had formed a slight acquaintance with Col. C—— in Mexico, and consequently did not need an introduction. When he entered the room, the colonel and Dick were engaged in conversation, which had been laid aside merely for the time, and the greeting over, Col. C—— continued:

"Mr. Hamilton, I have just been making a proposition to Mr. Wilson, to accompany me to Virginia, and there enter upon the practice of law. I have offered to him, if he will consent to do so, every facility, both in money and influence, which may be necessary for his success; and allow me to say, that if the beauty of our lovely country is marred by the existence of slavery, it is not like yours, blackened by the foul curse of alcohol, which does more to blight and blacken, to waste and wither, to degrade and stultify, than slavery in its most revolting form."

"Frank," said Dick, "I have almost made up my mind to go and try my fortune in the 'Old Dominion.' What do you think of it?"

"Do you think, Dick, that you will be better off there?"

"Yes, I should not be tempted there as I am here, and if I can be sure of that, I would like to go." After a moment's pause, he continued, with much feeling: "I may as well go there as anywhere. There are for me some precious spots upon the earth. There are graves I should like to visit; and there are living ones, the sight of whom, if it were only once more, would gladden my heart; but where they are I do not know."

"My dear friend, death has not disturbed the little flock. They are all living and well."

"Have you seen them? Do you know where they are? Who has seen them? Tell me, for heaven's sake," said he, while intense agitation was visible in his countenance.

"My sister has seen them within a few weeks, and they were well."

"Is it possible? Well, thank God, I may then see them again. This is more than I expected. Frank, you have always been to me the harbinger of good."

For a moment he was silent, but this unexpected

intelligence overcame him so suddenly, that he could not restrain his tears. At length he continued:

"Col. C——, I had almost concluded to go with you to Virginia, but I must give it up. I must go at once to those dear ones who are looking for me. They know in all probability, that I went to Mexico, and as the living are all returning, they will be looking for me too. Oh, yes! I can almost see the wild anticipations of their hearts, and feel the clasp of their arms about my neck. I am happy in the thought, that yet the warm breath of my mother may dissipate the fevered phantoms of my brain. Ah! but when they see me they will weep, and those are fearful tears which a mother pours out when compelled to look upon the victim of a rumseller in the person of her son."

"Richard, your mother is not looking for you."

"Ah! and has she cast me off? If she knew the sufferings through which I have passed, she would never do it."

"Oh, no, she has heard, and believes, that you were killed at the battle of Monterey."

"Then, I must undeceive her at once. Col. C——, you have been my friend. You have watched over me as a brother since the day I entered your command, in the city of Wheeling, until this day, and if it were not for the intelligence which Mr. Hamilton has brought me, I should go with you; but as it is, I cannot."

"Mr. Wilson," said Col. C——, "I am glad to see you manifest such feeling. It increases my friendship for you and my interest in you. It is best for you, however, to look at this matter free from all excitement; for you are now placed in a position in which you ought to act with remarkable caution. When you go home and have seen those who are still dear to you, what will you do? They and you are poor, and when the burst of joy and sorrow, which will attend your meeting, is over, will it not be succeeded by the cheerless vision of poverty rising before you, to chill you into despair again, and drive you to the rumseller's den? If you will go with me, I will provide you a home for your family, and the means to bring them to Virginia; and there, surrounded by new associations, and men who would not strive with each other to excel in making the child a drunkard, you will be comparatively safe."

"You are too kind, my friend," said he, with evident emotion.

"Never mind that, Wilson," replied Col. C——, "for kindness, if it is genuine, always brings its reward. I will do it cheerfully, as for a brother."

"Then, Col. C——, I will go. I would go to the ends of the earth to escape the ruin which I constantly fear."

Frank admired the noble Virginian, who, although a soldier, had still a heart filled with rich and gener ous sympathy, prompting him to offers of kindness, which would have been as readily fulfilled as they were cheerfully made. He, too, felt that he had a claim, and that it would be necessary for him to institute it at once, and accordingly, in the presence of Col. C——, he informed Dick that he had expected him to spend a few days with him before leaving the city, giving him to understand that it was the particular request of the family that he should do so. It was known to Frank that Col. C—— was about to repair to Washington city in a few days, and it was soon agreed that Dick could spend a few weeks in New York previous to leaving for Virginia. These arrangements being made, Dick stepped into another room to make preparations for accompanying Frank to his home, and while he was absent the colonel said:

"Mr. Hamilton, I feel very much interested in that young man, and would be willing to do anything within the range of possibility to save him. If he can be reformed, there is no honorable situation in life which he would not grace, and no position which he would not adorn."

At this moment Dick entered the room, genteelly dressed, and Frank involuntarily exclaimed:

"Why, I declare, you are very much improved in appearance, and bring 'old times' vividly to my mind."

As soon as they were fairly in the street, Dick said:

"Is it possible, Frank, that your sister has seen my family? And what must she think of me?"

"Yes, my dear friend, she has mingled her tears with those who love you, and understands the cause of your being brought to this sad state. You need have no fears, Dick, in entering my father's house, for they will receive you kindly, and do everything in their power to make you happy."

The conversation continued, and before Frank was aware of it, his home stood before him. They entered, and Frank, after seating his friend in the parlor, left him, and went to the room where his mother and Kate were. As soon as Mrs. Hamilton saw her son, and perceived that there was no unusual expression of joy in his countenance, she said:

"Ah! my son, it is as I expected: either death or the rumseller has anticipated you. You didn't find him. Well, I was fearful that something had happened to him."

"Well, mother," said Frank, "you are not often mistaken, I confess; but you are this time. I have fortunately found him; and he is now waiting you in the parlor."

"Is it possible?" said Mrs. Hamilton and her daughter in the same breath.

"Come and see," said Frank.

They entered the parlor, and Dick rose to meet them. His appearance was much better than they had anticipated, for they expected to have seen more distinctly the ravages of dissipation.

"We are glad to see you, Mr. Wilson," said Mrs. Hamilton, "and happy to make you welcome to our home. There," said she, pointing to his portrait, which Kate on that morning had replaced in the parlor, "for several years you have ornamented our parlor, and we hope now that you will feel yourself surrounded by the freedom of home."

"Thank you, Mrs. Hamilton," said Dick, and then added, as he looked at his portrait, and remembered the scenes through which he had passed, "This is a reminiscence of my better days."

Soon Mr. Hamilton came in, and, without an introduction, gave him a shake of the hand which told the cordiality with which he meet him more eloquently than his lips could have done, and then said:

"It seems to me, Mr. Wilson, that I have seen your face before."

"Yes, sir, you have," said he; "when the troops of the 11th regiment were landing a few days since, you inquired of me concerning your son."

"Upon my word," replied Mr. Hamilton, "it is so. You ought to have made yourself known, and come directly to my house."

"I had not permission to leave, until the regiment was disbanded, and, besides, the indisposition of Col. C——, who has been a very warm friend of mine, made it necessary that I should remain with him."

"Yes, yes, Mr. Wilson, always be grateful, and never forsake a friend in the time of his need. I would have been very glad to have had the Colonel here. Do you suppose he would be able to come and spend the evening with us?"

"I think he would be able and happy to do so," replied Dick.

"Then," said the old gentleman, with his unpretending suavity of manner, "we must have him here."

Orders were immediately issued to have the carriage in readiness. It required no lengthy argument to persuade the Colonel to accompany them, and he was soon in the carriage with them. He was manifestly in feeble health; but yet, according to the true Virginian style, he did his part to make everything pleasant, and when he entered Mr. Hamilton's house, he seemed at once to be at home. The evening was spent in hearing and rehearsing the life-like pictures of the scenes in which these young men had mingled, and the conflicts through which they had passed, with a continuous application from Mr. Hamilton, of the goodness of God, in saving their lives, and bringing them back to their native land.

After tea, Kate favored them with some excellent music, and to those young men it seemed to be doubly sweet, since for several years they had heard no music but the shrill music of the march, or the startling clangor of the battle-field, as it rose toward heaven, the harbinger of blood. At the request of Dick, she played with remarkable effect, "The Dead at Monterey," and immediately followed it with the cheering strains—"Home, home again from a foreign shore." When the last echoes of those strains were dying away, the glistening tear was seen in every eye—they could not be hidden, for they were the truth-telling oracles of their hearts, and told how the heart felt at the kindling recollections of home.

When the evening had been spent and enjoyed to a late hour, the colonel rose to depart, and thanking them for their kindness, said pleasantly,—

"Miss Hamilton, I am going to leave Mr. Wilson in your care for a few days, and hold you responsible for his safe delivery in Virginia."

"Very well," said Kate, blushing, "I will try to have him delivered to you safely."

Dick had spent a number of days with the family, and our hero could not doubt the genuineness of the spirit which he observed to be the governing principle of everything about him.

One day he ventured to inquire of Kate, in reference to his family, and the circumstances in which she had found them. She replied to his inquiries in a frank and feeling manner, and added,—

"Mr. Wilson, they will be rejoiced to see you. I

would like to share in the joys of that meeting, and I have been thinking of making a proposition to Frank, that we would accompany you home."

Dick was nearly overcome—"Home! home!" he ejaculated, "what a spell—what a subduing power there is in that word! But as yet, I must not see that spot—my exile is not completed. Oh! for a light to illuminate the darkness, and strength to overcome the perils which yet lie between myself and my mother's fond embrace. My way has been dark and gloomy, almost as the valley and shadow of death. I am going to Virginia. Col. C—— has made me an offer which I could not possibly refuse."

This, to Kate, was evidently unexpected, and, although unintentionally, she betrayed much surprise at his decision.

"Miss Hamilton," said he, "I am satisfied that it is best for me go."

"Perhaps you are right."

"I think I am," he replied, "inasmuch as it will afford me an immediate opportunity, not only to find a situation for myself but also for my little family, and this ought to be with me the great consideration."

After spending two weeks very pleasantly in their society, and feeling renewed in health and spirits, he intimated his intention on the next day to leave for Virginia. The family had become attached to him, and this announcement seemed to come prematurely.

They were loth to part with him, and if it had not been for the pressing nature of his engagement, he would not have gone; but he was sure that the offer made to him was prompted by kindness, and he did not feel at liberty to neglect it. During his stay, the whole family had done everything in their power to strengthen him against the insidious snares of the rum-seller. Mr. and Mrs. Hamilton had spoken to him as they would have done to a son, whom they tenderly loved, and were anxious to save from the most dread ful calamity; and Frank and Kate had done every-thing which they could have done for a brother, and they felt themselves to be richly repaid in the lively manifestations of gratitude, which were too plain to be mistaken, in every look and action of Dick.

The time of his departure came, and with tears they bade each other good-bye, and in doing so, Mr. Hamilton put a purse into his hand, saying—"God bless and keep you my dear young friend; may you be able to withstand all temptation, however disguised. Oh! beware of the wine cup;" and Dick was again a wanderer, in search of a retreat from the luring tempter.

CHAPTER XXIII.

THE EFFECT.—THE CAUSE.—THE REMEDY.

"Ah! Misery, how I feel thy power!
Long have I labored to elude thy sway,
But 'tis enough, for I resist no more."

THE destiny of the individual is often irrevocably fixed, who has formed a relish for the intoxicating cup. With him it is usually true,

"That one false step forever blasts *his* fame."

Mr. Hamilton greatly feared that this would prove true in regard to Wilson, and that, goaded on, as he constantly was, by the promptings of an insatiable appetite, he would be very likely to fall into the snares so thickly set in his way.

"I regret," said he to his family, as Dick Wilson left, "that there are so many dram shops scattered all over the land. But for these, this young man, with his firm resolutions to reform, would have little difficulty in effecting it. But as it is, he is constantly tempted to drink, go where he may; and however firm his purpose, it will be marvellous indeed if he long adheres to it."

"Father," said Kate, "I do not think so now. I had many pleasant conversations with him during his stay with us, and I am sure he will be able to withstand the temptations of those men who had nearly accomplished his ruin."

"I wish, my child," replied Mr. Hamilton, "that I was sure of it; but I am not."

"Don't you think, father," said Kate, "that he wishes to escape?"

"Of that, my daughter, there can be no doubt. All, no matter how degraded, who have become addicted to intemperance, regret it, and in their sober moments often weep bitterly over the desperation of their condition. They would abstain, but cannot. Their resolutions are strong enough, but they have not the power to carry them out. This I consider to be the case with Wilson. He wishes, he hopes, he may even be determined to reform; but he is not master of himself. His perverted taste, his burning thirst for the destroying beverage when excited by its presence, will overcome the calm teachings of reason and judgment, and he is, I fear, destined to be their slave. Yes, I consider his situation one of imminent peril, and the chances are a thousand to one against him. If he escape, his life must be a constant struggle. His watchfires must never go out, nor, for one moment, must the sentinel leave his post."

For many days after this young man left Mr. Hamilton's house, he was the subject of their daily conversation, and his ability to withstand temptation was thoroughly canvassed. Kate invariably maintained that she believed him to be beyond the rumseller's power, and often did she speculate upon the nature of the happiness which would visit Mrs. Wilson's lonely and cheerless dwelling, when tidings, as from the grave, should be borne to her, that the lost was found —the erring reclaimed—the son saved! Gradually but reluctantly, the cherished hopes of that family grew fainter and fainter. A month had passed away, and not a line from Wilson had yet been received, and all but Kate seemed forced to the conclusion that again he had fallen.

One morning Frank entered the room where Kate and her mother were sitting, and laid on the table an open letter, saying as he did so, with as much calmness as possible—

"That is from Dick Wilson."

"I knew he would stand firm," said Kate, while a flash of joy passed over her features.

"Read it," said Frank.

Kate took up the letter, and in an instant the truth flashed upon her mind, and laying it upon the table, she exclaimed—"Is it possible?" and left the room in tears. At the request of Mrs. Hamilton, Frank read to her the letter, which was as follows:

"*Dear Frank:* The rumseller has triumphed again, and I have fallen hopelessly beneath his stroke—fallen, to rise no more. They have made this poor life of mine an eventful one. You and your dear family have been very kind to me. You have tried to save me, but ah! in vain. A few years have made a great change in my character and destiny, such as I never anticipated. You knew me when my prospects in life were enviable, and you met me in the land of strangers, and there saw my misery, and you have known how I struggled against the ruin which beset me. I am passing away rapidly. I feel it bitterly. I had a constitution which for a time defied excesses, but at last it has given way, and now lies in ruin. I had hoped to look once more into my mother's face, and see her smile. I thought that once again I might be permitted to pronounce the names of brother and sister in the presence of those who gather with their griefs to my mother's side. That hope is dissipated forever. Oh! how I have thought of them, and longed for them. I have sat down by the camp-fire, on the plains of Mexico, to think of them when every eye, save that of the sentinel, was closed, and enjoyed sweet pleasure in the anticipation of a return.

"Ah! that hope will never be realized; for its last green leaf has withered and died, in the bleak wastes of my heart. Oh! it is sad to be a wanderer from home and its joys; but it is sadder yet to feel the burning thirst which consumes me, and to be powerless to resist its importunities. Oh! Frank, how often do I wish that I could commence anew the journey of life—that I could only be free from the snare which is leading me so rapidly to ruin. I now see the emphatic force of those truths which I derided at the time—that for the youth, or the young man, there is no safety, unless he inscribes upon his banner the motto, 'Touch not, taste not, handle not.' If I had done this, before the cursed taste was formed, I should have been spared the bitter pangs which I have been doomed to suffer. But, unfortunately for me, I thought that the exhilarating effect of wine, so far from being injurious, was positively beneficial. This was the sentiment in my father's family, and of the circle in which I moved in earlier life; and to this I owe the bitter scourge which now lashes me with such relentless fury. I never drank to intoxication until that fatal night, after my rejection at the village of B——. Yet I must say, that after taking the resolution, upon the death of my father, to stop drinking, I had constantly felt an almost irrepressible desire to continue a practice, the influence of which I knew not, until I sought to discontinue it. I had supposed that I could stop at any time, and without any difficulty; but no one can tell what a struggle I have had, save those who have been similarly situated. I have resolved, and re-resolved that I would never again touch the fatal glass; but when my eye rested upon it, and it was everywhere in my way, I was fired with such a perfect phrenzy of desire, that I could not resist. Frank, you will, I doubt not, think of me often; but I hope you will not be too severe upon my memory. Remember the *causes* of my ruin. Though I greatly erred in closing my ears to the kindly warnings which were given me, and in suffering myself to be borne thoughtlessly along by the social influences around me; yet I must plead in extenuation of my guilt, the great force of those influences, and my ignorance at the time, of the effect which they were producing. My fondness for society, and *the place* where I sought its enjoyment, laid the foundation of my ruin. That was done, though I did not know it, before I was eighteen years of age. The DRINKING SALOON, oh, that such a place had never existed—'*that was the rock on which I split;*' and the thought of its effect upon me is so paralyzing, that I can only add, that this is probably the last that you will ever hear of your early and grateful friend,

"RICHARD WILSON."

When Mr. Hamilton came in, the letter was handed to him, and he perused it carefully. It was evident that he was not disappointed in the result; indeed, he would have thought it miraculous if this young man, under the circumstances, had triumphed, but with such a conviction pressing upon his mind, he did not say, "It is no use to try—it won't do any good." But his was the language of the freeman, the Christian, and the philanthropist:

"I am not disappointed," he said; "this is what I feared, and just what will be found true in ninety-nine out of every hundred similar cases. While we should do what we can to restore those who are already fallen, we should, at the same time, remember, that in the case of the intemperate, 'an *ounce* of prevention is worth *many pounds* of cure;' and if we expect success to crown our efforts, we must seek the *causes*, and find and correct *them*, and the *effects* will of course cease. I have long been thoroughly impressed with the conviction, that if we should strike out of existence all the tippling houses of the land, that we should then have reached the fountain; and its streams, numerous and polluting as they now are, would be dried up thoroughly and perpetually. To effect this, stringent enactments are necessary, and I look forward with confidence to the time when the horrors of intemperance will be matters of history rather than the daily observation of all our citizens."

CHAPTER XXIV.

THE MISSION OF LOVE.

"For the poor make no new friends,
But oh, they love the better far,
The few our Father sends."

THE letter which imparted to the Hamilton family the intelligence of Dick Wilson's fall, brought also a smarting pang to each of their hearts; and gave to them a new illustration of the entire impotence of the best resolution, in contending with the temptations with which the rumseller besets the path of his victims.

They had hoped—fondly hoped, that those erring feet had been turned effectually from the path to ruin, and that he, in whose welfare they were so deeply interested, might yet be borne a victor to the threshold of his mother's door, and enter it again, amidst those mingling emotions of love and sadness which always hail the wanderer's return.

They were disappointed, however, and Dick Wilson had fallen again into the hands of an unrelenting enemy, whose cry is, *give*, GIVE, GIVE!

One evening, soon after the arrival of this letter, Mr. Hamilton's family were assembled around their quiet fireside, to talk over matters and arrange plans, in which the future comfort of Mrs. Wilson and her family could be secured.

"Something must be done," said Mr. H., with his accustomed cheerfulness of manner, "for the happiness of these suffering, yet, in this matter, sinless ones; who, to our knowledge, must now cease to hope, and who can expect nothing but sorrow in the future history of their son and brother. God send the day speedily when an enlightened and correct public sentiment, shall frown this horrid business of selling liquid poison, into the pit of darkness, whence it had its origin!"

Mr. Hamilton had just introduced the subject to his listening and delighted family, when Mr. W——, a princely *rum importer* of the city, was announced by the servant.

"Show him into this room," said Mr. H., whose orders were immediately obeyed.

After a few commonplace remarks, this gentleman, with unusual affability, said to Mr. H., "I came in, sir, to borrow of you five thousand dollars. I have made a very large purchase this afternoon, at a forced sale, of an entire cargo of the best foreign liquors. In fact, I suppose I got them at less than half their value. It's a fine speculation."

"I cannot accommodate you, sir," said Mr. Hamilton, frankly.

"Well," said Mr. W——, a little confused by the unexpected reply, "I thought that you would be as likely to have that amount of money on hand as any other person, and I knew that if such were the fact I could get it."

"You are mistaken, sir,—I have the money, and if you proposed to make any honorable investment, you should have it without a word; but into such a channel as you propose to put it, not a dollar of my money shall ever go, with my knowledge and consent. I am sorry, sir, that you do not know me better."

"Ah! very well, sir—no harm done, of course," replied Mr. W——; "but I can't, for the life of me, see why you should be so particular on this subject. This, sir, is purely a matter of business, and I should like to know what law could hold you accountable?"

"The law of God, sir—a *law* which neither you nor myself can violate with impunity. Ah! sir, the record of many a demijohn, cask, and barrel which you have sent out, and in which communities have been deluged with misery, will meet you in judgment. You say that you cannot see why I should be so particular on this subject. I think I can place you in a position where you can see, unless you are willingly blind.

"Can you, sir, look into the face of the dying drunkard, whose hopes for earth and heaven your business has enveloped in the very pall of despair?—can you look upon a reality of this kind without feeling that you stand in intimate and active connection with a business which is cursing humanity and defying Omnipotence? Oh! sir, I weep for that man who, in this day, can continue this business; and who has so well-nigh given away as worthless the last redeeming element in human nature. Yes, I do pity the man who, in reference to this *fathomless* and *shoreless* wickedness, is pulseless and motionless amidst the palpitations of an age trembling with the footsteps of advancing Justice."

Before this honest broadside of truth, the princely rumseller cowered; and soon Mr. Hamilton, relieved of his presence, was alone with his family.

"Father," said Kate, "I'll go bail that man will never trouble you again, either for money or influence, to put into the liquor traffic."

"Yes, that's a fact father," said Frank, "he understood you. It won't take him an hour or two, after he arrives at home, to learn your position, and he can't help but respect you for your candor. Many men who make the same professions that you do, would have acted differently; and would have strained every point to quiet their consciences and accommodate him; and then he, with a rumseller's generosity, would have said to himself, and chuckled over it too, what a heartless hypocrite *that man* is!"

"My children," said Mr. Hamilton, "there is nothing which these persons dread so much, and no agency which so effectually paralyzes them, as an honest expression of opinion, maintained by corresponding action. Their work is the work of darkness—they shun the light, and even now they tremble in anticipation of the people's voice of retribution."

"Come, come," said Mrs. Hamilton, "this won't do, this hour has been set apart for a sacred purpose, and we must not permit the shadow of the rumseller to darken it, and make us forget the labor of love which we owe to that suffering family. It is now settled that their hope is lost, and not a moment must be wasted in sending them relief."

"I will go," said Kate, "and bring Eliza Wilson home with me; and if she comes, I will promise to love and treat her as a sister."

"That won't do, my daughter," said Mrs. Hamilton, "the family must not be broken up. How do you think they could endure a parting of that kind? You can't have my consent to that arrangement, Kate."

"Let me settle the difficulty," said Mr. Hamilton. "I am for having the whole family come, and remain with us; we have plenty of room, and a good will in the bargain."

"That removes the difficulty," said Frank, "and chimes with my notions exactly. I did everything that I could for poor Dick, while I had an opportunity, and so did you Kate:—Now let us show to his afflicted family, that we really loved him. We have room enough, and heart enough, to make them as comfortable as they can be made in this world."

This was the very thing for which, from the day Dick Wilson left their door, Mr. and Mrs. Hamilton had been preparing; and it was a pleasure to them to witness the cheerful spirit with which their children concurred in the arrangement.

It was determined that, in a few days, Frank and Kate should set out for the village of R——, where Kate had seen them a few months before, and extend to them, and press them to accept, the invitation to accompany them to their city home.

They were intent upon their errand of mercy, and at the appointed time they were on their way to R——, at the outskirts of which Mrs. Wilson resided. A few hours' ride brought them to the place; and as they were leaving the cars, Kate pointed out to Frank the house in which she lived, and the antiquated grave-yard from which she had previously made her observations.

They entered the hotel near the depôt, when Kate proposed to her brother that they should go up and take a seat on the balcony; where, free from interruption, they might have a few moments to themselves, in thinking over the best way to introduce their delicate mission.

They were scarcely seated before their attention

was arrested by a small funeral procession which was just entering the grave-yard. There were but few in that train, and they principally women; and it was at once plain, from the handful of followers and the uncovered coffin, that the tenant was one taken from the humblest walks of life; and for whom there were but few to mourn.

"Let us wait here," said Kate, "until that solemn rite is over."

In the whole ceremony there was an unbecoming haste, and soon the last shovel-full of earth was pressed upon the bosom of the sleeper; and all but two—a little boy and a young woman—were on their way from the spot.

The two who still lingered by the side of that grave, seemed to have no disposition to leave it—they seemed to have laid in that cold, damp bed, a casket, in which the light and the life of all their love and hope had been treasured.

"Ah!" said Kate to her brother, whose eyes were filled with tears, "whoever these sorrowing ones may be, their hearts must be desolate indeed."

At length they rose from the spot where they had seated themselves, and placing a stone at the head, and another at the foot of the grave, they turned slowly away.

"Kate," said Frank, whose eyes were following those stricken ones who, hand in hand, were just passing out of the enclosure, "I thought that I had seen the rites of sepulture in all their forms, and felt the varied emotions which necessarily spring from them —but I have been mistaken. I have seen the city funeral, with imposing rites, of almost every class. I have stood by, when a hundred of my countrymen in a foreign land, mangled and torn by the havoc of war, were thrown into a common grave; but they never moved me as does that spectacle."

"See," said Kate, whose eye had been keeping pace with the mourners, "they are entering Mrs. Wilson's house,—my fears are realized—Eliza and little Harry are the mourners, and they are alone in their grief. Let us go to them at once, and share with them the sorrows of this bitter hour. How prophetic were her words, when she said to me, 'the sun of the coming summer will shine upon the grave of the broken-hearted Mary Wilson!'"

A few moments brought them to the door, about which the echoes of that sweet old song were lingering when first she entered it. It was a November day; and everything was chill and bleak without—a fitting emblem of the hearts of those within that humble enclosure.

As they entered, they found the first room tenantless, and Kate at once led the way into a little apartment adjoining, and then the truth was read at a glance. Mrs. Wilson was dead, and her two orphan children, unconscious of the presence of any one, were there alone in their grief. "My poor little brother," said Eliza, "what is to become of us now? Oh! how our dear mother loved us, and how she struggled to keep us with her! I am afraid we must part now. Oh how desolate has the rumseller's agency left us!"

"Fear not, sweet girl," was whispered in her ear by the sympathetic Kate; and the mourner turned as if an angel's voice had been commissioned to bring consolation to their hearts.

There are scenes, the spirit and the melancholy beauty of which, will forever elude both the tongue and the pen, and leave that description which would interfere with their sanctity lame in the extreme—and we pass this hour, in which broken hearts were made whole again, by the angelic love of this noble girl.

The little effects of the orphans were soon arranged, and having bowed together again by the grave of their mother, they were ready to depart with their benefactors; and as soon as they entered Mr. Hamilton's house, they felt themselves to be at home—a real home of tenderness and love.

They had heard the story of their poor brother, and knew that he was still a wanderer, tossed to and fro by this curse of mankind. Through the tender sympathy of the family by whom they had been adopted, they began to recover gradually—they soon became reconciled and composed, and the tide of an amiable boyishness began to flow freely from the heart of little Harry. On the cheek of Eliza, the rose which had prematurely wilted, began to bloom for a second time, with joy and love and peace.

CHAPTER XXV.

THE JOURNEY AND ITS RESULTS.

"'Tis woven in the world's great plan,
And fixed by Heaven's decree,
That all the true delights of man
Should spring from *sympathy*."

IT is a sad thing to turn from a new-made grave even under the most consoling circumstances which have ever hallowed such a spot; and it is all the more so, when one feels that it contains the most sacred treasure of earth, and leaves to be shrined in the cenotaph of the heart—the ever-dear name of *mother*.

From such a scene as this, and with all the holy feelings which pertain to it, Eliza Wilson and her little brother turned with their crushed and bleeding hearts, towards the home of the stranger; to mingle again in such society as that to which they had been accustomed, before the spoiler brought death, desolation, and misery to their door.

Light was sown for them in darkness, and it was impossible that, in the society of Mr. Hamilton's family, they could long be strangers. From the moment they entered that house, their hearts were made to vibrate to the gentle touches of unmistakable love and sympathy.

They had been there about two months, when Col. C——, of Virginia, visited New York, and although the acquaintance was only that of an evening spent with Mr. Hamilton's family, yet his visit was as welcome as that of an old friend. Six months in the balmy atmosphere of his native State, had wiped from his countenance the tinge which a soldier's life in Mexico had given him.

They were delighted to see him, and extended at once the hospitalities of their house during his stay in the city.

The Colonel participated with much feeling in the conversation over the history of poor Dick Wilson; and the probability that he with whom he had spent many pleasant hours in a strange land, was at that moment at the mercy of the *American legalized rum-seller!* brought a tear to his eye.

"You knew my brother once, did you, Col. C——?" inquired Eliza.

"I did, Miss Wilson; and when I saw him last in this very room, and knew how his heart melted under the influence of those sweet strains sung so tenderly by Miss H.,

> Home, home again from a foreign shore,'

I thought that he was safe. I saw your brother, Miss Wilson, at the battle of Cerro Gordo, in the advance line, when seven thousand lancers were dashing to the charge. I saw him also in that triumphal procession, as it entered the gates, and planted the American flag on the parapets of the Montezumas. Brave young man—but now how fallen! Strange that my country—the American's country—the exile's country—the world's home!—should permit this horrid work to go on!

"It has been to me, Miss Wilson, a matter of deep regret, that I urged your brother to come to Virginia. If I had not done so, you might have looked upon him once more; still, I do not think he would have been safe."

"Ah! sir," replied Eliza, "I hope this will not cause you any regret. It was an act of generous kindness on your part, for which none are now left to thank you, save myself and little brother. If he had not fallen there, he might have fallen elsewhere. These lures to ruin and death are filling every path; so that there is scarcely a square mile in the land in which temptations are not to be encountered, by just such noble-hearted young men as Richard. Oh! if rumsellers knew the character of those pangs with which they are piercing the hearts of millions, they surely would desist!"

"Ah! Miss Wilson," replied the colonel, "you misread the hearts of a large majority of those depraved men—they neither fear God nor regard man—the love of money is the prevailing, and the only sentiment in their hearts, and left to their own choice in the matter, the Ethiopian will change his skin, before they repent. The only repentance for them is a legal one!"

In this short conversation between Eliza and the colonel, and to which Mr. Hamilton's family were auditors—there was a feeling of evident pleasure. It gave them a deep insight into his character, and they admired the unequivocal orthodoxy of his sentiments upon the *great* evil which then as now, presented the mightiest obstacle in the way of civilization.

Col. C—— was far from being insensible to the worth of the family to whom, seemingly by accident, he had been introduced, and after a stay of several weeks, the greater part of which was spent in their society, he returned to his home.

One day Mr. Hamilton entered the room, where Kate and Eliza were seated, and laying a letter on the table, he said to Eliza, "Here, my dear, is a letter for you."

"Can it be from my brother!" she quickly exclaimed. "No, my child," said Mr. Hamilton, "you see it is from P——; perhaps it may be from some old friend of your family; open it, my dear, and read it."

She broke the seal, and found it to be from Mrs. Livingston. It was a kind, good letter—just such an one as orphans would be likely to prize. After many tender expressions of sympathy for them in the severe loss which they had been called to sustain, she informed them that Mr. Livingston had reclaimed from the parlor of a fashionable rumseller of P——, the fine portraits of her father and mother, which had passed from their possession under the hammer of the auctioneer.

"If we had these," she ejaculated, laying down the letter, "then we would have the images of all our dear loved ones now dead, but Ellen. Ah! would not their possession console my stricken heart!

Mr. Hamilton took up the letter, and looking over its contents said, with much tenderness; "yes, my sweet girl, you shall have these; they are yours of right, and they must be sent for immediately," and added, as he left the room, "give yourself no uneasiness."

The next morning Kate and Eliza, and little Harry, were together as usual, when Mr. and Mrs. Hamilton entered, and commenced a conversation,—

"We have been thinking," said Mr. H., "that it would be pleasant for you to visit P——; would you like to do so?"

"Yes sir," replied Eliza, "I would like to visit that place very much; but if I did, I must go at your expense, and that I cannot think of doing—you and your dear family have been too kind already; I never can repay you."

"My orphan child," said Mr. Hamilton, "speak

not in this way. Your presence and the gladsome heart of your little brother, more than repays us, every day that you are with us. You must go, and Kate and Frank shall go with you."

"May I go too?" quickly inquired Harry, as he fixed his full, inquiring blue eyes in the mild face of Mr. Hamilton.

"Yes, my dear little fellow," was the reply, "you may go too."

They at once agreed upon the time they should go; and while Frank was getting his business in order to leave, Kate and Eliza were busying themselves in making the necessary preparations for the journey, which was expected to consume several weeks.

With Eliza, thoughts of the unforgotten past would necessarily creep into her hours of preparation for a contemplated journey, in which she expected to have brought before her again in their vividness, the fearful scenes through which she knew none but the hand of God could have sustained her; and sometimes she ventured to hope that at least she might hear something of her brother.

The morning on which they set out for P—— was a beautiful one, in the early part of September. The trip was very pleasant, and each of them seemed to enjoy it, and soon they found themselves at the place of their destination.

As soon as it was possible, Frank called upon Mr.

Livingston at his counting-room, and informed him that Miss Wilson and her little brother were in the city.

"Is it possible?" said Mr. Livingston.

"Yes sir," said Frank, "they have become members of our family, and I have had the pleasure of accompanying them here on a visit."

"Thank you—thank you, sir," said Mr. L. "My carriage will be at the hotel for you in half an hour; all of the company must come."

Frank had scarcely found his way back, when a servant announced the carriage to be in waiting for them. They all entered it, and were soon in the hospitable mansion of one of the most worthy families of the city.

Mrs. Livingston inquired particularly of the later history of the family. She spoke of Dick with much tenderness, and as of one who, in all probability, was in the grave. Eliza, in her turn, inquired for many of those who were at one time intimate at her father's house, and was answered that already a number of them—ruined by the fashionable drinking customs of the day—had gone down to the cheerless grave of the drunkard.

Mrs. Livingston presented Eliza with the portraits which had been wrung from them to liquidate the demands of rumsellers; and it made her young heart beat again for joy, to look upon the dear faces of her departed parents;—they were always dear—now they were priceless. They all together visited the place where the dust of her father and sister was reposing. They lingered long but with a calm tranquillity around that spot; then turned from that place which had become the grave of their fondest and earliest hopes, and where in their very childhood they saw the openings of adversity's path.

When they had finished their visit in P——, and enjoyed for a number of days the hearty welcome of Mr. Livingston's family, they determined to visit the village of B——, to which place they arrived after a pleasant jaunt. It was soon understood after their arrival there, that they were interested in the history of Dick Wilson—a name which in that village had become a household word; and many, to their great annoyance, gathered about them at the hotel, to know who they might be, and if possible to find out their business. Mr. Watson soon heard of them, and at once hastened to make their acquaintance, as soon as he met them and knew who they were, he claimed them as his guests during their stay.

After a day spent in the society of each other, all reserve, which would have prevented a proper enjoyment of the occasion, departed; and they were—as was right they should be—free to converse in reference to those subjects which were of interest to them.

"Miss Wilson," said Mrs. Watson, "of yourself and

your little brother I had heard poor Richard speak with the tenderest affection. Oh! if you could have seen the noble manner in which—as he often used to say, 'more for his dear ones than for himself'—he contended with adversity, you would have witnessed a giant struggle.

"This was an unfortunate place for your brother—the rum influence was predominant—its emissaries were everywhere; and just when he seemed to have reached an eminence where he was safe, *they sacrificed him.* Judge L—— and old Stevens planned and executed that tragedy. Ah! yes; but Judge L—— and Stevens have not escaped the watchful eye of Providence—for God has written on the *uncared for* grave of one, and the *whirling* brain of the other, 'Let their habitation be desolate.'

"Stevens is dead; and his death was of the most miserable character. Remorse and terror filled to overflowing his last hours. His crimes were before him, and the drover's fate was revealed in the midst of one of his fearful paroxysms, upon which the stoutest heart could hardly bear to look. His confession was full; he acknowledged that by his own hand Mr Gilmore had been drugged into a sound sleep, and then murdered and buried; and, in connection with an individual already dead, that stone pile had been raised upon the drover's grave.

"In the midst of his ravings, he was often heard to

say, 'Wilson, this is a remarkable case'—'Where did this happen?' Again, he would call out to the grave-digger, as if he saw him opening that grave—'Jacob! Jacob! for God's sake stop!' &c.

"He has left a miserable son, who is good for nothing but the commission of crime. It could not be otherwise, for he was trained in vice; and although he is yet a young man, I believe that every sentiment of honor is erased from his being.

"Judge L—— was so criminated in the affair, by the confession of Stevens, that he was obliged to leave the country, and is now, we understand, a lunatic, and his family reduced to poverty. So, you see, justice, though sometimes slow, is always sure. Oh! Miss Wilson, the last word I heard your brother utter, will live in my memory forever—'I can't tell where this whirling brain may rest.'"

From this good friend, Eliza learned the history of her brother's struggle and fall; and having met and received the sympathy of many of his friends, they were ready to proceed on their homeward journey without interruption.

In making an inland tour through the country, they were subject to frequent interruptions and detentions, by reason of irregular conveyances, &c. After rendering many thanks to the kind family of Dick's early friends, the Watson family, they bade adieu. In a few hours after their departure, they came to a place where it was necessary for them to leave the cars and take to a canal packet, and in order to make this change, several hours were necessarily spent.

They entered a hotel, and after partaking of some refreshments, seated themselves together at a window which overlooked the beautiful bosom of the Ohio. At this moment, there appeared in full view a scene which attracted their attention, and awakened their deepest sympathies. There was before them, moving with slow and measured pace, two rough-looking boatmen, bearing in their arms in the direction of the hotel, an invalid, who, to all appearance, was in the last stages of a "*quick consumption.*"

As they came nearer, they saw that he was a young man; and Kate said to Eliza—"Poor fellow; he may be one who is struggling with disease, and striving to keep death at bay, that he may reach the home of his childhood, and feel the warm breath of his mother again, or the soothing hand of friends, before he dies."

"That is a sad thought," said Eliza; "but it may be so. I am afraid his earthly pilgrimage is doomed to terminate here. How hard it must be to die under such circumstances!"

By this time they had entered the bar-room, and Frank at once arose from his seat. He seemed to be intensely agitated, and stepped at once into the hall, closing the door after him as he did so.

He was standing near another door leading into the

bar-room, which was partly open, but not sufficiently so to give him a view of those who had just entered. From where he stood, he had a full view of the landlord, who, with an air of wonderful importance, was posted behind the bar.

"Has he any money?" were the first words Frank heard.

"I guess he hasn't," was the reply of one; "but then he isn't able to go any farther."

"The devil he ain't! Well, he'll have to go farther. It's no part of a landlord's business, this ain't. I can't afford to keep him a week or ten days, and then bury him, and I won't do it either! Go to the overseers of the poor, and if they will pay me, I'll do it; and if they won't, then I won't."

"I am in a dying state," began the invalid, with a tone hollow as the sepulchre itself. "I have vainly endeavored to reach my home; but that last fond hope is dead in my heart,—I must die in a few days. Keep me—you will not be troubled long—and God will reward you for it. I have no money, and no friend within three hundred miles."

"I can't do it! I've a family to look after; and he is worse than an infidel who don't do this."

"Oh! my God!" was the only reply of the dying young man.

"What is your name?" inquired the landlord, whose traffic had made his heart harder than the rock.

"Ah! my name!—It would do you little good to know it. I had thought to keep that to myself, and die unknown. My name is WILSON!"

At the mention of the name, Frank at once sprang into the room, and grasping the hand of the invalid, whose eyes were closed, he whispered "Dick!" A convulsive shudder passed through his frame, he opened his eyes, exclaiming—"Thank God! Frank, we meet again. You will stay with me until the struggle is over!"

"Yes," replied Frank, "I will remain with you—I will not leave you, while I can minister to your wants."

> "A friend's like a ship, when with music and song,
> The tide of good fortune still speeds him along;
> But see him when tempests have left him a wreck,
> And any *mean billow* can batter his deck;
> But give me the heart that sympathy shows,
> And clings to a messmate, whatever wind blows."

When this heartless man saw that there would be no doubt about his pay, he at once assumed a fawning attitude, and was willing to do anything and everything, that might be necessary. A room was at once prepared, into which Dick Wilson was immediately taken; and after he was made as comfortable as possible, Frank informed him of the others who were in the house, and he requested to see them at once.

Frank left him, and returned to the room in which he had left them. "You have a tender heart," said Kate, as he stood bewildered before them.

"I have seen enough, my sister, to soften the heart of any one but a rumseller."

"You never saw the invalid before, have you Frank?"

"Yes, a thousand times!" and approaching nearer, he said, "*The invalid is poor Dick!* I have seen him, and I thank God for the Providence which detained us here."

Eliza threw her face upon the shoulder of Kate, and ejaculated, "My poor brother—lead me to him. Oh! Where is he?"

As soon as the ladies could command sufficient calmness to make their entrance proper, Frank lead them to the room, and there stretched upon a bed, which was manifestly to be a bed of death, lay Dick Wilson. As soon as they entered he made an effort to rise in the bed, and his feeble arms were thrown about the necks of his sister and brother. "Where is mother?" he faintly inquired.

"She is dead," was the answer.

"Then you are alone. Oh! my sister and little brother, you little know through what scenes I have passed." * * * * *

After he had recovered from the exhaustion, into which this effort had thrown him, Eliza said to him, "No, dear Dick, we are not alone. Mr. Hamilton's kind family have taken us to their house and given us a home."

"God bless them," said he; "they did everything that was possible to save me, but I could not escape. Even now, if it had not been for you, Frank—with the visage of death stamped upon my countenance—this merciless rumseller would have refused me shelter in his house, and turned me into the street to die."

The next day found him somewhat revived, and he disclosed to them the history of his fall. "A single drop," said he, "wakened anew in my system those unquenched fires, before the fury of which I knew myself to be a life-long wanderer; and now in this feeble wreck of your dying friend, you see the result. Oh! Frank, bear witness for me, and let that witness have a trumpet's tongue, that the *rumseller is the great enemy of mankind!*"

He spent as much time in short conversations with his brother and sister, as was proper in his feeble condition. It was deeply affecting to see how tenderly he caressed that little brother, and how solemnly he warned him against those influences which had led him into the path of ruin; and now about to make for him an untimely grave. On the sixth day, the closing scene came. He seemed to be the first to apprehend its near approach; and calling them to his bedside, he calmly said, "I am dying. This is the last earthly scene in my history." And then taking the hands of those dear ones, who stood by his bed, he pressed them to his lips: then, without a struggle, the spirit of Richard Wilson, *The Rumseller's Victim*, with a trembling hope in the mercies of the Redeemer, passed into the presence of God.

It was on Sabbath morning when they made him a grave, in a lonely part of the little country cemetery at R——. The evidence of respect and affection was mingled with the clods that rolled in upon his grave; and they turned from the tomb of the brother and the friend, sad in heart, it is true—yet, with assurance that the rumseller's triumph with him was finished, that the victim was at last quiet in the grave. * * * * *

The amiable and lovely Eliza Wilson is now the wife of the high-souled Frank Hamilton; who, with a noble magnanimity and real devotion to the true interests of humanity, is contending with a giant's energy for the passage of the "Maine Law" in his native State; and Mr. and Mrs. Hamilton still live, to invoke the blessing of God upon the cause. Harry, whom they have adopted, and love as their own son, gives them every reason to hope for his future success as a scholar and as a Christian. It is said that Col. C—— will come again from Virginia, to transplant the beautiful, accomplished, and good Kate Hamilton to the region of sunny skies and milder days; where, may she long live to love and be beloved, as virtue's true heroines should ever be.

CHAPTER XXVI.

THE "MAINE LAW" OUR ONLY HOPE.—CONCLUSION.

"On the world's wide field of battle,
In the bivouac of life,
Be not like dumb driven cattle:
Be a HERO in the strife."

FRIENDS of humanity! you who have wept, and whose hearts have bled, at the sight of the fearful desolations which intemperance has made, what is to be done? A wary, gigantic, and interested enemy, feeding upon the hopes and happiness, and reddened by the blood of fathers, sons, mothers and sisters, is struggling to maintain an existence, which has already destroyed the hopes and happiness of millions; and which is ready, for a price, to revel in the overthrow of millions more, and scatter broad-cast over the land the germinating elements of disease, crime, poverty and death!

Is the contest to be given up, and hope surrendered to the spoiler, that his unslaked thirst for human blood may still delight itself in the warm, fresh current of new victims?

Is the banner which has floated proudly in times of darkness, and amidst many dreary vicissitudes, now to be furled? No! Hope, gathering strength from every element, which marks the progress of God's great purposes, answers, no! *no!* NO! but keeps the field; and let the banner, borne by stalwart arms and strong hearts, wave forth proudly as it ever did, displaying the simple motto, the "MAINE LAW," until every State shall catch the philanthropic inspiration, and drive this monster, Intemperance, from their borders.

The story of Dick Wilson is only that of thousands of young men, who, by the pernicious influence of the rumselling fraternity, under legal sanction, have been made to suffer, to bleed, and to die. This is but one of the ten thousand families which, by the power of this legalized wickedness, have been stricken down to the very earth; and whose agonizing wails are piercing the heavens, and calling down vengeance of the Almighty. Who are suffering at the hands of this desperately fortified organization, which has insinuated itself, with the stealthiness of a tiger's step, both into the ballot-box and the legislative hall—that it may control the one and overawe the other? Rather, who are not suffering?

Every relation in life has been chilled and torn by it, and its sacred sanctity has been wantonly violated by its accursed touch. You have seen the father, under its influence, tottering to his home, and through life—tottering even to the grave; and you have seen the mother and the children, who were as dear to her as if the munificence of a princess had been hers, subsisting upon tears and sorrow and poverty; for, locked in the coffers of the rumseller was the living of which she was the *rightful*, and ought to have been the *legal* owner. You have seen the strong young man going forth into the world, intent upon the prize for which he was struggling vigorously and with a high-souled magnanimity, each day removing obstacles and dissipating fears, until the end was full in view, and the reward was just within his grasp. Friends were attracted to him by the rich promise he gave, and upon him their earnest and admiring glance was fixed, as he passed another and another of those who were competitors in the same race, and they doubted not that he would reach the goal of his ambition. But in his, as in thousands upon thousands of similar cases, they did not know that a concealed venom was rankling in his veins, and that already the fatal fire was kindled within him, which, although smothered for the time, was only waiting an adverse gale of fortune, to fan it into furious and uncontrollable flame. It came: the victim struggled fiercely in the contest for life, but was overcome in the encounter, and sank into the dark and cheerless embrace of the drunkard's grave. And did he fall alone? Had that been so, the scene would have been relieved of more than half its horror. A mother, sister, and brother are again smitten by the crushing blow, their staff broken, and their earthly hopes and prospects blighted.

This is but a single case. Every city, town and village in our broad land presents a daily record of numerous cases, of which this is but a faint example. Few are the families even that have not been more or less directly scourged by this pest of the race. The long and full chronicle of crime, the baseness which gloats in its triumphs over propriety and decency, the broils which disturb public and private peace, the haggard ghosts of poverty and want, with all their suffering children, the madness which dethrones reason and demolishes "the dome of thought"—indeed, by far the greater share of all the ills that flesh is heir to, have their origin in the same prolific source of evil and of ruin.

In view of the devastation which it has wrought, and is still working, how humiliating the thought, that in this country, at this time, with all the lights emitted from the temples of science and the altars of religion, it should still go on, immolating annually its thousands of victims, and this, too, under the sanction of *American law!*

Again, the question occurs—What shall be done? Is the evil beyond our reach? Shall we abandon the field to the destroyer, and let his horrid work go on? Shall we continue, as we have heretofore done, to *aid* in the destruction of our countrymen and kindred, by giving to the rum traffic the positive sanction of law? "Forbid it, my country—forbid it, heaven!" Every motive which should control the actions of the philanthropist, the Christian, the political economist, the man of business, the friend of his family, or of himself even, impels to action. Humanity, in all her forms of wretchedness, is making her most earnest and solemn appeals. Her arguments are want and misery, sorrow and suffering, tears and trials, crime and blood. They are, however, utterly unavailing with those whose sensibilities have been benumbed, whose sympathies have been dried up, by the degrading associations and influences of the rum traffic. Gain is their only object, and the consequences which result to individuals or to society are nothing to them, if they only make it profitable. Disease and death may be before and around them—the fondest hopes and the dearest relations of life may be blighted and severed by their touch, without exciting one throb of pity in their callous hearts, or one purpose of amendment in their obdurate minds.

A business, therefore, the natural and unavoidable effects of which is to harden and degrade those engaged in it, and from which society so bitterly suffers, should obviously be prohibited by the strong arm of public law, from further riot upon social peace.

How is this to be done? All legislation upon this subject, with the exception of what is familiarly known as the "Maine Law," has been a failure. It has not been able to stay the tide upon which thousands have annually been drifted to ruin. *Entire prohibition* is the only legislation on this subject which promises safety; the only remedy that will secure the peace and happiness of future generations—from the curse of the monster evil. Help then! or your father—brother—child—friend—may be the next to fall within its terrible embrace and fill a drunkard grave!

THE END.